BREAKER

Speed Demons MC

Book Four

Jules Ford

ISBN: 9798857779354

Copyright 2023 by Jules Ford

All rights reserved.

This is a work of fiction. Names, characters, business, places, and incidents are either the product of the author's imagination or used in a fictitious manner. Any resemblance to actual living persons, living, or dead, or actual events is purely coincidental.

ALL RIGHTS RESERVED

This book contains material protected under International and Federal Copyright Laws and Treaties. Any unauthorized reprint or use of this material is prohibited. No part of this book may be reproduced or transmitted in any form or by any means, electronic or mechanical, including photocopying, recording, or by any informal storage and retrieval system without express written permission from the author/ publisher.

Cover Design by JoeLee Creative

Cover Model: Kevin K. Hessam

Photographer: Eric David Battershell

Formatting by: MD Foysal Ahmed
www.fiverr.com/foysalrumman

Proofreading by Nicola Thorpe & Jayne Rushton

Editor: Nicola Thorpe

With thanks

Dedication

For Mylene

Queen of voice notes.

Lover of laughter.

Keeper of so much beauty that your light shines all the way across the Atlantic.

He's here, babe. The messy little twat. ;)

Thank you for being Kit's cheerleader ~

You licked him, so he's yours.

Thank you for you.

XOXO

Other Books by Jules

Speed Demons MC

Bowie

Cash

Atlas

Snow

Breaker

Colt ~ Coming Soon

Soulless Assassins MC

Tyrant's Redemption (Co-author Raven Dark)

Note to Readers

Thank you for waiting patiently for the concluding part of Kit and Kennedy's story.

This book contains scenes of child abduction, graphic violence, and murder.

PTSD and its effects, and attempted suicide, also feature heavily.

And just like Snow, it contains Game of Thrones spoilers.

That ending, though...

Breakers Playlist can be found here ~

https://open.spotify.com/playlist/2YyiAuI7FIhv8UCOUL76vO

Glossary

SPEED DEMONS MC

OFFICERS

President	John 'Dagger' Stone
Vice President	Jameson 'Hendrix' Quinn
Sergent At Arms	Danny 'Atlas' Woods
Road Captain	Jacob 'Iceman' Irons
Treasurer	Xander 'Cash' Stone
Secretary (original member)	Abraham 'Abe' Decker
Enforcer	Gage 'Bowie' Stone
Tech	Colter 'Colt' Van der Cleeve

MEMBERS

Kit 'Snow / Breaker' Stone

'Shotgun'

'Chaps'

'Reno'

'Fender'

'Brew'

'Arrow' (was 'Boner')

PROSPECTS

'Sparky' (deceased)
Noah 'Billy the Kid' Thorne

ORIGINAL MEMBERS

Don 'Bandit' Stone (deceased)

OLD LADIES

Adele Stone, ex-wife of John 'Dagger' Stone

Sophie 'Stitch' Green, partner to Danny 'Atlas' Woods

Cara 'Wildcat' Landry, partner to Xander 'Cash' Stone

Layla Jane 'Doe' Hardin, partner to Gage 'Bowie' Stone

Kennedy 'Kitten' Carmichael, partner to Kit 'Snow / Breaker' Stone

Iris Decker, wife of Abraham 'Abe' Decker

Ashley Thorne, wife of Fender

Freya Stone, daughter of John Stone, sister to Xander, Gage and Kit

Rosie Woods, sister to Danny 'Atlas' Woods

CHILDREN

Sunshine Hope Hardin, daughter of Layla Hardin and Gage Stone

Willow Hardin, daughter of Layla Hardin and Gage Stone

Kai Carmichael, son of Kennedy Carmichael and Kit Stone

Kadence Carmichael, daughter of Kennedy Carmichael and Kit Stone

Gabby Thomas, daughter of Rosie Woods and John Thomas

DJ Thomas, son of Rosie Woods and John Thomas

Seraphia Reid, adopted daughter of Iris and Abraham Decker

Mason Gray, adopted son of Iris and Abraham Decker

OTHER CHARACTERS

Mayor Robert Henderson, mayor of Hambleton

Elise Henderson (nee Bell), wife of Mayor Henderson

Robert Henderson Jr (deceased), son of Elise and Robert Henderson

Anna Bouchard, salon owner

Tristan Forbes, salon employee

Callam O'Shea, owner of O'Shea's Bar

Donovan O'Shea, brother to Callum and Tadhg

Tadhg O' Shea, brother to Callum and Donovan

Captain Espinoza

Lieutenant Nate Hollister

SPC Kyle Simmons (deceased)

Private Sol 'Benny' Bendetti (deceased)

Table of Contents

Chapter One 1

Chapter Two 17

Chapter Three 29

Chapter Four 41

Chapter Five 56

Chapter Six 71

Chapter Seven 86

Chapter Eight 100

Chapter Nine 114

Chapter Ten 134

Chapter Eleven 151

Chapter Twelve 169

Chapter Thirteen 189

Chapter Fourteen 206

Chapter Fifteen 221

Chapter Sixteen 237

Chapter Seventeen 254

Chapter Eighteen 268

Chapter Nineteen 283

- Chapter Twenty 299
- Chapter Twenty-One 313
- Chapter Twenty-Two 321
- Chapter Twenty-Three 340
- Chapter Twenty-Four 359
- Chapter Twenty-Five 370
- Chapter Twenty-Six 383
- Chapter Twenty-Seven 394
- Chapter Twenty-Eight 409
- Chapter Twenty-Nine 425
- Chapter Thirty 438
- Chapter Thirty-One 459
- Epilogue One 466
- Epilogue Two 475

Chapter One

Breaker

My balls almost shrank into my stomach as I watched Atlas's smirk widen. "Yo, motherfucker," he nodded toward my mini-me son, who I hadn't known existed until five minutes ago, "I think you've got some explainin' to do."

I stared at Kai with a mouth so dry that I couldn't speak a word. The bitter taste of regret clawed at my throat.

Kennedy jabbed a hand to her hip and cocked her head, those cornflower-blues darkening as she curled her lip. "I think we should sit for this. He's got a lot of ground to cover." Her eyes bored into mine, her mouth twisting. "Maybe he should go back ten years and explain to the room why he told me his name was *Kyle fucking Simmons!*"

A throat cleared from behind us. "Umm. I hate to interrupt; I can see emotions are running high. But we've got a Celine Dion tribute act and her girlfriend waiting outside. If you want the wedding to go ahead, we need to start now."

Atlas turned to me, eyes narrowing before addressing Kennedy. "Look, babe. Know your head's spinnin', but it's our weddin' day." He gestured to me. "I know he's fucked-up big time, but you'll have to put it on ice for the next ten minutes."

Kitten's forehead scrunched up, and she shook her head blindly. "I'm out." A look of pain flashed across her face. "I can't do this. I need to get the kids out of here and make sure they're okay," she looked at Sophie, "I'm sorry."

I opened my mouth to tell her she'd do no such goddamned thing, but Soph beat me to it.

"No, Ned. Please don't go." She took Kitten's arm to stop her from walking away. "You're the only family I've got. I can't get married without you."

Atlas pointed to the space behind Sophie. "Blondie, stand there and don't fuckin' move." He turned to me. "And as for *you*. Get your ass behind me."

"I've got more important shit to do, Atlas," I retorted, gesturing toward the kids. "Have you lost your marbles?"

He rounded on me. "I told you, no goddamned shenanigans. This is my weddin' day. My woman's weddin' day, and you've flushed it down the fuckin' toilet bowl."

Kennedy turned to Kai. "Take Kady out to the waiting room. I'll be straight out."

"But Mom—" he began.

"Kai," she snapped, cutting him off. "Please do as I say."

My boy took his sister's hand while glaring at me. "Stay away from my mom," he spat before pulling his sister out of the room.

Every eye fell upon me as I ran a hand through my hair, staring after the twins.

My boy fucking hated me. He'd taken one look at me and made his mind up, but then if some asshole who'd professed to be my dad showed up at a family wedding when he was supposed to be six feet under, I would've had the same reaction.

My eyes slashed to my woman, who looked at me like dirt under her stiletto. How the fuck had the reunion I'd dreamed of for years turned into such a spectacle? Pulse racing, I turned to Kitten and spoke from the heart. "They're fuckin' beautiful, baby. Thank you."

Her head reared back. "Are you for real?" She stomped toward me, probably with the intent to break my balls, but Atlas stopped her. "Not now, Blondie. Stand in your spot, and keep it the fuck together until we say, 'I do.'" His gaze settled on me. "And as for you. Don't move, don't speak, don't fuckin' breathe until this is done. Any more bullshit, and you'll be sorry." He turned to the preacher. "Begin!"

Kennedy went to say something else, but Atlas slashed his hand through the air. "Hell to the fuckin' no. Stand there and keep it classy. You can turn ninja on his ass when we're done." His face jerked back toward the preacher. "Over to you!"

The older man looked nervously around the room, gulped, and, in a small voice, began. "Dearly beloved..."

My gaze returned to Kitten, and I winced at her hurt expression. I dropped my eyes, suddenly unable to look at her. It hurt too much.

Atlas's arm was around Sophie's shoulders, both of them taking in the preacher's every word. My throat burned as a thought hit me.

It should've been us.

I had to breathe through the clench of nausea in my gut to stop from throwing up. I'd screwed up badly, but I hadn't realized just how much until she called me Kyle.

One solitary word made my heart crumble, and my world darken even more.

Kyle. Kyle. Kyle.

How the hell could one small, stupid, throwaway lie fuck up the course of our lives so destructively? Had she been living with pain and grief? What had I done to her?

My stomach knotted as Kitten threw me a look that would've made a lesser man cry before turning to face the preacher, her jaw clenched stubbornly.

She hadn't changed a bit. She was still the most beautiful woman in the world. I watched, mesmerized, as she tilted her chin up, and my heart exploded in my chest. My girl was so strong, so fucking incredible. She raised two amazing kids and thrived without me, whereas, without her, I'd hit rock bottom.

Images of me, her, and the kids together laughing whizzed through my brain, causing my heart to gallop.

Atlas suddenly nudged me out of my trance, making me jump. "Ring, ya fuckin' fucknut," he whisper-shouted.

I whipped my hand into my pocket, pulled out a band of white gold metal, and handed it to him while Sophie turned to take another ring from Kennedy.

Our eyes caught again, and my heart thudded against my ribs as my head spun with questions.

What next?
Will she forgive me?
Does she hate me that much?

Staring at her, I tried to convey everything I felt. The problem was, I'd been numb for so long that I wasn't even sure what the feelings were. My eyes held hers, willing her to see how sorry I was, but she turned her face away with her lip curled as if she found me completely and utterly disgusting.

A muscle ticked in my jaw, and my hands clenched into fists by my side.

If it was a battle she wanted, she'd come to the right place. I wasn't giving up, not on her or my kids. For years I'd searched. Now I'd finally found her I wouldn't let her get away. By the time the day was done, I'd know everything about her, including her address.

I'd set up camp outside her house if I had to.

Kitten was mine. She'd been mine since she was a nineteen-year-old girl and would still be mine until she took her last breath. Other men, other women, none of it mattered. *She* was here now, and that was all I cared about. My kids were an added bonus. I knew I'd fucked-up, knew I had a lot of work to do if I was gonna make her want me again, but I was up for the job.

Everything had changed now I had her back. I'd move to Vegas, even get a regular job if I had to. I'd court her, make her remember how it was between us. I'd prove how much I loved her.

The preacher's voice registered in my brain. "Daniel and Sophie. I now pronounce you man and wife." He smiled at Atlas. "You may kiss your bride."

The SAA's hand flew out, grabbed Sophie by the nape, and tugged her into him. "Come 'ere, Mrs. Woods." He bent his head and kissed her hard while everyone whooped and cheered. Well, everyone except my woman, who was already trying to slip out unnoticed.

My throat went tight. "Kitten," I rasped loudly, stomping after her. "Get your ass back here."

With the door already open, she whirled around and jabbed a finger in my direction. "I'll get your number from Sophie. We'll organize access if I'm satisfied you haven't become a serial killer. But I promise you this, if my PI turns up any shit, you're not going near them."

Dad's forehead scrunched up. "Look here. We're a decent club, pillars of the fuckin' community. They're my grandkids, too. You can't just take 'em away."

"I can do whatever the hell I want," Kitten retorted. "I'm sorry, but I don't know any of you." Her eyes turned to me. "And the one I thought I did know turned out to be a liar."

She gave me her back and flounced out of the room.

"I'll talk to her," Sophie murmured, following her out.

My gut twisted.

What the fuck was she talking about? She knew me; she knew me better than anyone.

A hand clasped my shoulder. "Son," Abe murmured. "Just tell me one thing. Did you knock her up and ghost her?"

My throat burned as I turned to him. "I didn't know about 'em."

He nodded slowly, deep in thought. "Who is she?"

The love of my fucked-up, shitty life. I thought, but how could I say those words after what I'd done? "I met her just before my first deployment to Afghanistan. After a while, everything went south, and I ended it. I didn't know she was..." My voice trailed off because everything I said sounded like an excuse.

"Okay." His hand clasped my shoulder tighter, keeping it there as we walked out of the room. "Why the fuck did she call you Kyle?"

I let out a self-derisive snort. "Stupid prank me and my buds cooked up. As crazy as it sounds, I never got around to telling her the truth. I was deployed and only got a few visits before everything turned to shit. Kyle Simmons was a brother back in my unit. He was KIA during a mission our task force was ordered to carry out."

"You saw him die?" Abe asked, tone incredulous.

"Yeah. Ain't the worst shit I've seen either." I rasped, watching Kennedy crouch down and speak directly to the kids.

"Last question," Abe said thoughtfully. "You gonna step up for 'em?"

My heart plummeted because I'd dreamed of reuniting with Kitten for years. But I wasn't clean or good. What if I did something to hurt them?

I frowned. "I want to, Abe, but I'm scared I'm not good for them." I turned to him as a sudden heaviness weighed down my chest. "There's somethin' in me that ain't right."

Abe's hand slid up to the back of my neck, and he pulled my face closer, looking me dead in the eyes. "I know you as well as anyone, Kit. You do need help. Iris has been saying for years that she gets it. She understands what you're feelin'."

"Iris doesn't know shit," I snapped, thrusting a hand through my hair. "Nobody knows what I go through on the daily."

His eyes narrowed angrily. "You forget, boy, my Iris has been through somethin' more horrific than you can imagine. Don't fuckin' stand there thinkin' your pain's more deserved. My ol' lady went to Hell and came out the other side."

Shit.

"Me and Iris tried to get through to you for years," he continued. "But you slid so far down that we couldn't pull you up." He nodded toward Pop. "I told Dagger you needed help, but you know what he's like. I know the military changed you, Son; war changes everyone, but it's time to get yourself well again. You can't go on like this. You'll destroy yourself in ways you can't come back from. You've got somethin' to fight for now."

I glanced back at Kitten and cursed out loud as I saw her hand in hand with the kids, walking toward the exit, Sophie following. "Where the fuck are you going?" I yelled, heart in my mouth.

She craned her neck and shouted, "Fuck off."

"I've been waiting to speak to you," I bellowed, stalking toward the door with my fists clenched. I'd finally found Kitten—discovered I had twins—and all she could do was run? If she thought I'd let her go, she could think again. She'd had nine goddamned years of raising what belonged to me while I'd been left to fall apart.

I ignored the shouts and footsteps from behind me as I jogged to catch up.

Kitten swept through a small garden where a photographer was taking photos. "Come on, kids."

I ran up next to her. "You're not leavin'. We need to talk."

"I need time," she gritted, keeping her eyes ahead, not even looking at me.

"Please don't leave, baby," I begged. "There's so much I need to explain."

She kept her face forward, pretending I wasn't even there. I sped up, running ahead of her, walking backward. "Kitten, stop!" I bellowed, teeth almost gnashing together.

"Get lost," Kai yelled, pulling his mom past me.

"Breaker," Sophie's voice carried a hint of warning, "calm down. You're too heated to have a civil conversation. It will be better to talk later when emotions aren't running so high."

I ignored her, instead addressing Kennedy. "Please don't leave, baby."

"I need time to talk with the kids," she muttered, heading for a white Range Rover. "They're my priority. Not *you*." Her voice dripped with disdain.

Every emotion I'd buried over the years clawed at my organs, and slowly, I felt the monster rising. I grabbed her arm and got in her face. "Why won't you talk to me?" I snarled.

"I need to make sure my children aren't scarred for life because the father they thought had been dead for the last eight years has suddenly appeared and is actually very much alive." She shook her head slowly as if she couldn't believe what was happening. "How could you? I gave you *everything,* and it wasn't even real."

I tried to take her hand, but she pulled it away and stared at me, her eyes glistening with tears. "Don't you dare!" she rocked up on her heels, getting in my face. "Don't touch me! You don't get that right anymore. You lied to me! I fucking *grieved* for you for eight years. You're *sick*."

For a split second, I lost my shit. The monster surged, and adrenaline pounded through my veins. Without thinking, I dug my fingers into my girl's shoulders, tugging her hard toward me before leaning until our noses were an inch apart. "You're not fuckin' leavin'!" I roared.

She let out a yelp, wrenching herself away from my hold. "You better get him in hand," she snapped over my shoulder. "He's out of control."

Atlas and Cash started to crowd me, herding me away from her. Teeth clenched, I shoved my brother hard, watching with a satisfied sneer as he fell backward and sprawled across the ground.

"Breaker. Calm the fuck down," Atlas ordered, pushing me away from my woman.

I let out another roar, and bedlam broke out.

Dad ran toward us, yelling, with Abe on his heels as screams cut through the air. Cash jumped to his feet, cautioning the women to get back before coming for me again.

Atlas hauled himself between me and Kitten, creating a barrier. "Keep it together, fucknut," he told me, voice hard. "The kids are goddamned terrified, and if my wife gets caught up in your bullshit, I'll take a baseball bat to ya. Now take a fuckin' breath."

"Fuck you," I spat, trying to get past him, but he was like an unmovable mountain. I heard a yell and felt pain radiate from the back of my knee. I spun around, pulling my arm back, ready to punch, when I saw Kai standing there, fists raised.

"Leave my mom alone!" he yelled. "You're an asshole. I hate you. I hate you."

Every piece of anger drained out of me, and my body slumped. "Kai," I croaked, raising my hands to show him I wasn't a threat. "I'm not gonna hurt her."

"It's okay, Son," Kitten murmured soothingly as she approached us, my dad by her side. "Come on, let's get you in the car."

My heart sank when I noticed Kai's little hands tremble. Golden eyes, just like mine, filled with tears, and his face paled.

Fuck, my own kid's scared of me.

"Son—" I whispered before he yelled again, cutting me off.

"I'm not your son. I wish you'd stayed dead. You're not my dad. My dad's a hero who died for his country. You're a monster."

My heart ached. I raised a hand to my chest to rub away the pain. "I'd never hurt your mom or you. I'd never do that. I just need a chance to explain."

"Get in the car, Kai," my woman ordered gently.

"But Mom—"

"Son," she reiterated. "Please don't argue with me. Get in the car."

Kai muttered under his breath as he turned and banged his shoulder into my ribs on his way to the Range Rover.

Kennedy heaved out a sigh. "Jesus, save me from alpha sons and dead baby daddies."

"I'm sorry, baby," I rasped.

"You!" Kitten said accusingly, pointing a finger at me. "Believe me, we *will* talk, but I need some time to come to terms with all this bullshit."

"Okay," I raised my hands, holding them up defensively. "We'll speak tomorrow."

My girl cocked a perfect eyebrow. "I need time. I'm talking weeks, not days. Don't you get it, Snow? They've grown up thinking you died in an explosion. They thought you were a war hero, but now you're standing here, flesh and blood, and they know you've lied. This is the kind of shit that stays with a kid. This is the kind of shit I'm supposed to protect them from."

Breaker

Heat exploded through my chest. "You don't need to protect them from me," I bellowed. "I'm their goddamned father."

Kitten let out a frustrated scream as she pushed past Atlas. "Oh my God, don't you get it?" she shrieked. "You're *not* their father. Their father's called Kyle Simmons, and he's fucking dead."

Her words stabbed my heart like tiny knives. "Baby. I've searched for you for years. Don't fuckin' leave. Give me a chance to explain."

"You mean like you left me," she ground out, eyes shining.

I hung my head, all anger draining from me.

"What the fuck do you mean 'years to find her'?" Dad piped up. "Can somebody please tell me what's goin' on?"

"Dagger!" Abe admonished. "Let him fuckin' speak."

I tried to take another step toward her, but Atlas's hand clamped down on my shoulder, stopping me. "Give her what she needs, Breaker," he muttered quietly. "If you push too hard, it'll do more harm than good. I'll make sure you get your chance, brother, but you have to trust me to sort it."

"At least give me your number, Kitten," I pleaded. "Don't shut me out. Please. I've been searching for so long, baby."

Raw pain slashed across Kitten's beautiful face. "You'd know all about shutting people out, right, *Kyle*?"

My stomach clenched as my thoughts returned to that awful day when I'd left her sitting in her living room, staring into nothing.

I'd thought about it every day since it happened. The moment I lost her was when I gave up on myself. Now, I'd been given the chance to get her back, to have something to fight for again, and I wasn't gonna waste it.

"I'm not leaving Vegas until you talk to me," I declared, voice suddenly full of bravado.

Kennedy's shoulders went back, and I knew I was about to have a fight on my hands. "Stop pressuring me, Snow."

"I'm not leaving. I've got rights." I jerked my thumb toward her cage. "They're my kids, too. You can't just keep 'em from me." The moment the words left my lips, I knew I'd fucked-up—even more.

"You've got rights?" she questioned, her tone deathly quiet.

I winced. "Well—"

"You gave me a fake name almost ten years ago, knocked me up, and walked out on me, effectively deserting me. And now you think you've got rights?" Her eyes narrowed. "If you try and force those kids into something they don't want, I'll keep you in litigation until they're eighteen, and no court in the land would give you access to them. Test me, Snow, and you'll lose. When it comes to them, there's no compromise. I'll fight to the damned death."

My heart stuttered as I watched her raise a hand to rub her temple.

"I thought you were dead," she whispered. "All this time, I've told them their father died before he could meet them, and all along, you were alive." Her face paled. "I've *never* lied to my kids, but *you* made a liar out of me."

I closed my eyes. "I'm sorry."

"So am I." Slowly, she turned to address Sophie. "Will you give me his contact information when I'm ready?"

"Of course, Ned," she replied softly.

Kitten turned back to me. "I'll talk to the kids; if they want to meet you, they can, but I won't force them. If you don't like it, by all means, take it to a judge." She started for the car.

"Don't leave," I begged, about to go after her, but Atlas grabbed my shoulder and pulled me back.

"Get the fuck off," I bit out.

"Nah!" His grip tightened. "If you've got even half a brain, you'll stand the fuck down and give her the time she's just fuckin' asked for."

I started to struggle again. "Atlas. Get the fuck off me,"

Cash stomped over. "Do as he says, fucknut. You'll be lucky if she ever speaks to you again."

"I'm going after her," I snapped, trying harder to get out of Atlas's hold.

"Kit," Dad shouted. "Let her go."

I roared, nostrils flaring as I watched Kitten strap the kids into the car before jumping into the driver's seat. I snarled, trying to push the SAA off.

Cash grabbed hold of my arm. "Get the fuck away from me!" I tried to pull away, but Atlas's muscular bicep snaked across my windpipe from behind, cutting off my airway. "Calm the fuck down," he muttered in my ear from behind. "You're scaring the kids."

Still struggling to escape their hold, I bellowed out a roar as the Range Rover pulled away. Kitten's head swiveled to face me as I helplessly watched her drive away.

Atlas relaxed his hold across my throat, and I stumbled free. My lungs burned as I turned and glared at Cash and Atlas. "Fuck you!"

Cash smirked. "Well, you've fucked everyone else in Wyoming. It was only a matter of time until you moved on to the men."

"Cash. Shut up!" Cara shouted. "You're not helping."

He shrugged. "You've got a screw loose, Kit. 'Bout time you went to see a shrink."

"Why? So I can be like you, *brother*?" I sneered. "You're just a spoiled prick. You wouldn't survive a month in the places I've been." My stare slid to Atlas. "I expected more from you."

The SAA's eyebrows knitted together. "You were acting the fool, Breaker. Little Kady girl was crying. You scared the shit outta her. How are those kids meant to wanna have a relationship with their pop when he acts like a lunatic? Add on the fact you got rough with Ned, and I doubt you'll get within ten feet of 'em. You'll be lucky if she doesn't slap a damned restraining order on ya."

"Did you see Kai kick his ass?" Cash barked a laugh. "We should'a let the little ninja kid beat his fucked-up brains in."

My fingers tensed. "Go on, asshole," I muttered. "Get it all out. It's no wonder everyone thinks you're such a jerk." I turned to Pop, who was watching the scene with his arms folded across his chest. "God only knows why you're so proud of your future prez here," I nodded toward Cash, "he's as useful as a bible in a whorehouse."

I went into my inside pocket and pulled out my cell phone.

"What ya doin' now, Kit?" Abe asked gently.

"Calling Colt," I replied, stabbing at my phone. "Need an address."

Dad eyed Atlas and Cash. "You're not getting it."

"Watch me. And Pop, fuck you and fuck your club. You've proved where your loyalties lie, and like always, they're not with me." I held the cell to my ear, waiting for Colt to answer.

"Kit," Iris wailed.

"Don't bother calling Colt," Dad retorted. "He's had orders not to help ya. If you see Kennedy now, you'll fuck everythin' up. Why can't you see how over-the-top and irrational you're bein'?"

I ended the call, trying to keep my shit together and not go postal on my dad.

Whenever they needed me, I was there.

Breaker

Jesus, it wasn't long ago that I'd sneaked into the Sinner's compound and blown their clubhouse sky-high. But the minute I needed help, everybody turned their backs on me.

When Cash fucked-up with Cara, Dad supported his ass. The same happened when Bowie fucked and chucked Layla. I got more understanding from Abe, Iris, and Atlas than from my family.

Like ten years before, Kitten flipped a switch inside me and brought me back to life. My emotions were out in force. No more passivity, and no more pushing shit down. My family was about to reap what they'd sowed. If they wanted to treat me like I didn't belong, they'd get their wish.

"I understand how you feel, Son," Dad said, tone low. "But making rash decisions now won't help. I'll bring our flights forward. We'll go home and cook up a plan."

My throat heated. "I don't have a home with you anymore."

Iris sniffed. "Please come back to the club, Kit."

I shook my head jerkily. "I'm staying. I wanna be near my kids."

"You can't, Breaker," Atlas insisted. "Keep the peace now, and it'll be easier later. Give her time to come to terms with everything."

"I'm not leaving," I repeated. "Gonna check into a hotel. Don't need her address. I've got her place of work. I'll go there." I went to walk away, but Cash placed a hand on my shoulder. "Dad said no," he muttered.

"Dad can eat shit," I retorted. "I'm not his problem anymore."

Dad stomped over until he faced me. "Kit, stay away until she's ready."

"It's not your business what I do." I snapped, shoving Cash away. "Would you treat *him* like this?"

Dad released a frustrated sigh. "You're coming home with us."

I rounded on him, getting in his face. "I don't have a home with you."

"Careful, boy," he warned. "I can still put you on your ass."

"Please, Kit," Iris begged. "I promise I'll help you. But come back with us first. You have to plan what you're gonna do, and I'll help."

My eyes slid to the woman who'd been like a mom to me.

She'd always had my back. I had no reason not to believe she had my best interests at heart. My thoughts went to five minutes before when I grabbed Kitten. I didn't mean to hurt her; it was just that everything came on top, and I'd led with my emotions. I wasn't used to feeling so out of control.

My gut clenched painfully.

Maybe I had acted irrationally. But it didn't take away from the fact that, like always, my family and so-called brothers didn't back me up. I was sick of being an outsider. What was I staying in the club for? I didn't get the same brotherhood everyone else did. I didn't get respect or the opportunities everyone else did.

A plan formed in my mind.

I'd return to the club, sort my shit, and leave. I'd pack everything and move to Vegas. Kitten may not want me, but if I could prove to her I was steady, she may eventually give me a chance. I needed to be close to my kids.

There were counselors all over Vegas. Maybe I could contact the VA Center in Grand Junction again to see if they'd take me on.

The burn of self-disgust in my throat, which had suffocated me for years, suddenly cooled.

Only when I thought of leaving the club did I realize how stagnant I'd become. The MC was great in a lot of ways, but it wasn't great for me. The idea of getting away from my old family and building my new one made my heart settle.

I should've left the Speed Demons years ago.

Chapter Two

Kennedy

Pressing my foot on the gas, I sped out of the parking lot and joined the stream of traffic heading toward the north of the city. My heart leaped into my mouth as sniffles sounded from the backseat.

"You okay, Kady?" I asked. "Don't worry, baby. You're safe."

"My head hurts," she whispered, sniffing back the tears.

I heard a rustle as Kai leaned over to comfort his sister. "It's okay, Kady," he muttered. "I won't let him get to you."

Every nerve ending tingled, and my thoughts raced.

Snow was out of control back there. At one point, I thought he was going to hit me.

My knees almost gave out when I walked into the chapel and saw his ghost there. Then, when he spoke, and I realized he was flesh, blood, and bones, something clicked, and for the first time in years, I was whole again. I yearned to throw myself in his arms and never let him go before it hit me like a ten-ton trailer.

For years, I'd mourned a man who wasn't dead.

My cracked thoughts suddenly twisted together, forming a plan. The first thing I had to do was protect my kids. My jaw clenched as clarity shone through my mind.

"Gonna make a quick phone call, babies," I said soothingly before loudly barking, "Call Scotty." The in-car phone rang a few times before a soft voice greeted me.

"Lorraine. Put me through to him," I ordered.

My partner's secretary must have heard my desperation because he'd picked up within seconds. "What the fuck, Ned? I've got a meeting with Tote in three minutes. If I'm late, he'll break my fucking kneecaps."

"Snow's back," I breathed.

The three-second silence was so deafening it almost burst my eardrums before my partner suddenly snapped, "Tell me!"

I sighed deeply, letting Kennedy Carmichael, the lawyer, take over. It took me about ninety seconds to calmly relay everything from walking into the chapel and seeing Snow to jumping in my car to escape the crazy, screwed-up nutjob ghost from my past who was hell-bent on getting to my kids.

Scotty made all the right noises as I spoke. The second I finished, he barked two words at me. "Restraining order."

"Yeah," I confirmed. "Ask Lorraine to send it straight to Judge Browning to get signed off, but don't file it until I say. He owes me a favor. If Snow turns up at the house, I'll file it. After what just happened, I don't want him within ten feet of my kids."

Scotty let out an audible sigh. "Agreed. Leave it with me. Get the twins home and lock the goddamned doors."

"Don't worry, Scotty," I said, taking the turn for Summerlin. "My security system's the best on the market. If he shows, I'll get the kids straight into one of the panic rooms."

"I'll tell Tote to get a couple of men over for protection."

I almost winced. "Don't tell the Kings yet, Scotty. If Hustle finds out, he'll hunt Snow down. The last thing we need right now is a club war." I paused as I turned onto Reverence Parkway. "I've got enough to deal with without defending my uncle for first-degree murder."

"How about I put the PI on him then?" Scotty suggested. "He can arrange a tail. At least we'll know if he's making moves to come for you."

"Okay. Good idea. I'll let you get everything set up." I paused for a second. "Thanks, Scotty."

"Get the kids home. I'll call you later," he advised me before the line went dead.

The second he hung up, ringing sounded through the car.

I looked at the display and saw Sophie was calling me. Taking a calming breath, I psyched myself up and touched the screen. "Hey."

"Thank God," Sophie breathed, relief flooding her voice. "I've been trying to call."

"Had Scotty on," I admitted. "I needed to get ahead of this shit."

"I can't believe it happened," Sophie murmured. "I've never seen Kit like that before. Usually, he's, well—unemotional. It went even crazier after you left. They had to bundle him into Abe's car to stop him from going after you. Cash and Bowie are with him in case he tries to follow you."

I glanced in the rearview, looking at Kady's tear-stained cheek as she looked out of the window sadly. "He's a lunatic," I snapped. "If he comes near me or my kids, I'll get him arrested."

"I'm so sorry, Ned. You must be in pieces, seeing him like that with no warning. I never put two and two together, never even suspected that your Snow was Kit."

"Why would you?" I demanded. "I thought his name was Kyle Simmons, and he was dead. How could anyone suspect that, actually, he was Kit Stone? He lied to me,

Soph. What kind of person does that? All these years, I've been mourning the wrong man."

"He's sick, Ned," Sophie breathed. "Remember what we talked about back when he left you? Remember what happened? Now I know it's him; everything's slotting into place. I haven't been around Kit enough to know he's got severe PTSD, but he must've had it for years."

"That doesn't give him a pass to do whatever he likes, Soph," I spluttered. "He's a grown man. He knows right from wrong."

"I know," my friend said resignedly. "Please don't do anything drastic. I'll make sure Atlas keeps him away. We're returning to Hambleton to let things settle down, though John wants to contact you about seeing the kids. I can't believe the Stones are the twin's blood family."

My stomach clenched with nausea as I glanced into the rearview again, catching Kai's eyes narrow as he listened in on the convo. He held his sister's hand while her eyes drooped, and my heart plummeted. That scene would've taken a lot out of Kady. "I can't even think about that yet, Soph. Me and the kids need to have a conversation. Whatever happens next is their choice, not mine."

"I know. Look, I have to go; Atlas needs me. It may be about Kit." My friend's tone dropped. "I'll call you later. Love you."

"Love you too," I replied as the line went dead.

I took the turn leading to my house and checked Kady again, who by then was breathing rhythmically. "I'm sorry you had to see that, Son," I told Kai gently. "You and your sister are too young to witness that behavior. Are you okay?"

"Yeah," he murmured through clenched teeth. "Why did he lie?"

My heart squeezed as I thought about it. "I don't know. The last time I saw your father, he was ill. It's not an excuse, but maybe that was part of it."

Kai shook his head, turning his face toward the window, effectively ending the conversation. "He's a lying asshole," he whispered.

I stared back at the road, allowing my boy his space. He needed to think everything through, and he wasn't the only one. How sick did someone have to be to put someone they professed to love through that for nothing?

I couldn't wrap my brain around it. That was why I left so suddenly. How was I supposed to stand there acting like nothing had happened when my heart was bleeding out on the floor?

Escaping wasn't cowardice on my part. Anybody who knew me also knew that cowardice wasn't my jam. I couldn't think straight, and before I confronted Snow, I needed to calm down and come to terms with the fact that the so-called love of my life was still alive after eight years of believing he was killed in action.

When he chased us down, and I finally looked him in the eyes, I immediately noticed the same blank expression he'd had when he ended us. I wanted no part of that version of the man. My only thought was getting Kai and Kadence out of there and ensuring they were okay. My children were my priority. Not him.

How could he do that to me? To us? He was everything to me, and he lied.

His actions made a mockery out of everything we shared, everything we were. He'd given me somebody else's name, for God's sake.

Everything was a lie.

We were a lie.

My thoughts and memories were tainted. Loving Snow and then mourning him didn't mean shit. Emotion built in my chest like a pressure cooker. My golden boy never existed. The man I'd loved, adored, and yearned for every day for years was a liar.

My Snow had betrayed me in the worst way possible.

Fuck him.

Fuck him!

I pulled up to my house, pressed the remote button to open the gates, and drove through. I was so deep inside my head that I didn't notice Kady had woken until a melodic little voice startled me out of my thoughts.

"Mommy. Kai needs us."

My head jerked around to see Kai red-faced with his fists clenched. "I hate him," he growled.

"His heart's sick," my girl whispered, "And his head's stormy inside like thunder and lightning."

I thoughtfully regarded my little empath.

Kadence could feel moods and emotions, but none like her twin's. She'd take one look at Kai and know his mood instantly. Kady's sweetness radiated from her. She never got angry or bitchy. The only time she ever showed any sadness was when Kai struggled.

And struggle he did.

My boy never felt like he fit in anywhere. Kady was surrounded by friends at school, whereas Kai was a loner. He felt aggravated by everyone except me, his twin, and Sophie. My son didn't give any fucks about social norms, hated them even. He isolated himself, withdrawing to the point where I had him tested for ADHD and autism, but both tests were negative.

Turned out it was just the way he was. It was Kai, and although he seemed unconventional to others, to me, he was perfect.

"Come on. Let's get you inside." I unclipped my seatbelt and jumped out of the car, inwardly berating myself for allowing the kids to witness so much drama. Opening Kady's door, I helped her out before telling Kai, "Come on, Son."

I slipped my hand into my girl's and looked down at her pretty face as we walked around to get Kai. "How do you feel about what happened?" I asked.

"I'm okay." Kady's smile faded a little. "Our daddy's just like Kai. He had thunder and lightning in his head, too, but his was more painful. He's sick, mommy. He needs a doctor."

My heart dropped like a dead weight.

Helping Kai out of the car, I lowered to my haunches, drawing eye level with my girl, and asked, "Where was he sick, baby?"

She tapped my forehead. "He's sick, there," her finger lowered, and she touched my heart, "and there. He's sad, Mommy, but when he saw us, he was happy. Then, when everyone started shouting, he was sad again."

My throat thickened as a years-old memory of lying in a bath with Snow flickered through my mind. It was the night everything fell apart. The night he nearly destroyed me.

I knew he was sick. He'd changed so drastically in such a short amount of time.

The first time I saw him, his eyes were clear and full of hope and determination to make the world safer. Such a massive contrast to the last time I saw him.

Since he'd died, I'd done a lot of legal work with Vets and seen more blank eyes and tortured expressions than I cared to admit. I tried to help men who'd been discarded after they risked their lives for their country. It was my way of honoring the man I'd loved, the missing half of my soul.

What a joke that turned out to be.

I'd witnessed what war did to people, but Kady hadn't. She couldn't have known, and she was too young to understand the bad shit in the world.

Bad shit that I had to protect her from, even if it meant keeping her away from her father.

"Okay," I tucked a lock of blonde hair behind her ear before rising to my full height. "I get you're worried, but you guys are my priority. We should have a family meeting, talk it out, and sleep on it."

"I know," she sang as we walked to the house. "Please don't be grumpy, Kai. I know you're angry, but everything will be okay."

I looked at Kai thoughtfully, worrying about how my boy seemed to be taking Snow's return from the dead almost as badly as I was.

He was his dad personified in looks and personality, especially his protectiveness, which Kai possessed an abundance of. My son was so watchful of Kady and me that it was sometimes over-the-top. He assumed the role of the man of the house so wholly that he stopped being a kid a long time ago, which gave me many sleepless nights.

I'd hear him creep downstairs in the dark and check the doors and windows were locked. He'd watch Kady, not in a weird way, but to ensure she was safe and happy. He'd tested the only two men I'd brought home to meet them in ways that surprised even jaded old me.

He wasn't an asshole kid. I had guys as friends who he was great with, and of course, he had Uncle Hustle. But he was an ass toward the only two serious boyfriends I'd had over the years.

The way his eyes flicked over them, all blank and assessing, kept me awake at night. Kai may have had an old head on young shoulders, but it was a lot for a boy his age.

I talked to him about it, but he said they didn't feel right in our space. His instincts turned out to be spot-on. Both men were nice guys; fun, handsome, and successful. More importantly, they made an effort with my kids and tried everything to win them and me over.

They were perfect on paper but were missing one vital thing.

They weren't *him*.

And maybe, deep down, Kai felt that too. When I thought about it, I realized Kai must have possessed some level of spirituality because he felt Snow's absence just as painfully as I did. Now his dad had appeared, and my kid was hurting and confused, so I had to tread carefully with this entire fucked-up situation.

I opened the door and ushered the kids in, sighing as I took in Kai's look of pure anger. "Hey, Son," I murmured as Kady took one of his hands, me the other.

Kai's body jerked. He hated being touched. Usually, only Kady could get close, but tonight, we needed to support each other. I wouldn't let my boy bottle everything up like he usually did.

He clenched his jaw. "I'm okay, Mom. Don't need anything. Don't wanna hug, don't wanna feel better. I just wanna be left alone."

My heart ached for him. I could feel his pain; it was the same as mine. Kady took everything in her stride, but my boy didn't like to be blindsided. It sent him out of whack and unsettled him. Today must've been his worst nightmare.

Leading the twins into the kitchen, I gestured for them to sit at the table while fetching them both a juice carton from the fridge. "We've got to talk about what we'll do, Son. First, I need to ask something, and I need you to be truthful. Do you want to get to know your—dad?" The last word came out almost strangled.

I felt Kai let out a huge sigh. "No. He lied to you. He's not dead, and his name's not Kyle."

I swallowed past the lump in my throat. "Okay," I agreed. "You don't have to do anything you don't want to."

Kady snuggled into her brother and looked at him with wide eyes. "I want to talk to him," she said quietly.

Kai's eyes jerked toward his sister. "No, Kady! What about Mom?"

I stroked Kai's soft, dark hair—so much like Snow's—swallowing my tears.

This was my son to a tee, loyal and protective. However, he needed to understand I was the parent, not him. It was my job to look out for them, not the other way around. The thought of the kids spending time with Snow made me want to puke, but I knew if it was safe for them, I'd allow it. If I didn't, they'd always wonder.

Kai needed a dad—or at least a father figure—to take the pressure off him.

People talked about those times when we had to put our feelings aside for the sake of our kids and do what was best for them, even if it killed us.

After what happened at the chapel, I was loath to let them anywhere near Snow, but was that me being a petty bitch? I had to remember he left me, not them. Snow didn't know of their existence until today. I hated him and despised what he'd done, but if he wanted to get to know the twins, didn't he have a right? Could I, in all good conscience, refuse contact?

I winced when I recalled the restraining order that had no doubt already been signed. I wouldn't file it unless Snow made me. I needed him to disappear until the kids—and I—had time to come to terms with everything.

Conditions would have to be implemented, and I'd need to closely monitor Snow's anger issues. It was clear his mental health had declined further, but I could offer supervised visits. Why should the kids miss out on meeting their flesh and blood who seemed eager to get to know them?

As much as it pained me to lose a bit of them to *him*, my gut told me it may also help, Kai especially. And I was a girl who always listened to her gut.

Inwardly bracing, I spoke the words that made my stomach turn over. "I want you to do what's best for you, Son. Forget what happened between me and your father; it's nobody's business but ours. We may be angry with him now, but he's still your dad, and you have a big family to get to know. I won't be hurt if you're curious about them. It's natural to have questions." I gently turned Kai's face and looked into his golden eyes. "We talked about visiting Sophie. We still can. Maybe it will help you and Kady make your minds up about your dad. And your grandpa—John—seemed really happy to meet you. That's cool, right?"

Kady nudged her brother gently. "Daddy's not a bad man, Kai. And did you see our grandpa and our uncles? I know they were a bit weird, but Sophie likes them, so they can't be bad people, right? We like Atlas, don't we? He's their friend."

Kai shook his head. "He lied to us all. And what if we hate them?"

"Then we jump on the first plane home and forget we ever knew them," I reassured him.

His shoulders slumped. "I dunno."

"So, take some time and think about it," I suggested. "You've still got a week of the semester left. Plenty of time to decide." I purposely kept my tone light. "You know what we should do?" I waggled my eyebrows.

Kai let out a cry of, "No!" While Kady giggled and yelled. "Dance party!"

I gently grabbed my son's arm. "Come on, grouch, let's dance it out." I started to tickle his pits, making him yelp loudly. "Momma wants to dance! Come on! I'll even let you choose today's song."

Kai held his head in his hands and groaned. "Kady can choose."

Kady squealed, throwing her arms around him and giving him a quick hug before bouncing to the floor. "Alexa. Play Shake it Off," she yelled excitedly, jumping on the balls of her feet.

Kai groaned again.

I laughed.

And as I danced around the kitchen with my kids to Taylor's cheesiest song, my smile assured them everything would work out.

However, inwardly, my thoughts churned. I couldn't get Snow and what he'd done out of my head.

Every day, I'd spoken to his ghost. Every day, I'd made a silent promise to keep his memory alive through our kids. Every day, I'd told him how much I adored him and how I'd do anything to see him one more time. A piece of me died the day his commanding officer told me he'd been killed in action, and it had never come back.

Not like him.

How could I get over such a colossal betrayal when he'd destroyed me all over again?

Chapter Three

Breaker

The flight home was the stuff made from nightmares. Abe, Atlas, and Iris formed a protective bubble around me from the minute we left the chapel. They wouldn't let Dad near me. Bowie and Layla had been pretty great, too. However, Cash sat behind us on the plane, cracking jokes at my expense.

With the heightened emotions hijacking my brain, I couldn't seem to block him out.

I'd been pacing all night, trying to shut down the pain like I'd done for years, but it hadn't worked. Seeing Kitten again and discovering Kai and Kadence's existence had flung the door to my feelings wide open, and I couldn't seem to lock them back inside again.

In the space of twenty-four hours, I'd gone from blank and emotionless to a tweaker.

Every organ burned when I remembered how Kitten had run from me. The only woman I'd ever loved took my kids and left, and I wasn't sure how I was keeping my shit together.

I'd dreamed of our reunion for years, of walking down the street and catching sight of each other. I imagined her throwing herself into my arms and everything suddenly being better.

Should've known she'd loathe me. Jesus, I loathed myself.

My emotions were unraveling. A dark pit enveloped my chest, and it hurt to breathe. My fingers tremored so severely that I had to hide my hands in my pockets.

The thought of Kai and Kadence's upset expressions kept swirling through my mind. How the fuck had I caused so much damage to my family in so short a time?

Kitten hated me. The only person who'd kept me alive through all those lonely nights probably now wished I *was* dead.

Maybe I should've gone boom years ago. At least that way, she'd have had something real to mourn.

Going boom would do Kitten and those kids a favor. You're evil.

You're no good to anyone.

You're a disgrace.

You don't deserve a family.

I leaned forward, holding my head in my hands. The voices in my head were driving me goddamned crazy.

"You okay, Kit?" Abe asked, looking at me in the rearview mirror.

"Yeah," I croaked, sitting up to not worry Iris.

We'd been on the road for about ten minutes when she cleared her throat, pulling me out of my destructive thoughts.

"Will you tell us about her, Kit? I've never seen you like that over a girl before. She must be extraordinary."

Heat scalded my throat as the memories I'd pushed down for years started swirling through my mind. A movie reel flashed behind my eyes: the night we met, watching her dance in a smoky club, and finally, the marks and bruises I left on her skin. Images of us doing the simplest things flickered, and every one of them sent an ache through my bones.

I hadn't spoken about her to anyone except Benny and Simmons, so I struggled to find an explanation. How was I supposed to encompass everything we were to each other in mere words? How could I explain a love like that? And how could I even try to justify what I'd done?

"I was twenty-one when we met. Full of good intentions but no clue about anything, really. The first time I saw Kitten, I was on leave just before we deployed. She was the headline act for an exclusive strip club."

Abe barked a laugh. "Only you, Kit."

I smiled at the beautiful memory. "That's what I thought at the time, typical me. A buddy had just gotten an NJP. He'd met a girl who turned out to have a screw loose. She kept showing up at Fort Campbell causing shit."

Abe's gaze caught mine through the mirror. "So, you and your buddies had the bright idea to give the women you were undoubtedly aiming to fuck some fake names to stop history repeatin'." His mouth set in a thin line.

"Better than that, Abe. We gave our girls the names of all the assholes in our unit we clashed with. It was a stupid prank, but it seemed like a good idea at the time, funny almost. You get where I'm going with this?"

"Fuck!" he muttered. "Kyle Simmons."

"Yeah," I muttered. "The same Kyle Simmons whose vehicle I watched get blown up by an IED just outside Kabul eight years ago. Three of our five-man team were wiped out in the blink of an eye. The other was almost crippled. I was the only one to walk away more or less unscathed."

"Oh, Kit," Iris murmured sadly. "I'm sorry you had to see that."

My eyes flicked right, and I stared out the window, thinking about the explosion that haunted my dreams. "Ain't the worst thing I've seen. Hell, I've done stuff that would give a serial killer nightmares. I turned into a monster years ago."

Silence fell over us, everyone turning to their thoughts.

Discussing what happened to Benny, Simmons, and Espinoza made my head spin.

I'd shut it all down for so long because the onslaught of remembering made me ache.

Seeing Kitten again slashed my fucked-up soul wide open and let all the nasty out. The blood flowing through my veins burned like acid, contaminating me.

My mind's eye relived Benny's Humvee blowing up every night in my dreams.

I'd never understood why it happened like that. Benny and Simmons were good, decent men. What God would take them and leave a monster like me breathing? How was that fair?

Not for the first time, I wished the IED had hit my vehicle instead of theirs. At least that way, I could've spared Kitten and my kids the trauma of seeing me alive again. Maybe going boom had been the answer all along, but I was too weak to go through with it.

Maybe I could do better in the next life and be the man who deserved them.

It was apparent Kitten didn't want me, and I'd already scared my children away. I'd exposed them to the worst excuse for a man they'd ever meet.

Their father.

"What happened with Kennedy? Why didn't you go back for her?" Iris asked, pulling me away from the dark voices in my head.

"The last time I saw her, I ended it," I said quietly. "I wasn't myself, 'Ris. I went into some kind of trance and got physical with her. Didn't know about it until the next morning. To this day, I dunno what happened, but I knew she was better off without me." I let out a self-derisive laugh. "Funny thing is, years later, when I finally left the EOD, my head was even more fucked-up, but it didn't stop me from searching for her then. Thinking back, I'm glad she disappeared. I would've ruined her. Yesterday proved that."

Iris twisted her body around to glare at me from the front seat. "Stop that, now! You're a good man, Kit. You just went through some awful stuff. When we get home, you're moving in with us, and we'll help you. It's time for you to take responsibility for your health. This has gone on long enough."

"She's right, Son," Abe concurred. "War changes the best of people. Saw it with Bandit and your pop."

My eyes darted to look into his in the rearview mirror again. "Huh?"

One side of his mouth lifted wryly. "Yup. I think it's why Dagger stays away from ya. He sees the same in you as he's got in him, and it fucks with his head." Abe grinned. "Ever wondered why Bandit was such a crazy fucker? He came back from 'Nam with a fuckin' screw loose. Same as you have."

I barked out a laugh as Iris simultaneously slapped Abe's arm hard. "Shut your mouth, old man," she scolded.

He looked at me in the rearview again and grinned. "He knows I see him like a son. Hope he knows I love him just as much, too."

I rubbed my forehead, trying to stop the voices.

He's lying. You're not worth shit.
Nobody cares about you.

I had to bring my hands up to clasp the sides of my head to ease the painful thump. My senses were overstimulated with everything I'd felt over the past twenty-four hours. Seeing that billboard released something inside I hadn't felt in years.

Hope.

But why hope when everything I'd lived for was lost to me? I didn't know how I'd go on anymore. I didn't fuckin' want to, not without *her*.

My entire body ached, and my skin felt too tight to contain my blood and bones. Everything was jarring; the light was too bright, the sounds too loud.

I'd dreaded this day, and I was right to.

By the time we pulled up to the compound gates, I was a mess. I could feel my insides cracking apart. My mind kept going over the pain in Kennedy's face; the pain I'd caused.

I was holding myself together by a thread.

Abe muttered something to himself as he lowered his window and shouted, "What the fuck's goin' on?"

My gut had churned for the last few miles, reminiscent of how it did when I shot an insurgent. I'd gotten so attuned to danger by the time I left the military behind that I could sense trouble from miles away.

I craned my neck toward the clubhouse.

A group of people stood over something lying out on the ground. Hendrix tried to push a couple of the whores back, who were hugging and crying.

Something was wrong.

Billy sauntered over to let us through the gate.

We'd recruited him as a new prospect after the way he handled a shotgun when the Sinners attacked the clubhouse. His name was Noah, but Atlas christened him Billy seeing as he shot up those fuckers like Billy the Kid.

He leaned down to Abe's window, resting his arms on the pane. "You just missed all the fun. Sinners dumped a dead chick at the gates about ten minutes back. VP, Colt, and Iceman carried what's left of her inside the compound before the cops came sniffing around." He jerked his head toward a huddle of people in the lot. "She was already dead. I don't know her, but one'a the boys said she used to whore for you guys."

Something punched me hard in the chest. A part of me knew who it was.

Blindly, I opened the door and hauled my ass out of Abe's cage. The thud of car doors filled the air as Dad and the others jumped out of their vehicles.

"Who is it?" Dad shouted.

Hendrix turned, saw us, and beckoned.

With Abe beside me, I moved toward the huddle of people. I heard Cash mutter something disrespectful to Dad as they followed behind.

Hendrix shook his head as we approached. "Not the best welcome home, huh?" His eyes went over my shoulder to Dad. "She was dumped outside the gates, Prez. We brought her straight inside to work on her, but I think she's been dead a while."

My eyes dropped to the heaped body sprawled on the ground.

My gut dropped. I could hardly recognize April's face because it had been battered almost to a pulp, all swollen and misshapen. Her blood-soaked shorts were familiar, and I saw a ring on her index finger that she never took off.

The voices in my head became almost unbearable.

You did that.

It's your fault.

You threw her to the wolves.

Sophie rushed past us and lowered to the ground, quickly examining April's corpse. She glanced up at Atlas. "Looks like she's been dead a while. The blood's been dried for days."

"What about the baby?" Dad asked, tone thick with disbelief.

Soph gently pulled April's shorts down to reveal her stomach. "Look." She pointed to an extended, jagged cut across her abdomen. "She's had some kind of C-section," Sophie traced her fingers over the broken, bloody skin, "but it wasn't done by a professional. She's been ripped apart. It was done about a week ago, see? The wound has already started knitting back together." Her fingers moved from the cut to the long, purple stretch marks covering April's saggy stomach, and she shook her head. "It looks like she went to term before they took the baby."

I sucked in air through my nose, hands clenching into fists.

April was a cunt. She fucked me over, and Cash. But did she deserve that? Did any human being deserve to be tortured that way? At least when I murdered, I made it quick. I'd never made anyone suffer.

You're still a monster.
She's dead because of you.

"What we gonna do with her?" Abe asked, eyes still glued to the body. "Her folks died before she joined the club. Does anyone know if she's got any family?"

I rubbed at the ache in my chest before lifting my hand to massage my temple as adrenaline pumped through my veins so hard it made me dizzy.

"I'll take her to our burial site," Atlas muttered. "She was a traitorous bitch, but she still deserves to be buried properly."

"I'd burn the whore," Cash muttered. "She got everything she deserved. Buryin's too good for her."

Heat swept through my chest like wildfire.

My head swiveled to face Cash. "Are you for fucking real? She's been tortured and murdered. You've got no respect for anyone."

He shrugged, glaring at the body on the ground. "Got no respect for her." His stare lifted to mine, mouth twisting with malice.

I knew that look. He was about to get nasty.

"You've been let off the hook. The baby wasn't yours. If she was at term when they beat her bloody, she was way further along than she told you." Cash smirked. "At least we know you've only been a deadbeat dad to two kids instead of three."

His words stabbed my brain like tiny blades.

Almost deafened by the rushing in my ears, I ground my teeth, clenching my jaw tight.

"Wish we got to her first," Cash added with a quiet snort. "Right now, I envy Bear."

Without a thought, I turned, pulled my arm back, and punched Cash across his jaw. As he staggered, I grabbed the back of his head, dragged him up, and jabbed my fist in his face.

Suddenly, I was back in the ring with Espinoza and my boys. The vision of my buds sitting on the gym floor, watching with grins spread across their faces, seemed so real that even the sunlight dimmed as if it was one A.M., and I couldn't sleep. I could smell Sarge's sweat and hear his grunts as we sparred.

"Kick his ass, Snow," Benny shouted.

Simmons laughed.

"That's it, princess," Espinoza rasped through the gumshield, his black eyes burning into mine. "Come show papi what you got."

Roars filled my ears, along with demands to punch harder.

My fists pummeled bone, causing a crunch that made my stomach soar.

Sarge's fist hurtled toward the side of my face. I ducked left and right, avoiding his flurry of punches.

"Fuckin' asshole," he panted.

I bounced on the balls of my feet, landing another jab across his head.

Laughter went up from the boys standing outside the ring. "Harder, Snow. Fuck him up."

I pulled my gloves up in front of my face and punched him repeatedly. The last pummel hit, and he let out a quiet groan. Encouraged, I did a flurry of two-one punches.

Shouts and cries filled the air as I methodically kept pummeling, not that they registered. I was so caught up in the vision that I couldn't stop. Emotion rushed through my chest. I had to get the pain out, and the only way I knew how was through violence.

The monster roared to life, taking over my mind and body. I punched, kicked, and snarled like a wild animal, doing everything I could to feed my innermost cravings and desires. My sense of awareness was comatose. I didn't think or feel; I just kept punching until all I could see before me was blood.

Suddenly, hands grabbed me and hauled me backward.

My mind whooshed again. Suddenly, the gym I'd been in just seconds before disappeared. The harsh sunshine almost blinded me, and I gulped in air when I saw the Demon's lot all around.

Still disorientated, I felt strong arms banded around my chest, and a deep voice murmured, "Calm down, Kit," repeatedly in my ear.

"No," I snarled. "I wanna go back to Benny and Simmons." Disorientated, I swung again before horrified screams cut through the air, jarring my over-sensitive brain. My throat thickened as pain ricocheted through my body, highlighting the acute ache radiating from my clenched fists.

I glanced down at my hands, almost mesmerized by the blood oozing from my knuckles and covering the sleeves of my shirt. That was when my blood-covered hands began to violently shake.

"W—what happened?" I asked, my tone tortured.

Movement caught my eye. I turned to see Dad and Bowie kneeling on the floor, helping someone up. A flash of tan skin and tribal tattoos caught my attention, and I watched as Cash slowly rose to his feet, his face a mangled mess.

"Jesus, Kit. I thought you were gonna kill him." Hendrix's voice emanated pure disbelief.

"I dunno what happened." I tried to step forward to help Cash, but the arms keeping me contained pulled me back again. "No!" I bellowed. "Let me help him!"

"No," Hendrix murmured. "It's gone too far. This won't stand, Kit. Now you're really fucked." The thread of disgust in the VPs voice wound around my heart and squeezed until I couldn't breathe. Air sawed in and out of me, and I started to hyperventilate.

Everything that happened over the last ten years flickered through my mind. Love, death, violence, murder, and destruction.

The clouds in my mind parted, and clarity finally shone through.

Everything about me was wrong. Everywhere I went, I left pandemonium in my wake.

I'd damaged the only family I'd ever want. Of course, my kids hated me; I hated myself. I'd murdered people and brought torment to so many others. Everything about me was vile.

I couldn't even save April. Months ago, I'd handed her over to a monster even more fucked-up than me, and I hadn't lost a moment's sleep. Now, her dead body lay mutilated in the goddamned parking lot of a biker compound.

There was no hope for me. The best thing I could do for everyone was leave the earth; it would be a better place without me. At least that way, I could save the people I loved any more heartache. I couldn't live with the agonizing pain, making it impossible to breathe.

I knew it as well as I knew the back of my hand.

It was time to go boom.

Do it. You may find peace in Hell.

Everyone will be happier without you.

You're a demon.

Finally, I listened to the voices in my head. It was the only solution.

My hand went to my inside pocket for the Browning BDA my gramps left me when he died, but my holster was empty. My nostrils flared when I recalled I'd been on a flight and left it locked away safe in my room.

The disappointment faded when my eyes caught a flash of metal.

Hendrix didn't go to Vegas.

My hand flew toward the open holster he'd fastened over his tee and snatched his firearm.

Veep's eyes filled with shock, the same shock which no doubt made his arms loosen from around me. I took the opportunity God had granted me by stepping back, dropping to my knees, and butting the gun's barrel against my temple.

Screams, cries, and shouts filled the air, but it didn't matter. Nothing would matter soon.

My eyes darted around to see Pop barreling toward me, his face pale and stricken. "No!" he bellowed.

"I'm sorry," I croaked, closing my eyes and slowly squeezing the trigger.

A deafening gunshot cracked through the air just as my entire body jerked with the impact of the bullet.

My spirit sank into darkness until there was no more pain.

Chapter Four

Breaker

Rock bottom.
I'd often dissect the phrase in my mind, thinking about what it really meant.
Over the years, my imagination often threw up mental pictures of my body, lifeless in a ditch somewhere. Or drinking too much whiskey and choking to death on my own puke. I knew things had deteriorated over time, and I knew I was a fuckin' mess. Still, I never thought I'd hit the elusive rock bottom for one straightforward reason.

I always imagined I'd kill myself before then.

But whether it be divine intervention, fate, or simply God's will, I was still alive, and logic told me I should've been grateful for that. But when I woke up in bed at the clubhouse, I wasn't sure how to react.

In a way, I felt cheated.

After all the heartache, pain, and torment, I reckoned I had the right to go out on my own terms. I wasn't much good to anyone the way I was, so why couldn't they give me that? I wanted to stop hurting myself and everyone around me. It wasn't about being selfish or even courageous. It was just what I believed to be right.

Knowing what I'd done to the only woman I'd ever loved was the tipping point. Then, seeing April that way and knowing I could've stopped it was the final straw.

When I saw Benny, Simmons, and Espinoza, the pain receded, and for a moment, I was happy. Where did a man who was too fucked-up for the military and too fucked-up for society belong?

Nowhere.

The only places that had ever felt right were with my buddies and by Kitten's side. But, I was too far gone for the latter to ever happen. The problem was, now I'd found her, and *them,* there was nowhere else I wanted to be, even though I was too broken to become the man they deserved.

So, what was the point of anything?

When my eyes flickered open—and the realization that I was in bed at the clubhouse, instead of burning in Hell, hit me—I didn't feel any gratitude for being given a second chance.

Instead, I felt resentful.

Why couldn't they let me find peace?

Someone was in my room with me, but I didn't know who until Dad spoke.

"I'm sorry I let you down, Kit. I'm so fuckin' sorry. Never again do I wanna see my boy with a gun against his head. Never fuckin' again, Kit. I admit I ignored the signs. I admit I should've done better."

"What happened?" I croaked. "Why am I not dead?"

"Atlas shot you in your shoulder. You jerked, and the gun moved as you fired," Dad choked out. "There wasn't time for anythin' else. I couldn't get to you in time."

My mind drifted as Dad went on for what seemed like hours.

He promised he'd try to be a better father in the future and support me. He said he'd do everything it took to get me well again. I heard it, but I wasn't listening.

Breaker

It wasn't his fuck-up, and it didn't really matter how we got to where we were at. The fact was, for me, death had been a long time coming.

I was empty, my insides a void where evil reigned. I wasn't good for the world and certainly wasn't good enough for Kennedy.

Every sick act I'd done throughout the last eight years had become a noose around my neck. All I could do was lay there, numb. I had nothing inside left to give.

Pop called Sophie in. She gently examined me while talking in her soothing doctor's voice. My pain subsided a little after she gave me an injection, but the aching of my shoulder and head didn't compare to the ache in my heart.

It was a shame she couldn't fix that.

Dad eventually left, and someone else came in; then they left, and they were replaced by another person. Didn't look to see who came to babysit me; I didn't care. I just wanted to be left alone.

I slept on and off until, at one point, I awoke to Abe. The pain in my soul intensified as he told me how much I'd hurt Iris and how if I ever tried anything like that again, *he'd* put the bullet in my ass. He told me everything would be alright, and they were getting me help. On and on he went, trying to pull me out of my stupor, but he couldn't get through to me.

That shit would take an army.

'Take cover!' A voice yelled as an explosion rocked the air, the Humvee shaking with the force of it.

'Benny! No!' I screamed. My emotions ignited and surged; love, hate, and fury rising through my body, making me tremor violently. The pain was so excruciating it made me double over.

'Take evasive maneuvers. Evasive maneuvers.'

Bullets pinged off metal. I looked outside the Humvee to see Benny standing in the moon dust, his body in flames.

'Weapons ready, Snow. It's an ambush.'

'But I gotta save Benny,' I screamed, trying to stand, to get outside and stop him from burning, but suddenly I was paralyzed. I couldn't move a muscle.

'That's not the mission, Snow. Stand down.'

More explosions cracked through the air as Benny held his hands out to me, imploring, 'Help her, Snow. Help her.'

I watched, frozen with horror, as Benny's skin slowly charred and blackened. 'Help her, Snow,' he screamed. 'You gotta help her.'

I looked down. My breastbone protruded, pulsing in and out with every thump of my heart. I started to choke, suffocating on the smell of Benny's burning flesh.

Then, Hollister's voice. 'Shut it down, Snow. The mission is all that matters. If you don't do it, I will. That's an order, soldier.'

'Help her, Snow.'

Benny's voice jerked me awake. My eyes slashed to the corner of the room where my best friend faded away to nothingness, his eyes black voids, staring and haunted.

I braced myself for the onslaught of feelings to maim me down to my bones. It was always like that when I first woke. For a split second, I'd be at peace, then everything would come rushing back and sicken me again.

Acid burned the pit of my stomach because now everyone had seen me raw. For the first time in my life, I didn't have a plan. Offing myself wasn't an option now. My pop would do his best to ensure I didn't get another opportunity.

What the fuck am I gonna do?

My thoughts turned to Kitten and the twins, and a pinprick of light shone. But then I recalled the hardness of her stare, and the light receded. My own kids fucking hated me, and I couldn't blame them. I hadn't done right by them or their mother. If they hated me now, imagine how they'd feel when they discovered something wrong inside me?

I was fucked because I didn't know how I was supposed to exist in a world without her and now without *them*. The only real home I'd ever had was by Kennedy's side. Without her, I didn't belong anywhere.

The pain lancing through my heart took my breath away.

I didn't have the strength to carry on. Every piece of hope I possessed was snuffed out because I'd only stayed in the world for her, and she didn't want me.

Footsteps sounded from down the hallway. The walls in this place were pretty thick, so whoever it was must've been making a racket. Another set joined the first, then another. Eventually, it seemed like a herd of wild animals was coming for me.

I tried to sit up, but I was hindered by the gunshot wound in my shoulder and my bandaged knuckles. After several attempts, my back finally hit the headboard, and I steeled myself.

For years, I'd masked how messed up I was. Obviously, something was off, but Dad, my family, and the club had no idea how bad things really were.

Now, my day of reckoning was finally here.

The door to my room flew open, and Dad walked in with Abe. Cash, Atlas, and Bowie followed single file behind.

My body locked as I caught sight of Cash.

One eye was swollen shut, his nose obviously broken, and his face was cut and bruised. I'd never seen my brother like that before. He was a tough man. He'd breezed through prison because his reputation preceded him. Nobody would have dared try their hand.

Someone had fucked him up, and badly. What the hell had been going on? What had I missed? I couldn't help staring at him as the guys lined up beside my bed.

Pop's eyes softened as he regarded me thoughtfully. The last time I'd seen that expression directed at me was when I came home after my first deployment. It struck me at that moment how much I'd missed it.

Abe sat on the edge of the mattress, his eyes flicking over my face. "You look better, Son."

My throat became so thick with emotion that I couldn't speak, so I just nodded, even though I didn't feel remotely better.

"You were nearly fucking comatose yesterday," Dad interjected. "At least you know we're in the same fuckin' room now. You gave us all a scare, boy," he let out an amused snort, "even Cash."

My eyes darted back to my oldest brother. His stare hadn't left mine the entire time he'd been in the room. He seemed wired. I opened my mouth and, in a voice croaky with underuse, asked, "What happened to you?"

A hush fell over the room.

Cash's good eye sliced to Dad as he muttered something under his breath.

Atlas barked out a laugh.

Bowie covered his grin with his hand.

"Don't you remember?" Dad asked in a confused tone.

I cocked my head to one side. "Remember what?"

Laughs rose through the room.

"You beat the fuck outta him," Atlas said with a chuckle.

Eyes lowering, I took in the dressings wrapped around my knuckles. What were they talking about? I would've remembered something like that, for God's sake. My head wasn't fucked-up to the point that I couldn't recall beating my brother.

Goosebumps skated over my skin as a memory came to me of Kitten's throat, bruised by my hand, and the marks I'd inflicted on her perfect body. I did that and didn't remember. It'd happened many times since. I zoned out during sex. Fuck, I'd nearly killed April without knowing a thing about it.

What was wrong with me?

"We've been in officer's meetings on and off for two days." Dad waved a hand between me and Cash as his voice rose. "This shit's gettin' outta hand. For months Colt's been looking into rehab centers, but that was before you tried to goddamn off yourself."

I flinched, watching Pop take a deep breath, trying to calm his shit instead of doing what he wanted to do and cussing me out. Not that I really cared. Either way, I was fucked.

"You need to let me walk away," I said matter-of-factly. "You've seen what I'm dealin' with up here." I tapped a finger on my head. "None of you get it; you never did." My eyes slashed to Atlas. "You were so hell-bent on getting me back here that you took me away from something that might have got my head right again."

Atlas nodded thoughtfully. "You think I don't know that, Brother? Jesus. It's not fuckin' rocket science. The military fucked you up so bad that you shit PTSD outta your goddamned asshole. But you forget, I tried to make it right, too. I fuckin' begged you go back to Grand Junction, but you told me you didn't need it. I fucked-up, and that's somethin' I'll regret until the end of my days, but you had chances to get yourself straightened out, too, Breaker. Instead, you partied and fucked until you passed out."

"I never wanted to be here," I muttered, ignoring the stab from his comments. "This place makes me worse."

Dad rubbed his beard thoughtfully. "It's your home, Kit."

"It doesn't feel like home?" I retorted, my eyes sliding to Cash's fucked-up face. "I apologize for doin' that, but I can't help thinkin' it's been a long time comin'. I'm always the butt of the joke with you. Never mind that I killed more people than I dare to remember to keep assholes like you livin' the life of a fuckin' king."

"You seem bitter, brother," Cash fired back.

"You're right, *brother*. I am bitter," I agreed. "I'm bitter and twisted 'cause I sacrificed everything for this country but still get treated like a goddamned joke by the likes of *you*."

"Son—" Dad began.

"So it's, son now, eh Pop?" I glared. "Usually, it's fucker, little shit, or goddamned dog's dick. Every time you put me down, it fucks me up a bit more 'cause I gave up everything that meant anything, only for my so-called *brothers* to treat me like a fuckin' idiot. It makes me sick to my stomach." My heart raced, and my hands tremored as all the pain flooded back. Something caught the corner of my vision, and my stricken eyes veered to Benny, silent in the corner.

"What did you give up, Son?" Abe asked quietly.

Stare still on Benny, I rubbed at the tightness in my chest. "Her," I croaked. "I gave up her."

Cash snorted derisively and stomped toward my bed. "Don't blame us for that. It was your choice to ghost Kennedy." He glanced at Dad. "Don't let him guilt trip you about that."

"Cash!" Dad bellowed so loud that I flinched. "For once in your goddamned life, shut the fuck up!"

The room fell silent as Cash's stare hit his boots.

"Tell us, Kit," Abe encouraged quietly. "Why did you give her up?"

I closed my eyes and exhaled.

The thought of sharing my screwed-up feelings made me wanna hold another gun to my head, but I'd gone this far, so I had let them have it all. They'd seen everything. I had nowhere else to hide.

"You saw me after my first deployment, right?"

The guys nodded.

"When we returned to Fort Campbell, I got recruited into a task force alongside two of my buds. Things went downhill from there pretty quickly."

"What did you do?" Bowie asked.

"Bombed, killed, murdered, and maimed," I replied. "It didn't take long for things to go bad."

Mutters filled the air.

Abe held his hand up for silence. "You told Iris and me that your buddies were killed," he prompted.

I nodded, thinking back to that fateful mission. "We'd been sent into Kabul to take down an insurgent on the FBI's most wanted list. It was either bad intel or a setup. They were waiting for us."

"Fuck!" Dad murmured, scraping a hand down his face. "Is that why things went bad with Kennedy?"

"No," I confirmed. "Things went bad with her way before that. I had a choice to make. Leave the military or leave her. It was clear I couldn't have both, not with what it was doin' to me...." My voice trailed off as I thought back to that night. "I remember goin' to see her. We'd just finished a tough mission. I had to put two men down who turned out to be teenagers. My lieutenant told us to take the weekend and get our heads together. I remember goin' to her club, but everythin' else is a dream. I can only remember flashbacks. The next morning, I woke up feelin' okay. Then I saw what I'd done to her, and I didn't believe it at first. I loved her so much. I'd never hurt her...." My voice thickened with emotion. "I left her 'cause I couldn't risk staying in case I did it again. I never knew she was pregnant."

Dad eyed Cash's beat-up face before turning back to me. "How often do you have blackouts, Son?"

I shrugged. "I dunno. Not all the time, usually when I'm highly emotional, or when I'm fucki...." My voice trailed off again.

Atlas grimaced. "Yeah, okay. No need to spell it out."

Dad rolled his eyes as snorts and snickers rose through the room. "Fuckin' schoolboys." His gaze rested on me again. "I'm sorry about April. Not sorry she's dead, Son. She did nothin' but bad shit to this club, but I'm sorry it affected you that way."

"It wasn't like that, Dad," I explained. "It was the way she went out. Nobody deserves that." Heat hit the back of my throat 'cause Pop usually looked at me with contempt, but all I could see was concern. It was nice. "On top of running into Kitten, I saw the twins and just lost my head." My eyes lowered. For the first time since I woke, the thought of what I'd done seemed like an overreaction. But then, lately, the highs were incredible, and the lows tortured me in ways I couldn't comprehend.

It was no wonder I broke.

Pop's face took on a determined look. "I've spoken to the director of the Vet Centre in Grand Junction. I want you to complete their program and get yourself well again."

My pulse began to pick up speed. "No," I insisted. "It's too late for me now."

Dad folded his arms across his chest. "It's never too late, Kit, and what's your alternative? Shooting yourself again? Think how that would affect Kennedy and your kids. How would they feel if you hurt yourself instead of fighting? You're a father. They need you, and we need you."

My chest felt so tight I could hardly take a breath.

"I'll talk to Blondie," Atlas interjected. "I'll tell her what's happened. She's a tough bitch. She'll understand."

My heart raced faster, and I felt my face drop. "What if she takes those kids away from me after what I did?"

"All the more reason to beat feet toward Colorado. I can't see her lettin' you loose on 'em if your head's still fucked." Atlas deadpanned. "Won't let my kid near a nutjob like you." He winked to take the sting out of his words. "Speaking of kids, guess what?"

All eyes turned to the SAA.

"My Stitch is knocked up." His grin grew so wide that he resembled the Cheshire cat. "I'm gonna be a dad."

Shouts of congratulations cut through the room, followed by the thud of back claps. I looked at the men's smiles and grins, wondering in another life if they'd be happy that I was a dad, too.

My heart jolted as the faces of the twins flashed behind my eyes.

Kadence, my girl, seemed curious about me. She was all smiles until I caused that scene in the parking lot. As much as I knew I'd fucked-up, a part of me felt she wanted to know me better.

All thoughts turned to Kai, and a heavy weight settled in my stomach. My boy was protective. He'd be a harder sell. Would he understand how I stayed away so I didn't hurt his mom? Would it appeal to his protective instincts? Maybe he'd be more receptive toward me if he knew I was trying to do my best for them all along.

Could I do this? For them? Was it even feasible?

Second chances were all very well, but I needed a fucking miracle to get Kennedy on my side. Could I ever be the man she fell for again? She loved the old Kit so goddamned beautifully back then.

I owed Kitten so much. Even after what I did to her, she'd had the backbone to raise my kids magnificently. Her strength of character put mine to shame.

Even if I never got my girl back, just having her in my life could help keep me on the straight and narrow. Anything she gave me was better than being without her at all. If the past eight years had taught me anything, it was that.

And didn't I owe it to my kids to at least attempt it?

I wasn't sure I'd survive what was ahead, but maybe I should take one last shot at giving it a go.

My voice was steely as I said, "Pop."

Silence fell over the room once more, and Dad turned to me.

He was a handsome guy. Usually, he looked good for his age, but right then, he seemed older and tired. My gaze sliced to Abe, my second dad, who looked just as ravaged, and it hit me.

Doing what I'd done hurt them. Maybe what I was about to do would hurt me more. Perhaps attempting to process my emotions would destroy me. But they deserved some fucking effort.

My kids needed a dad who put them first, just like their mother had done for the last eight years.

I raised my eyes and looked my dad straight in the eye. "We'll go to Grand Junction. I doubt it'll work, but I'll give it a go."

Dad's shoulders slumped, and his frown relaxed suddenly, making him look years younger. "Good." He smiled. "That's good, Kit. You can do this, Son." His voice sounded determined like he was trying to convince himself.

A light knock sounded on the door. Everyone turned as it opened, and Sophie walked in.

Her eyebrow cocked as calls of congratulations rang through the room. Stomping over to Atlas, she narrowed her eyes. "I thought you didn't want to tell anyone until we got to twelve weeks," she snapped, giving his chest a hard poke.

The SAA rubbed at the spot she'd prodded, looking affronted. "I didn't mean the family, baby."

The pretty doctor pursed her lips. "So that means we're telling everyone now."

Atlas made a 'meh' face.

Sophie rolled her eyes. "You just wanted to be the one to tell them, didn't you?"

His lips twitched.

She shook her head at her husband before eyeing me softly. "Everyone out, please. You're exhausting my patient."

Relief made my shoulders droop. I could've kissed her. Admittedly, their visit made me feel a little better, but there was a lot to process.

The men filed out except for Cash, who touched Sophie's shoulder. "Can I have a quick word with him in private?"

She went to say no, but something in his face made her stop. Soph looked between us quickly. "I'm timing it. You've got three minutes." She smiled at me reassuringly before joining the line of men walking out the door, closing it gently behind her.

My skull flopped back against the headboard.

A showdown with my asshole big brother was the last thing I needed, especially while my mind was still so confused. It was hard to argue with someone who always thought they were right. Never mind, I felt so goddamned fragile.

I set my shoulders, bracing for Cash's angry accusations, but instead, he raised a hand to rub the back of his neck and quietly said, "Brother, I'm sorry."

I froze.

"Look, Kit. I know I'm a dick. I mean, Cara tells me every damned day, so it's not like I can miss the fact I'm an asshole most of the time. I know I've been too hard on you." He stepped forward and lowered his ass onto the side of the bed. "I ain't apologizing for the stuff I did when we were kids 'cause I had it worse than you and Bowie put together. Gramps gave me a ton more bullshit than I ever gave you, and the oldest brother toughenin' up the younger ones, well, it's a rite of passage." His eyes glazed over as he thought back. "We drifted apart when you enlisted, but I still thought about you all the time, especially when you were deployed. When I got outta the slammer and saw you with April, I felt betrayed 'cause I was tryin'a make things work with Cara, and you bringin' her around made it harder. So, I took my shit out on you."

Something loosened in my chest.

This was the first time my oldest brother ever apologized to me in thirty years. Cash was sorry for the wrong thing, though. He had every right to be an asshole after I almost saddled myself with the club whore who purposely fucked us both over.

Now Kennedy was back in my life, albeit precariously, I could see where Cash came from. It didn't take a genius to work out that I went with April to piss him off. But after the way things went south, the joke was on me.

"Remember when you blew up the Sinners' clubhouse?" Cash asked.

I deadpanned. "Well, yeah."

"That was the first time I saw the soldier. The way you went in there and single-handedly took 'em down and walked out with a prisoner slung over your shoulder. That was some cool shit, brother, and just now, when you told us what you did in the military," he reached out and curled his hand around my nape, looking hard into my eyes, "it proved you're a fuckin' asset to this club. Get your ass to that hospital, and I'll do everything I can to have your woman and kids here, waitin' for you when you get back. There ain't nothin' wrong with admitting your weaknesses, Kit. If a dick like me can see a shrink and admit my faults, anyone can. I know from experience you've got a long road ahead, but I'm gonna help. You get me?"

Heat hit the back of my throat, and I nodded.

He jerked one nod, slid his hand away from my neck, and rose to his feet. "Good luck, Kit." And with that, my brother turned and sauntered from the room.

I stared after him with my mouth hanging open.

What the fuck was that?

Growing up as the youngest Stone brother wasn't easy, but it wasn't horrific either. We were loved and cared for. I remembered Bandit taking Cash off by himself. At the time, I was jealous he was getting Grandpop's attention, but after what he'd told me, I realized it wasn't easy for him. Bandit put him in the ring with grown men when he was fourteen. In Winter, he'd take Cash up into the woods and make him do target practice until his hands were numb with cold.

As much as Xander was revered as the eldest son of the eldest son, I was starting to understand he had his own pressures. Probably more than me. Cash had been going to therapy for months. At first, it cut him raw, but after a while, he settled and made positive changes.

After that conversation, I could see how speaking to someone had helped him more than I knew. The asshole would never have apologized to me like that before.

That got me thinking. If therapy could mellow out the likes of Cash, could it help me vanquish the monster? The idea of exposing how dark I'd become made me wanna curl up and die, but if I wanted a chance at being what Kitten and my kids needed, there was no choice.

I had to give it a go.

Chapter Five

Kennedy

I tucked the comforter tighter around Kady's little body as she winced in pain. "Can I get you anything else, baby?" I asked, sitting on the side of the bed. I touched the backs of my fingers to her forehead, checking her temperature.

Kady shook her head and whimpered, making me almost weep. I hated seeing my kids in pain.

My girl got headaches, but nothing like this. It seemed to be a full-blown migraine, but instead of lasting for hours, it had gone on for days. I'd called the doctor out to examine her, but he said it should ease anytime. When it didn't, I called Sophie for advice but couldn't get an answer.

Two days passed, and I kept trying, but she hadn't replied. Not only was I frantic about Kady, but I was also going out of my mind about Sophie. Even if she was at work or couldn't answer her cell, she'd always call me back without fail. After running into Snow like that, she would never have dreamed of disappearing on me.

Something was wrong. I could feel it. My stomach had been in knots for days, and my hands trembled constantly. The only positive spin I could put on the situation was that it stopped me from stressing about Snow.

I caught my son's shadow at the bedroom door. "Hey."

"I'll lie with her," Kai told me as he approached the bed. "She'll feel better if I'm there."

I nodded blindly. "If her headache doesn't ease soon, we're taking her to hospital. I don't care what the doctor says." I could've kicked myself that I'd let that asshole stop me from taking her to be examined properly. If anything happened to my baby, I'd drag his ass into court faster than he could say 'struck off the medical register.'

Kai slipped under the comforter and cuddled my girl into him. "It's okay, Kady," he murmured, gently stroking her hair. "It'll go soon. You'll be fine."

My heart swelled at the sight of my son looking after his twin. They were always like this, and it usually worked, too. The way they cared for each other made me thank God for the amazing kids he gave me. I just hoped that Kai could make his sister feel better soon.

I jumped slightly as the peal of my ringtone drifted up the stairs.

"Get it, Mom," Kai ordered gently. "It's probably Aunt Sophie."

"Will you be okay?" I asked, rising from my position on the bed,

He nodded, still stoking Kady's hair.

Swiftly, I left the room just as the ringtone went silent. My heart leaped into my mouth when I recalled how sick Kady seemed. If it wasn't Sophie calling, I'd bundle the kids up and drive to the hospital. A three-day migraine was atypical, especially for an eight-year-old.

As my feet hit the bottom step, the cell phone pealed again. "I'm coming," I breathed, heading into the kitchen and snatching it off the counter. My shoulders slumped when I saw Sophie's name written across the screen.

Stabbing the answer button, I heaved a sigh and lifted the cell to my ear. "Thank God it's you. Kady's ill, and I don't know what I'm doing. I called Doctor Hollifield, but he said to keep an eye on her for now."

"Ty knows what he's talking about, Ned," she replied. "I worked with him for three years, and he's a talented doctor, but if you're worried, take her to the hospital."

"Yeah," I agreed, blowing out a relieved breath. "I've been trying to contact you. Is everything okay?"

"No," she replied. Her voice was so quiet I had to strain to hear her. "Something happened. Are you at home now?"

"Yeah. We've not left the house for days." My heart thudded against my ribs. "Are you alright, Soph? Is it Atlas?"

"I'm fine," she reassured me. "Atlas, too. But something happened a few days ago. I've just got back from Colorado. Atlas and Cash have already landed at Harry Reid. I tried to come, but he wouldn't let me." She paused for a few seconds. "Ned. I'm pregnant."

Warmth flooded my insides as Sophie's news sunk in. "That's amazing. Congratulations. You'll make the best mother, Soph."

"Thanks, babe. Look, I'm sorry, but I have to be quick. The boys should get to your place anytime now. Atlas will tell you what happened. Just keep an open mind, okay?"

The sick feeling returned, and bile rose through my throat because, somehow, I knew. "It's Snow, isn't it?"

"Yeah."

The pinging of my security system cut through the kitchen. "That must be them," Soph whispered. "It's best they tell you face-to-face."

The hand holding my cell phone trembled, and my throat almost closed. "What's happened?" I demanded, moving into the hall.

"Atlas will explain everything. You said you were already coming to Wyoming, but can you leave earlier?"

"I think so. School's out this week, but I told the principal the kids won't be back this semester with Kady being sick. Scotty knows I'm going away for the Summer. I just need to clear my desk at work and pack."

"Layla and Iris are heading to the rental," Sophie told me. "They'll make your beds and leave food and snacks for you and the kids. It will be ready by the time you get here."

My front door loomed ahead of me. A part of me wanted to run away and hide. I hated what Snow had done to me and the kids, but I couldn't help the joy that shot through me in the chapel when I realized he was still alive. I didn't know what Atlas was about to tell me, but I worried from Sophie's tone that it wasn't anything good.

I peered at the camera to see Atlas and Cash waiting outside on the porch. "What's going on?" I murmured. "Tell me."

"It's better if Atlas explains," Sophie replied. "Let them in. I love you, babe." Before I could tell her the same, she disconnected the call.

I tapped in my security code and swung the door open.

"Yo!" Atlas greeted me. "You spoke to Stitch yet?"

"Yeah," I confirmed. "What's going on?" Lack of sleep from looking after Kady and worry for Snow took over, and I began to sway on my feet.

"Whoa," Atlas called out, grabbing my arm. "Sit down before you fall down." He led me back into the kitchen and settled me at the table before going to the fridge and grabbing a few bottles of water. He threw one at Cash before opening another and placing it before me. "Drink, Blondie," he ordered gently.

My eyes widened as I noticed that Cash's face was beaten. It was black and blue. One eye was swollen shut, and his nose had strips stuck vertically across it.

My head reared back. "What the hell happened to you?"

Cash threw me a lopsided grin, wincing as the action pulled the stitches on his lip. "Kit 'Tyson' Stone's what happened."

I closed my eyes, suddenly exasperated by the fact that everyone was speaking in damned riddles. Raising a finger, I jabbed it toward Atlas. "You better tell me what's going on, or I swear I'll give you so much shit your balls will run back into your scarily toned stomach." My jaw clenched. "Is he dead?"

Atlas held his hands up defensively. "Calm down, Blondie."

"Atlas," I shrieked, about to lose my shit.

He rolled his eyes. "No. Kit's not dead, but it was a close call."

A sense of dread blanketed my stomach, and all the fight left my body. I rubbed at my aching temple. "What happened?" I whispered.

"When we got back to Hambleton, he lost his head. I reckon everything got on top of him 'cause all it took was shit for brains here," he nodded at Cash, "to open his asshole mouth before Kit beat the crap outta him." Atlas paused and lowered his voice. "I didn't know how badly Kit was sufferin' with PTSD until he grabbed our VP's gun and tried to blow his own brains out."

My whole body jerked from the impact of his words. "What?" I shrieked.

"He's okay, Ned," Atlas said reassuringly. "We got lucky."

I shook my head disbelievingly. "How did it come to this? How did he get this bad?"

Snow had all the symptoms of PTSD, even when we were together. He'd been restless when he'd first visited after his deployment. I'd lie awake, feeling him fidget. More often than not, he'd pace my apartment when he thought I was asleep. I didn't know enough about the condition then, but he'd already displayed symptoms.

After faking his own death, it was apparent he didn't want me, but I still would've helped him if I could, if only for the twins' sake. My work with Vets gave me the tools to understand how far soldiers could fall through no fault of their own.

When I thought about the beautiful man who'd watched the sun rise over Vegas with me ten years ago and compared him to the Snow who'd left me, it was hard to believe they were the same person.

He'd changed drastically in less than a year. He'd gone through something terrible. God only knew what he'd experienced to alter his spirit that way. My stomach hurt when I remembered how I'd treated him at the chapel. Maybe that was the catalyst.

I was shocked when I walked in and saw his ghost. A part of me wanted to throw myself in his arms the second I realized he'd been alive for all those years, but then everyone started to call him Kit, and my heart felt like it was cracking in two.

I'd wanted space to build my walls back up. The kids and I needed time to come to terms with Snow being alive and what that meant. My decision was for the kids, but what if it was part of why he did something so drastic?

My stomach dropped.

Was it all my fault?

My eyes turned to address Cash. "He's okay, right?" When Cash nodded, I asked, "Did someone talk him down?"

He glanced at Atlas. "Well..."

Atlas picked at the label of his bottle. "He was too far gone, Ned. Couldn't have talked him down if we tried. Had to resort to the old-fashioned method of stoppin' him."

My forehead furrowed. "Huh?"

"I shot the fucker." He grimaced. "Hit him in the shoulder just as he squeezed the trigger. His hand jerked, so he missed his target but grazed there." Atlas tapped the side of his head. "It'll heal, and it's an improvement on him blowin' his brains out."

My brain went numb as I glared at Atlas and shrieked, "You shot him?"

"There wasn't time to do much else," Atlas retorted. "Kit was about to..." Atlas's voice trailed off.

My thoughts raced. "Where is he now?"

The two men glanced at each other again, conversing silently.

My eyes bugged out. "Please tell me you took him to the hospital."

Atlas held his hands up to me defensively. "Calm down, Blondie. Sophie patched him up. As of last night, he's at a VA hospital in Colorado. They've got a treatment facility there that can help him,"

"After it happened, he had some kind of mental breakdown," Cash explained. "He was goddamned catatonic for almost two days. Dad called an officers' meetin', and we agreed it'd be better if he got specialized treatment." He leaned forward in his chair. "Atlas remembered he'd settled on the place years back. We thought he'd be more comfortable somewhere he knew."

My nod was automatic. Of all the words Cash relayed, three, in particular, leaped out and made my heart feel like it was withering away.

Breakdown?
Catatonic?
Treatment?

I turned to Atlas, my face twisting incredulously. "How the hell did Snow get that sick? How could you live with him for years and not notice his PTSD?" I stood so forcefully my chair scraped back loudly across my flagstone tiles. "If he's been sick all this time, it's hardly a shock that he got in that state. How's he even functioning?"

Atlas exchanged a look with Cash, who scraped a hand down his face—forgetting his bruises—and winced in pain.

I'd have laughed if the entire situation wasn't so screwed up.

Atlas's mouth twisted, but he didn't reply. He knew I was right.

They'd let Snow down badly.

His family and friends must have noticed considerable changes in his behavior. Still, they stood by and let one of their own self-destruct.

MCs banded together but were notorious for not getting involved in each other's personal shit. I'd seen it with the Three Kings. There was help and support available, but only if sought out. The brothers didn't ask questions. They just accepted each other for who they were.

Still, my blood boiled at their complete lack of care and attention. If anyone had the right to watch Snow self-destruct, it was me. After all his lies, I wanted to slap his face and tell him what I thought of him, but I'd never want this for him or anyone. He'd been living in Hell, and everyone who should've helped him ignored his pain.

I leaned back against the countertop, rubbing my forehead as I tried to think. "Where in Colorado is the treatment center?"

"Grand Junction," Atlas confirmed. "No point runnin' down there, though. He can't have visitors for the first week. They need to get him clean before he can start the program. Breaker's stuck there for a couple of months, maybe longer. He'll go through physical and mental therapy. It'll get worse for the poor bastard before it gets better."

I fixated on Atlas's words. "Get him clean?"

"Drugs. Booze." Cash's gaze lowered. "Women."

A wrecking ball smashed into me. I squeezed my eyes shut, desperately trying to fight back the rush of tears.

Of course, he hadn't waited.

It wasn't like I'd waited, either, but then I thought he was dead.

Logically, I knew addiction was one of the most significant behavioral changes PTSD caused, and sex was often part of that. Still, the idea of him with other women still made me feel sick.

He'd never really been mine. It was probably why he stayed away. My golden boy lied about his identity, and as soon as things got tough, he ran out on me. Snow had hardly proven himself to be devoted. What did I expect? Years of celibacy? An internal battle raged inside. He'd left me hollow. Everything I thought we meant to each other was a wicked lie.

So much for fucking soulmates.

I tilted my chin up.

I had to put it to one side for now. Kai and Kady deserved the chance to know their father. Family was everything, and I didn't want them to live without those relationships. My feelings about Snow didn't matter. All I cared about was what my kids needed.

Throat still burning, I turned to Atlas and croaked, "So what now? I'm assuming you want something seeing as you're standing in my kitchen resembling two very butch, leather-clad Village People."

Atlas's lips twitched.

"She's a smartass." Cash declared before lowering his voice, mumbling, "Cara's gonna fuckin' love her."

"Is Cara moving to Vegas?" I asked sarcastically. "Because you talk like we're going to be in close proximity."

He looked up at the heavens and sighed audibly.

I knew I was being obtuse. I also knew they wanted something from me—and I didn't need two guesses as to what that was. If they needed my help, they'd have to lay it on the line. And, if they were about to ask what I suspected they were, it would mean involving my kids, which was pretty goddamned huge.

A favor equaled a marker in my world, including for my babies.

"Well?" I cocked my head, waiting.

Cash rose from his seat, his eyes never leaving mine, even his beat-up one. "We need you." He ran a hand across the top of his head frustratedly. "Kit needs you so fucking badly he's lost the goddammed plot."

I opened my mouth to curse at him, but Cash raised his hand. "Please, let me finish."

My jaw clamped shut.

Cash glanced nervously at Atlas before continuing. "He looked for you, Kennedy. Every day since he left the EOD."

Tears hit the back of my throat.

"He spent years searchin' the entire fuckin' country. He went to Vegas, then Harvard. Were you there at some point?"

I held onto the countertop, casting my mind back to all those years before. "Originally, I planned to go to Harvard Business School, but everything changed. I discovered I was pregnant with the twins and changed my career path to law. Duke offered me a place, and I got the opportunity to share an apartment with Sophie. It was no brainer, really." My eyes widened as a realization hit me. "Snow didn't know my plans had changed. It all happened after he left me."

"I'll be damned," Cash said quietly. "That's it. We couldn't work it out." He and Atlas stared at each other, another one of those silent conversations passing between them, before continuing. "He gave our tech guy the name Kitten or Kenny. Atlas already explained everyone called you Kitten back then."

I froze as a memory floated through my mind.

"You never even knew my name... My uncle calls me Kenny. He has since I was a little girl. It's the one thing of any importance I kept."

"Kitten's my middle name," I whispered. "I had a shitty mother, but she had a sense of humor."

Cash let out a humorless snort. "Look. I fucked-up with Kit. We all did. There's a history between us that we need to work through. I dunno if you're aware, but I went to jail for three years for beating a man."

My jaw dropped. "And you want me to bring my kids around you?"

"It's okay." He shrugged nonchalantly. "Turned out he was a rapist piece of shit."

"Oh, well. All good then." I deadpanned.

"I'm a reformed man." He puffed his chest out. "I'm gonna be a dad soon. I'm sorting my shit, and I've got my woman. I know from experience Kit needs the same. I was locked away when he came home from the military. I never understood how fucked-up he was. I was an asshole to him; we all were. I'm the oldest brother; it's my responsibility to look after him, and I'll do anything to make it up to him. So, name your price."

My eyes narrowed to tiny slits as I took in Cash's expression.

This guy was unbelievable. If he thought I would let him use me and my kids to ease his guilty conscience, he'd lost his damned mind. I was about to open my mouth and tell him so when Atlas spoke up.

"You were comin' to Hambleton anyway, Blondie. Just stick with ya plans and play the rest by ear. Dagger's desperate to get to know the twins. They've got a big family who'll fuckin' worship 'em. The club wants to make shit up to Kit, but also you, the boy, and little Kady girl. Let 'em."

Jesus. These two had raised my blood pressure. I pressed a hand against my churning stomach while I tried to think about everything logically.

Snow betrayed me. I didn't owe him anything, but he was still the kids' dad.

I wasn't the type of woman who could kick a man when he was down, especially a man I used to love with everything in me. And I had to admit, Cash revealing that Snow searched for me made a slight difference.

It wasn't my decision, though. All I could do was tell Kai and Kadence the facts and let them choose their paths. They'd always be my babies, but they were intelligent and independent with individual minds and feelings. I'd never make them do something they didn't want.

"I need to speak to the kids," I murmured, still deep in thought. "We'll decide together."

Cash grinned. "We've got all day."

A quiet scuffle broke out, and a little voice said, "Mom?"

I turned to see the kids hovering by the kitchen door. Kady looked up at me bright-eyed. "I feel better now. I'm thirsty." Her big eyes went to Cash, then Atlas. "Hey!"

I took in my little girl's face. Her cheeks had some color back, and she smiled for the first time in days.

"Yo, little Kady girl," Atlas approached the kids and fist-bumped them, making them giggle. He got down on his haunches to speak to my girl. "Bit early to be in your night clothes, ain't it, princess?"

She gave him a toothy grin. "I was in bed. My head hurt, but it's okay now. Where's Sophie?"

Atlas grinned. "She's at home cooking my baby."

Kady's face went white as a sheet. A squeak escaped her throat.

"He means Sophie's keeping the baby warm in her tummy, Kady." I fetched some fruit juice from the fridge and beckoned the kids into the kitchen. "Come here, baby." I put the drinks down and lifted Kady, plonking her tiny ass on the counter before smoothing her hair back. "You're headache's gone completely?"

She nodded enthusiastically, wide-eyed, and sucking her juice through the straw. Her gaze slid toward Cash, and she beamed. "Hi! You've got eyes like my brother."

"Hey, pretty girl." He moved toward us, holding his hand out. "I'm your uncle Cash."

She shook fingers, laughing, just as Kai muttered. "Stupid name," under his breath.

Atlas barked out a laugh. "Yeah, boy. It is."

Cash jerked his eyes to my son. "It's a cool name when you think about why the club calls me it."

Kai cocked his head to one side questioningly.

"It's 'cause I'm good with money." Cash shot him a knowing wink. "I've made 'em all rich."

"Cool." Kady swiveled her head toward Atlas, furrowing her brow. "Is your name Atlas because you know where the countries are?"

Atlas's lips twitched as Cash started to laugh.

Kai approached, scrambling up on the counter with his sister.

I bit my lip, dreading the conversation we were about to have. "Now you're both here, I need to talk to you." I took a hand each, looking between my two amazing kids.

Luck was too small a word when it came to them. I felt their souls from the moment they were born—so different but still entwined beautifully. Kady was just a dream, and Kai, even with his grumpiness, tried so hard to do the right thing for his family. I wondered how they'd take what I was about to tell them.

"Cash and Atlas came to tell us something. It's about your father."

Kady's eyes grew massive while Kai's narrowed.

"He's really sick," I told them quietly. "Your grandpa, John, wants us to go to Wyoming. He thinks maybe we can help." I squeezed their little hands gently. "Have you made up your minds' yet?"

Kady nodded. "I want to go." She nudged her brother. "Kai said he'd do whatever I wanted."

I smiled at my boy. "This is your decision, too. I don't want you to regret it."

Kai's eyebrows drew together for a minute while he thought it through. After a while, he turned to Cash. "What's it like there?"

A massive grin spread across Cash's face. "Home. For me, it's like home, Kai. The club's like a big family. You know Sunny, right? Well, there are other kids there, Gabby and DJ. Baby Willow's sweet, and my Cara's gonna have a baby boy soon. Iris and Abe'll go crazy for ya. There's laughter, music, and motorbikes. It's not perfect, but it's pretty close for me."

"What about our dad?" Kady asked. "Is he there?"

Atlas shook his head. "Nah, princess. He's in the hospital, but maybe soon we can take you to see him if it's okay with your ma. If you come to Hambleton, you'll mainly spend time with the rest of your family until your dad's well enough to come home."

"Is it like Uncle Hustle's MC?" Kai asked.

Atlas's head reared back. "Hustle?"

"My uncle's part of the Three Kings MC," I said innocently. "Do you know them?" I almost laughed as Atlas scraped a hand down his face and mumbled to Jesus.

"It's crazy how close you were all this time," he said, voice low. "Kit's been to almost every state looking for ya, and you've been right under his nose all along. We were at their compound not long ago. He'll fuckin' die when he finds out."

"I'm pretty sure Hustle will have a few things to say, too," I mused.

Kai pulled at my sleeve. "Can I get a motorcycle?" he asked innocently.

"Yeah," I retorted. "When you're eighteen. Until then, you've got a got a skateboard and your mountain bike."

Kai huffed, folding his arms across his little chest.

"I think we should go," Kady announced. "We can meet the other kids, and maybe we can get a weird name, too."

I didn't know whether to laugh or cry.

It was apparent the twins had already made their minds up. They may have had a lot of unresolved feelings for Snow, but they were also curious. The thought of getting to know a big family appealed to them too much to pass on the opportunity.

Kai huffed out a breath. "Okay. We'll go."

Kady's eyes lit up, and she squealed.

My heart went out to my kids.

This was big for them. The only family they'd known was Sophie, Hustle, and Katie.

My kids weren't spoiled brats, but I worked hard to give them a private school education. They received extra tutoring and music lessons. Every Summer, I took them traveling to exotic places in every corner of the world, but not this year. Instead of the three weeks I had planned in Sydney, Australia, they'd meet their biker family in small-town cowboy country.

I was so proud of Kai and Kady. They were good kids; I just hoped this debacle didn't hurt them. They didn't deserve bad things. They just wanted to know their family.

I hope Snow appreciates how amazing his kids are.

My stare slid to Cash.

Thank you, he mouthed.

I nodded before turning to Atlas and raising one shoulder in a shrug. "You'd better get the flags out, boys. Looks like we're all going to bumfuck Wyoming."

Chapter Six

Breaker

Grand Junction was a pretty town in Northwest Colorado. It was a mix of old and new, modern and quaint. The town was much like any other, except it was surrounded by beautiful mountains and rivers.

It wasn't gonna be a hardship looking out of the window, that was for sure. I wondered if the natural beauty was therapeutic for the men and women at the VA hospital Dad was driving me toward.

Thinking back years ago to my time here was bittersweet.

Memories of holing up in that house at the foot of the mountains played through my mind as I stared out the SUV's window. It seemed like a lifetime ago. I was so fucking desperate for help. My drug and alcohol dependency at the time was out of hand.

Why didn't I explain to Atlas that day how much I needed to stay?

Pride? Guilt? Ego? Fear?

All of the above?

Even thinking back to that time felt like a bad dream. I'd been caught so deep inside a haze of cocaine and tequila that it seemed like my life was a TV show where everything happened to somebody else.

When had I disassociated? And not only from the people close to me but also from myself?

Was that why I'd held a gun to my head?

Since I'd woken with a bandaged skull and a tortured brain, I'd done some soul-searching, and through it all, one question remained.

Why did I want to go boom when, after years of searching for Kitten, I'd finally found her? The thought of us being together again one day kept me alive on the nights I'd been so tormented that ending it all seemed like it would be a relief. I never pulled the trigger, though. So, why did I attempt it when I finally found my light at the end of a long, dark tunnel?

It didn't make sense.

Dad leaned forward to turn down the radio, pulling me away from my thoughts. "We're here, Son." He stopped the car at the gates, murmuring something to the security guard.

Gut churning, my eyes lifted slowly to take in the large white building that would serve as my home for the next two months. The vast structure was square in shape, with additional annexes added on. It hadn't changed since I was here last. It still looked clean and clinical, pretty much what you'd expect from any hospital.

Dad gave security a one-finger salute before driving around the side of the building to the parking lot. "Place looks okay." He glanced at me and maneuvered the SUV into a parking space near the building.

"Yeah," I said, watching him switch off the engine. "I liked it when I came before. They've got good facilities, and the staff I met were cool. That was why I chose it."

Dad sat back in his seat. "If I'd have known then what I know now, I never would've sent Atlas for ya."

I let out a self-derisive snort. "Pop. If I'd known then what I know now, I'd have never let him take me home."

Dad nodded thoughtfully. "There's been a lotta fuck ups made on both sides, Kit. Let's hope bein' here stops history repeatin', 'cause if I lost any of you kids, I'd be fuckin' destroyed. For as long as I live, I'll never forget the image of you fallin' to your knees with a gun to your head. I keep waking up in a cold sweat."

My throat thickened. "Sorry, Dad."

"Me too, Son." He turned to look me in the eye. "Are you ready to do this?"

"No." I looked up at the building. It seemed intimidating, especially when I thought about the work ahead. But a feeling of acceptance settled over me. "It's time."

It was do or die. I couldn't go on the way I had been. And now I was here; a part of me was impatient to get in there to find out which way it would go.

We got out of the car, going to the trunk to get my case and rucksack. When Dad opened the door, I saw another large bag beside mine.

"What's this?" I asked, gesturing inside the trunk.

"It's mine," Dad confirmed. "I'm staying at a hotel tonight. I wanna see ya tomorrow before you start the program. I'll be comin' down to see you every week. I'll bring Gage, Xander, or Freya with me. We're doin' family therapy."

My eyes rounded. "What? You're doin' therapy—?"

He held a hand up to silence me. "I'm fuckin' disgusted it went this far, Kit. It won't hurt the family to learn how to communicate better. It may even bring us closer." He shook his head sadly. "After your ma left, everythin' turned to shit. I know it started before that for you, but Cash went off the rails, Bowie turned into a shell of himself, and Freya lost time with Adele she'll never get back. We never talked about it, and that's on me. We'll face things instead of sweeping them under the rug. It starts now."

I stared at Dad, throat burning with emotions I didn't want to feel.

I'd never heard him speak like that before. Usually, he said the club and the brothers were all we needed, but his little speech had just blown every perception I had of him outta the water.

Seemed you *could* teach an old dog new tricks after all.

Dad clapped me on the shoulder. "Don't look so shocked. I'm not that much of a dinosaur. I've seen what therapy's done for Cash, so I'm not averse to tryin' it. Though, I don't mind admittin', the thought of talkin' about my poor old feelin's is makin' my ass cheeks clench like a motherfucker."

My heart flipped inside my chest, suddenly feeling lighter than it had for years. "Your wrinkly ol' ass could do with the workout, Pop."

He barked out a laugh, eyes twinkling with mirth. "You're probably right, Son." Our stares locked, and he nodded toward the building. "You ready to take the first step, Kit? Ain't gonna be easy, but it's like they say. Nothin' worth havin' ever is."

I didn't reply immediately. I wanted to absorb everything because, standing in a strange parking lot with my Dad baring his soul to me for the first time ever, I started thinking a bit clearer.

If he could burn his comfort zone to pieces at his age, why couldn't I? There were so many things I had to fight for, but suddenly, they didn't seem quite as far out of reach as they had a few days before.

I loved my kids without ever speaking a word to them, and I loved their mother with every goddamned bone in my body. Surely that counted for something?

Dad gave me a concerned look. "You okay?"

I went to say an automatic yes, but instead, I clamped my mouth shut.

How could I explain to Dad that the thought of failure made me wanna run and never come back? He'd moved heaven and earth to get me here, and I didn't wanna seem ungrateful, but I'd had no time to get used to the idea. I wanted to get better for the sake of Kitten and my kids, but I was so used to being this way I didn't know who Kit Stone was anymore. I certainly wasn't the young soldier who wanted to change the world.

What if the man under the monster wasn't worth shit?

I was more terrified of walking through those doors than any of the countless missions I'd endured. From when I was a kid, I knew exactly where I was going. Even later, when I roamed the country, it was with the purpose of finding Kitten.

It seemed symbolic because, for once in my life, I didn't know what to expect. The pressure weighing on my shoulders made my heart race inside my chest.

This was my last chance. If I failed, I'd lose everything that mattered, and the mere thought of that goddamned terrified me.

One Week Later

The last seven days had been a whirlwind of blood tests, a mix of physical and psych evaluations, and getting to know how things worked.

I felt the same way as I did those first weeks at Camp Eggers. Jumpy, out of place, and way out of my depth.

I'd hardly slept for the first few nights, but as time passed, I needed ten hours straight, plus I napped during the day.

Maybe my body was trying to catch up from the years of missed sleep, or perhaps the booze was finally leaving my system.

Thankfully, it didn't matter because I'd been mostly confined to my room, a ten-by-ten-meter box with an attached bathroom. It reminded me of the CHU I'd shared with Benny on our first deployment to Afghanistan.

I'd always assumed the hospital would be like a prison where we were only allowed out of our rooms for exercise and mealtimes, but I was wrong; it was nothing like that.

All the staff were friendly and personable. They checked in without being intrusive and even bantered with me on occasion. My room had a small flat-screen TV attached to the wall, which allowed me to set up my streaming services. What really blew my mind was that I could keep my cell phone on me on the premise that I kept all calls and messages between six and seven P.M.

On day three, at six o two, I switched my cell on, and a message came through.

CASH: Ure girl n kids arrive tomorrow. Mission completed. See ya soon.

I slumped down on my bed, not quite able to believe what I was reading. My hand raised to rub my heart, which was doing backflips at the mere thought of Kitten being around my people.

A question kept nagging at me, though. It was clear Kennedy was a lioness who protected her cubs. How did my brother persuade her to take them to a goddamned MC? She was a successful, brilliant lawyer. I assumed she'd run a mile when she discovered my lifestyle.

For days, I tried to wrap my brain around Kennedy, rubbing shoulders with a clubhouse full of bikers. However, as time went on, memories flooded back into my mind. It seemed the longer I went without booze, the clearer my head became, and I began to really think about the girl I knew from ten years ago.

"Follow me," she ordered gently. "Ed's shy around new people. Let me go first." She turned toward a narrow alley between a small grocery store and a laundromat.

A knot formed in my stomach.

"Kitten," I snapped. "Get back from ther—"

"Ed? Are you home? Breakfast time," she called out.

After a few seconds, a dude lumbered from the alleyway. He was dressed in dirty clothes, and his hair was unkempt—obviously a homeless guy. "Morning, darlin'," he greeted with a deep scratchy voice. "You look pretty today."

My heart bloomed as I recalled how she looked that morning and how the sunlight made her blonde hair gleam with its rays. I could almost smell the sweet scent of peaches as I remembered how I nestled my face into her throat.

As the days went on, more memories assailed me.

"I've never seen anything more beautiful," she said, laughing. Her head turned, and she looked at me over her shoulder, her grin brighter than any morning sun.

I took a mental snapshot and tucked it away before grinning back at her and murmuring, "Neither have I, baby. Takes my goddamned breath away."

For the first time in a long time, Benny wasn't in the room staring at me with haunted voids for eyes. It was just me and her, and I realized that over the years, I'd pushed it all away because remembering what we had hurt too much. Kitten was coming back to me piece by piece, and a part of me loved it, but I was still numb underneath it all. The pain of missing her still made the breath catch in my throat, but I couldn't escape her, and because of that, I was forced to think.

Kennedy, as a young woman, befriended the homeless and made elderly shopkeepers happy by waltzing down store aisles with them. My girl was no snob, and she wouldn't raise our kids to be that way, either. Kitten gave a shit, even though only a couple of friends and an uncle cared about her.

I'd pushed the essence of who Kitten was away because remembering made me ache.

She'd be determined to give our kids something she'd never had but always yearned for. Of course she'd taken Kai and Kadence to Wyoming. She'd suffer Hell to give her kids something she never had.

Family.

Day Ten

The mere idea of group therapy made my palms sweat. I wasn't a man who'd ever be comfortable sharing his feelings, but it seemed a little easier with strangers and men in the same position as me.

The counselor, Ken, told me not to join in on my first group meeting and just to listen, which I found weird.

But as I sat there taking in everyone's stories, I started to understand they weren't so different from mine, and the men telling them were as screwed up as I was.

Many of our tales ran parallel, and our trauma came from similar places.

It wasn't just me who zoned out and imagined myself back in the EOD. Others did, too, and in some cases, carried out violent acts, just like I did. Many men hid monsters, all of which they wanted to extinguish, again, just like me.

In a way, being at the Vet Centre invoked the sense of camaraderie I'd lost the day Benny and Simmons died.

Like the military, we were all here trying to achieve a goal together while supporting our brothers in arms. I hadn't connected with anyone since losing Benny, maybe because I was so terrified that my new friendships would eventually get shattered the same way.

A man around my age rose from his chair and addressed the room.

"My name is Michael Martinez. Until twelve years ago, I was a sergeant in the U.S. Marine Corps. I lead my battalion through two tours of Iraq." He let out a humorless snort. "I guess I was lucky there, saw some action, but we were at the end of that war, so we served mainly as peacekeepers. Then, me and my unit got deployed to Afghanistan."

Quiet murmurs of encouragement rose through the air. Of the fourteen men I sat with, around ten were nodding along, obviously remembering their own time there.

"The day we landed at Bagram was surreal. Everyone was running around on the flight line as we exited the plane. We were sent to a tiny room for a briefing. I didn't even get to see the mountains because the dust had kicked up from a bomb that had detonated just outside the base about an hour before we arrived. On that first briefing, Command told us, 'If you're not in shape, you'll die, so get down the gym.' I envied the soldiers I commanded because they didn't have clearance to see the intelligence reports, which told us how much danger we were in, even at the base. I didn't sleep for the first week. I couldn't get the statistics of that report outta my head. And the stats were proven right because I lost thirty percent of my men on that deployment." He shook his head sadly. "Command turned out to be right. The poor souls who got KIA had the lowest fitness levels in the unit."

Ken spoke up. "How does that feel years later? In what ways has it stayed with you?"

Michael smiled wryly. "I survived because I could run faster than them. How fucked-up is that? If I'd pulled a muscle or didn't work out quite as hard as my team, I'd probably be one of the men lying in a grave. In my dreams, I'm always running. Last week, I looked out the window of my house and saw a kid sprinting down the street. Suddenly, I was there again amongst all the chaos and confusion. I could even smell the stench of death." He raised a shaking hand and thrust it through his hair. "My wife walked in on me while I was losing my shit. I dragged her outta there, trying to save her. I pulled her hand so roughly that she dislocated three fingers..." His voice trailed off before he croaked, "I hurt my woman."

My throat heated, amd my mind flew back in time.

"Are you saying I did that, Kitten?"

Her hand stroked my face, and she smiled brightly, too fucking brightly. "It's fine."

"I left, made inquiries, and checked myself in here," Michael continued. "I dunno what to say to her. How do you explain the horrors you've been through? How do you live life remembering events the closest people to you will never understand? And more importantly, what if next time it's worse than three dislocated fingers?"

Ken looked around the room. "Any advice? Who thinks they can help Michael communicate with his wife in a way he feels safe and comfortable?

"He could write to her." A big guy who looked to be in his late forties turned in his seat toward Michael. "That way, you can control what you tell her, and if things get too much, you can take a break and go back to it."

Ken nodded. "Good idea, Mack. Tonight, I want you all to write a letter to someone who's seen you at your worst. It could be a partner, a family member, or even a son or daughter. Explain to them what happens when you're triggered. Tell them a story about your time in service. See if you can make them relate. Treat it like an exercise in talking about what you did and how you feel about it. You don't even have to send the letter if you don't want to. Just get it out there."

Michael thought for a minute. "I used to write to her all the time on deployment. She used to love getting mail from me. She's kept every letter. Maybe she'd like that."

I stared at the man standing before me, noting how our lives were so similar.

Kitten told me back then how much she looked forward to my letters. She used to carry them around with her and read them all the time. She said they made her feel closer to me.

It was a nice idea, but I couldn't stop doubt from mind twisting my mind.

My girl would probably tear up the letter if I wrote her. Hell, she'd probably set fire to it and watch it burn.

But maybe that wasn't the point. Perhaps the process of writing it in the first place could help me get to a place where one day I could tell her the things I needed to say. And even if she never read it, the fact that I made an effort could help thaw the wall of ice between us.

"If you want to post your letters, then by all means, do it," Ken said, interrupting my thoughts. "But before you seal them, show them to your therapists. There may be things in there they can help you with. Maybe there are things you'd like to express, but you don't know how. You're here seeking help, so let us help you." Ken glanced at his watch and looked up. "We're fifteen minutes over. Sorry 'bout that, but I didn't want to interrupt the flow. For the ones who've just started, we don't advise too much therapy for your first couple of weeks; we don't wanna overwhelm you. Go for lunch and start thinking about who you'll write to and what you wanna say. Tomorrow morning, you've one-to-one sessions with your therapists. Don't forget to take your letters if they're done."

Words of assent sounded through the scrape of chairs sliding across the tiled floor as everyone made to leave. I stood and followed the men who were already clustered into friend groups.

As far as I could tell, me and Michael were the only ones at the start of treatment. Most of the patients had been here much longer, so they'd already formed connections. It was weird; since I'd left the military, I'd been a loner and preferred it that way. But here, I felt like the kid who'd moved schools in the middle of the semester.

Then again, I'd felt that way for years. Being an outsider was nothing new for me.

Michael glanced at me, face ravaged. He lifted his chin, gave me his back, and walked off. I got it; he needed to be alone. After opening up the way he did, I couldn't blame him.

He was clearly way out of his comfort zone, just like me. I couldn't imagine telling a room full of strangers what I'd done. I had to hand it to him; at least he had courage.

Muscles suddenly weak, I shuffled to the elevator and pressed the button for my floor. Thoughts crashed through my brain so forcefully that my head spun. I had to suck it up and do the one thing I'd dreaded since the second I'd seen Kitten at Atlas's wedding.

Somehow, I had to explain myself.

My shrink was an ex-lieutenant who served in the Medical Corps for twenty-five years. She was also an attractive woman with a sense of humor.

When I walked into her office and saw who I'd been assigned, I turned, ready to walk back out again, but her laughter stopped me in my tracks.

"You can quit your tantrum, Stone. Come sit down and stop being a baby."

I turned back to face her and blinked.

"I'm Lieutenant Nina Blackrock." She nodded toward the chair in front of her desk. "Sit your ass down."

I hesitated momentarily, watching her pick up my file and start reading. "Says here you have absence episodes." She looked up at me. "You zone out? Lose time?"

I nodded my reply.

She went back to her notes. "You deployed to Kabul?"

My feet moved toward her desk. "Yeah."

"I was at Eggers at the same time as you," she murmured. "We overlapped by two weeks." She looked up at me again and smiled. "I know your Lieutenant Hollister; well, I did. I turned him down when he asked me out on a date."

My mouth dropped open.

"Don't look so shocked, Stone," she waggled her eyebrows. "I may be old enough to be your intelligent, beautiful, and very youthful aunt, but I'm not past my prime yet, and I certainly wasn't ten years ago."

My lips twitched. "Why'd ya turn my LT down?"

She shrugged. "I was seeing a beautiful captain at the time," her eyes glazed over with a faraway look, "he had a face like an angel. Pity he was only good for one thing."

I barked out a laugh. This woman was a trip.

Her eyes met mine and softened. "Are you more relaxed now, Kit?"

"You're good, Lieutenant," I said with a hint of admiration.

"I've had lots of practice. You wouldn't be the first man to see I've got tits and want to walk. I got you to sit down, didn't I?" She grinned. "So tell me, how are you doing?"

I dipped my chin. "Not great. Or else I wouldn't be here."

The doc's mouth twisted to one side like she was trying to stifle a laugh. "I meant today in particular. How do you feel?"

My eyes hit my sneakers as I thought about her question.

Should I gloss over it like I had every other time I'd seen an Army shrink, or should I let her have the truth?

I raised my stare until it hit hers and just let her have it. "I'm numb."

She nodded slowly. "Thank you for being honest. How long have you felt that way?"

I thought about her question, and my throat thickened as something struck me.

I'd been numb since I'd first walked into Eggers.

Kitten and the young girl I found in the aftermath of a bomb were the only people who'd brought out flashes of emotion since then.

Hollister's voice floated through my brain.

Shut it down, Snow. Shut it the fuck down.

I'd obeyed those orders for the last ten years; it was the only way I could push through. I shut it down because being numb was preferable to being in pain. Numb was safe, but to be who *she* needed meant feeling everything again, and that made my chest feel like it was about to cave in.

Here I was again, staring at another fork in the road. One leading to my self-destruction, the other toward my salvation.

An image of Kitten, her skin bruised and marked, flashed behind my eyes. Then April, cold and lifeless, after I'd almost strangled her to death. My thoughts then turned to Cash with his eye swollen shut and strips across his broken nose. Then finally, to Benny and how I wished every fucking day I could take his place.

Giving up would be so simple. All I had to do was get up, walk out, and disappear. No more pain and no more torment. I could remain numb forever.

What stopped me was the memory of Michael and how he'd stood in group therapy the day before, shaking like a leaf in a storm. The way he'd stood with his head high in a room full of strangers, telling them about his shame, impressed me. The pain ravaging his face was a mirror image of everything I felt inside.

Still, he did it because he was a decent man who wanted to fight for his family.

Now, it was time to decide *my* path.

No more half-assed attempts. It was do or die. I either gave it my all, or I walked.

Did I want to feel numb? Or did I want to feel everything?

My hands shook at the mere thought of what I was about to do. I'd run away from my emotions for so long that I didn't know who I was anymore.

The young soldier who'd loved Kitten so completely died the minute he pulled the severed body of a girl from the wreckage of a VBIED.

Swallowing down the lump in my throat, I brought out a mental snapshot of the night I stood in an airport lounge, regretting how I'd let my girl go. I smiled when I remembered her running into my arms minutes later. I closed my eyes, recalling how she looked at me with so much adoration, the way she smiled, and how she made me feel like I mattered.

And I made my decision.

"When I was a small boy, I sat in front of the TV watching the Twin Towers burn, and I decided there, and then I wanted to serve my country..."

And over the next eighty minutes, I didn't stop talking.

I told Nina everything.

Chapter Seven

Kennedy

My eyes bored into the massive one-story building. God knows what I'd expected, but it wasn't anything like this.

MC clubhouses were usually dark and dingy, but this place was the opposite with its whitewashed walls and silver corrugated iron roof. The double doors leading inside were dark oak, traditional, warm, and welcoming. Beyond the building was an incline of woods with fields on either side for as far as the eye could see.

Its green lushness was a far cry from the arid desert appeal of Vegas. This was a place where kids rode horses after a swim in the river. A place of barn dances, hayrides, and where the seasons changed every few months. Cowboy country at its finest.

However, I was a city girl, used to blistering heat twelve months of the year and red sand getting into every nook and cranny. Bright lights and brash people represented home to me. It was all I'd ever known.

A prospect picked us up from Rock Springs the night before and drove us straight to the rental we were staying in, which the club owned. The kids were exhausted from traveling, so we ate and turned in early.

That morning, some guy called Billy had dropped an SUV off at the house. Before he'd left, he relayed that every place we'd need to go was already programmed into the GPS, and John would love it if we went to the clubhouse later.

So, here we were.

The same guy who dropped off the SUV let us through the gate, and quickly, I found myself standing open-mouthed, gazing up at the place that made me feel the same way I did years ago when I took the Nevada Bar. Quietly confident while also unequivocally goddamned terrified.

The double doors ahead began to open. I snapped my spine straight, taking the kids' hands as I waited, shoulders tense to see who was greeting us.

Show no fear, Kennedy. I told myself, watching the doors open wider.

I didn't know what to expect, but what happened next never entered my head.

A deep voice bellowed, "Get that fuckin' dog away from me!" before a man with soaked clothes came streaking out the door with the ugliest dog I'd ever seen snapping at his heels. The guy squealed like a pig as he sprinted across the parking lot.

A little girl who, on closer inspection, I recognized as Sunny, stomped through the doorway, also soaked from head to toe. "You're a bad man, Icemans," she shrieked. "You got my party dress alls wet. Bites his hiney, Jolly Batman!"

The dog barked and growled as he threw himself after the guy, who by then had climbed onto the bed of a blue truck, yelling and shouting at the dog, who was jumping up and down, trying to get to him.

"Mommy!" Kady breathed, eyes shining up at me. "It's so much fun here."

I froze, glancing down at Kai, who took in the crazy scene with a small smile playing around his lips.

My eyes jerked up again to see a crowd of people appear in the doorway. "They're here," a voice yelled as

I watched Sophie push through them and run toward me. "You're here!" she shouted again excitedly.

The crowd of people at the door began to fly in all directions as Atlas threw them out of his way. "Stitch! Be fuckin' careful, will ya!" he barked before running after his wife.

I let out an 'oof' as Sophie barreled into me, throwing her arms around my neck. "I'm so happy to see you," she said, burrowing her face against my shoulder. "We've been waiting all morning."

Another piercing yell cut through the air as the dog leaped onto the flatbed of the truck and started nipping at the guy's ass. "Get this mutt away from me!" he shrieked, jumping down and running back through the lot. "He's rippin' me a new one."

"Good!" Atlas bellowed. "You got little Sunshine wet with that goddamned water pistol. I told you not to bring 'em inside the clubhouse."

My head reared back slightly. "Water pistols?"

Kady tugged on my sleeve. "Can I play water pistols?"

"Yeah," Kai agreed. "Me too."

Atlas folded his arms across his chest. "They're all out back acting like fools." He shook his head exasperatedly. "When Prez sees the state of the clubhouse, he's gonna blow his fuckin' top. He had the prospects cleaning it at eight this mornin'." He jerked his thumb around the side of the building. "Go around the back and tell those idiots if they get too rough with ya, I'll kick their asses."

The twins nodded eagerly and scampered off.

"Can I play too, Assless?" little Sunny called over, pointing toward the twins.

"Thought you wanted to keep your little frock nice for biker boy and little Kady girl," he replied.

She looked down at her dress, lifting her arms to the side. "Assless, are you blinds? I'm all ready all wets now."

I cocked my head, mouth twisting. "Assless?" I asked quietly.

"It's what Sunny and Gabby call him," Sophie whispered. "It's hilarious. Wait until she shouts it across the clubhouse; he literally winces. He won't tell them to stop, though. I think deep down he loves the attention."

Wide-eyed, I looked around the parking lot.

Men in cuts whooped and hollered at the guy still being chased by the ugly dog, snarling and baring his teeth.

Atlas started yelling at him again. "I swear, Iceman, you're a goddamned prick. You're lucky I don't take my slugger to you again." His voice lowered to a mutter. "Fuckin' idiots. The place is s'posed to be a biker clubhouse, not a kid's playground." He caught Sophie's eye and pointed to the clubhouse. "Get your ass in there, woman. Told ya to rest; instead, you run at Blondie like she's a long-lost sister. You only saw her a few days ago."

"Stop being an asshole," she yelled at him. "I'm pregnant, not an invalid."

His eyes narrowed. "You were unsteady on ya feet this mornin'."

"I just got up too quickly," she snapped. "I hadn't eaten breakfast. My blood sugars were just a bit low."

He pointed at the clubhouse. "Get in there."

Sophie let out a loud harrumph. "Come on, Ned." She grabbed my hand, dragging me toward the clubhouse. "I need to get away from Captain Caveman here."

My stomach leaped. "You're all crazy."

Sophie shrugged. "You'll get used to it. In a way, you've been initiated slowly. At least there hasn't been an attempted kidnapping or a shootout today."

My heart stopped dead. I shrieked, "What?"

Sophie craned her neck as she dragged me through the door. "It's fine. We're due some peace and quiet."

The clubhouse's interior felt cool after standing in the sun's heat. The room we entered had a long wooden bar running across the back wall with chairs and tables dotted around. To my left was an elevated games area with pool tables, a dart board, and an old games machine flashing in the corner.

Immediately, I knew Kai would love it here. It was so him. Dark and a bit rough around the edges. My boy didn't like fluff, and this place was everything but.

Suddenly, I heard a frustrated screech. My head jerked right to see Cara up on her toes in Cash's face. "I've told you, me and the baby are living at the gallery. It's none of your business."

He folded his arms across his chest. "Don't fuckin' think so, Wildcat."

"You're such an asshole," she spat.

He grinned. "Yup."

Sophie rolled her eyes. "Ignore those two. They're always arguing. I blame it on the sexual tension; it rolls off them in waves. If she wasn't already, I swear he could get her pregnant just by throwing her a look."

"This place is crazy," I murmured, watching Cash run after an angry Cara, who was storming off.

Sophie smiled, her eyes following them, too. "Yeah. It's certainly interesting." We moved toward the couches lined up against the wall and sat down. "Welcome to Hambleton, babe." My friend smiled indulgently. "I'm so glad you visited, especially after all the Kit business. How are you feeling about it now you've had time to come to terms with it all?"

I sat back and thought for a minute.

I didn't want to offend Sophie, but I felt tweaked. A week ago, Snow was dead, then he wasn't. Just as I'd started coming to terms with his return from the dead, he'd tried to kill himself and now was being treated for PTSD. My head was aching with it all, along with my heart.

But still, if it wasn't for the kids, I wouldn't be here. I felt like I was swimming in the ocean without a life preserver.

"Honestly. I'm confused and embarrassed," I admitted.

"Oh. Ned. There's nothing for you to be embarrassed about," Sophie assured me. "If anyone should be embarrassed, it's him."

I didn't know if it was the kindness in Sophie's voice or that Kai and Kady weren't around, and I didn't have to hold it all together, but tears filled my eyes. "Why didn't he tell anyone about me?" I sniffed. "Why was I such a big secret? He obviously had no intention of ever introducing me to his family. Was he ashamed of me?"

"Jesus, Ned. No," she insisted. "How could he be? You're smart and gorgeous. How could anyone be ashamed of you?"

I deadpanned through my glistening eyes, sweeping a hand down my body. "Well, duh. I know I'm hot. It's not that. I just don't understand why Snow lied to me. He obviously didn't want me to track him down, or he wouldn't have lied about his name."

"Wellll," Sophie drawled, cringing slightly. "Kit may or may not have told Iris why he did it."

I froze, eyes narrowing. "What did he say?"

Sophie made an 'eek' face. "So, a guy in his unit had some fun on leave with a girl who turned a little crazy and kept showing up at Fort Campbell. He got some kind of court-martial. After that, Breaker and his friends decided to give false names so the same thing didn't happen to them."

My brow furrowed. "But the guy's name he gave me wasn't fake. Kyle Simmons existed. He died."

Sophie winced. "Iris said Breaker and Kyle were rivals. That was why he gave out *his* name. If anything came back on him, it would be Kyle who took the heat. She said it was more of a practical joke than anything."

"What?" My tone dripped with disdain.

Soph shook her head disbelievingly. "I know it's ridiculous. I'm pissed for you. If Atlas did that to me, I'd cut his balls off. When I think about it, most men in this club, including Atlas, don't use their smarts much. It's a proven fact that Cash and Bowie's brains reside in their dicks. Apparently, he wanted to tell you the truth when he returned for his visit but never got around to it. The next time you saw him," her voice dropped, "he wasn't in his right mind."

I sat there with my jaw on the floor and my heart aching painfully. A memory hit me from out of nowhere, taking me back to the time when a friend introduced me to a handsome soldier in a Vegas diner.

Something pinged suspiciously as a look passed between the two men sitting with us in the diner. They seemed to be having a whole other conversation telepathically.

"Is everything okay?" I asked.

"Yeah," Chloe's guy assured me. "Let me introduce myself. I'm Lee." He nodded toward his friend. "This is Kyle."

Kyle's stare veered down at his hands. His face flushed almost nervously as he slid his eyes back to mine. It seemed like he wanted to say something, but he rolled his lips together, staying quiet.

That look, that stain on his cheeks, it all made sense now. He was reacting to the lie.

Heaviness formed in the pit of my stomach when it struck me how I'd never really known him at all. *My* Snow was brave and courageous, whereas Kit Stone was an immature coward.

It was unbelievable how grown men could behave like idiotic schoolboys. Did he and his friend laugh about getting one over on me? Did he feel like a big man for misleading a young girl in love who would've given him the world if she could?

My hand raised to rub my forehead, feeling sick.
What an asshole.

"Iris said he wanted to tell you, Ned." Sophie took my hand in hers and squeezed. "I'm mad at Breaker for doing that, and I'll tell him so as soon as I get the opportunity. But I believe him. I think he got caught up in a stupid prank and backed himself into a corner he didn't know how to escape."

"But he could've told me when he came back," I said, incredulous. "But instead, he made me believe he was somebody else. Did he think I was gonna go running after him? Jesus, how fucking arrogant can one man be? He's not *that* irresistible. He must have an inflated ego if he thought I'd moon after him like some lovesick schoolgirl?"

A muttered curse sounded from across the room. "Thought I told you to let Breaker explain, woman," Atlas muttered.

We both turned to see him entering from a corridor leading off the bar.

"Yeah, you did," Soph retorted, "I just didn't listen."

Atlas's face took on a bemused look as he sauntered toward us. "I put it down to youth. He was a fuckin' kid who saw his bud get a hard time and didn't want to go the same way. He was all about the military at the time."

"Don't make excuses for him," I snapped angrily. "Snow fought for our country; the government put a weapon in his hand and sent him to war. He couldn't have been that immature."

Atlas grinned. "You're wrong, Blondie. Men don't grow up at least until we hit our thirties—"

"And even then, it's hit or miss," Sophie drawled, looking at her husband with her eyebrow cocked.

Grinning, Atlas turned to me, ignoring his wife. "Prez said he'll be out to talk to ya soon. He's just finishin' up with Veep."

I caught movement out of the corner of my eye. Cara was walking back into the room from another corridor with Layla. I took them in, marveling at how beautiful they were but so different. Layla's face was kind and open, whereas Cara had swagger.

They both gave me a tight hug, murmuring words of welcome.

Layla released me and laughed. "I've got to hand it to you, Ned. I know weddings—especially of the biker variety— are known for drama, but you and Breaker take the cake."

My cheeks pinked as Sophie and Cara laughed.

Atlas narrowed his eyes. "Gonna remember this shit when she marries Cashy boy," he said, jerking a thumb toward Cara. "Gonna cause a stink at all the future nuptials and see how they like it."

Cara waved her hands in Atlas's face. "Ooh, I'm so scared. Do what you want. I couldn't care less, seeing as I'll never marry Cash."

Layla laughed again just as Sophie went to stand.

Atlas ushered her back onto the couch. "Whoa, whoa, Stitch. Where the fuck you think you're goin'? Will you sit the fuck down?"

"Oh my God, this is ridiculous. I was only going to get a tray of snacks," she retorted. "I can walk."

He glared at he as if she were a naughty child. "Don't fucking think so, Stitch. Anywhere you wanna go, I'll carry ya."

My head reared back. "Are you crazy? She's not a baby."

"She's carryin' my kid," he said, eyes still on my best friend. "I can do whatever the fuck I want."

"Aren't you gonna kick his ass?" I asked Sophie, throwing my thumb in the direction of her husband.

She sighed and looked to the heavens before saying something that made my eyebrows shoot up my forehead. "Okay, Atlas, have it your way. Go get some tea from the fridge and bring us some snacks, seeing as you won't let me do it."

Atlas gave her a cool nod, turned his back, and disappeared.

Layla and Cara craned their necks, watching him leave before turning back and grinning at Soph. "Can't believe he hasn't caught on yet." Cara laughed as she sat down on the other side of Sophie.

I looked at the girls quizzically. "Are you gonna let me in on the joke?"

Layla's pretty grey eyes shone with mirth. "Cash and Bowie were laughing about Atlas being an expectant father. The smartasses said he won't lift a finger to help. Sophie bet them that Atlas would wait on her hand and foot for a week to prove them wrong."

Cara laughed. "Sophie's blood sugars were low this morning, and she nearly fainted. Atlas hasn't let her lift a finger since. The boys are gutted. They couldn't exactly point out she was lying because pregnant women faint. Plus, Atlas would've beat the fuck out of them if they accused her of putting it on. Now those assholes have to stand by while Atlas runs around after her like his ass is on fire and watch a thousand bucks slowly slip away."

My stare shot to Sophie. "Were you pretending?"

"Not entirely," she explained. "I wobbled when I stood, but it wasn't as bad as Atlas assumed. I had to play along because I'd already spent the money. I've ordered a gorgeous bassinet and a sweet decoration that hangs above the crib."

I threw my head back and laughed. "You're an evil genius."

"She didn't have to try too hard," Layla murmured. "Cash and Bowie aren't the brightest. They know how protective Atlas is of Sophie. Their minds aren't entirely focused, especially Cash, whose head's up his butt because of the whole Kit thing. He's taken it really hard."

Sophie leaned toward me, her hand covering mine. "We were all saying we couldn't believe it at the wedding when you breathed 'Kyle.' And then Kit's face when he realized it was you. He looked wrecked."

"Of course he was wrecked," Layla agreed. "I don't think he ate or slept for days before or after, which didn't help his state of mind. Then, getting home and seeing April's body like that. It probably tipped him over the edge."

A chill raced down my spine. "Who's April?"

Sophie smiled sadly. "I'll tell you everything later when we're somewhere quiet. It's a lot to take in." She looked pointedly around the room, which was beginning to fill with men.

I was desperate to know more about this April girl, but if Soph was about to tell me she was Snow's ol' lady, I'd rather not be in a room full of bikers. It was bad enough hearing that shit from Cash standing in my own kitchen.

The main doors flew open, and peals of laughter went up from the kids as they ran inside the bar. Kai and Kady headed straight toward me, Sunny on their tail.

"Mom," Kai said, his breath sawing in and out. "We went up the woods. There are ghosts up there. The Demons have their own graveyard."

"Yeah," Kady squealed. "And we saw Sunshine's hors—" She suddenly clamped her mouth shut, her eyes rounding.

I cocked an eyebrow. "What have you been up to?"

Kady looked down and toed something across the floor, her little face sheepish. "Nothing!"

I looked my girl dead in the eyes. "You remember the chat we had before we left? I told you to be good and not get up to mischief."

Kady's eyes slashed to her twin's face, desperately looking for help. Her expression froze, and a look of pure shock spread across her features. "Look," she whispered.

I turned to Kai, whose eyes were darting around the room, excitedly taking it all in. He wore an expression I'd never seen before. His golden eyes were big and round as his gaze went from one biker to another, his face flushed. "Wow!" he breathed.

My jaw went slack as something incredible happened, something extraordinary I'd never seen before, and it made my heart soar. Kai's handsome little face broke out into a beautiful grin. "This place is the shit!" he yelled.

"Language!" I snapped.

Kady pulled on my sleeve and whispered, "Mom. He likes it here."

My skin prickled as I took in his bright stare and hopeful expression.

Nothing impressed Kai. He didn't like people or crowds. He didn't like going to new places because he never felt comfortable. But right then, the joy on his face was unlike anything I'd ever seen. He almost shimmered with excitement.

Kai's lack of social skills often kept me awake at night. I worried he'd always feel like an outsider. I didn't want him to be a sheep and follow the crowd or lose his quirks. I just wanted him to feel comfortable in his surroundings.

I glanced at Sophie, taking in her shocked expression as she stared at Kai. We'd talked for hours about him. Soph had assured me Kai was healthy; he just thought differently from his peers. She told me one day, he'd find his happy place.

Thank God, it seemed she was right.

I glided a hand across his back. "You okay, Son?"

He nodded blindly, turning to watch John, Bowie, and Cash walk into the bar. "You know you said I can be anything I want as long as I'm happy?"

Butterflies danced in my belly. I smiled, recalling the thousands of dollars I'd wasted on Kai's education. I knew exactly what he was about to say. I squeezed my eyes shut and laughed. It was either that or sob. "Go on, Son."

Kai whipped around to face me. His eyes shone, and his little chest puffed out proudly. "Mom, one day, I'm gonna be prez of the Speed Demons," he announced, voice heavy with determination. "Just like my grandpa."

John's steps faltered as the smile on his face grew to the size of Kansas. He almost skipped toward Kai, which looked comical from a bearded biker with massive muscles.

"That's my boy," he crowed, giving Kai a gentle clap on the shoulder. He jerked a finger between Bowie and Cash. "See? Ya brother got started on the next generation years before you two clowns. He got on the job early, *and* he gave me twins. You fucknuts are slackin'."

Cash let out a growl. "You can't just click ya fingers and twins appear. I thought you had to have 'em in the family?"

"We have," John said with a shrug. "Bandit was a twin. His brother died at birth. It was different back then; having kids was dangerous." He puffed out his chest, glancing at Cara's pregnant belly. "These days, you can churn 'em out, no problem."

Cara dipped her head, glaring. "I think what you meant to say was, us women can churn them out. All you men have to do is pump, dump, and roll over."

Bowie barked a laugh as Cash grinned. "Yup!" they said in unison.

John crouched down until he was eye-to-eye with Kai. He ruffled his hair lovingly before booming out, "Son. You ever been on a motorcycle?"

"Can I?" Kai yelled almost beside himself, hopping from foot to foot.

My heart dropped. "No!" I shrieked.

"Ned," Sophie whispered. "I think you're in trouble."

My heart twisted as I imagined my boy flying from a motorcycle. "He's too young to ride, John," I insisted. "There's no way I want him on a bike."

"I'll work on her, boy," I heard John murmur to Kai. "Your grandpa'll sort it."

I looked up at the ceiling as my chest curled inward. How had this happened?

A week ago, we'd never heard of the Speed Demons. Now, it had come to light that my babies were legacy kids, and Kai wanted nothing more than to be part of the club, including riding a motorcycle.

My stomach gnawed as another thought suddenly came to mind.

How was I meant to take Kai away from here now?

It was clear the place gave him a sense of identity and belonging. I'd kept the kids away from Hustle's club because it wasn't a place for them, but on the rare occasion I had taken them, Kai had never settled the way he did here.

It wasn't that the Demons were more kid-friendly; maybe this place was in Kai's blood, and he felt a kinship.

Sunny ran around the compound without a care in the world. John and the club members obviously adored her, and now they loved the twins, too.

The second Kady saw Snow and his family, she was all in. Even though Kai was more reserved, I suspected his being here and meeting these people would do him good, but I never imagined this.

My boy had found his happy place in small-town, bumfuck Wyoming, which meant one thing.

I let out an audible sigh, pursing my lips.

I was screwed.

Chapter Eight

Breaker ~ One Week Later.

Once I decided to give my time here a chance, I threw myself into it.
After my first session with Nina, where I'd purged myself until I was raw, I'd returned to my room and written my letter. I figured the best time to do it was when old emotions flooded my bloodstream.

There was a list of people as long as my arm to who I could've addressed it. But of course, Kitten won out.

Maybe it was because of what happened the night before I left her when I was a young soldier who'd lost his way. Or because I never went back for her until it was too late. Or maybe it was because I'd left her holding the babies, even though I had no clue about them.

What I wasn't sorry for was their existence; I'd never be sorry for making babies with Kennedy. If one thing in life had gone right for me, it was that. It was hard to convey in a letter how I felt disgusted for so many things I'd done but not at what came from them.

Most of the other guys in the group sent their letters within days of putting pen to paper, whereas I still mulled over whether to send mine at all.

I knew there was a lot to say—I'd probably be explaining myself until I met my maker—but didn't I owe it to Kitten to do it face-to-face? At least that way, if she wanted to kick me in the balls, I'd be there in person.

It was fucked-up how one letter could cause so much indecision and self-doubt. In turn, it caused my mind to almost self-destruct because feeling that way, hell, feeling at all, was unfamiliar.

The more I talked, the more I felt, and the more I remembered.

To help me understand it, Nina told me to look at it like I was a recovering amnesiac. As I opened up and talked about what I'd gone through, the little things came back.

I was still numb. Years of conditioning myself to push everything down couldn't be reversed in days or even weeks. But Nina and the other guys were slowly helping me not only remember but also how to deal with the onslaught.

Group therapy was nothing like I envisaged on my first day. We didn't only talk about the bad shit; we also remembered the brotherhood and the camaraderie many of us struggled to live without. Just like the military, we all had a shared goal, and over the two weeks I'd been at the clinic, against all odds, a new sense of belonging formed.

I wasn't a 'joiner inner,' but I commented and added anecdotes to stories the other guys told. We often end up almost pissing ourselves laughing, which for me was probably the best therapy considering it wasn't something I'd done much in the last ten years, and even when I had, it'd been forced.

The group had just discussed how combat caused soldiers to develop a dark sense of humor, probably as a coping mechanism for the bad shit we'd encountered.

It often created a bigger divide between us and our friends and loved ones purely because they didn't get it. What soldiers found funny, civilians found distasteful—

even disrespectful—and it made the barrier between us and the rest of society grow bigger.

There were probably hundreds of psychological papers on it, but for us, it was just the way it was. Ken explained how humor built rapport with the people around us, so it made sense that the differences in what we found funny often pushed people away, which added to our feelings of isolation.

I admired how Ken broke down the simplest things. He made so much sense and made me feel vindicated in many ways because it wasn't just me who'd gone through it.

One of the guys, Harris, was in the process of telling us a tale about how his unit had to battle the elements in Afghanistan. The entire room busted a gut as he relayed his story.

"Our usual pilots had been given a few days R&R, so we were being transported by an aviation team we didn't know. We were loaded onto two Chinook helicopters with orders to take down a small group of insurgents hiding out in the desert." His lips twitched. "Do you guys remember how strong the winds blew in that place?"

"Those desert storms could blind a man," Ken confirmed.

"Amen," someone else muttered.

"That day, the winds coming down the mountains made flying conditions testy as fuck," Harris continued. "So, when the Chinook me and my team were in tried to touch down, the pilot couldn't land it. Whenever he attempted it, the wind caught the underside of the copter and flung us ten feet into the air. It wasn't too long before we started to spin." He barked out a laugh. "I remember thinking, *well, Harris, you've had a good run*. It was obvious we were gonna crash and burn."

Snorts and chuckles rose up.

"After a minute of white-knuckling it, one of the boys started singing Disney songs, shouting, 'Come on boys, best Disneyland ride ever.'"

I laughed, imagining Harris's copter spinnin' like a motherfucker, while a unit of big, hairy soldiers yelled out Disney tunes. The other men laughed along with me until the room was filled with the sounds of us all busting a gut.

Harris rolled his eyes, chuckling as he continued his story over the laughter.

"We had a blast, laughing and hollering, pretending we were at fucking Disneyland." Harris looked around the room, a massive grin on his face. "Eventually, the pilot landed us perfectly, and off we went to kill the T-Man."

The men were still in hysterics.

Ken wiped his eyes. "It reminds me of the term 'laughing in the jaws of death.' Only military personnel can do it, and it proves my point. Our humor doesn't resonate with civilians."

"Yeah," Harris agreed, his smile fading. "When I told my wife the story, she started crying. I was only trying to make her smile by telling her what I thought were funny stories, but I upset her." His eyes rested on Ken. "Nobody understands me anymore. I've changed so much from being deployed and fighting in wars. I see the world so differently from my wife and family. We've got nothing in common. I love Suzie, and she loves me, but I'm not the man she married. She can't handle who I've become, but I can't change back to the man she wants after seeing the shit I've seen."

Ken looked around the room. "Who else feels that way?"

My hand shot up at the same time as everyone else's.

"It was the same for me," Ken admitted. "When I came home from Iraq, the world was skewed. Eventually, I rediscovered myself by doing things the *old* me used to do. My father was a carpenter. Growing up, I spent hours helping him. So, I built myself a shed and started playing around. It brought back memories of the man I was before I enlisted," he smiled thoughtfully, "and I got enough of the old Ken back for my wife to recognize me again and put her mind at rest." He looked around the room, catching our eyes as he talked. "War changes us, but not our core values. You still have your memories. My suggestion is to tap into them. Remember the way you used to feel. Think about conversations, the people you had them with, and the circumstances around them. You're different now—and that's okay—but your sensibilities are still the same."

My mouth opened before I could stop it. "What if they're not? What if you've become someone you don't recognize?"

The room went quiet until Michael spoke. "I'd like to know, too."

Ken looked around the men. "Does anyone want to answer that?"

A guy called Lou stood, scratching his head as his eyes took on a faraway look. "I think the point is to tap into the men we were before, then look at who we've become and reconcile the two. The shit we've seen and done is a part of us now. We need to come to terms with it. In a way, we need to forgive ourselves."

"That's the one thing I can't seem to do," I explained. "I remember what I did and the friends I lost and wonder why God spared me."

"Not one man here doesn't think the same way, Kit," Ken murmured. "But we *were* spared. Can't say I'm a religious man after the bullshit I've witnessed. Maybe you're right, and a higher power does decide our fate. Maybe there's no such thing, and it comes down to plain old being in the right place at the right time. But, I do know that your brothers who didn't make it wouldn't begrudge you peace. They'd want you to live your best life. It's shit you can't change, so eventually, you just have to let it go."

Mac leaned forward to address me. "When I was in Iraq, I was incensed. I felt a huge betrayal by the Iraqi people. We were there to help them and give them a better way of life; in return, they'd turn around and try to kill us. I didn't kill indiscriminately, but I killed, probably when I shouldn't have. I believed it was for the greater good. I left the military six years ago, and it was only in the last year I started to feel. It hit me: the military turned me into a killer. They put a gun in my hand and told me to kill or be killed. So I did, and it took years for that mentality to wear off and the guilt to set in. It took me that long to get my head around the idea that killing wasn't my right. They drum it into you; it's for your country, you're heroes, thank you for your service. But people don't realize how every day is a struggle. They don't hear the voices in my head telling me to shoot a driver because he cut me up on the freeway. They don't see me counting to ten because some dick closed a door in my wife's face instead of holding it for her, and I wanna break his neck with my bare hands."

Murmurs of agreement sounded as the men nodded.

Mac's words resonated deep inside me.

The military made me a monster. I had nightmares about what I did in the name of my country. Through it all, I'd discovered the world wasn't fair. Good men died, and justice failed while evil prevailed. Life wasn't as black and white as I'd always believed.

Deep down, I wondered if that was part of the reason I lost myself.

I grew up in a world of superheroes and the Taliban. Good versus evil. Right versus wrong. The news channels dedicated hours to the war against terrorism, and boys like me wanted nothing more than to fight the good fight.

But the good fight included picking up pieces of little girls caught up in explosions or killing kids recruited to fight for oppression before they killed you. Those things affected me more than I'd admitted, even to myself. Eventually, my world became so ingrained in violence that I was desensitized.

I became disillusioned, and to continue my work, I pushed everything down until the only time I felt anything was when I blew shit up, maimed, and killed. Eventually, I got addicted to the violence; it became the only way I could feel.

My thoughts immediately turned to Kai and Kadence, and my heart flipped over because I *had* given good to the world through them. They could be my gift to compensate for the evil I'd inflicted.

I had to succeed in my recovery to be a role model and ensure my kids were decent people. But to do that, I also needed to be present in their lives.

I sat up in my chair, and my spine snapped straight.

It was time to resurrect the man behind the monster.

One week later

The following weekend, Dad brought Cash for family therapy.
Michael and Lou waited with me in the garden. I figured talking to Mikey would calm his nerves, seeing as his wife was due to arrive any minute. It was the first time he'd seen Claire since the 'dislocated fingers incident.' His hands tremored so hard he couldn't hold his coffee cup.

"It's gonna be okay," I said reassuringly. "If she wanted to 'Dear John' you, she'd have done it in writing. Chicks never do that shit face-to-face unless they have to, especially if their husband fucked their hands up."

Leo barked out a laugh.

Mikey grinned, shaking his head. "Asshole."

I leaned back on the bench, face to the sun.

I'd started to make friends again, which was weird. I swore I never would after Benny and Simmons died. Over the last few weeks, I'd stopped stressing so much. Once the booze was out of my system, Nina started me on anti-depressants, so I wasn't sweating over the small stuff anymore.

I felt Michael stiffen from beside me. "There she is."

My eyes lowered to see a brunette woman walking toward us, waving.

Michael jumped up and sprinted toward her, arms pumping to help him speed up.

"There's a man in love," Lou murmured as our friend picked up his woman and swung her in a circle while she laughed.

A lump formed in my throat, but I smiled for Michael, happy Clare was still standing by him. "Yeah."

My thoughts turned to Kitten like they seemed to every other fucking second of the day. *Wonder what she's doing?* I mused, staring at Michael as he flung an arm around his wife's shoulder and pulled her into him before walking her inside the clinic. *I wonder if she ever misses me the same way I miss her?*

Clarity of thought was good, but it also threw up questions I didn't have answers to.

I knew Kitten and my kids were in Hambleton, and she'd agreed—with conditions—I could spend time with them when I got home. That was the extent of what I'd learned. Dad didn't want to say too much over the phone. He told me to concentrate on getting well and leave the rest to him and Cash.

Movement caught the corner of my eye. Speaking of the devil, I watched Dad and Cash saunter around the corner of the building wearing cuts over their tees, showing off their straining muscles, jeans, and biker boots.

I nudged Lou. "I'm up." I jerked a thumb toward my pop and brother.

"Jesus," Lou said under his breath. "It's like Sons of Anarchy on steroids. Is that your dad?"

My lips twitched.

"Fuck me," Lou muttered. "He's a big boy."

Dad raised a hand. "Yo!" he shouted as he approached. "Lookin' good, boy. Come and give your old man a hug."

I laughed as I stood, making my way to meet them. "Hey, Pop." I nodded at his attire. "Good to see you dressed up for the occasion."

He laughed. "Thought you'd be in your jim-jams, wearin' your straitjacket," he barked. "Didn't know we had to wear evenin' attire." Dad's gaze went to Lou. "Yo. You a friend of Kit's?" He walked forward, holding his hand out. "Any friend of my boy's a friend of the Speed Demons."

Lou stood and shook Dad's hand, introducing himself.

"Pop thinks he's a new man," Cash told me quietly. "He's tellin' all the boys they should look into therapy. They're shittin' 'emselves in case he makes it mandatory."

I rubbed my forehead, "Fuck!"

Cash laughed. "He's drivin' us fuckin' crazy."

Shaking my head, I took in my Dad as he gave Lou his card and an invite to hang around with a view to prospecting. Pop's expression was open as he talked about the club and the businesses. He turned to me and Cash. "My boys there are part of the legacy," he said, puffing his chest out. "Kit's boy's already wanting to join; he's only eight."

My heart stopped, eyes widening. "Oh fuck!" I breathed.

"Yeah," Cash deadpanned. "That's what your girl said."

I gaped at Dad, then at Cash, who pursed his lips. "He hasn't stopped complaining that me and Bo haven't given him twins. Bowie's fuckin' Layla three times a day. He's exhausted. Said there's no way you're gettin' one over on him. Reckons he's gonna knock Layla up with twins, then he'll do another set when she's ready. Just so he can go one better than you. Bandit was a twin, so it's in the family."

My head reared back. "It's not a competition. You don't just magic twins out of thin air."

Cash shrugged. "Tell that to Bowie."

"Jesus," I muttered. "It's no wonder we're all in therapy."

Cash laughed and clapped me on the shoulder. "You're preachin' to the choir, bro."

I looked at him, then at Dad, who was showing Lou pictures on his cell. I assumed of the kids, and I started to chuckle.

Cash looked at me and grinned quizzically. "What's so funny?"

I looked at Dad, puffing his chest out, and laughed harder.

"What?" Cash asked, joining in the mirth. Within seconds, he was laughing, too, and before long, we were both busting a gut. I looked at Cash, who had tears streaming down his face. My chest tingled with warmth as we chortled and laughed together like brothers should.

And it was amazing.

Family therapy went surprisingly well.

At first, it was less like therapy and more like a funny family squabbling session.

Cash laughed at how Dad went to his therapist's office and told him he'd set him up with the best blowjob of his life if he wiggled his appointments around so Dad could get in early.

Pop's face was a picture when the receptionist snapped that Mitch gets mind-altering blowjobs at home, and because of his offer, he was going to the back of the queue.

Turned out the receptionist was Mitch, the therapist's wife.

Pop's face flushed and flustered before he said, 'Deary me,' like some grandma.

Later, he'd stupidly relayed the story to Atlas, who then relayed the story to all the other officers. The next church meeting turned into chaos.

"Dad asked Abe how the new house builds were comin' along?" Cash said, grinning. "Abe just stared at him and said. "Deary me!"

Nina covered her smile with her hand.

"Then he asked Bowie if Callum O'Shea would send a couple of bartenders over to work for your welcome home party." Cash laughed. "Guess what Bowie said?"

I started to chuckle.

Dad looked to the heavens. "Fuckin' idiots," he grumbled. "Bandit'll be rolling over in his grave. Church was serious business in his day."

Nina looked at me curiously. "Both your brothers are officers?"

I nodded.

Her brow furrowed. "Why aren't you?"

The room went silent for a minute until Dad cleared his throat. "Kit isn't an officer 'cause I never gave him the chance."

Automatically, I went to excuse him, but he held his hand up to stop me.

"The fact is," he continued. "At our vote for Road Captain, you were nominated along with Iceman."

My eyebrows snapped together. "What?"

Dad's stare hit his boots. "I blocked it."

My heart plummeted. "Why?"

Pop's stare lifted to mine. "You were drinking a lot and takin' god knows what. I didn't think you were ready, but now I reckon I dealt with it wrong. Abe and Atlas took me to task at the time and told me that you should at least get a chance. They said some responsibility might straighten you out, but I was so fuckin' scared I didn't listen."

I took in his red-stained cheeks, maybe a sign of embarrassment.

Dad leaned forward, resting his elbows on the table. "When I came home from the military, I was just like you, Son. I saw shit I never spoke of, and it affected me badly. Back then, PTSD wasn't heard of, and there was a stigma attached to seein' a shrink." He rubbed his beard thoughtfully. "There was so much goin' on. The girl I loved married someone else, and to top it off, your grandma was sick with cancer. I kept it together in public, but I was a mess in private."

"What did you do?" I asked.

Dad grinned. "I met your ma and got her knocked up straight away. When I asked her to marry me, she agreed as long as I talked about what happened. Adele's a smart woman and wily as fuck. She saw what clamming up did to me, so she made me go out with her brother, your Uncle Derek, who was goin' through the same shit. It helped, but then your grandpa pushed me too hard too soon."

Me, Cash, and Nina all leaned toward Dad, straining to hear.

"One night, I blacked out and half-killed a member of the club, my best friend who tried his luck with your ma. He was just bein' drunk and stupid. One minute, I was in his face; the next, I was standin' over him with his face mangled, and I was covered in his blood."

I rubbed at the pain in my chest, my heart hurting as I took in the look on my dad's face.

"It was my cousin, Seth," Dad said quietly.

A memory pinged, making my gut jump.

"Seth was in a wheelchair," I pointed out. "How could you have beaten him if he was in a wheel..." my voice trailed off as Dad's eyes turned stricken.

Awareness washed over me. "Was it you? Did you put him in it?"

Dad nodded, scraping a hand down his face.

"Fuck!" Cash snapped.

Pop shook his head sadly. "I didn't wanna give you too much, Kit, but in doing that, I never gave you enough. I was scared I'd push you too far, scared you'd snap like I did. But also, I admit, you being the way you were reminded me of my own issues. You held a mirror up to my weakness, and 'cause of that, I neglected you." His chest contracted as he blew out a breath. "I love you, Kit, but you scare me."

I scared him? Jesus.

Growing up, my Dad was my hero, and in a way, so was Bandit.

They'd both enlisted and served their country, and I wanted to follow in their footsteps. The MC was secondary to me, which, in a way, later drove me and Pop apart. I'd always thought I was like my Mom, but I was starting to see I was more like John Stone than I ever realized.

Dad straightened his back, looked me in the eye, and, in a clear voice, said, "I'm sorry."

The heavy knot inside my chest slowly unraveled, freeing something inside me. My heart bounced, and I sighed so hard my cheeks puffed out as Ken's voice from the last group meeting suddenly went through my mind.

Eventually, you just have to let it go.

Maybe that could be my new mantra.

With that in mind, I leaned across the table, clapped Dad on the shoulder, and smiled. "Apology accepted, Pop," I told him quietly. "Let's just move on."

Movement caught the corner of my eye. Turning, I saw Nina close her notebook and gently place it on the table before lifting her eyes to meet ours. "Good session, guys." She said, turning her smile directly on me. "You made excellent progress."

She was right; we had. There was still a long way to go, but after Dad opened up, I was more confident we'd be okay.

Being here, talking shit out, and coming to terms with everything in my past was helping. I felt stronger already but still had a lot of shit to deal with.

The letter I'd written Kitty weeks ago was still on my dresser like a red flag waving at me whenever I walked into my room. I'd gone back and forth debating whether to send it at all. The relationship—if that was what you could even call it—with my girl was in dire straits.

But talking had helped today; in fact, talking had been helping for the last few weeks. I knew Kitten was furious at me, knew she had her walls up, but what did I have left to lose?

It was time to explain myself. Maybe I'd never get her back, perhaps a part of her would always resent me, but Kitten being in my life was enough. Anything was better than nothing, and I'd take any scraps she threw at me.

It was more than I'd had for the last nine years.

Chapter Nine

Kennedy

"We're not leaving!" Kai yelled, his handsome little face turning an angry red. "Kady and me wanna stay with our family. I can't believe you wanna take us back to Vegas. I hate it there."

"It was only ever meant to be a vacation, Son," I reasoned, cocking my hip. "I have a job to get back to."

His hands clenched into fists by his side. "You can work anywhere. You said one day you'd go to New York and open an office. Why can't you do it in Wyoming instead?"

I closed my eyes, trying to keep my shit together. Wyoming was hardly a metropolis, but try telling that to Kai. "School starts up in a few weeks," I explained gently. "I have to get you and your sister organized."

"We can go to school here!" he cried. "The Demons are building houses down by the creek. We can live there, too, with Sunny and Willow!"

Looking upward, I let out a deep sigh, my stare falling on the bar area where Bowie, Colt, and a few other men sat on stools, pretending not to listen. "Did you put him up to this?"

Bowie barked out a laugh. "Nope. Told him he had to talk to you. Can't say I'm against the idea, though. Pop would pay you good money to stay."

My eyes dropped back to Kai, who looked close to tears. "Honey, I can't magic a job out of thin air. I'm a partner in the firm now; it's not fair to just up and leave. I've got responsibilities."

"Well, actually, Mr. Stafford, the town lawyer, retires next month," Colt called out. "The town's gonna be needin' a new lawyer."

I looked around to see Colt tapping on a tablet. "Huh?"

"The town will need legal counsel," he continued. "You could buy his buildin' and open up a new practice. His client reach is massive. You'd do well."

"See, Mom?" Kai breathed, face shining with a look of victory. "It's like... fate."

My eyes narrowed on the good-looking bastard who'd just fucked me over without a care. "Great," I gritted out. "Thank you so much for that!"

Chuckles rose from the bar area as Colt flashed me a sexy, panty-disintegrating grin. "No problem, Kennedy. Want me to make you an appointment to view it?"

"Why not?" I snipped. "You've been so helpful. Remind me one day to return the favor."

He smothered a laugh with one hand, still typing with the other. "Anytime."

"The price is excellent for a three-story building in this part of town," Harry Stafford advised the following day as he gestured for us to precede him up the stairs of his law offices. "I've lowered it for a quick sale."

I looked around the plush carpeted space, smiling as I recognized the original coving and sash windows that gave the place an expensive, classy feel.

"Do you need all this space?" Sophie asked me as we ascended onto the floor above.

Harry gestured around the vast room. "I used this floor for filing and paperwork, but when everything became digitalized, it became redundant. I considered renting it to another business but decided to retire instead."

I ran my fingers lovingly over the dark mahogany banister and smiled as my imagination started to run wild.

This place felt good. It was big enough to run a practice and hire new talent fresh out of law school, just like I'd always wanted to. My dream was to work pro bono while the other lawyers earned money to keep the firm afloat. I wanted to represent the people who life screwed over. Vets, abuse victims, and people walked all over by companies and businesses out to make a quick buck off people's backs.

I could take the top floor for myself and divide the lower floors into offices for at least another eight lawyers and still have room left for a nice reception on the ground floor. The place had planning permission for an elevator to be put in, and it already had internal stairs. However, everything would probably have to be brought back up to code.

"What's the town council like?" I asked Stafford.

He smiled like the cat that got the cream. "The mayor who's head of the town council is a close personal friend of mine. I can have whatever plans you have signed off within the week." He cocked his head, his eyes skating from my head to my toes. "I'll have to give the mayor some background information. The town's very particular about who it welcomes into the fold. The mayor likes to keep out any unsavory types,"

I opened my mouth to cuss the stuck-up asshole out, but Sophie stopped me.

"Kennedy is from an old southern family. You've heard of the New Orleans Carmichaels, right? Well, Kenny here is the youngest daughter. She followed in the footsteps of her grandaddy, Senator Calvin Carmichael, by becoming one of the country's top defense lawyers. She's moving to Hambleton to be closer to family," she nudged me sharply, "isn't that right, Kennedy?"

The pageant queen smile that flashed across my face was obviously fake, not that Stafford noticed, seeing as his eyes lit up excitedly.

"I'll pass that onto Mayor Henderson, dear," he said in a low tone. "I'm positive there will be no issues at all." He patted me on the shoulder. "I'll leave you two lovely ladies to look around. I'll be over the next street at Magnolia's if you want to talk."

We smiled and nodded our goodbyes as Stafford descended the stairs and slipped out the front door. The minute he left, I whirled around to face my friend. "New Orleans Carmichaels? Where did that come from?"

"I know!" she cried. "Wasn't I awesome? The mayor would've blocked the sale if he knew you were tied to the Demons, so I thought on my feet. You can thank me later."

"What if he does a background check, Soph?"

"Got it covered." She pulled her cell from her purse, stabbed a few buttons, and put it on speaker.

After several rings, Atlas barked, "Yo, Stitch, baby."

Sophie looked at me, waggling her eyebrows. "Big man. I need you to speak to Colt and ask him for a favor. Kennedy needs some information added to her background."

"Wait!" I hissed. "I haven't decided what I'm doing yet? You can't just add a good ol' family onto my history, Soph."

She dismissed me with a wave while relaying everything that had happened to Atlas.

"Soph!" I snapped, but she waved her hand again as if to shut me up.

Blood heating, I cursed under my breath and stomped to the window.

I hadn't even spoken to Scotty about branching out, but Sophie acted like it was a done deal. I knew my friend would love to have me and the kids close, but she had to understand that I already had a life I loved in Vegas. Blistering heat, sand, and casinos weren't to everyone's taste, but it was all I'd ever known. Vegas was a town that would eat you up and spit you out in the blink of an eye, but it had been good to me, and I was hesitant to leave it behind.

I'd been in control of my own destiny since I was sixteen. The only time I pinned my dreams on somebody else was the year I was with Snow, and look how that turned out.

The memory of him made my heart clench.

If I were to move here, it would be because I wanted to, not because the kids or Sophie backed me into a corner. It was a big move to make when I was so unsure.

But what if it would make the kids happy?
What if it's what Kai needs?
What about Snow?

Questions raced through my mind, but my decision couldn't be just about the kids or their father. I had to make the best decision for my family, even if it wasn't the popular one.

Mama had to be happy for everything else to run smoothly, and Vegas was our home. We had a beautiful, big house with a pool and decent lives. The kids had music lessons and attended an outstanding private school. My job wasn't only exciting but also fulfilling. Hustle and Katie were in Vegas, as was Scotty.

There was no way I could leave the only place I'd ever called home. The kids and the Speed Demons would just have to deal. We could visit, and I could even look at buying a home here for vacations.

This was a battle Mama was determined to win. I had to for my own sanity.

"Okay, honey. See you later," Sophie said before disconnecting the call. "Colt's on the case already." She walked across the room to join me. "It's a great space. Stafford was right when he said it was a prime location."

My mouth twisted. "Such a prime location; he hasn't had a buyer yet?"

"Hambleton's mostly stores. There are limited uses for a building like this. The town needs another lawyer."

I stared down at the street below. "I can't buy it," I explained quietly. "The thought of leaving Vegas gives me hives. It's my home."

"But what about the kids?—"

"The kids will be fine," I assured her. "We'll visit during school breaks. They'll be okay once they get used to the idea."

My friend leaned her head on my shoulder, and together, we gazed out of the window.

"I got my hopes up," Soph whispered. "I miss you so much, Ned. Life's not the same without you in it."

Tears burned the back of my eyes. "Hush now. I'm at the end of a phone, babe. I was there for all your Atlas bullshit. I'll always be there."

"What about Kit?" She sniffed.

"What about him?"

"You love him," she turned her face toward me, "you've always loved him."

I couldn't stop a lone tear from escaping. "Babe, I always will, but it doesn't mean he gets a pass. Anyway," I shrugged, looking out the window to the street below, "he hasn't made any contact with me."

"You told him not to," she reminded me gently.

I turned back to her and smiled. "Yeah. 'Cause, like I said, Snow doesn't get a pass."

"Right," my friend said sadly.

Silence fell over the room as we got lost in our thoughts.

Loving Snow was so easy, even after what he'd done. Every girl experienced one relationship that shaped them above all others, and Snow represented mine.

He was the first man who I thought gave a shit. We were so in tune we didn't even have to speak to know what the other was thinking. It was crazy how he kept giving me so much beauty and then so much pain. I'd be forever grateful that I met Snow because he gave me my babies. It was like I always said. Everything happens for a reason, right?

Since he'd been back in my life, my heart had been heavy, like it was weighed down with grief. It was absurd how I could hate a man for dying and living.

Time was a great healer, though. Even though I missed my golden boy so much it hurt, I knew I'd be able to finally let him go once I'd worked through everything. The version of Snow I missed was a beautiful soldier who danced with me on a mountaintop. That man *was* dead or never really existed. That was the Snow I'd love until the day I died, but it was one-sided. He never loved me, at least not enough to tell me his real name.

Acceptance was wonderful because, along with it, came clarity.

Sophie gave a heavy sigh. "Shall we get out of here? Atlas will send out a search party if we don't return soon. He's crazy possessive." She rubbed her tiny baby belly.

"I'm sorry I can't stay, Soph," I murmured, hugging her tighter. "I've loved him for so long that I don't know how not to anymore, and if I stay here, I'll never find out. I need to accept what's happened and move on. I can't do that when he's in my face every day. I need a clean break."

She moved until she faced me. "I'm sorry."

I smiled through my sadness. "No need to be. That's life. Love doesn't cancel out the lies. Sometimes, I wish I could be softer or more forgiving. I'm just not that girl."

"I don't want you to be," she said, looking into my eyes, "'cause it wouldn't be you. Now wipe your eyes. You look like Alice Cooper."

A laugh escaped me, fresh resolve making me pull my shoulders back. "Alice wishes he could carry it off like me." I reached into my purse, pulled out some wipes, and cleaned my face.

"I can love you just as hard from Hambleton, Ned," Sophie said, voice full of conviction.

I rubbed her arm. "And I can love you harder from Vegas."

"Then everything will be good, right?"

I nodded, silently thanking God for giving me such an amazing woman for a best friend. "Yeah, babe. Everything's gonna be great."

To our surprise, the Demon's parking lot was deserted when we pulled in thirty minutes later. It was full of vehicles but no people, which was weird. Usually, the place was packed with men who hung outside shooting the shit while cleaning their bikes.

"It's like a ghost town," Sophie mused, looking around. "I'm expecting a tumbleweed to roll through the place any second."

"Come on," I said, pointing toward the doors. "I'm not in the mood to play spot the biker. The sooner we get in, the sooner we can see what the hell's going on."

We got out of the car and slammed the doors shut just as a loud roar went up from inside the clubhouse. My eyes snapped to Sophie's. "Is it the Superbowl, and nobody told us?"

"It's bizarre," my friend drawled. "Atlas didn't say there was anything special going on."

I started toward the doors. "Come on, I need to check the kids are okay. If the guys are getting rowdy, I'm gonna take them home."

Soph fell into step beside me. "John will have them safe. He'll close the place rather than let the kids get caught up in biker crap." She grabbed the handle and went to push. "Come on."

We walked in and immediately encountered a wall of cuts in front of us. The men held their backs to us while focusing on something by the bar.

Sophie grabbed my arm, pushing through the crowd just as the sounds of guitars strumming filled the room.

As we pushed through the men, Sophie suddenly stopped dead. "Oh my!" she breathed, raising her hand, and pointing across the room. "Look."

My gaze snapped toward the bar, and I stilled as I took in the sight before me.

Kady sat on a stool, strumming her guitar with Colt and another man I hadn't seen before. I would've remembered if I had.

He wore black jeans and a cut over his muscled, bare chest, covered by a myriad of black and grey tattoos. His hair was long but fastened in a man bun, the dark strands lightened by the sun. Bright blue eyes aimed at Kady, and he gave her an encouraging smile.

"What d'ya wanna play next, little bit?" he rumbled in a deep, rich voice.

"Do you know August?" she asked, squirming excitedly on her stool as she looked up at him with shining eyes.

"Oh!" Soph murmured. "Hendrix is back from Virginia."

My nipples tingled as I watched the guy grin at my girl. I swear every woman in the room sighed as he began strumming out the chords to one of Kady's favorite Taylor Swift songs.

Colt joined in, then Kady, until the room was filled with the folky intro as they played the melodic chords together, and my girl began to sing.

The sweet, clear tone of her voice rose above the guitars as she sang the lyrics she knew by heart. Her eyes closed, and a small smile played around her pretty lips as she began to feel the words.

Kady's love of music was soul-deep. It was her outlet for the emotions she took on from the people around her. I believed singing and playing instruments was her way of purging them so they didn't weigh her down.

"Jesus, Ned," Sophie whispered. Her eyes rounded as she stared at Kady with a shocked expression. "She's amazing."

"She is," I agreed softly. "Her music teacher says she's incredibly gifted. She plays guitar and piano at the level of a professional. Reading music for her is as simple as reading the alphabet. She can also hear a song once and immediately play it by ear."

"I never realized," Sophie murmured. "Why don't you send her to a school for musicians?"

A lump immediately formed in my throat. "She's too young. I can't let her go yet. I want her to have a normal, happy childhood. If she wants to pursue a music career when she's older, I'll do everything I can to help her, but I want her to go to school, have fun, and be a kid."

"Yeah," my friend breathed. "I agree."

"In the meantime, I just have to put up with Taylor," I muttered, lips twitching. "But it's a trade-off I'm good with as long as Kady's happy."

"Oh, my God!" Soph's fingers dug into my arm. "Look at John."

My eyes slid to the kid's grandfather. My heart bounced when I saw the delighted awe all over his face as he leaned on the bar, smiling down at Kady with his hand settled on Kai's shoulder. His chest was puffed out proudly, which made me smile. But seeing the love shine in his eyes made me think about my plans for the future.

This was all I'd ever wanted for them.

Since we'd arrived here, the twins had flourished under the care and attention of their grandpa, uncles, aunts, and cousins.

The club devoted itself to family. The kids were encouraged to play, explore, have opinions, and voice them. There was no attitude of 'children should be seen but not heard' like my mother's, and it made me wonder if taking them away was the right decision.

My eyes went to Kai, who looked up at John with the same golden eyes as the older man as they exchanged identical grins.

Heart thumping, I turned my gaze on Kady, who strummed her guitar, eyes still closed as she sang the bridge.

Heat burned my skin as something pulled my gaze to the right, where it met blue, as the handsome biker shot me a sexy smirk.

His stare flicked down my body before he lifted it again to meet mine.

My throat closed as I took in the sheer beauty of the man.

I wasn't looking for a baby daddy. I knew better than anyone how the biker world worked. I had kids with a brother, which made me off-limits. Even if something could happen, I wouldn't want it to, but there was no rule to say I couldn't enjoy the view. It wasn't like Snow had saved himself for me.

Pain shot through my chest, breaking the spell that Hendrix's gaze weaved. Pushing it down, I turned my attention back to Kady, who strummed the last chords of the song.

Somebody started clapping. More people joined in until the noise almost deafened me. Cheers went up, and feet stomped, making my baby girl's face break out in a huge smile as she took in the men's adoration.

John went over, crouched, and hugged her before standing again and turning to the crowd, still shouting their appreciation. "My little Kady girl's gonna be a huge star one day!" he exclaimed proudly.

A laugh escaped me as Kady jumped down from her stool, her little guitar still strapped across her body. She slipped her hand into her grandpa's, her little eyes shining. "Can we play Taylor Swift, Grandpa John?"

The claps and cheers faded, groans and mutters taking their place.

John turned to Colt. "You heard my girl. Sort it." He ignored the rumbles of complaint from the men as curses turned the air blue.

Colt tapped on his cell and grinned as 'I Knew You Were Trouble' started pounding through the speakers. "Thought this one fit." He chuckled.

Sunny came flying through the bar from the corridor leading to the kitchen. "I loves this song!" she squealed, grabbing Kady's hand. "Let's dance." Kady took off her guitar, propping it carefully against the bar before allowing Sunny to pull her toward the middle of the room, tugging John. "Come on, Grandpa. You dance with us, too."

All color drained out of John's face. "Err... Umm... Girls," he pointed toward his office, "I gotta go do some work. How 'bout I get young Billy to dance with ya?"

"No, Grandaddy!" Sunny shrieked as she spun in a circle. "Please do twirls with us first."

"Yeah, Grandpa. Please." Kady begged.

John's cheeks went from white to scarlet. He shuffled his feet in a circle, caught between wanting to make the girls happy or running like the devil was on his ass.

A "whoop" sounded from the doorways. Cara stood in the same corridor Sunny came from. She began to circle her hips. "Woohoo!" she yelled. "Shake that ass, John! Show the ladies what you've got." She let out another hoot, waving her arms slowly in the air as she swayed from side to side.

John's eyes snapped to her. His stare hardened, and he snarled.

Sophie and I glanced at each other, laughing.

Cara cackled loudly before shooting us a wink. She looked hilarious, heavily pregnant, baby bump out to there, swaying seductively while shouting at John. "Shake that jelly, Prez!"

All the men began to bust a gut as John skewered Cara with another look.

"Hold it there, Prez," Abe snuck through the crowd, holding his cell from up high, videoing the scene. "Say cheese, Dagger."

Bellows of laughter rose up.

"You're just like Tinkerbell, Grandaddy John," Sunny cried. "You're such a pretty twirler."

John's face reddened as the crowd roared.

Atlas walked into the bar, his steps faltering. "What the fuck is this music?" He caught sight of his prez and barked a laugh before howling so hard he had to bend over and clutch his stomach.

Sophie and I giggled.

Abe had tears streaming down his face, hooting as he filmed John shaking his ass to Taylor.

All the men shouted encouragement to their prez. "Go on, Dagger. Show 'em how we do it old school." "Somebody call Dancing With The Stars."

John's cheeks burned as he held the girls' hands, shuffling his feet, shaking his head at his own hilarity. "Bandit would kick my ass," he muttered, obviously mortified as the entire room cracked up at the sight of him twirling to Taylor.

Kai sidled up to me and took my hand. "Please don't make us leave, Mom?" he begged. "Uncle Cash was right. This place *is* home."

My stomach dropped as I took in the pleading look on his face.

Taking Kai away from this would break his heart. I fully expected countless women to do that to my son in the future, but I didn't want the first to be me.

I looked at Kady laughing with her grandpa and then back at Kai, whose expression turned joyful. He loved Hambleton so much; it was the only place he'd ever felt comfortable in.

What the hell was I going to do?

I was still mulling the same question over hours later when I ushered the kids into the rental house.

After Kady and Sunshine finally let the guys change the music, they had a mini impromptu party. Abe brought Iris out to do some old-fashioned jiving.

I loved watching them. Abe doted on his wife, and she looked at him with so much love I almost wanted to cry. John made Mason show everyone his body-popping breakdance moves and tried to do a dance-off with him. It was hilarious, and we ended up laughing all night.

Eventually, Iris brought out a feast. Cara made some picky plates, so we pushed tables together and ate.

Layla and Cara entertained me with a story about Sunny from last Christmas. Layla went bright red as she told how me she'd never live the pussy story down.

Cara and I almost fell on the floor laughing.

The kids went off to play for a while before we headed home, and I chatted with the girls about my dilemma.

"Their school is amazing. It's private, but I only sent them there because my partner, Scotty, knows the principal. State school would be fine, too."

"Hambleton's Elementary and High Schools are excellent," Cara confirmed. "Their teacher-to-pupil ratio is great; most go to college or trade school when they graduate. Though by the look of Kai, the only college major he'd wanna do is Biker one-oh-one."

I watched as he chased through the bar after Sunny. "He does love it here."

Layla laid back with a blanket over her shoulder, nursing Willow. "I understand why you're confused, Ned. All I can tell you is that the Speed Demons gave me the family I never had. Cara and her parents were always great to me, but when I met Bowie, he also opened up a whole new world for Sunny. I've never been happier than I am now, and neither has she. They've taken her on as their own. As far as Bowie and everyone else is concerned, he's her dad, even though she's not his blood. They're good decent men, and I know there's a lot of history with you and Kit, but he's decent too. He did a lot to get Bowie and me together, and after the shooting, he was amazing." She gently moved baby Willow over her shoulder to burp her.

"Atlas loves having him on his team," Sophie interjected. "He says Kit's a natural. He's well-trained, smart, and thinks on his feet. I guess it's his military training."

"He was bomb squad," I told them. "He's highly trained in explosives. My uncle says they diffuse bombs but have a darker side, too."

Sophie leaned forward. "What's that?"

"I don't know exactly, and even if I did, I couldn't say," I looked furtively around the room, "*they* might be listening."

Sophie's face scrunched up. "Who?"

"You know... Big Brother," I whispered.

Sophie's eyes went big with shock.

Cara and Layla's stares began to dart around the room.

A grin spread across my face, and I began to laugh.

Sophie rolled her eyes. "Ned! I thought you were being serious."

I laughed harder.

"Oh my, God," Layla said with a huff.

Cara began to giggle.

"Look," Sophie said, getting back onto the subject. "I know you love Vegas, but here the kids have everything they need; emotionally and physically. Just think about it and have a chat with Scotty. We're not as isolated as you think. We're in driving distance of Colorado and Wyoming's cities, so there's plenty of scope for work." She shot me a pleading look. "You can keep your Vegas house to visit and vacation. Hell, we'll even come with you."

Cara's eyes shone. "Yes! We'd never even have to see the boys. We could chill at yours and send them down the strip. Can you imagine the peace and quiet?"

The girls began to talk excitedly as they planned their vacation to Vegas. In contrast, I began to think seriously about what they said. So many factors and moving parts were involved that I didn't know what to do next. I loved Vegas; it was my home, but Hambleton was where the kids wanted to be, and if I was honest, I liked it here, too.

With my mind still going over the conversation, I locked the front door to the rental and watched the kids run to their rooms to play. I moved to the kitchen and sat at the kitchen table, weighing everything up.

It was okay for the girls to say I should relocate here, but it was a big decision. In a way, I was scared I'd make the wrong choice and fuck everything up.

Perhaps I needed a sign.

"Mommy, there's a letter here for you." Kady bounced into the kitchen, waving an envelope. "I just saw it on the hall table."

My brow furrowed as I took it from her with a thank you.

Who the hell was writing here for me? If Scotty needed me, he'd call.

The first thing I noticed when I examined the letter was its lack of a stamp or postmark. It had been hand-delivered. The second thing I saw made my heart leap into my throat.

Snow's handwriting.

Dumbfounded and nauseous, I stared open-mouthed at the envelope while Kady fetched a drink from the fridge.

"Goodnight, Mommy," she said, kissing me on the cheek before wandering to her room.

"Night, baby," I croaked, eyes still glued to the letter as I tried to work out how it got here. John and Cash had returned from Grand Junction a few days before. One must've brought it back with them and left it here while we visited the clubhouse today. My money was on Cash; he'd been scarce all day. Cara told me he was working, but he obviously had time to slip out without anyone noticing.

I'd been waiting to hear from Snow for what seemed like forever.

Counting up in my head, I realized he'd been there five weeks already. I'd started to wonder if he would reach out at all. In a way, I was glad he left it a while. It gave me time to calm down and think rationally about our situation.

A big part of me didn't want to read it. But a bigger part of me did, so with my heart still in my mouth and trembling fingers, I slowly slid my finger under the seal and gently tore the top open. Then, sitting back in my chair, I began to read.

Jules Ford

Dear Kitten,

I'm so fucking sorry.

As stupid as it sounds, throughout all the years I've thought about you, it never once occurred to me that you had the wrong name.
Isn't that ridiculous?
Maybe, it was because it was never about that for me. What we had transcended trivial shit. You knew me soul deep, so a name meant nothing to me because you were just Kitten, and I was Snow, and nothing else mattered. I didn't need your name to know how much I loved you; how much I still love you.
It's not an excuse. There's no excuse good enough for what I put you through, and for everything I was never there for.
I haven't forgiven myself for hurting you on our last night together. I regret so much shit in my life, baby, but nothing as much as that. To this day, I don't know how it happened, but I'm sorry for that, too. I'm working on so much while I'm here, so please don't think I'll ever hurt Kai and Kady like that. Please don't keep them away from me. I need my kids in the same way I need you, baby, like you're my air supply, and without you, I can't breathe.
If it wasn't for the thought of you out there somewhere, I would've put a gun to my head years ago. I hoped we'd find each other again, and even when I lost hope, there must've been a part of me that knew one day we'd be reunited. Some nights I'd dream it, and it was so beautiful that I'd wake up, and my heart would burn to ash because it wasn't real.
In the parking lot after Atlas's wedding, you said we were never real, baby, but we were. You're the only real thing I've ever known. My name may have been fake, but

the way we loved each other wasn't. I never want to hear that shit out of your mouth again.

Us being together has been my dream for so long, but just being in your and the kids' lives is enough. Being without you made me realize that I don't need anything except for you to be happy and healthy. Even if we're never together again like we were, I'd be the happiest man alive if you were just present. But I'm gonna try to win you back. I remember everything now, and I'll spend my life making you remember too. You may hate me, and I'll understand if that's the case, but I'll settle for what I can get. Any scraps of you are better than nothing. I know that from experience.

This may be asking too much, but will you visit me?

Don't bring the kids. The thought of them seeing me here makes me wanna throw up, but I wanna share this part of me with you. The Snow you loved is hovering. He's standing on the edges looking in, but I can feel him, baby. He's so close.

I'm sorry for every tear I caused you. I'll spend forever making it up to you in every life we'll ever live.

Your idiot,

Snow

One Week Later

Harry Stafford pointed to the pile of papers on the desk we were leaning over. "I just need your signature here and here," he prompted.

With a flourish, I signed my name and, just like that, bought myself a law practice.

Harry invited me to stay for a celebratory glass of champagne, but I refused. I had to go home and get an early night because after reading Snow's heartfelt words and thinking about them for days, I'd decided to do as he asked and go to Grand Junction.

The letter he sent made me cry myself to sleep because even though it was apparent his feelings for me hadn't changed, he'd still thrown me away. Love was never our issue, but the only time he ever genuinely communicated with me was in writing, and I needed him to apologize face-to-face.

Our showdown had been a long time coming.

And after eight years, it was time to give that asshole a piece of my mind.

Chapter Ten

Breaker

On Friday afternoon, I asked for an extra therapy appointment with Nina. Kitten's visit was due the next day, and I needed help to work through all the thoughts and feelings racing through my body.

Nina asked me to try and convey my emotions and how I saw Kennedy's visit.

"I guess it's a feeling of being on a high ledge and looking down on the street below," I explained carefully. "I've dreamed of being down on that street with everyone for years, but being alone on the ledge is all I've known for so long it's like I'm scared to take the leap in case it hurts."

"What's happening on the street below?" she asked.

I shrugged. "People going about their business and living their lives."

"And you're stuck on the ledge watching and listening?"

I nodded. "It never bothered me until now."

"Are you ready to take the leap?"

I sat back in my chair, thinking about Nina's question.

Was I?

I felt ready. The weeks spent here had made me stronger. I didn't push anything down anymore; I felt it, dealt with it, and let it go.

Therapy with Dad and Cash had helped, too. They made me see myself as part of the family again and not an outsider, which was a relief after last year's events. It was like someone opened the drapes, allowing me to see clearly again. However, a lot of that was because of the medication Nina prescribed for me.

I worried about addiction. I'd taken enough synthetic substances to last me a lifetime, and I wanted to interact with my kids and not be spaced out. Nina assured me the anti-depressants I was prescribed were worth the risk. Later, when I was ready, I could be weaned off them. Alternatively, I could be on them for the rest of my life because, as my shrink said, millions of people took lifelong medication. It was preferable to falling into depression again like I did before.

"I think I'm ready," I informed her. "But I can't help worrying it's too soon? What if I take the leap and fall flat on my ass?"

She leaned forward, clasping her hands on the desk. "That's where your dad and brother come in. We've talked extensively in our sessions about your triggers and how to deal with them. You'll have days where you wonder if it's all worth it, Kit. Let's face it: nothing in life goes to plan, but they'll help you. You've built a support system. Now's the time to utilize it."

"What if I end up back here?" I asked, a heavy weight pressing down on my chest.

Nina skimmed my file. "You've got support at the Sheridan Center in Rock Springs. You got along great with the outpatient coordinator there. If you feel like you're slipping, Steve will help you, and you know you can always call me. It's onward and upward for you now. I don't release patients back into the wild if I don't believe they can handle it." She closed my file. "I know you've had past issues with your family, but your dad and brother have stepped up. Trust them and trust yourself. Starting Monday, I want you to leave the center during the day, interact with as many people as possible, and get yourself used to new situations. There are always groups going out for a hike and to the gym in town."

"Okay." I smiled wryly before slowly standing and heading for the door.

"Good luck tomorrow," Nina called out as I grabbed the handle.

I stopped and craned my neck to address her. "Kitten's gonna cuss my ass out."

"You can handle it," she said with a laugh. "You blew up an entire mountain, for God's sake. You can handle a teeny, tiny spitfire."

I barked out a laugh, marveling at how easy humor was these days. "Doc. I'd take a fight with a mountain over my girl any day. My Kitten's got claws."

I felt her before I saw her; her pull was still so magnetic.

Everything inside me screamed to turn around and look, but I resisted the temptation. Instead, I lifted my face to the sun and reveled in the love she evoked inside my heart.

My body was clear of booze and drugs, and my medication made me feel present again. My senses were magnified, and I was connected to the world around me for the first time in a long time.

I was alive and about to meet with the woman I'd loved ever since I was a young, dedicated soldier, ready to change the world.

And I was grateful for it.

Being in her presence elicited such pure, unadulterated excitement that my heart bounced joyfully inside my chest. I couldn't help smiling at the rays of warmth from the sun kissing my skin.

I felt my heart thud back to life as her footsteps got louder.

Even the sound of her approach made my nerves settle. I remembered how she'd always had a calming effect on me. Facing her was the most challenging and the most exhilarating thing I'd done in years. Surprisingly, it didn't faze me one bit. I was so fucking ready to live again.

I'd left my soul with her for safekeeping but now wanted to take it back. It was the only way I could be the man I needed to be for my beautiful family. The mere thought of being a father made me wanna punch the air with joy, and even if Kitten wasn't by my side, I'd still be lucky she was in my life.

Inhaling the sweetness from the roses surrounding us, I thanked God for the opportunity to make things right again. My blessings were abundant, and I knew whatever happened next, I'd be okay.

Her footsteps got louder as she approached me, and I knew it was time.

Three.

Two.

One.

I spun around, and my heart bloomed as I watched Kennedy's approach.

The girl I knew was beautiful inside and out, but the woman she'd transformed into was incredible. The sun's rays hit her from behind, making the beams of light reflecting in her white-blonde hair appear like a halo of spun gold. My cock twitched at the memory of its softness when I fisted the tresses while kissing her soft lips in a smoky nightclub.

My stare slid to her face, and our eyes met.

One side of Kitten's mouth curved up into the same smirk she'd shot at me from a dark Vegas stage ten years ago, making goose bumps scatter down my arms. Her cornflower-blue eyes traveled from the top of my head to the tips of my toes, assessing the man I'd turned into during our years apart.

The space between us almost crackled with electricity. I couldn't look away. I never wanted to tear my eyes off her again; I'd been robbed of her for too many years.

She wore tight black leather pants and a bubblegum pink tee, which molded itself to her perky tits, a little bigger than before. Her hips swayed seductively as she strutted toward me on sky-high heels, making her long, shapely legs look like they were carved by the Gods.

Just like years before, I swore she'd never know what I knew or what I'd seen. Never would she feel the darkness. I'd make sure she lived out every dream and succeeded in everything she did. Kitten was the only speck of light in a world of darkness, and I'd keep her shining brightly if it was the last thing I did. I'd protect her and keep her safe. I'd always put her above me, every fucking time. No question. No doubt. But now I'd put Kai and Kadence on the pedestal with their mom and worship them all.

I knew how hard she'd fought for the last eight years. No woman was stronger than one who strived to be a mom and a dad. She'd raised my kids like a warrior, and it only made me love her all the more.

My fingers itched to touch the feather-soft skin I'd dreamed of caressing for nine long years. How was I supposed to stop myself from gathering her in my arms? From telling her how much I loved and needed her? How was I supposed to keep my goddamned hands to myself when my reason for living was standing right before me?

Kennedy's steps faltered as she approached, stopping about a foot away. Her hand went to her popped hip, and a shapely leather-clad leg kicked out. I always loved it when she gave me shit, but at that moment, the defiance rolling off her in waves was magnificent.

I almost moaned out loud as I felt my cock harden even more painfully.

Her bright red pillowy lips twisted into a sexy pout as she raised one perfectly shaped eyebrow. "Well, well, well," she drawled. "If it's not the artist formerly known as Kyle Simmons."

My body jerked as an invisible wrecking ball smashed into my chest.

The military, missions, and war had all affected my state of mind in the worst way possible. They'd changed the man I was, turning me into something dark and vicious. But walking away from Kennedy was the catalyst that broke me. Without her, I was incomplete. My soul withered away when it didn't have my Kitten to feed it. It was starved to death without her.

She'd belonged to me since she was a nineteen-year-old girl with a head full of dreams. It didn't matter if we weren't together. She'd still be mine until the day they buried me. Kitten owned my heart and soul. She always would. I wasn't me without her.

My eyes flicked over her face and locked with hers. The need to take her in my arms was overwhelming, but again I resisted. If I wanted her forgiveness, I had to go at her pace.

With that in mind, I stepped forward, erasing the distance that seemed so cavernous between us, and gave the woman who owned my heart my best panty-dropping smile. Someone once told me I could charm the birds out of the trees; I just hoped my girl was susceptible, too.

I thrust a hand out toward her. "Hey, beautiful. My name is Kit Stone. I'm so fuckin' sorry it took me all these years to tell you."

Our eyes locked, her brows drawing together like she was trying to work something out before her pupils expanded slightly. The corner of her mouth hitched as she looked down at my outstretched fingers like they were damned rattlesnakes.

Silence enveloped us for what seemed like hours while she stared at my hand. Then, her eyes lifted to meet mine, and something amazing happened that made me wanna take my Kitty in my arms and cry for everything we'd missed.

Instead of taking my hand, she raised her fingers and touched my face, staring deep into my eyes like she was searching for something. My heart did a backflip as she murmured her following words.

"I see you." She smiled. "My Snow's back, isn't he?"

A shiver skated down my spine, and I closed my eyes, committing her touch to memory. A thousand mental snapshots flashed behind my eyes like a movie playing in my mind.

I pushed my cheek into her hand, trying to get closer because I'd missed the softness of her skin. Kennedy was my fire. She only had to look at me to make me burn for her.

I must have stood there for a full minute before Kitten stepped back, leaving me bereft. My eyes snapped open, a thread of panic weaving through my chest. I didn't want to stop touching her, but I understood her anger toward me.

My pulse thrummed when I saw her watching me with narrowed eyes. Her lips twisted, and I knew I was about to get a verbal ass-kicking.

"You!" she said accusingly, poking her finger into my chest. "Are an asshole."

A slow smile spread across my face, and my inner voice whispered, *there she is*.

"Why didn't you tell me your real name?" she demanded, thrusting a hand back to her hip. "You had nearly a week when you came to Vegas to tell me the truth. Six days, Snow, to open your mouth and say something as simple as your name. And you know what's *really* maddening about the entire fucking shit show? I would've understood. I probably would've laughed about it. I loved you so much I would've forgiven anything."

A lump formed in my throat. "I'm sorry. I tried to tell you the night before I left for Fort Campbell, but I knew you were already hurting. I didn't wanna make it worse or ruin our time together." I gently took her hand, stroking her thumb with mine, and stared into her eyes, willing her to see the honesty in my eyes. "I'm so sorry for lying to you, baby. I'll never do it again."

She gently pulled her hand away from mine. "Stop."

I stared at my sneakers, hiding my pained expression from her.

I'd expected her to be resistant. For weeks, I'd told myself to take whatever she gave me. Kitten's anger was justified. I'd lied to a girl who'd been good to me. She was entitled to feel a certain way. I had to let her work through her anger and not force her hand. That would just make it worse.

She nodded toward one of the benches. "Can we sit?"

"Yeah." Resting my hand on her back, I guided her across the grass to the seat. My body sang from our physical closeness. I loved how she made my blood heat and my skin zing. "You want anythin'?" I asked, shooting her the sexiest grin I could muster. "Coffee? Tea? Me?"

A laugh sounded from inside her throat. "That one's as old as Abe."

I chuckled, plonking my ass beside her, and my heart melted as the sweet scent of peaches wafted under my nose. "How are you getting on at the club?" I asked, willing my dick to deflate.

She turned her face toward me, a small smile playing around her lips. "Great. Kai fits right in. I guess the apple doesn't fall far from the tree."

My grin faded.

Breaker

I appreciated the sentiment of Kai being like me. Any man who denied wanting a son just like them was a liar. The male species was comprised of ego-driven assholes, and I was no different. Knowing Kai was similar to me was bittersweet because I'd missed so much of him and Kadence growing up. But nobody else should have had to tell me shit about my kids. I should've already known.

I nudged Kitten's arm with mine. "What are they like?"

"They're great kids," she replied, voice full of admiration. "Very spirited. Kai's perfectly complicated. He's headstrong, protective, smart, and stubborn. Kady's the opposite. She's a dreamer, sweet, and kind. She knows how you're feeling because she can feel it, too."

I looked down at my hands, marveling at how there seemed to be parts of us in both of them.

Kai definitely had my traits, but the knowledge that Kadence felt everything spoke to me on a deeper level. My emotions were such a force they sometimes overwhelmed me. It was the reason I pushed them down; it was easier to do that than have to deal, especially on deployment when I had to stay upbeat for the sake of everyone around me.

My gut panged as I wondered if my baby girl had inherited the most damaged part of me. I didn't want that for her, but at least I could help and guide her. "They're beautiful kids. I loved them the second I saw them." My heart twisted at the next question I needed to ask. "Do they wanna meet me?"

Her face scrunched up. "Of course. Why do you ask that?"

I flinched at the memory of our recent parking lot encounter. "They saw me at my worst. I was a disaster waiting to happen. I still can't believe I let them see me melting down like that. They must think I'm a goddamned lunatic."

Kitten rolled her eyes. "They're not stupid, Snow. They know you were sick. I talked to them about it, and they understood. Stop feeling sorry for yourself."

My head reared back as my shocked gaze hit hers. "What the fuck, Kitten? I'm just concerned."

She sighed audibly. "It's not about you, Snow," she murmured. "It's about what the twins want. When you get back, say hi, but let them come to you in their own time. They're good kids. Kady will probably be all over you like a rash from the second she sees you. Kai will be less receptive, but that's how our boy is. He'll need time to work it out. He's strong-minded, and nobody will sway him unless he wants them to."

Leaning forward, I rested my elbows on my knees, my lungs aching in my chest. "I've fucked-up so badly. I've missed every milestone because of one throwaway lie."

"Yeah, you did fuck up," Kitten agreed. "And you missed a lot, but you were sick, Snow. Don't beat yourself up for that."

My heart clenched at the kind words I didn't deserve. This was just like my woman. She had a knack for letting me know what I did wasn't okay but not wanting me to feel badly about the things I couldn't control.

I turned my face, looking up at her. "It's no excuse, baby."

"Yeah, it is," she replied, her voice catching. "PTSD wrecks relationships. We were young; what chance did we have? I forgave you a long time ago for hurting me that night. I knew things had deteriorated when you turned up at Crimson Velvet, but I still took you home. I was naïve in thinking I could fix you. I wasn't equipped for that."

There was my Kitten, showing her humility.

Even back then, she was kind and understanding. Her spark drew me to her, and I'd kept it with me during my darkest days in the military. Being without her light made everything seem so bleak for the years she wasn't there.

"Thank you," I choked out. "But it was my fault. I should have never gone to you that night."

"I don't agree," she argued gently. "Everything happens for a reason. When I thought you died, I was a wreck. Then, when I looked down at my babies, everything changed. I had to keep it together for them; they got me through my grief."

I stretched my pinky, lightly touching hers. "Nah. You're the strongest woman I know. Look at everything you've built from scratch. I never doubted you'd achieve everything you said you would."

My woman stared down at our hands as I linked them, and her brows furrowed in thought. She gnawed at her bottom lip for a minute before lifting her gaze to meet mine. "You wrote that you still love me in your letter. Why?"

My throat thickened with emotion. "'Cause I never stopped."

"I don't understand," she whispered. "You ended it years ago. I don't know what you want from me now?"

I gazed into her cornflower blues and just spoke from the heart. "I want everythin', baby."

Kitten blinked away the tears hitting her eyes and tilted her chin up defiantly. Anger and a hint of regret flashed across her face.

I knew she was about to shatter me, and even though I'd expected it, a part of me had still clutched onto a thread of hope that what we had would see us through. Somewhere along the way, though, I'd forgotten how prideful my woman was. Kennedy didn't suffer fools, and she didn't put up with shit. It was crazy how the thing I loved most about her was the same thing taking her away from me.

Clenching my jaw, I held on and braced.

"It's over, Snow," she said in a voice husky with tears. "I can forgive a lot of bullshit, but I can't forget. It wasn't just the lie, though that was bad enough. It was the way you left. I loved you so much, but you didn't fight for me. You walked out and left me heartbroken. I believed in you, but you didn't believe in me until it was too late."

I closed my eyes and allowed the pain to sweep through me.

Every organ ached, and my heart felt like it'd been scooped out with a rusty spoon. I brought a hand up and rubbed at my sternum. God only knew why it hurt so much; it wasn't like I hadn't expected it.

My thoughts returned to that awful morning when I woke up and realized what I'd done to her. Kitten was right; I hadn't fought, but leaving her was still the right thing to do at the time. I knew she would crucify me for what I was about to say, but I had to try.

"I get it, baby, and you're right; I didn't fight for *us*. But leaving was my way of fighting for *you*."

Her eyes narrowed to angry slits before she opened her mouth to spit vitriol at me.

I held up my hand to silence her. "If I'd have stayed, it would've ruined you, Kitten. You would've given up everything for me, and it would've destroyed you. Leaving you killed me, but it was still preferable to staying and slowly killing you."

I caught a flash of pain behind her eyes. "You didn't even give me a chance."

"That's right," I confirmed, my tone low. "And if I had to do it again tomorrow, I would. It's been you before me since we first watched the sun rise over the city, baby. It always will be. My job was to protect you and keep you safe, even if it was from myself. I accept I went about it the wrong way, and I'll deal with the consequences, but don't ever ask me to sacrifice you or my kids 'cause I never will."

A pink stain spread across her cheeks. She stared at me for a full minute before she shook her head dismissively. "Nice speech. Shame it's nine years too damned late." She crossed her arms across her chest with a huff.

"I didn't have a choice," I went on. "Staying would've destroyed you over time. You've got no idea how bad things got." I lifted my hand and skimmed a finger down the delicate skin of her throat. "Remember what I did to you? Right there?"

She jerked a nod, her nostrils flaring.

My fingers slid down to her shoulder, then her arm, before gently taking her hand in mine. "I was violent, and eventually, I would've turned it on you. Jesus, I already did. I'll apologize for a lot of shit, Kennedy, but I won't feel bad for leaving. You were safer without me, and so were Kai and Kadence."

Silence fell over us for a full minute as we stared into each other's eyes. I could almost see the cogs turning in her head as she weighed my words and their connotations.

"Blame me for everything, Kitten," I told her, gently squeezing her hand. "I deserve it, but please don't hold that against me."

She looked down at our entwined fingers before nodding. "I never saw it from your point of view before. You make it sound almost noble in a dark and twisted way."

I let out a humorless laugh. "That's me, baby. Dark and twisted all over."

"But this place is helping, right?" she asked softly. "You seem much more like the Snow I first met."

"Yeah," I agreed. "It's taken a lot of therapy and a few meds, but I'm better than when you last saw me. I was a prick and lost my head, but the last thing I meant to do was upset the kids."

She rested a hand on my arm. "Talking of the kids. I brought some photographs of them. Is that okay?"

My heart jumped. "Jesus, woman. Yes!"

She went into the small bag hoisted across her body, brought out an envelope, and handed it over. "The kids want you to keep them."

"Tell 'em I said thanks." I tore open the paper and pulled out the wedge of glossy images with trembling fingers.

My heart flipped as I examined the first photograph.

It had been taken the day they were born. The twins were swaddled in white blankets and laid next to a light-up box with the date. "June eighteenth," I said in a husky voice. "That's around the day Benny died."

She cocked her head. "Benny?"

"Remember Lee?" I grimaced, placing the pictures on the bench beside me.

The look she shot me was venomous. "Any more surprises, Kit? A secret wife or ol' lady? A few more kids scattered around the country?"

Her words robbed me of all breath. "Say that again," I said huskily.

"Huh?" she said, looking confused.

"My name. That's the first time you've said it." My hand snaked up to cover her fingers, still touching my arm. "You don't know how many times I've dreamed of you saying my name. I must have imagined the sound coming from your lips a thousand times."

She pulled her hand away. "If you hadn't lied, it wouldn't have taken so long, but that's water under the bridge. After today, it's history. We need to move on and stop living in the past."

My stomach tightened at the mere thought of her leaving. "I don't wanna stop living in the past, baby. I was happy there, with you."

She nudged me. "Don't say that." Her tone was matter-of-fact. "It complicates things. John said he'd already told you we're staying in Hambleton, so we'll be in each other's lives. Maybe we can try to be friends, but it won't be anything more." Her face took on a pained expression as she clasped my hand. "I want us to be okay, especially because of Kai and Kady, but I know myself, Snow. Even if we tried again, I resent you so much that it would eventually contaminate us."

"I don't care," I said pleadingly. "I can take anything you throw at me."

"No," she insisted. "I don't want to live like that. It will hurt the twins. You know I'll be here for you. We've got two amazing kids, and I think we'll be great co-parents. You gave them to me, and I'll always be grateful." Her eyes shone with tears. "You were the first man ever I loved."

I reached up and cupped her face, angling it so she could see how much I meant what I was about to say. "I'm gonna be the last man you ever love, too, in this life and the next. You'll always be my fire." I watched the tears hit her eyes before one tracked down her cheek. I leaned forward and pressed my mouth against her soft, damp skin. "That's the last time you'll cry for me, baby. I'll only ever make you smile from now on."

Her hands covered mine, and my heart dropped as she gently pushed me away. "I've told you what I came to say. Now I have to go. It's a long drive, and I want to get home in time to say goodnight to the kids."

I watched, transfixed, as she slowly stood. "Why you runnin' away, Kitten?"

Her lips twisted. "You'd know all about that, wouldn't you?"

Emotion burned my throat. "Low blow, baby," I gently scolded.

She bobbed her head in agreement. "Like I said, I've got a lot of pent-up resentment." She turned on her heel and began to strut away on her sexy as fuck heels.

"I'll be home next weekend, Kennedy," I called after her. "Don't make any plans. We've got a lotta catching up to do."

She whirled around. "Haven't you listened to a word I've said?"

My eyes raked up and down her body, leaving her in no doubt about what I meant by catching up. "Take care, baby," I smirked. "You know I love you, right?"

She pointed an angry finger at me. "Don't get any ideas."

I shot her a wink, my smirk growing wider.

She huffed, turned, and weaved across the gardens, her swaying hips drawing every male eye. A low growl escaped my clenched jaw, my blood boiling as I watched a couple of guys try to get her attention.

She was beautiful and sexy but with an air of vulnerability that appealed to the opposite sex. I didn't like it—it had maddened me since the day we met—but there wasn't a damned thing I could do about it stuck in here.

Watching her stomp toward the corner of the building, where she'd soon disappear out of sight, my thoughts went back to the last few years and what she'd been doing. Cash had already told me she didn't seem to have a man in her life, but that didn't mean there hadn't been any.

Since my first week here, dark images of my Kitten sprawled out underneath some faceless man had tormented me. I'd driven myself crazy with the idea of her fucking them, even though I'd done much worse.

I'd whored myself out to nameless women for years, and it had slowly snuffed out whatever light I had left because none of them were her. Nina determined I wasn't addicted to booze, drugs, or sex. Fucking a woman was never about being close or intimate. It was merely an outlet for violence and a way to subliminally punish myself for what I'd done, not just in the military but also to Kitten.

I'd suspected it throughout the years, so it wasn't a shock. But, getting confirmation from a professional who dealt with similar cases was good. I knew it didn't let me off the hook. I hated myself for my reckless behavior, but I had to forgive myself, or I'd never be able to move forward.

I knew Kennedy still loved me as much as I'd always loved her. She was at the center of my universe. Kitten had belonged to me mind, body, and soul ever since we'd sat on a mountain, watching the sun's rays race across the city. It wasn't logical; it was just us.

And whether she liked it or not, I was gonna make her remember everything.

Chapter Eleven

Kennedy

Deep in thought, I stared out the window of my new office, looking down on the street below.
"The equipment's gonna be here at four, so I'm going out now to grab a bite before it gets here. Are you gonna be okay?" Hendrix asked.

I swung around to face him, my eyes flicking over the black tee and jeans molded to his perfectly muscled body. He had the sexy man-bun thing going on, which on a typical day would have me panting, but today—nothing.

"Of course," I replied. "Sophie's bringing Kady over soon. I won't be here when you get back."

His eyes gleamed. "Cool. See ya later, gorgeous." He sent me a sexy smirk before turning around and disappearing through the door.

I let out a quiet curse, inwardly asking myself what was wrong with me.

Hendrix had been flirting with me since we met at the club when he played guitar with Kady. I'd flirted back a little—what was a girl to do?—but my heart wasn't in it. It didn't take a genius to work out why.

Thoughts of Snow had consumed me for the week since my visit to Grand Junction.

Being a lawyer, and a good one at that, not much shocked me. I prepared for every outcome and eventuality, but walking through the hospital's gardens and being met by the same Snow who was with me for that week in Vegas had disarmed me. The thing between us that made us so goddamned perfect for each other was still there. I wanted to deny it, to look at him and feel nothing, but it was impossible. So now, I was caught in a conundrum I never saw coming.

How was I supposed to live in the same town and share my children with a man I fell in love with when I was a nineteen-year-old girl? Snow cherished me and probably would've continued to do so if the military hadn't gotten to him. He was halfway back to being my golden boy, so keeping him at arm's length would be challenging.

I wasn't a kid ruled by hormones; it wasn't the sexual side that concerned me. Just being with Snow, him touching me, and saying all those beautiful things was admittedly a bit of a love bomb. But I knew I could stick to my guns. It was like I told him; I held too much resentment to make it work between us. I loved him, and I'd still fight for him to the death, but only because he was the twin's dad.

Talking of the twins, Kai and Kady were full of questions when I got home.

I'd told them Snow loved their pictures and was desperate to get to know them. We'd talked about how much better he was and how he seemed more like the man I thought the world of years ago, but it was a hard sell, especially for Kai. He was still unsure, whereas Kady couldn't have been more excited. Her dad was somebody new for her to love. I liked the idea of Kady helping him heal with her smile and sweet nature. It was a given that her daddy needed her as much if not more, than she needed him.

I'd kept myself busy with the new building all week, which helped keep my mind off Snow. The Speed Demons owned a big construction company, so John spared a few men to come in and put up partition walls on the lower floors to create offices. They'd completed the work in two days. Now, they were rewiring and fitting new electrical points.

I was impressed by how quickly the work had moved along. The flooring was due to be delivered later that day, along with the industrial refrigerators and microwaves I'd arranged to be installed in the new lunch room. It was exciting stuff, made all the better by the thought of interviewing three law school graduates coming in the next week.

Scotty was encouraging about opening the new offices of Clarke and Carmichael. He'd told me to go for it. The Three Kings still wanted me to represent them, which I would. I'd decided to keep the Vegas house for vacations and when I needed to fly in for consultations and court cases. I'd already agreed to represent the Demons, so I had a shiny new client.

Work, career, and the kids were all ticking over brilliantly. It was my love life that left me feeling queasy. Snow was coming home the next day. John was riding down to Grand Junction with a trailer for Snow's motorcycle, and they were riding home together. My stomach was jumping with nerves.

The club wanted to throw Kit a party Friday night, but he'd said it would be too much. All he was interested in was seeing me and the kids. In light of that, plans were changed. John arranged a family barbeque on Saturday instead so Snow could meet the kids in an environment where they were all comfortable.

He'd been warned about Kai, and John told me he was prepared for a hard time, but I was still concerned my boy would say something that would push Snow toward relapse. I'd spoken to the kids and talked about

Snow's condition and where he was mentally. I'd also told them I'd forgiven him for his wrongdoings, blaming them on his illness. After that, it was out of my hands.

Kai could be distant, bordering on dismissive, but he wasn't purposefully rude. I just had to trust that his protectiveness would shine through and he'd do the right thing, but this time for his dad.

A smile slid across my face as I spied Sophie walking down the street, holding hands with Kady and Sunny, who skipped down the street on either side of her.

She looked so pretty with her slim, toned figure and thick dark hair, which she wore down. Sophie had always lacked confidence, made worse by her fuckface of an ex-husband, who, over time, ground her down and destroyed her spirit.

When Soph first told me about Atlas, I told her to go get herself some and not take it too seriously—he was a slutnut biker, after all—but he'd surprised me. He adored her, and as a result, her confidence had grown. He locked her down pretty quickly; she was already blooming with the first flushes of pregnancy. Though secretly, I put her glow down to being deeply in love and being loved back just as hard.

Sophie saved me the night Snow ended things between us, and I'd never forgotten it. She'd helped me raise the twins and was Godmother to them, so we were stuck with each other for life.

Kady must've sensed me because she looked up, saw me in the window, pointed me out to Soph, and waved.

Smiling, I waved back, motioning for them to wait down the street before grabbing my purse and hurrying down the stairs and out the door to meet them.

We were heading over to the salon for some girlie pampering. The girls had told me about Anna and Tristan, so I couldn't wait to get there and make more friends. What I was most excited about was that Snow's sister, Freya, had come home from Med School in Colorado the night before and was meeting us there, too.

I was new to town and looked forward to creating a new friendship group.

After Sophie left Vegas, I threw myself into work. I had friends back when I danced, but the girls drifted away when Marcus had to sell the club. I loved Cara, especially when she gave the men shit. Layla seemed sweet, and of course, Sophie was my girl, but I was a great believer in the saying, 'You can never have too many friends.'

The second I pushed the door open, Kady ran for me. "Mommy!" she squealed. "Me and Sunny are getting our nails painted, and Auntie Sophie said Miss Anna can do our hair."

I went on the back foot, bracing as my girl flew into my arms. "That's amazing, baby," I said, trying to match her excitement as I bent at the waist to bury my face in her beautiful blonde hair.

She looked up at me, eyes shining. "I'm gonna be pretty for Daddy."

"You'd be pretty anyway," I murmured. "You don't need painted nails for that." I glanced at Sunny. "You okay, honey?"

Sunshine nodded enthusiastically. "I gets to see Tristan today. He's sooo funny."

Soph nodded her agreement. "She's right. He's hilarious. He's also gonna love getting his hands on you. He's the same guy who does my hair. You'll be like a shiny new doll for him."

We set off toward Main Street, adjacent to my offices in the much quieter Monument Street. The salon was just a few minutes away through an alleyway. Sophie and I shot each other amused looks as the girls chatted about the color they would get for their nails.

As we emerged onto the street close to our destination, I heard something that stopped me.

A high-pitched and loud *"ladieeeees"* filled the warm Summer air.

I whipped around to see a beautiful, tall man with bleached, cropped hair come prancing up the street, holding coffee holders filled with cups in both hands. "Oh my laaawdy!" he drawled excitedly. "You girls looked like Charlie's Angels the way you came supermodel stomping outta that alleyway."

"Hey Tristan," Sophie called out.

"Afternoon, Meredith," he called back. "Hair's lookin' good, girl. How's that big lump of hunk you've got pantin' after you? He hasn't been in for his prison buzz cut in weeks."

"Who the fuck's, Meredith?" I asked Sophie, tone confused.

"Meredith Grey, honey," Tristan called over. "Our pretty little doc puts me in mind of a younger and prettier Meredith Grey, you know, from the show Grey's Anatomy?" His eyes caught on my face and traveled down my body and back up again before his steps slowly faltered. "Oh my!"

"Told you so," Sophie murmured. "I just heard a thud as he fell for you."

"Little baby club princess, Little Miss Sunshine," Tristan squealed. "Help a boy out and introduce me to Farrah Fawcett reincarnated and her little baby mini-me."

Sunny bent her neck back, gazing up at Tristan. "This is my new friend Kady. Uncle Kit's her Daddy, so she's my cousin. That lady's her mama, and she's called Kennedy."

"Well, aren't you a lucky little girl?" he breathed, eyes flicking toward Kadence. "I'd do *anything* to have Kit as *my* daddy."

A bubble of laughter escaped my throat as Sophie simultaneously giggled.

"I can share," Kady offered. "I'm sure my daddy won't mind, but I have to ask him."

Tristan laughed. "I think he's delighted being your daddy, little Miss Flower Petal, but thanks for the beautiful sentiment." He nodded toward the door. "Usually, I'd be the chivalrous one outta the bunch, but I got my hands full of skinny caramel lattes. Can you believe our little Magnolia's shuttin' up shop? Her Momma's sick and needs help, so she's closing the coffee shop and goin' back home to Indiana."

"Oh no!" Sophie exclaimed as she pulled the door, gesturing for us to go through. "I hope it's nothing too serious. I'll have to chat and see if I can help her out. While I'm there, I'll get her lemon heaven bar recipe. I'm addicted."

The girls rushed inside, full of excitement, followed by Tristan. "Anna, sweetheart," he sang. "Caffeine's here!" Sophie and I entered just as he called out a hesitant, "Anna?"

My ears pricked up as I heard murmurs and whispered shouts from a back room.

"Oh, shit," Tristan muttered just as he spied a tall figure appearing in the doorway of the room where the sounds just came from. "If it isn't Anna's long-haired lover."

Hendrix's stare hit his boots before lifting to me. "Kennedy," he said sheepishly. "What are you doin' here? Thought you were at the office."

I glanced at Sophie, who stared at Hendrix open-mouthed.

"We're getting a makeover," Sunny informed him. "What were you doing backs there?" She paused, then squealed, "Hi, Miss Anna!"

My gaze swept over Hendrix's shoulder to see a beautiful redheaded woman appear behind him from the same room, looking pink-faced and disheveled.

"We were talking about a new hairstyle for Hendrix," she rambled, fixing her buttons as her cheeks burned scarlet.

Tristan put the coffee holders on the reception desk, popped a hip, and glared at Hendrix with his lips pursed disapprovingly. "You wanna take a seat, handsome? I'll give you a trim."

Hendrix's stare hit his boots again, and he scraped a hand down his face. "Just remembered, Ned's deliveries are due. Gotta go." He glanced back at Anna before giving us a loose salute and hurrying out of the salon, slamming the door behind him.

You could've heard a pin drop as all eyes turned to Anna.

"What?" she demanded, red-faced. "Hendrix wanted a private consultation."

Tristan pointed a finger and waved it downward. "Na ha, girlfriend. Your lipstick's smudged, and your buttons are all askew. You can't kid a kidder."

Anna's shoulders slumped. "Tristan, stop. You're embarrassing me."

His face softened. "Anna," he said gently. "He's not gonna make an honest woman outta you. He doesn't even take you out on dates. That man isn't worth the heartbreak."

Sophie's eyes rounded. "You're seeing Hendrix?"

My heart gave a nervous jolt as I thought about all the times he'd flirted with me over the previous few weeks. He'd made it clear he wanted to get to know me better, but he'd been seeing Anna all along.

What an asshole.

Anna exhaled deeply, raising a hand up to rub her forehead. "I wouldn't exactly call it seeing," she said quietly. "We're umm," her gaze fell on the girls, who were listening to every word, and she winced slightly, "special play friends?"

"Does that mean you go on the swing with him?" Kady asked excitedly. "Me and my play friends like the swings."

Tristan let out a snort while Sophie giggled.

I smothered a laugh with my hand.

"Oh, my Gods! Do you play doctors and nurses?" Sunny asked excitedly. "That's my favoritist game."

Tristan's face turned purple with the effort not to choke, but Sophie and I didn't have the same restraint. We looked at each other, and both burst out laughing. Even Anna's lips twitched as she shook her head at us.

Voices came from the door as it opened, and Cara, Layla, and a beautiful brunette walked inside.

"Freya!" Sunny screeched, rushing toward her before throwing her arms around the woman's legs.

"Hey, Sunny Sunshine," the brunette breathed as she bent to kiss Sunny's head.

A beautiful smile spread across Kady's face. It was a sure sign that she got a good vibe from the woman I suspected was about to be introduced as her new aunt. Even if Sunny hadn't yelled her name, I would've known she was Snow's sister by her eyes, which were the same golden color as his.

Her gaze darted between Kady and me as if weighing us up. "I'm Freya," she announced. "I'm happy to finally meet you."

I approached her, stretching my hand out, but she waved it away and hugged me tightly. "You're gorgeous. It's no wonder Kit fell like a ton of bricks." After a beat, she let me go and crouched to pull Kady toward her. "Hey, pretty girl. Dad hasn't stopped talking about you and your brother. It's great to finally meet you." Her eyes flicked over my baby girl's face. "You're so beautiful, just like your mom."

Kady nodded enthusiastically. "Thank you. And Kai's just like Daddy."

Freya's eyes softened. "That's good for Kai when he grows up. Your dad's very handsome." She rose to her full height, turning to me. "I hear you paid him a visit. Pop said he's much better, but Dad sometimes buries his head in the sand, especially regarding Kit. Tell me, how's he really doing?"

I examined Freya's sparkling golden eyes and open smile and decided we would be friends. Sophie told me she was in med school and was a talented doctor. She was as beautiful as her brothers were handsome, and I got a sense of kindness from her.

"He seems much more like his old self," I assured her. "He's worked really hard at changing how he processes things. His doctor didn't go into great detail with me, but she said he's continuing treatment at Rock Springs when he gets home. She seems really happy with his progress."

Freya nodded, regarding me thoughtfully. "Thank you for standing by him, Kennedy. He's been so sick for so long. I'm away more than I'm home, but when I did try to speak to him, he brushed me off. It seemed as if he was always trying to avoid me. We're not close, but I hope that will change now he's getting help."

I acknowledged Freya's words, thinking how her story was a lot much like others I'd heard.

Sufferers of PTSD often withdrew, especially from family, and for many reasons. They didn't feel like they fit in and didn't want to cause their loved ones any heartache. Vets I'd worked with often needed friends who'd been through the same thing as them to come to terms with how they felt.

"Avoidance is a huge part of PTSD," I advised her. "Sufferers often unplug from the people around them. Many have little triggers that affect them in ways we don't even realize. From what I've heard, your brother disassociated from everyone, too, starting with me. I wouldn't take it personally."

She gave a little shrug. "Admittedly, it's not a field I'm familiar with. I'll read some studies on it over the next week and work out healthy ways to support him. Dad's all over it. He's realized that therapy can help, thanks to Cash. He's finally joined us in the twenty-first century."

Layla nodded knowingly while Cara burst out laughing.

I regarded Freya thoughtfully. I liked her; she was smart and cared about her brother. He'd need people to talk to during his recovery. Grand Junction had been instrumental in putting him on the right path, but he still had a long road to walk.

I startled slightly as Tristan's hand cupped my elbow and led me to a workstation. "I love your girlie bonding session, Farrah, but you need to get that perfectly formed tush in my chair of dreams and let me get my magic fingers into those gorgeous tresses." He gestured for me to sit, then swung the chair around so we faced the mirror. "How about we put a toner on to brighten it up, and I'll style it big and bouncy." He waggled his eyebrows. "Those bikers like a little va va voom. Don't they, Anna?" he asked, his tone turning steely.

Every eye turned to her, and her cheeks burned red.

"Anna? Is there something you're not telling us?" Freya inquired before her expression became knowing. "Hendrix?"

"Anna said Hendrix is her special play friend," Sunny squealed.

"About time," Freya said under her breath, her expression turning deadpan. "You two have been dancing around each other for a year now. It was only a matter of time." She leaned forward, waggling her eyebrows. "How is he?"

"Freya!" Layla jerked her head toward the girls who were looking at the selection of nail polishes on the wall. "Little ears."

Freya smirked. "We don't want a repeat of last Christmas, right?"

Layla blushed prettily.

"So, Farrah," Tristan said, running his hands through the lengths of my hair. "Tell me. Where did you get your boobs done? They look as perky as a Dallas cheerleader's."

"They're all mine," I informed him. "Cop a feel if you don't believe me."

Tristan bounced on the balls of his feet, clapping his hands excitedly. "Oh my! I've always wanted to touch a lady lump."

"Have you never touched one at all?" Cara asked, eyes shocked.

"Na ha." Tristan swept a hand down his body. "Does it look like I touch boobies on the daily?"

"Did you tell them what you did to Atlas?" Sophie asked, her mouth twisting into a wry smile. "I think you frightened him half to death. It's no wonder he won't come here anymore. He bought some hair clippers from the internet so he can buzz his hair himself in the future."

Tristan let out a loud squeal. "I tripped, I tell you!"

"Of course you did," Anna teased.

"I just wanted to know if it was true," Tristan cried. "That lucky bitch Meredith gets all the fun. And she's such an itty bitty little thing. They'll have to bury her in a Y-shaped coffin the rate she and King Dong bump uglies."

"Mama," Sunny called out. "What's bump uglies?"

"I'll tell you when you're thirty-five," Layla advised her daughter, directing a stern glare at Tristan.

"Get to the point," Cara demanded. "What happened with Atlas?"

"The last time Atlas came in for his buzz cut, Tristan just happened to trip over and fall in his lap. My poor man's scared to come in now. He swears Tristan tried to cop a feel."

Tristan stamped his foot. "I did not. I just wanted to know if what you said about the Coke can was true."

"Tristan," Sophie hissed. "I told you that in confidence."

"Wait!" I held my hand up to interject. "What Coke can?"

Tristan's mouth hitched, and he looked down pointedly. "You know," he gestured to his groin. "Coke can. And I ain't talking 'bout no choad. It's got length *and* girth."

"Oh!" Layla exclaimed.

Cara's eyes rounded. "Oh!" she parroted.

Anna's eyes rounded as her gaze darted between Tristan and Soph.

My spine stiffened. *Coke can? Jesus!*

I caught Sophie's shocked gaze in the mirror, raising an eyebrow. "Well, you kept that quiet, girl. I thought we were BFFs forever. Aren't you meant to tell your BFF everything? Especially things like *that*. I mean, *Coke can*? Jesus, Soph. I'm suddenly filled with a whole new sense of admiration."

"Sorry, Ned," she snipped, not sounding apologetic at all." But I know that mouth of yours. Thanks to Tristan, the entire clubhouse will be riding Atlas's ass by the end of the weekend because you go in hard. I love you, and I'll admit your shit's amusing when it doesn't involve me. Still, now you know, I'll probably be looking for a divorce lawyer by Monday."

"Hey! I exclaimed. "I can keep a secret. Keeping secrets is my damned job. But don't worry, I know a good lawyer, just in case."

Sophie's face paled.

"It's fine," I said, waving a hand nonchalantly. "Atlas's secret's safe with me."

"Yeah, right," Soph retorted. "The instant he says something to piss you off—which will probably be the second you next see him—you'll start shit."

I went to deny her accusation, but the words caught in my throat. Actually, she made a good point. "Yeah," I admitted. "You're probably right. But you gotta keep your man on his toes, babe. It's like I always say, treat 'em mean, keep 'em keen."

"I like her," Tristan announced gleefully. "She's got class and *beautiful* hair."

I raised my hand for a high-five. "Thanks, Tristan."

He tapped my palm with his before grabbing my fingers and shooting me a mega-watt smile through the mirror. "Anytime, Farrah. You're my kinda girl."

Two hours later, we waved goodbye to Tristan and Anna as we exited the salon.

"I can't believe Magnolia's is closing," Cara whined, rubbing her pregnant belly. "Her cakes have gotten me through this pregnancy. This baby will come out yellow with the number of lemon heaven bars I eat daily."

"It's a shame her mom's sick," Layla agreed. "But with all the shootouts, crime, and disappearing women around the area, she's probably looking for excuses to get out."

My steps faltered at the curb, a knot appearing in my stomach. Cold fingers crept down my spine as I watched a black sedan drive past us. "Wait. What?"

Sophie's eye held mine. "I told you about the war with the rival club," she reminded me.

"You did," I agreed. "But you didn't tell me about shootouts and disappearing women. Part of my decision to relocate here was to get the kids away from all the crime in Vegas. Are you telling me I've jumped out of the frying pan and into the fire?"

Soph's eyes glazed over in thought. "I'm sure I told you about the shootout at the club."

My eyes bugged out. "No! You didn't tell me about that. Jesus, Sophie. Are you crazy?"

She winced. "I'm sorry. I thought you knew. The Burning Sinners are into some nasty stuff. We've been on lockdown more than once because of them."

"The boys think they're behind the disappearance of women and young girls from the area," Cara added. "It's come to light they're trafficking them."

The tension behind my eyes threatened to build into a full-blown headache. "Oh, my God," I mumbled, rubbing at my temple. "Let's get out of here."

Taking Kady's hand, we walked through the alleyway toward Monument Street, where my rental vehicle was parked. Another cold trickle trickled down my spine again as the black sedan drove past us, parking close to my car.

A knot formed in my stomach.

Cara came to a halt beside me, automatically glancing around. "Are you okay?"

"I don't know if it's because we were talking about the Sinners, but something feels off." Goose bumps trailed down my arms as I scanned the sedan. The windows were tinted, so I couldn't tell who was inside.

"I can't see anything," Layla murmured, glancing over her shoulder. "But if something feels weird, maybe we should call the club."

I bit my lip. "Do you know that car?"

Cara peered closer. "I don't recognize it."

"Neither do I," Layla confirmed.

My heart jumped as I caught a bright flash through the open window. "Did you see that? Is he taking pictures of us?"

Cara began to hurry toward the vehicle. "Come on."

My ears pricked up at the sound of the engine turning. The car pulled away from the curb, picking up speed as it headed toward us.

I took a deep breath, trying to calm my spike of adrenaline. I needed to calm myself down so I could take a mental note of the car's license plate.

Why would a stranger take photos of us? Kady and I had been approached by modeling scouts in the past. They were always upfront and never took pictures without our permission.

I squared my shoulders, my nostrils flaring as the car came closer.

Later, thinking back, I knew what I did next was stupid, but at the time, I was so incensed that I wasn't thinking straight. Without hesitation, I ran, positioning myself on the road to prevent the asshole from getting away. Straightening my spine determinedly, I held my hand in the air, signaling the car to stop, but instead of slowing down, it accelerated.

"Ned!" Sophie screamed, but it was too late; the car was already barreling toward me. Heart thudding out of my chest, I closed my eyes and prayed for divine intervention as the engine's sound roared louder.

My life flashed before my eyes. Images of me, Snow, Sophie, and the kids filled my mind as I silently prayed for my life.

The high-pitched squeal of tires filled the air. Heart racing, I cracked one eye open just in time to see the vehicle suddenly swerve last minute and accelerate past me.

The relief sweeping through my body was so palpable I almost sunk to my knees. If Sophie and Layla hadn't rushed forward and grabbed my arms to keep me upright, I probably would have collapsed on the sun-heated asphalt.

"What were you thinking?" Sophie yelled. You could've been killed."

A wail filled the warm air, and my heart stopped for a beat.

Kady.

Pushing past Sophie, I ran to her, arms pumping as I tried to gather speed. As I approached, I fell to my knees and gathered her in my arms. "Hush, baby girl," I said soothingly, stroking her hair. "I'm okay. Don't be scared." I pulled back, heart aching as I took in her red eyes and tear-streaked face. "Don't cry, Kady. Look at me. I'm fine."

My girl bowed her head. "That man was bad," she whispered. "He was looking at me and Sunny."

An icy chill hit me, even though it was a sweltering hot day. The mere thought of any adult looking at my daughter nefariously chilled me to the bone. "What do you mean, Kady? Why was he looking at you?"

"I don't know how; I just know he was. He was taking pictures of me and Sunny, and I didn't like it."

A shadow fell over me. I craned my neck to see Layla standing directly at my back, holding Sunny's hand. Sunny's grey eyes were huge with fright, her bottom lip wobbling as if she were about to cry.

I watched Layla's face pale as Kady's words registered. Moisture hit her eyes, and she pulled Sunny protectively toward her.

"Did you hear that?" I demanded quietly.

"Yeah." Her eyes shone with tears. "Let's get back into the salon. We'll ask Anna to lock the doors until Bowie comes for us." She went into her purse and pulled out her cell phone.

I stood, and we all began to hurry back the way we came. Cara and Sophie stood to the side, shielding us, but I was so inside my head that I hardly noticed.

Why would somebody be taking pictures of random little girls? I asked myself.

A dark pit formed in my stomach. There was only one reason I could think of, but I didn't dare let my mind go there; it was too awful.

When I decided to move here from Vegas, a big plus was that it was safer for the kids.

Growing up in a city opened my eyes to the heinous crimes that went on. Prostitution, drugs, and trafficking.

You always heard about kids and girls going missing, never to be seen again.

I was lucky; dancers, showgirls—and especially strippers—were often attacked or hurt throughout their careers, and even though I was young when I stripped for a living, I was protected. I could've easily ended up as just another statistic in different circumstances.

Our relocation was designed to build family connections and a sense of belonging for the twins. I didn't want them touched by darkness, and I certainly didn't want them constantly looking over their shoulders for danger.

And just like that, I regretted my impulsive decision to move to Hambleton. I should've held off for longer instead of allowing myself to be pressured. But, even as I berated myself, I knew the kids wouldn't want to leave here, even after what had just happened. For them, it already felt like home.

Hambleton gave off the air of a quiet, small town untouched by crime, but was that just a façade? I needed to make some inquiries and find out if there was more going on than met the eye.

A plan formed in my mind. I'd talk to the club. If I was dissatisfied with their solution, I'd look into hiring private security. It may have seemed a little over the top to others, but in my mind, there was only one way forward.

I'd do anything to keep my kids safe.

Chapter Twelve

Breaker

At six A.M on a warm Friday morning in August, I sat on a mountaintop, waiting for the sun to rise over a pretty Colorado town.

In a matter of hours, I'd be leaving Grand Junction in my rearview.

I reflected on how the most pivotal moments of my life always occurred on a goddamned mountain. I fell in love with Kennedy Carmichael looking over the city of Vegas. Now, on a rocky peak in a small Colorado town, I contemplated how to bring her back to me.

Michael, Ken, and Tony, another guy who'd completed the program with us, kept me company. We were all heading home later, but I wanted us to share something memorable before we went our separate ways.

Window Rock was an easy hike that took us about forty-five minutes to complete. We took the level loop trail through woodland made up of pine and juniper just so we could watch the sun come up over the beautiful views of Monument and Wedding Canyons.

It was dark when we set out, and I wasn't used to being awake so early, but at that moment, sitting on a rock five and a half thousand feet in the air, shooting the shit with some good friends, it was worth every bit of effort it took to get here, just not physically, but symbolically, too.

Since Kitten visited, so much had changed.

Before, the thought of leaving the clinic made my gut roil. But after seeing Kennedy, my new focus was her. If I was gonna make her love me again, I needed to make amends, and I couldn't do that stuck here.

Still, for now, I was in good company and determined to make the most of my last hours with the men who'd supported me through the last couple of months.

I turned to Ken, sitting on my left. "How long?"

He checked his watch. "'bout five minutes, give or take."

I looked ahead again, taking in the purple glow, signaling the sun's imminent return. The sky was even more beautiful than before in some ways. The dark night was over, and that resonated deep within me because where there was even a ray of light, there was hope.

Lighter days were coming, especially now I had so much to look forward to. Sitting with my ass in the dirt, looking out over the canyon, I couldn't help thinking it was the first day of the rest of my life.

And I couldn't fucking wait.

"You okay, Kit?" Mikey asked from beside me. "You're not usually this quiet."

I rested my arms on my knees, unable to tear my eyes away from the purple hues turning to shades of pink as the seconds passed. "I was just thinking how Benny would've loved this. All the boys, sittin' on a rock, havin' a bonding moment, would be right up that sappy fucker's alley."

Mikey nudged me. "He'd be proud of ya."

My heart swelled at Mikey's words.

I'd been talking about Benny, Simmons, and Espinoza for the last couple of weeks. It felt good to remember them the way they should've been. I felt like I was honoring them, just like they deserved.

Benny wasn't in my head anymore. I stopped seeing him about a month into the program. Probably when the meds worked their way into my system. I didn't miss the ghostly version I saw in my nightmares, but I did miss the funny, loyal guy who made me laugh when life got heavy.

Noticing the sky turn a shade paler, I reached into my pocket, pulled out my cell, found the song I wanted, and pressed play.

I'd rediscovered Raleigh Ritchie again about a week ago when a few of us reminisced about our time at Eggers. But it wasn't 'I Can Change' that resonated deep inside my newly forged soul; it was another track called 'Stronger Than Ever.'

The opening bars of a lone piano playing before Raleigh's masterful lyrics mingled with the cool mountain air, weaving their magic as the first ray of light pierced the dark sky.

"Hold onto your hats, boys. Here it comes," Ken murmured.

Seconds later, the sun burst over the horizon, filling the world with oranges, reds, and pinks as the words to the song's chorus filled the air.

My heart swelled at the beauty of the sky and the meaning behind the words, which seemed to chase away the last piece of the dark void that resided inside me.

My chest warmed for the first time in years as I watched the sun racing toward us across the canyon, lighting up the world, and how it made me feel at peace.

The air stroked across my skin, and as I breathed in its clean pine scent, I swore I'd never give up.

Whatever happened, I was going to be okay.

Shifting my stare to meet Michael's, I took in his wet eyes and smiled because my cheeks were damp, too. We laughed, swiping at our faces, and again, I couldn't help wishing Benny was with us. Some of the best moments in my life included him, and from now on, those moments were what I'd remember. For once, happy memories assailed me. The laughs and how we always bet on who'd best predict the bomb blast. He was here with me; I could feel him, and I knew exactly what he'd want me to do.

"Hey, Mikey." I nudged my friend to get his attention.

He turned and cocked his head questioningly.

"Did you ever hear the one about the Air Force lieutenant?" I asked.

My bud shot me a grin. "No."

"Well," I continued. "A sergeant in a parachute battalion was participating in a shitload of nighttime exercises..."

"You take care, brother." I gave Mikey a clap on the shoulder.

We were leaving. Clare had arrived ten minutes ago. They were going to a hotel to get reacquainted before returning to pick the boys up from their Grandma's house the next day.

Lucky fucker hadn't stopped talking about it since we'd walked down the mountain and back to the center a few hours before.

Mikey clasped my shoulder. "You sure you don't want us to wait with you for your dad?"

"Get the fuck outta here." I laughed. "You're the one needin' a babysitter, bro." I leaned down to address Clare. "You know, he wouldn't have lasted a day in this place without me."

She patted my arm. "We'll wait with you. It's fine."

I was about to tell her to beat feet when I heard the roar of tailpipes in the distance. My ears pricked up at the din, which got louder each second. Pop told me he was driving one of the club's SUVs to collect me, but it sounded like he'd brought his bike, and he wasn't alone, either.

I stood straight, holding my breath and peering down the street curiously.

Suddenly, the sun glinted off metal, and Dad finally rode into sight. "Jesus," I breathed as I caught sight of a large convoy of bikers on Pop's tail and a flatbed truck bringing up the rear. I'd never seen anythin' so damned cool as the sight of my brothers out in force.

The sun beat down, glinting off the chrome of the motorcycles heading my way, and it hit me that they'd all come to take me home.

Dad saluted Mikey before he slowed to a stop ahead of me and kicked his stand on. He lifted his helmet, jerking a thumb toward the boys. "Thought you might wanna blow away some cobwebs. The boys caught wind of why I was coming and insisted on joinin' me."

I threw my head back and let out a hoot. "Fuck yeah!"

Hollers and laughs filled the air as the men all shouted greetings and good wishes. It suddenly occurred to me that they'd come in solidarity. They wanted me to feel appreciated and part of things instead of like an outsider. And I couldn't have been more grateful.

I turned to Mikey, pulled him in for a hug, and clapped him on the back. "You've got my number. Make sure you use it."

My bud pulled back and nodded, giving Dad a chin lift. "Ditto." He walked around to the driver's seat and slid inside. "Take care, bro," he yelled through Clare's window before starting the engine and pulling away to begin his own journey home.

It was bittersweet. On the one hand, I was so fucking happy Mikey got to go home to his family and live a beautiful life, but on the other hand, I was gonna miss him. But that was life. It was like Kitten said—everything happened for a reason, and whether I saw Mikey on the daily or not, he'd still be at the end of the phone.

The sound of metal clanged as some men started hauling Veronica down from the truck.

"Jesus Christ!" Cash yelled. "Be careful, will ya?" He dismounted before charging over. "Stop that shit. You're gonna scratch her."

Dad shook his head good-naturedly. "Those fuckers couldn't organize a game of beer pong in a frat house. They had one fuckin' job." He gestured toward the line of bikes behind him. "Is this okay, Son? They heard I was comin' to get ya, and I couldn't stop 'em. They just wanted to show their support."

I looked down the line at the guys chatting amongst themselves and found it didn't bother me. They weren't crowding me or asking questions. It seemed much like any other ride.

"It's all good," I assured him.

Dad heaved out a hard breath. "You better prepare yourself. Something happened yesterday. We've got Church at five. I want you in there."

My gut knotted at Dad's tone. "What'd happened. Is it Kennedy? The kids?"

"We dunno, Kit," Pop replied thoughtfully. "Nothin's concrete, but I think the Sinners are stepping their game up. Kennedy and the kids are fine, but there was an incident."

An icy chill ran down my spine. "Right." I started for the truck as I reached for my cell to check traffic conditions, which would determine the best route to take.

"Where you goin'?" Dad called from behind me.

"Getting Veronica," I yelled back. "We need to jet, now! I gotta family to protect."

We rode steady all the way home.

Dad took the front spot. Me and Cash side by side behind. I took Ice's spot, which surprised me, seeing as I should've been somewhere at the rear of the convoy of bikes. I wasn't an officer, but none of the other guys were except my dad and brother, so I didn't read too much into it.

The minute we hit the outskirts of Hambleton, my shoulders relaxed. Cash had been calling the clubhouse every half hour to check everythin' was okay. We both wore radio helmets, so he kept me updated all the way home.

He told me Hendrix had gone back to Virginia because his pop was in a bad way.

Ice had gone with him for some reason, which was weird in some ways but not in others. I'd never known Drix to take any of the boys home with him, but Ice was his best bud, so I assumed he went to show his support.

Riding through my hometown clear-headed and back on track was a strange experience.

Hambleton was a pretty little town just north of the Colorado border. It boasted a lush, green landscape due to its close proximity to Green River. It was the perfect place to grow up and raise kids, except for the Burning Sinners MC, whose illegal shit seemed to overflow into our town an awful lot lately.

I'd heard through the grapevine that Dad and the other officers were planning to take 'em down. I'd already blown up their clubhouse, which was good because it put them on their asses for a few months while we trained the men in hand-to-hand combat and drew up tactical offense and defense plans. They'd already attacked our clubhouse, so I couldn't help wondering what they'd been up to while I'd been in Grand Junction.

All too soon, we hit the road leading to the clubhouse. As we neared the building, the electric gates automatically opened like a welcoming hug. The roar of tailpipes was deafening as the thirty-strong line of motorcycles all rode into the parking lot together.

I followed Dad, who slowly aimed his bike toward the President's parking space outside the doors. Surprisingly, Cash followed him, parking in the VP's space to Dad's right and gesturing at me to park beside him in the Road Captain's spot.

My eyebrows knitted together.

Weird.

What were they playing at? Everybody knew the officer's parking spaces were sacred. Bigger men than me had gotten their asses kicked for daring to assume they could take one. Dad was a stickler for the rules, so the fact that I'd been ordered to park in Ice's spot indicated something big was happening.

I removed my helmet, hung it from Veronica's handlebars, dismounted, and turned to Dad. "Where's Iceman," I demanded. "And why am I in his space?"

Dad threw Cash a look before replying, "Church now," and nodding toward the main doors.

Cash shook his head as if telling me to keep my mouth shut before following Dad through the main doors and into the bar. With a mind full of questions, I stepped behind my brother and entered the clubhouse.

An almighty roar went up the second my sneakers hit the threshold. Heart thudding, I looked up to see the bar packed with my brothers, who began stomping and cheering me as I entered the room.

"Welcome home, Breaker."

"You're a sight for sore eyes."

"Enjoy your little vacay, ya lazy bastard?"

Chuckles and hollers sounded through the earsplitting thump of pounding boots.

I looked around the room at the wall-to-wall cuts, feeling slightly overwhelmed by all the love being thrown my way. For years, I'd mostly kept myself to myself. I had my crew of boys, and of course, I'd been working with Atlas for the past six months, so I'd developed other somewhat fragile connections. But it was mainly all surface because, underneath the mask, I'd disassociated. I became numb, so being around real people with real feelings and emotions was frustrating. It seemed preferable to keep my distance.

Because of that, I hadn't expected a welcome party. This was surprising, to say the least.

Dad rested a hand on my shoulder. "The boys wanted to be here, Kit. It's about time you understood that you're part of a family, you always have been, and that ain't gonna change."

I cleared my throat to eradicate the lump that had formed. "Thanks, guys," I croaked. "Didn't expect it, probably don't deserve it, but thanks."

The crowd parted to allow Abe to step through. It was crazy how everything seemed so much brighter now. The world around me had been muted for so many years. The only way I could describe it was that my brain had dials like a TV, and the contrast had been turned down.

But not anymore.

Abe's fingers curled around my nape. My throat tightened as I saw tears spring into his eyes. "Jesus, Kit. You're back," he rasped. "You're you again."

I looked up at him and smiled. "Hey." Raising a hand, I rested it on his shoulder, my heart squeezing with love and appreciation for the man who'd stuck by me when everyone else had given up. "There's so much I need to thank you for, Abe. But I dunno if I've got the words in me."

He dug the heel of a palm into his eye and laughed. "You don't have to thank me for a fuckin' thing, boy. Seein' you like this is all I wanted."

I looked around. "Where's Iris?"

"She'll be here. All the women wanna see ya. We told 'em to stay away while we had Church, but they'll pop up anytime now."

He must have seen the question in my eyes because he nodded thoughtfully. "Kennedy's a good girl, Kit. Gotta say you picked a spitfire there. She's been sending the boys all in a tizzy while givin' 'em so much shit they don't know their asses from their elbows. She's a looker, alright."

"She is, Abe," I agreed. "But she's also more than just tits and ass. She's got the same qualities as Ris and my ma."

"Yeah." He squeezed my nape. "She'd have to be special to keep you interested."

Footsteps sounded from the corridor. "Alright, motherfuckers. You can all blow smoke up Breaker's ass at the barbeque tomorrow. We need him in Church." His eyes fell on me and softened. "Where's ya cut ya fuckface? You know the club rules." His eyes slid down my body, and he grimaced. "Fuckin' grey sweatpants? You're just like Bowie, waving ya dick in my face." He bent down, eyes narrowing as he examined my crotch. "I can see the fuckin' outline. Are you even wearin' shorts?"

Hoots of laughter rang through the bar.

"I just walked in the place, asshole," I said defensively. "Haven't had time to change."

"Well, it's too late now," he snapped. "We're runnin' late as it is." He looked up at the crowd of men watching us with interest. "As you fuckin' were, ya nosy bunch of bitches."

The crowd began to thin out, the men goin' back to their games of pool or makin' their way toward the bar to grab one of the beer bottles readily lined up.

The SAA turned for the hallway he'd previously come from. "Chop, chop, motherfuckers. We ain't got all day."

I stepped behind the men, wondering why they wanted me in Church.

The room had been off-limits to me ever since I patched in. It was reserved for officers only. Members could enter, but only under Dad's strict orders. Colt had changed the locks out for fingerprint recognition years ago, so nobody could get in there unless they were authorized.

The room was the last one at the end of the corridor, opposite Dad's office.

Atlas approached, held his thumb up to a pad on the wall, and waited for the locks to disengage. After a loud beep, the SAA held it open and gestured for us to go through.

Bowie was already in there, waiting. When he saw me enter, he stood and walked around the table to greet me. "Ain't you a sight for sore eyes," he said, clapping me on the back. "I never thought I'd hear myself say this, but I've missed seein' your miserable face. Ya feelin' okay?"

Out of all my family members, Bowie was probably the one I was closest to. Last Summer, when he got shot, I was the one who was at the hospital every day, helping him. Dad had a club to run, Abe had to help him, and Cash was still in jail at the time.

Bowie was in a bad way, and even though he made a full recovery, initially, he needed help to do things as simple as taking a piss. Unfortunately, that was where I came in.

I must say, I've had better jobs.

"I'm good, bro," I assured him. "Though it's like I've been away two months, and now I've entered the twilight zone." I looked around at the faces watching me with interest. "Can somebody please tell me what the fuck I'm doin' in Church?"

Dad sat in his seat and instinctively touched the gavel, eyes still on me. "Take your seats," he ordered.

Eyebrows drawn together with confusion, I watched as the men sat in their allotted positions. Pop in the middle of the long table, dented with years of being pummeled. Abe took his seat at one end. Bowie sat on the other side, next to Cash, who plonked his ass in Hendrix's seat to Dad's right. There were two vacant seats: Cash's Treasurer chair and Iceman's.

Dad placed his elbows on the table and leaned forward. "There's been some changes happenin' in the last few weeks, Son," he began. "Hendrix's dad's been sick, so he's been back and forth to Virginia to help. We've been talkin', and now, we think it's time."

"Time for what," I asked after a few seconds of hesitation. "Why are you all talking in riddles?"

"The officers already know, but the men don't. In the next few days, I'll announce that the Speed Demons are expanding," Dad informed me. "Hendrix has asked my permission to open a new chapter in Virginia. His pop's getting older now, so he wants to be closer to home."

My head reared back.

A new chapter? This shit didn't happen overnight. Opening a new chapter of the Speed Demons was a huge deal. Men had wanted to before but never gotten permission. Bandit was a control freak, and Dad took after him.

"How long has this been in the pipeline?" I asked. "Veep couldn't have woken up one day and decided to open a new chapter."

Dad lifted a hand to stroke his beard. "When he took the VP role initially, I made it clear the presidency would one day go to Cash. Hendrix is a born leader. I knew he wouldn't accept VP unless there was a way for him to be Prez one day, so I agreed that he could open a new club somewhere else when the time was right."

"Why didn't you just give Cash VP at the time?" I asked, confusion lacing my tone.

Dad's eyes narrowed. "He was too young, and I didn't think he was ready. I was right, too; the stupid little shit got himself locked up six months later."

Cash rolled his eyes.

Atlas's lips twitched.

"And what's Ice got to do with anythin'?" I asked, ignoring the amused faces of the men. "Is he startin' another chapter, too?"

Dad winced. "Lord. No. That fucker's trouble. He wanted a change of scene and a new role, so Drix asked him to go to Virginia as his enforcer. It makes sense. They're good buds, and Drix will need his help with recruitment and settin' up the new place."

Dad was right; it did make sense. Besides the two men being close, Ice boxed for the Air Force when he flew jets back in the day. It was clear he'd been restless for a while 'cause lately, he'd caused a lot of trouble. He went after Sophie, knowing full well that Atlas was into her, though I reckoned he liked her more than he admitted.

"So what's this got to do with me bein' in Church?" I asked Pop. "Want me to step in until you run a new ballot?"

"Already ran a new ballot, Break," Atlas interjected. "Last week, in fact. Eighty-seven percent of the vote for the new Road Captain went to you."

My heart stopped.

What the fuck?

Me?

"Last week, I was still in the VA clinic," I argued. "How could so much have happened in eight goddamned weeks? Things change, and life goes on; I get that more than anyone, but why would the members vote for someone who's fucked in the head?"

Atlas went to argue, but I cut him off.

"How? Why?" I demanded. "Half' a those men don't even like me, so how the fuck am I suddenly in a position where they have to respect me?"

"I think you're wrong there, Son," Dad said, regarding me thoughtfully. "It's true you only socialize with a select few and don't know the other men very well, but you are well respected. When word got around that you totaled the Sinners' clubhouse last Winter, half of them looked at you with stars in their eyes. Durin' the trainin', you were out in the snow helping 'em with their aim. You were great with Sophie when the others gave her shit 'cause of this prick." He nodded to Atlas. "Then you kicked the living snot out of mouth almighty here." He pointed to Cash. "He's such a bastard that half of them wanted to shake your hand, and the other half wanted you to be godfather to their newborns."

Abe barked out a laugh.

Bowie and Atlas chuckled.

Cash glowered.

I understood what Dad was getting at. Cash was an asshole to everyone. The members would've been all over him getting a bloody nose. But the majority votes came from the officers, so I was more than a little shocked that I got through.

My eyes settled on Dad. "Last time, you nixed me 'cause I wasn't ready. I was in hospital when the ballot got called, so what makes me ready now? What's changed?"

Dad slowly rose from his chair and leaned forward across the table. "*You've* changed. *You've* taken responsibility, gone away, and got yourself sorted out. Why the fuck wouldn't I vote for you to be our new Road Captain? I told you things were gonna change around here. Plus, you know I like to keep it in the family."

Cash's face swiveled to face Dad. "You know what that phrase relates to, right?" he asked incredulously.

"What?" Dad demanded.

"You know," Cash said, nodding toward Dad's crotch. "*Keeping it in the family.*"

Chuckles rose through the air.

Dad looked at my brother as if he was crazy. "What the fuck are you gabbin' about now, boy? Have you been watching that Sister Wives show again? I knew that shit would melt your brain one day."

Cash smirked. "Cara watches it. I don't have a choice."

Dad's nose scrunched up like my brother gave off a bed smell. "You dirty bastard. I wonder about you sometimes. Of course, I didn't mean that, ya stupid fucker."

Bowie tipped his head to the side, lookin' at Atlas. "Did you see VPR yet?"

"Yip!" Atlas jerked one nod. "It's TV goddamned gold. That forty-year-old fucknut runnin' around behind his ol' lady's back with one of her crew. Even I was ready to punch his fuckin' lights out."

Bowie chuckled. "Did you see that crazy English dude givin' him shit at the reunion?" he asked with a shake of his head. "'You're a worm with a mustache!'" he crowed in a ridiculous British accent that sounded more Aussie to my ears.

Atlas barked out a laugh. "He's a fucked-up motherfucker, but I nearly pissed myself laughin' when he called the worm with a mustache and his Bambi-eyed bitch goddamned poo-poo heads."

Bowie began to chuckle. "He's a crazy little skinny dude, but I like him."

Dad's eyes slashed between Bowie and Atlas. "What the fuck are you two talkin' about now? Who's a worm with a mustache?"

"Vanderpump Rules," Bowie confirmed. "You know, the whole 'Scandoval' thing." He made speech marks with his fingers.

Dad's head reared back, his stare locking with Abe's as his eyes bugged out. "Did I ride through a fuckin' wormhole on the way back from Grand Junction and end up in an alternate universe where my middle son's turned into a bitch?"

Abe raised a hand to cover his laugh.

And as for you!" Dad said, turning to Atlas. "You better go ask Stitch if you can borrow a tampon. You'll be on the rag before we know it." He shook his head, eyes shocked as he turned back to Abe. "I'm in a livin' fuckin' nightmare."

My lips twitched as I watched the guys continue to banter. I'd always assumed Church meets were serious, but this was a goddamned comedy show.

"Don't care what anyone says." The SAA sniffed haughtily. "I've put that stuck-up English bitch on my 'shouldn't but would' list. She's as old as the pyramids, but God help me, I'd Vander*pump* her into a coma. Bet she'd like a bit of ol' Atlas's big dick, seein' as her husband's an Ozzy Osborne clone. Poor old fucker would probably need a crane to lift it." He circled his hips in a slow fuckin' motion, causing a chuckle to rise through my throat.

Bowie and Abe laughed with me as a buzz sounded from the door.

I turned to see Colt entering, face in his iPad as usual. "Yo!"

"Why are you meant to be the smartest of all of us, but you can't tell the goddamned time?" Dad snapped. "You're always fuckin' late!"

Colt checked his watch and winced. "Sorry, Prez, I was on a roll. I found the black sedan."

Dad glanced at Cash before shifting his stare to me and nodding to one of the empty chairs. "Take your seat, Kit. We got somethin' to tell ya, and you ain't gonna like it."

A jolt of panic hit my gut. "What?"

Dad nodded to the empty seat again. "Please, Son."

My mind started to go crazy with scenarios. If something so bad happened that Dad wanted me in on a Church meeting, why didn't he tell me when he called me last night?

Pop must have read my mind because he rasped. "I didn't wanna tell you while you were stuck in Grand Junction simply 'cause there was nothin' you could've done. I didn't want you goin' outta your mind when we've already got it under control."

"Got *what* under control?" I demanded, sitting my ass down, still glaring at Dad.

He nodded to Cash. "Tell him."

"Yesterday, Layla, Sophie, and Kennedy took Sunny and Kady to the salon in town," my brother explained. "On the way out, they noticed a car parked up, and Kennedy got the heebie-jeebies." He leaned forward, arms to the table, to look me in the eye. "They noticed a flash comin' from inside the car. Like someone was takin' photographs. Whoever it was saw they'd been made and took off."

My eyebrows knitted together as a dark feeling crept through my gut. Closing my eyes, I tried to beat down the thread of panic rising through my chest. I moved my face from side to side, allowing myself to feel it without letting it control me.

"What the fuck's he doin'?" Bowie muttered.

"Shut the fuck up," Cash snapped. "Leave him to process it his own way."

After a few beats, I lowered my face and stared at Colt. "You say you know who the cage belongs to?"

He nodded, his lip curling slightly. "It's a company car owned by the Mayor but used by Brett Stafford. We think he was takin' photos of the girls to pass on to the Sinners."

The meaning behind Colt's words made my hands itch with the need to kill.

"Funny how that little prick keeps poppin' up whenever there's trouble," Bowie stated, his face like thunder. "Maybe we should grab him and have a little chat?"

Cash dipped his head. "Agreed. We should hunt the fucker and take him down the Cell for questionin'. I could make the scrawny little rat squeal within five minutes.

"Do you think he's involved with the Sinner's trafficking business?" I asked. "And why's he driving a car that belongs to Mayor Henderson?"

"We think he's involved," Dad confirmed. "Stafford was best buds with Henderson Junior, who we know was set on selling Layla. He was also buds with the rapist piece of shit back when he drugged those girls. Stafford covered for Robbie when the fucker got to Layla years ago, tellin' her a load'a bull about who she was with that night 'cause she'd been drugged so badly she couldn't remember a thing. He's been working for the mayor since he came back to town, but we think it's a front for what he's really involved in. The fucker's probably using Henderson Senior as a foil to cover his ass." He looked between Bowie and me. "It's your women, your girls, your call."

I pondered Dad's statement, weighing up the best way forward.

Every paternal instinct I had screamed at me to nab him. The thought of anyone hurting my Kady made my blood boil. My little girl was already at the center of my universe, along with her brother and mom. The thought of some sick bastard tryin' to take my Kadence from me brought out protective instincts I didn't even know I possessed.

The problem I faced was that I could kill Stafford in my sleep, but it wouldn't take the mark off Kady and Sunshine. Once the Sinners had them in their sights, we were fucked.

As satisfying as watching the life drain from his eyes would be, we'd achieve more by using him to our advantage. Sooner or later, he'd lead us to the sick fucks who pulled the strings. Bear and his crew were the ones we needed to take out.

"I say we put a tail on him," I suggested. "He's Harry Stafford's son. If he goes missin', the cops will get involved. Instead, we could use him to lead us to the perverts at the top of the food chain. Questionin' him would be pointless 'cause he won't be clued into the important stuff." I shifted my gaze to Atlas. "If he was taking pictures of the girls, he may be scouting. Sunny and Kady would fetch stupid money on the black market, so they gotta be covered. We also need protection for Kennedy and Layla."

"Already on it," Atlas told me. "They've got armed guards with instructions to shoot first; ask questions later."

It was good to know Atlas was taking it seriously, but it didn't stop dark images from flashing through my mind. Breathing through my scalding chest, I cleared my throat, trying to keep my mind on business.

Losing my shit wouldn't help my family.

I fixed my gaze back onto Dad. "Do we know where Bear's holed up yet?"

"No," Dad rumbled. "We've pinpointed his second in command. His ma died a few months back, and she left him her house. We've been watchin' his movements, but he hasn't led us to Bear yet."

I turned to Bowie. His face was set in a snarl, and his fingers into fists. "You've been quiet during all this, bro. What do you think?"

His expression morphed into a snarl. "Me and you are gonna pay a little visit to Bear's VP's place. I'll keep watch while you bring out your hidden soldier boy and rifle through his shit. If it's proven that they've got their sights on my baby girl, I'll hunt every Sinner down and put a bullet in their heads." His eyes narrowed. "But you're right. Let's make sure we pinpoint everyone involved first. You up for some brother bondin' time, Breaker?"

I knew what he wanted me to do, and I was all in.

My lips twisted as I shot Bowie a determined look. "Yeah, bro. Let's do it."

Chapter Thirteen

Kennedy

I'd hardly slept a wink all night. Even when I did manage to drop off, my dreams were plagued with shadowy figures trying to claw at my kids while I looked on helplessly.

The incident outside the salon affected me on a cellular level. It was all I could think about. Of course, the more I tortured myself, the jumpier I became. Luckily, it hadn't affected Kady; she was fine as soon as she'd calmed down.

Kai wouldn't let her out of his sight, which, for once, I was grateful for. He'd locked all the windows and dragged his comforter into her room to sleep at the foot of her bed. I knew this because I woke up every hour, crept in, and checked on them.

Today was the welcome home barbeque for Snow.

I wanted to cry off, but the kids needed to spend time with him, and I hoped I could snooze in the sun if he was there to keep an eye on them. Maybe I shouldn't have expected him to take over parental duties so soon, but he'd gotten away with it for eight years, so it was tough.

I got up early to take a shower. After I'd dried off, I slipped on a red silky sleep short PJ set and wandered into the kitchen, still towel drying my hair. Walking through the door, I caught a dark shadow from the corner of my eyes. "Fuck!" I screeched, almost jumping ten feet in the air.

Holding a hand to my thumping heart, I stared into the golden eyes of the father of my children and blew out a relieved huff.

No man had a right to be so beautiful so early in the day. Snow's curly dark hair was perfectly messy, and his skin was tanned from spending time outside. Black jeans matched his tee, the tight arms showcasing large biceps, flexing as he folded his arms across his hard chest.

"Morning, baby." He smirked, eyes flicking down to my boobs and then to my bare legs.

I rubbed at my racing heart, wondering why it suddenly thudded so hard. "You moron!" I whispered so as not to wake the kids. "You almost gave me a fucking conniption. Jesus. My heart's beating out of my chest." I sent him a glower. "You idiot!"

He lifted a sexy eyebrow. "Did you think I was the boogeyman?"

Incensed, I stomped over and slapped his chest. "Did nobody tell you what happened the other day? Jesus, Snow. I've hardly slept a wink for worrying. You scared me half to death."

His face fell. "Fuck! I'm sorry, Kitten. I didn't think. I took over from Arrow early this morning. Atlas gave me a spare key 'cause I didn't wanna disturb you. I thought I could drive you all to the shindig later. I've been looking forward to seeing you and the kids."

"I thought you wanted to wait for the barbeque?" I reminded him.

He shot me a sheepish smile. "Easier said than done, baby. Couldn't wait another second."

"You should've let me know," I berated.

"I messaged you three times," he informed me.

"So take the hint, Snow. Do not disturb!" I took in his beautiful, handsome face and flattened my lips. "You look well," I told him begrudgingly. "How do you feel?"

His lips twitched. "I'm good now." His voice was low with innuendo as his eyes flicked down my body again. "But I'm more worried about you and Kadence. Tell me what happened."

I went over to the coffee pot. "It was weird," I replied, setting a big pot of java up. "One minute, everything was fine. The next, it turned crazy."

He followed me, sitting at the table as I explained what had happened the day before. I kept my tone emotionless, sticking to the facts. I'd just gotten to the part when I ran into the road to stop the car when I felt a chill in the air. My stomach constricted as I craned my neck to see Snow's eyes harden.

"You did what?" His voice was deceptively low.

I sighed. "Yeah. I know it was stupid, but I—"

"Stupid?" he roared, rising to his feet, palms to the table. "What the fuck were you thinkin', woman?"

My heart jolted, eyes widening as I took in the horrified expression on his face.

"He could've run straight into you," he rasped, stomping toward me. "Jesus fuck, Kennedy, he could've fucking killed you right there in the street." He grabbed my arms. "If you *ever* risk yourself like that again, I'll tan your ass."

I stared up at him open-mouthed.

I'd never seen this side of Snow before.

The man who spent a week with me in Vegas was protective but not overtly. However, this reaction was over the top. A tiny part of me understood why. Still, I'd managed like a fucking trouper for years without alpha Kit Stone thinking he could talk to me like a five-year-old.

"Step back," I ordered, voice taut.

His beautiful golden eyes narrowed. "Don't get snippy, Kennedy. Promise me you'll run for the nearest cover and call me for help if anything like that happens again."

"I said, step the fuck back," I barked.

He did as I demanded, but only by an inch.

I pulled my arms free from his hold and popped a hip. "You!" I screeched, poking his chest. "Can fuck right off." I jammed my hands to my waist and leaned forward, getting in Snow's face. "Shame you weren't so protective nine years ago, asshole. You walked out on me without a second thought." I poked his chest again. "I've raised two amazing kids without incident, so I suggest you stop acting like a fucking Neanderthal and cut out your ridiculous alpha bullshit."

His hard stare softened as he gazed into my eyes. "I love you. Kennedy." He said, tone low.

"Oh, please," I rolled my eyes. "This already?"

"Please, hear me out, baby. If anything happened to you..." Snow's voice trailed off, and he raised a hand, curling it around my nape and stroking the back of my neck. "I was broken without you for years, even knowing you were out there somewhere. If you got hurt, I'd never recover, baby. I'd burn the world down for you."

My heart bloomed at his sentiment, but I straightened my spine, steeling myself against him.

He couldn't just waltz in here saying all the right things and expect me to fall on my back with my legs in the air. He left me, then he fucked his way through Hambleton like I didn't exist. His words didn't match his actions.

"Stop that shit," I told him. "Do *not* think for one minute that those bedroom eyes can get you back in my good books. Keep those thoughts to yourself. You're here to see the kids, not me. I'm not gonna fall for your smooth talk."

His lips hitched. "You think I've got bedroom eyes?"

"Ugh!" I exclaimed, my heart suddenly thudding in my chest. "You're incorrigible. Step back, Snow."

"Yeah," a voice said from over Snow's shoulder. "She said, step back, asshole."

Kit's body locked, his eyes closing as he muttered, "Fuck."

"Yay!" I exclaimed, relieved that I'd been saved from having to beat Snow off with a Keurig. "Kids are up." I shoved Snow's bulky body to one side, looking around at Kai and Kady. "Morning, babies. Look who's come to see you. It's Daddy Dearest."

A weird squeak escaped Snow's throat.

Kai's eyes narrowed as he took in the scene. "You okay?" he asked. "He givin' you shit?"

"Course I'm okay," I assured him, a little too brightly. "Breakfast?"

My son let out a huff.

Kady stood all cute and sleepy, thumb in mouth, wearing her Taylor Swift nightie. The minute Snow had whirled around to face them, her eyes went so big they almost took up half her face. "Hey!" she greeted, peering at him closely.

He cocked his head and stared, and his body locked again. I could've sworn his eyes filled with moisture, but he blinked it away. "Fuck me," he breathed. "She's fuckin' spectacular."

My heart melted at the look of adoration in Snow's gaze. "She is," I agreed softly.

Kai folded his arms across his little chest, skewering Snow with a look as Kady blushed prettily, coyly swinging from side to side.

The room fell silent as Snow took in the sight of his lovely daughter. Then his shoulders tensed, chest contracting as he heaved in a hard breath. "Jesus Christ. You can never date." His head swiveled to me, his stare hardening with shock. "You hear me. Kenny? She can never date."

I rolled my eyes. "She's going to date, Snow. We'll have boys breaking the door down to get to her."

A groan escaped him, and he rubbed at his chest as his golden eyes slid toward our son. Snow shook his head disbelievingly as his stare swept over our boy's face, identical to his. "Your gramps told me you're a biker in the makin', Kai. A natural."

My boy narrowed his eyes, his way of resisting his father's considerable charm.

"I know you're angry with me, Son," Snow explained. "I'm angry with me, too. But I'm here now, and I'm gonna look after you and your mom."

"I don't know you," Kai sneered. "Your promises don't mean shit."

I opened my mouth to tell him to mind his language, but Snow beat me.

"I get you feel a certain way, Son, and I don't blame you for bein' hostile. I can handle hostility, but don't use language like that anymore in front of your sister. Get me?"

"You did," Kai muttered accusingly. "Hypocrite."

Snow nodded. "Right. So I'll try to curb my language around the women, and you do the same. Deal?"

Kai glowered at his father, but to give Snow his due, he didn't back down. His cool stare remained on Kai like they were battling for alpha male supremacy.

Kady staggered to the table, still half asleep, and slipped onto a chair. "What's for breakfast?" she asked, utterly oblivious to the stare-off between the alpha idiots.

I tapped my lips. "How about we celebrate finally meeting your 'not so dead after all' father and have ice cream?"

Kai's eyes snapped to me, effectively breaking the stare off. "Really?" he breathed, suddenly perky. "Ice cream?"

"Nope." I chuckled. "You've got bran flakes."

He groaned. "I hate bran."

I maneuvered around Snow, walked the few steps to my boy, and grabbed him, smothering his handsome little face in wet mom kisses. "You love bran." I teased, lightly swatting his tush. "It keeps you regular."

"Ugh," he groaned again. "You're so embarrassing. I'm going to shower." He whipped around to head toward the hallway, but before he sauntered out, he muttered, "I'll be back in ten for my bran. Don't make it yet. The flakes will go soggy."

Snow watched Kai's retreat open-mouthed, eyes glued to the spot our boy had just vacated. "Is he always like that?" he asked.

Kady folded her arms onto the table, resting her head on them. "That's a good mood. You should see him when he's really grouchy."

"That's a good mood?" He scraped a hand down his face. "Jesus."

Kady turned her head toward Snow, regarding him thoughtfully. "Your head's not stormy anymore. Mommy said you saw a doctor. You're better now?"

He looked at me inquisitively before turning back to Kady. "Yeah. I saw a doctor, and I feel good." He paused, looking thoughtfully at his daughter. "You could see inside my head, pretty girl?"

"No, I could feel it," she explained in a matter-of-fact tone. "Do you like Taylor Swift?"

I covered my smile with my hand, watching Snow's eyes bug out, suddenly looking lost and a little nervous.

I knew right then that the kids would run rings around him. He did the right thing, putting his foot down with Kai straight off the bat. Even if he didn't show it, my son was the type of boy to respect the way Snow told him to watch his language but assured him he'd do the same. It was a good idea that put them on a similar level and stopped Snow from coming across as preachy. He'd built a tiny rapport with his son and didn't even know it.

I was sure Kady would be all over him by the end of the day. She was probably feeling him out so she could report back to Kai. In fact, he probably put her up to it. Her brother knew she could get the measure of a person, and he was using that to his advantage.

They were effectively tag-teaming Snow, and it was hilarious. Their father had to pay his dues as far as they were concerned. Certainly, in Kai's mind, he had to earn his place, and this morning's antics were just the start.

My mood was dark by the time we drove to the clubhouse.

Snow had spent the morning mowing the lawns and doing odd jobs around the rental. He was probably trying to get into my good books, but I didn't mind, seeing as he took his shirt off. When he walked up and down with the lawnmower, the view from the kitchen window was impressive.

He'd always been built. When I first met him, he was sinewy with tight muscles like a runner. Later, he bulked up, but now he was bigger still. My gaze fell onto his tanned skin, gleaming under the sunlight, watching the way his muscles flexed as he worked. I couldn't help admiring the physical attributes he'd grown into. Although I hated to admit it, he was even more beautiful than before.

During the morning, he'd come into the kitchen to get a drink, and my eyes flicked over the tattoos he'd gotten while we'd been apart. Without thinking, I'd asked him about them.

He'd pointed to the bull's head on his pec and the tiny writing around it. "I had this one done when I left the military. It says, 'When the sun rises, I wake up and chase my dreams. I won't regret when the sun sets because I live my life like a beast.' It's a quote from a Rob Bailey song. Originally, I envisaged the beast as the one I felt lived inside me. But after the Vet clinic, I changed my perception. Now, I imagine it as a motivational tool. I envision myself as the beast who conquers his demons. I fashioned the beast's head into a bull because my Zodiac sign's Taurus." He pointed to the words on his forearm. "I got this the night before I went to Grand Junction. It's a Lance Armstrong quote that I'd read in a magazine earlier the same day. It seemed like a sign. It says, 'Pain is temporary. It may last a minute, or an hour, or a day, or a year, but eventually, it will subside, and something else will take its place. If I quit, however, it lasts forever." His eyes softened as they took me in. "That's about getting myself right again, of course, but it's also about never quittin' you, baby. I've lived in pain without you for so long, and now you're all with me; it's true. The pain's been replaced with something else."

Our gazes locked. The love shining in his eyes made my throat thicken with tears. "Stop saying things like that. I don't want you to have false hope. We're not together."

He'd smiled at me. "It doesn't matter if we're together or not. I'll never quit trying." He'd turned and walked back into the yard without a backward glance, leaving me a gooey mess in the kitchen.

He'd always been able to make me feel like the only girl in the room. Even that first night when we bared our souls in the diner. He'd looked at me with such intensity that nobody else existed. My heart ached, though, because other women *had* existed for him, and from what I could gather from the chatter I'd overheard from the club girls, there'd been a lot.

Thoughts of him with other women had driven me crazy ever since Cash had implied it when he came to my Vegas house with Atlas. I couldn't get them out of my head.

My blood turned to acid when I thought about all the women he'd had after me. I was never jealous before, but somehow, imagining Snow with his harem burned me from the inside out. I knew promiscuity was often a PTSD symptom. Many men found sex a way to find relief, albeit fleetingly. Still, my mind kept throwing up images of him with faceless women, and it ate away at my sanity.

When we spoke at the Vet Center, and he told me why he'd left me, I got it. I could forgive him for that because he thought he was doing the right thing.

But there was still a gaping lie between us, along with a harem of women. It was clear he hadn't even thought about waiting for me.

I'd slept with other men, but I thought he was dead. Snow knew I was alive somewhere in the world, but instead of putting all his energy into finding me, he spent it fucking around.

His actions didn't match his words, and the more he implied he'd always loved me, the more my mood darkened. By the time we pulled up to the clubhouse gates, I was hardly speaking to him.

"You okay?" he asked me carefully from the driver's seat as we drove into the parking lot.

I ignored the urge to slap his face. "I'm tired. I didn't sleep well last night."

He snaked his hand across the back of my seat, looking in the rear window as he reversed the SUV into a parking space. A fresh scent of sandalwood wafted under my nose, throwing me for a loop. I closed my eyes, steeling my heart against him.

The rear doors opened, and the kids jumped out of the car.

"See you out back," Kai muttered excitedly before the doors slammed, leaving us in silence so awkward it was jarring.

Breaker

Snow broke the deadlock first. "I'll see to the kids today, Kitten. You relax and have a drink. I'm off the booze, so I'll be your designated driver. I'm guarding you tonight anyway."

Something dark unfurled in my chest.

I didn't know if it was frustration at the memories coming to the surface or disgust at myself for responding to him after everything I felt inside, but I needed to put him in his place.

Turning to Snow, I poked his chest. "Don't do me any favors, asshole. I've been a parent for eight years. I've had more sleepless nights than you've had easy women. I can look after my own kids, thank you." My lip curled as my mouth went into overdrive. "You sit there talking like you're the father of the year, but you don't know shit. You waltz into our lives after missing the hard part of parenting and talk like you're perfect. I see through it, Snow. I see through you." I went to click my seatbelt off so I could escape, but his hand covered mine, stopping me.

"What do you know about the women?" he demanded. "Whose been fillin' your head with shit they know nothing about?"

"You don't need to be James fucking Bond to pick up snippets of conversation, Snow. I know you've been with countless women. You say you love me, but you were more interested in dicking around than finding me."

"So that's why you're being bitchy." His eyes glowed as strong fingers curled around mine. "Why are you so concerned about me? I doubt you've been celibate for the last nine years, Kitten. There's no way you've deprived yourself."

I snorted quietly. "You know nothing, Jon Snow."

He shifted his entire body to face me. "So, you never fucked anyone after me?" His voice got louder. "Did you build a shrine to me and worship at it every night?" He huffed out a humorless laugh. "Bullshit."

I glared into his stern eyes, almost gratified at the jealousy in his tone. My jaw clenched, and I suddenly yearned to hurt Snow the same way he'd hurt me. The need to bring him down a peg or two overtook my senses.

I shot him a smirk. "I wasn't celibate, Snow. Not in the least. I had boyfriends. I was even close to accepting a proposal a couple of years ago. Just think, I could've been married to someone else now."

His grip on my hand tightened almost painfully. "Don't, Kennedy," he grated out. "Or I'll fuckin' show ya who you belong to."

"Like how you belonged to me?" I retorted. "The man whore of Hambleton. I'm so fucking proud my kids' dad's got a reputation of being community dick."

His nostrils flared. "It wasn't like that."

"Course it wasn't." I let out a brittle laugh. "Don't you dare tell me you buried yourself in women every night while imagining it was me because I'll slap your fucking face."

"I never thought of you once," he muttered.

"Standard, asshole behavior," I banded back. "You're stating the obvious."

He tipped his head back exasperatedly. "Drop it, Kennedy."

"Like you dropped your pants?" I sneered. "And your fucking standards. Tell me, Snow. What was it that turned you into a walking STD? Or was fucking women until your dick was raw the only way you could sleep?" I *tskd*. "How cliché of you."

The atmosphere turned thunderous.

Snow's breath sawed in and out like he was trying to keep his shit contained, but I kept pushing. There were so many conflicting narratives; all I wanted was the truth.

I glowered, eyes narrowing as my lip curled into a sneer. "You say leaving me broke you, but you soon replaced me with a hundred others."

Breaker

Snow's eyes darkened. His jaw clenched so tight I saw a muscle tick. He moved me around to face him, and then, leaning forward, he bellowed words that made my heart explode.

"*I choked them out, Kennedy!*"

My eyes rounded as he pulled his tee away from his neck like it strangled him before he continued.

"The only way I could function was to wrap my hands around women's throats and half fuckin' kill 'em. It wasn't sex I was addicted to; it was violence. I hurt women who liked that shit 'cause it took the edge off. I half choked them to stop myself walkin' the streets and punching innocent people out." His tone became agitated. "What I did to you the last time we were together, well, it got worse. A demon lived inside me, and I only found peace when I let it out."

A cold tremor went through my body as a memory flashed through my mind.

Snow completely zoned out the night he hurt me. He was there physically, but his mind disappeared into another world. When he realized what he'd done the following day, he wept and felt so ashamed he could hardly look me in the eye.

Snow hung his head. "I was fucked-up, baby. The only way I could feel normal was to do the most abnormal shit you could imagine. It was never about intimacy or feelin' close. It wasn't even about the relief of emptying my balls. I got off on the violence, not the act of sex." He slumped back in his seat, staring unseeingly out of the windshield. "I never thought of you once because I didn't want you to be part of it. The memory of you was the only clean, decent thing I had left. It was never about love because whether you believe it or not, that always belonged to you. Could I have looked harder for you? Maybe. But what bullshit would I have brought you, Kai, and Kady, into? It got so bad that I once went into a trance and almost killed some bitch. I had to breathe life back into her, Kennedy. Do you think I'd ever want you to suffer that shit?"

I waited for my mind to catch up with Snow's explanation. "Did you tell your therapist at Grand Junction all this?" I asked gently. "What did she say?"

"She said it's common. The military trained me to shut my emotions down until the only time I felt anything was in combat or on missions. When I killed, I got a high that eventually became addictive. The only time I felt anything was when I was violent, so over time, my brain retrained itself to need it in order to feel. I don't know the psychology behind it, but my shrink told me that sex became an outlet." He turned his head to look me dead in the eyes. "You want me to tell you about what I was doin' in the EOD? I warn ya, baby. It's not noble or heroic."

"Tell me," I said almost pleadingly. "Make me understand."

His eyes glazed over as he began to think back. "I'd been put on a task force. Instead of diffusing bombs, we made them to take out the enemy. We played the Taliban at their own game, Kitty. The unit built bombs and took them into caves, houses, and villages. We were often stuck inside tight spaces and populated areas. We couldn't draw attention to ourselves, so my weapon of choice became my knife. I slit more throats than I care to remember, Kitty. Nina reckons it's the reason I was so fixated on women's necks and throats. Can you believe that shit? How fucked-up is that?"

Again, I remembered the marks he'd left on me that night. He'd hurt me all over, but the bites and bruises were more concentrated around the area of my throat.

"You never said a word. When did you join this *task force*?" I demanded.

He bowed his head again. "When I got back from our week in Vegas."

I closed my eyes, fighting against the tide of sorrow sweeping through my body.

Breaker

I remembered everything about our week together.

Snow had trouble sleeping. I assumed it was because he'd not long returned from deployment. But in the weeks after he left, his personality changed drastically. He became unreasonable and accusatory, turning aggressive over the slightest thing.

Even though my head swam with all this new information, I felt relieved that I finally knew why he'd changed so much.

Jesus, shit like that would blacken anyone's soul.

"I had every intention of owning up about the lie, Kitten," he admitted. "I was gonna tell you that week, but it went so fast, and I didn't wanna ruin it for us. The thought of returning to Fort Campbell and leaving you upset and alone almost killed me. I didn't wanna tell you over the phone, but by the time I got back to you, I didn't even think about it. I was so far down the rabbit hole by then that it never occurred to me." He banged his head back gently on the headrest of his seat. "Then I hurt you, and I knew I had to leave if you were gonna have any chance of realizing your dreams. I remember sitting on the bed with you in my arms, knowing what I had to do, and it broke me, baby. When I left, I threw myself into the missions just because shutting it down stopped me from missin' you so goddamned much. Then I saw Benny and Simmons and our captain die, and that was it. I didn't wanna feel shit after that."

"You saw it?" I breathed, my heart breaking for him.

He nodded sadly. "I was behind them in another Humvee when theirs exploded. We were under heavy fire. After the explosion, a bird flew in to help us, but we crashed. I took a blow to the head and was put into an induced coma for weeks while they waited for the swelling in my brain to go down. My lieutenant lost a leg. We couldn't even go to their funerals because our recoveries took so long." He hung his head again, rubbing at his temples.

Snow and Lee—or, should I say, Benny—were so close. I saw it on the night I met him. They had a friendship where they knew what each other was thinking. In the diner, I remembered their silent conversations. Later, when Snow initially rejected me, Benny knew him well enough to find me at Crimson Velvet and get me to the airport to say goodbye without Snow knowing a thing about it.

For me, the equivalent would have been Sophie dying, and the mere thought of losing her, especially in such a violent way, made me want to curl up in a ball and sob. I ached inside because he'd been through much worse.

It went a long way in helping me see him in a different light.

Snow had overcome so much, suffered for years, and still found the strength to check himself into a place hundreds of miles away from home and get help for his issues. I knew he was a tortured soul—even back then—but I still had no idea how deep it went.

How did he get out of bed every morning?

The jury was still out on whether Kit deserved my love, but I didn't doubt he deserved my respect and support.

Something tickled my pinky.

I glanced down to see Snow's little finger touching mine.

"So now you know," he said pointedly. "The question is, what happens next?"

My heart drummed against my ribs, his question whirling around my brain.

It would be easy to fall back in his arms and tell him everything would be okay. But the fact remained, I wasn't the same forgiving, open-hearted girl I used to be. I'd loved him since I was nineteen, but it didn't mean he got instant forgiveness.

Breaker

After what he'd told me, I knew there were grey areas, where initially, I only saw black and white. But the Kennedy, now, was jaded.

I looked at Snow, and my mind blanked because as much as my heart begged me to jump back in, my head told me it would be a huge mistake.

For the first time in my life, I had no clue what to do next.

Chapter Fourteen

Breaker

The barbecue was already in full swing when Kitten and I walked in.
All eyes sliced toward us—no doubt wondering what the fuck we'd been doing in the car for thirty minutes while the kids were already here—but I ignored all the knowing stares.

Instead, I approached Dad, Atlas, and my brothers while Kitten sauntered in the opposite direction to hang with the girls.

I rubbed my clammy palms down my jeans as I walked.

Admittedly, I knew there were difficult conversations to be had, but not so goddamned soon. This morning was the first time I'd seen her since leaving the Vet Center, but I thought I'd at least get a few days' reprieve. The deep dive into the sordid details of my past had blindsided me.

"Jesus, Break," Atlas boomed, eyes flicking over my ravaged expression. "You look like you've gone five rounds with Bowie. Lighten up, will ya. Today's meant to be a celebration."

Dad grimaced. "What the fuck happened to you, Son? Everythin' okay?"

My nostrils flared. "Had a run-in with Kitten. She's bustin' my balls."

Cash grinned. "Welcome to my world, motherfucker."

Bowie's mouth flattened into a line. "Dunno how you put up with those ball-breaker women. Give me a cute lil' thing with a sweet disposition any day."

"You dunno what you're missin'," Cash muttered. "There's nothin' like a wildcat spittin' and snarlin' while she bounces on your dick."

"Amen, Son," Abe crowed.

"Surprised your celibate brain remembers," Atlas banded back. "From what I can tell, you've not fucked her since Christmas." He took a swig of his beer while chuckles rose through the air.

"Not sure I could get to her anyway," Cash mused. "Her baby belly gets in the way of everythin'. It's typical; Cara's never more gorgeous than when pregnant, but fuckin' her's impossible."

"Never stopped me with your ma," Dad muttered.

I almost gagged.

"Shut up with that talk," Bowie said, outraged. "That's my mother you're boastin' about. Is nothin' in this place sacred? It's weird how you tell us about you and Ma."

Dad laughed and took a swig of his beer.

A peal of child's laughter sounded from my right. I turned to see what was happening, and my mouth fell open at the sight ahead of me. "What the fuck?"

Yesterday, the area was unused land, which we usually filled with an overflow of cars from the auto shop. But overnight, a children's playground had appeared from nowhere, though I used the term loosely, seeing as it was more like something I'd imagine you'd find in Disneyland.

Breaker

The back of the area housed two bounce houses. One was pink; the other blue. They must have been twenty feet high and at least thirty wide. They were massive.

The three swings and merry-go-round were vintage and big, made of metal and wood. They were the style that'd graced playgrounds back in the eighties, which would've made me nervous if the ground hadn't been covered in springy green AstroTurf.

My breath caught as I watched Kai start to climb the tall, metal slide that stretched twenty feet in the air. "Wait! That wasn't there yesterday. I would've noticed."

"You couldn't fuckin' miss it," Abe said, cursing under his breath.

My shocked eyes jerked to Dad. "Did you know about this?"

He puffed his chest out. "Course I did. I bought the fucker."

My eyes rounded. "What the hell did you do that for?"

Dad grinned. "My little Sunshine asked me for a playground months ago. Then little Kady girl asked too, so I thought, why not?"

"But Pop," I protested. "It's archaic. There's a reason they got shot of those old playgrounds. Kids probably died on 'em."

"I told him, Kit." Abe sighed. "But the tightwad went for the one listed at half price."

Atlas rumbled a laugh. "Nothin' wrong with it." He nodded toward Kai, who was shooting down the slide at fifty miles an hour. "Look, your boy's havin' a ball. It'll put hairs on their chests. Kids nowadays need toughenin' up. Fallin' off that fucker will do it."

I watched, horrified, while Sunshine stood pale-faced at the foot of the slide, gazing up fearfully. "Look! Sunny's too scared to even go up the steps. She's goddamned terrified. Makin' her climb Mount fuckin' Everest would be kinder."

Cash let out a cackle.

Abe snorted.

"She'll be alright," Dad assured us. "She just needs to get used to it. The kid's a bit apprehensive about the height, is all. My Sunshine's a brave little thing. She'll be good as gold in a few hours."

"She'll be splattered on the ground more like." I pointed over at the little girl, who by then was almost crying. "She's too small for that shit. She's fuckin' six years old."

"That's why I made the boys lay AstroTurf," Dad explained. "They doubled up. Anythin' fallin' on that from a height will bounce straight up again."

By then, Cash had doubled over. He pointed a finger toward the playground, almost unable to speak through his laughter. "She ain't goin' up there." Tears streamed down his face. "She's scared outta her fuckin' wits."

Abe hooted, holding his stomach and busting a gut.

I shook my head as I watched Kai go over to try and help Sunny. He held his hand out, beckoning for her to follow him up the steps.

She shook her head obstinately, folding her arms across her chest. Her face turned red like she was about to burst into tears.

"Poor little thing's upset," Bowie griped. "She was so excited when you said you'd built her a playground. She fucking twirled all morning at the thought of gettin' her hands on the goddamned thing. Then, lo and behold, we get here, and it's a fuckin' death trap."

Cash nearly fell to the ground, cry laughing.

Abe howled.

Dad looked sheepish. "It was the only one I could get on such short notice. All the others would've taken weeks to be delivered."

Bowie's lips thinned. "You're just a cheapskate. Didn't it occur to ya that they delivered it so quickly 'cause nobody else wanted to risk their kids on it? The thing's uninsurable. It's a public liability."

I choked out a laugh.

Cash cried.

Sophie's voice floated through the air. "It's okay, Sunny. I'll take you up later." The doc shot Cash and Atlas dirty looks. "We'll go on it after we've eaten."

Sunny beamed.

Atlas turned to his wife and scowled. "Don't fuckin' think so, Stitch. You're not goin' up there in your condition."

She waved him off. "I'll be fine. Cara's too pregnant. Layla's scared of heights, and Ned said you'd have to pay to get her up there. I'm the only one willing to help the poor kid out."

Atlas's hands went to his hips, and he looked to the heavens. "I'll take her up," he bit out.

"Yayyy!" Sunny cried. "I loves you, Assless!"

Sophie jabbed a hand to her hip. "Don't be stupid, Dan. You're too big. You'll break the thing." Her eyes slid toward an eager-looking Sunny and softened. "I'll take you up, sweetheart."

"Let him do it, Soph," Bowie called over. "He'd be doin' us a favor. Better for Atlas to break his fuckin' neck on that thing than you or one of the kids."

"You're crazy if you think you're goin' up there, Stitch," Atlas argued. "I'm the SAA. I keep the club safe. It's my job. Now zip it, woman."

"You've been drinking," Soph reminded him. "You'll be sorry if you go up there."

"*You've been drinking. You'll be sorry if you go up there*," Atlas mimicked sarcastically. "It's a fuckin' slide, woman. Get a grip. I lived on those things when I was a nipper, not like these pussy bitches." He jerked a thumb in mine and Bowie's direction.

Soph held her hands up defensively. "Okay. Go up the thing half-drunk if you must. But don't come running to me when it ends in tears. I won't be putting lotion on your hairy ass when you get burns off the thing. It's metal, the sun's been heating it, and your backside's too big for comfort."

He patted his ass. "My backside's perfect, Stitch. Just like my dick."

Kennedy began to choke. "*Coke can*," she coughed.

My forehead scrunched up.

Coke can?

Sophie shot my woman a glare before turning back to her husband and shrugging. "If you say so, big boy."

Atlas preened. "Come on, little Sunshine. Your favorite Uncle At will take you up on it now before we eat." He walked over to the slide, beckoning for Sunny to jump into his arms.

The little girl threw an arm around the SAA's neck, punching a fist in the air with the other, squealing, "Yay. Me and Assless is going high."

"That's right, little Sunshine," he agreed, voice cocky. "Uncle Atlas will sort ya."

I watched as he ascended the steps with Sunny snuggled in his arms. A coil of nerves threaded through my stomach as I watched him climb higher and higher. "Is he gonna be okay?" I asked Dad quietly. "I'm surprised he offered in the first place. Isn't he a little bitch when it comes to heights?"

"He's been drinkin' all mornin'." Dad's mouth twisted ironically. "It's probably Dutch courage gettin' him up there."

"Say what?" Abe interrupted. "He's drunk? You can't put a drunk Atlas in charge of Sunshine, especially twenty feet in the fuckin' air."

"He's not drunk," Pop insisted. "He's just a bit tipsy, is all."

"Too late now," I muttered, heart in mouth as I watched Atlas settle his ass down on the top of the slide and reposition Sunny.

"Hold on tight," Layla shouted up at her daughter as she looked on nervously. "Don't let go of Atlas."

"Give it a rest, woman," The SAA shouted as he launched his ass down the slide, gathering speed as he headed toward the ground with Sunny on his lap, shrieking. "Weeeeeeeeeeee!"

A split second later, an almighty squeak filled the ether, and Atlas ground to a halt part way down. His eyes widened as he stared at us. Gingerly, he rocked his hips, trying to work himself loose, but his ass wouldn't budge. "Goddamnit!" he roared.

Abe looked up, a massive grin stealing over his face. "The stupid fat fucker's got himself stuck!" he hollered. "His ass is too fucking wide."

Silence filled the air for a split second. Then, roars of laughter went up, the men shouting and hooting at the sight of their SAA stuck halfway down the slide.

A wail pierced the ether. "H—H—Help me," Sunny stuttered. "I'm scared." Her face twisted in terror, and she began to sob.

Layla ran toward the slide. "Help her, Bowie."

But my brother was on his knees, roaring with laughter.

"Oh, my God!" She sighed, looking helplessly up at her daughter, who by then was wailing.

Abe pointed up, then doubled over, howling. "W—We told ya that ass was too fat."

Atlas looked down at us from fifteen feet in the air. "Fuck me!" he murmured, obviously mortified.

Dad looked to the heavens, heaving a breath out, laughter still cutting through the air as the boys rolled around holding their bellies. "Prospect!" he bellowed.

Billy came sauntering over, trying to keep a straight face. "Yeah, boss?"

"Go get some engine oil from the auto shop." Dad cursed. "We'll have to try and grease him out."

I laughed just as Abe fell on his ass with a loud hoot. "I—I—I can't." he roared with a laugh. "I—I just can't." He pulled himself to his feet and began to stagger toward the clubhouse door, hands covering his crotch. "Gonna p—piss myself." He howled. "Jesus Christ, I—I need the can."

Another bubble of laughter rose through my throat as I stared at the SAA stuck halfway down the slide, trying to console little Sunny, who was beside herself.

It was one of the most comical sights I'd ever seen.

Dad glared at me. "Not you. You're as bad as these assholes." He peered upward, shielding his eyes from the bright sunshine. "Look. Poor little Sunshine's scared to death." I watched as his lips twitched. "Fuckin' idiot." He chuckled.

My gaze swept to the benches to see Kennedy pointing toward Atlas as she roared with laughter, with Sophie and the other sixty people all joining in.

My stomach warmed as I took in the happiness etched on her face.

I hadn't seen her laugh like that since I visited her in Vegas years ago. She looked so young and carefree.

I always wanted to see her smile like that. She deserved everything good, and I'd make sure she got it. My heart was full of her, and I knew it always would be. Kitten would always be mine.

My stare lowered to little Kady smiling brightly as she looked up at Sunny on the slide. She was the double of her mom. I wouldn't have wanted her to be any other way. She was damned perfect.

Kai stood at the bottom of the slide, hands out, trying to calm Sunny. "You'll be okay, Sunshine," he soothed. "We'll get you down. I promise."

I marveled at his kindness and how he hated seeing the little girl cry, even though she was perfectly safe in Atlas's arms. My boy was a born protector, and I loved that about him, even though the same trait made him wary of me.

An emotion pinged deep inside. Warmth spread through my chest as I recognized it from nine years before when my girl threw herself into my arms as I walked through arrivals at Harry Reid airport.

A smile spread across my face, and just for a second, I could've cried because recognizing the feeling was fucking incredible.

For the first time in a long time, I was happy.

Eventually, we got Atlas down.

I'd run up the slide, grabbed Sunny, and carried her safely back to her mom. I'd gone back up to try and pull Atlas out, while the men laughed and catcalled, but he was wedged in too tightly.

Dad ordered the boys to put the grease inside used beer bottles and give them to Atlas, who poured it down the sides of his jeans. It took so long that Dad thought we'd need to take an angle grinder to the slide, which caused another round of laughter, but Atlas refused.

It took a good hour, but eventually, he got loose and knee-walked down to the ground, red-faced.

"Well, it serves ya right," Dad told him through a mouthful of cheeseburger. "You got up there after you were specifically told your ass was too fat. But did you listen?" He shook his head exasperatedly.

Atlas narrowed his eyes. "You bought the fuckin' thing in the first place, Prez. Nobody else offered to help poor little Sunshine, and I wasn't lettin' Stitch up there in her condition."

"You should've done," Dad insisted. "She would've been down in a jiffy. But no. Fat ass thinks he knows better."

"My ass ain't fat," Atlas muttered. "I'm big-boned."

"You ain't got bones in your ass, fuckwit," Pop retorted, pointing at him with a half-eaten cheeseburger. "If Bandit was here, he'd have *shot* you in the ass."

Atlas huffed.

"Now I've gotta order another barrel of engine oil 'cause my SAA thinks he's still an eleven-year-old boy and likes to play on the kids' slide." He shook his head again. "It's like tryin' to wrangle a bunch of lunatics on a full moon." He pointed at Cash. "Mouth almighty here thinks he's all that 'cause he got his ol' lady knocked up without her knowin'. And my SAA gets his fat ass stuck down kids' play equipment." He scraped a hand down his face. "Thank God for Kit and Freya."

Atlas's head reared back. "Your tune's changed, Dagger. I was singin' Break's praises not long ago while you called him a dog's dick."

Dad looked affronted. "Well, he was, but Kit's sortin' his shit now, and his old man couldn't be prouder."

I let out a chuckle.

Atlas was right. Not long ago, Pop thought I was a waste of space. He'd done a complete one-eighty, and it was nice to have my father on my side for a change.

I looked around the area and smiled.

Twilight had hit, and the place looked fantastic. The younger guys had left to party in town, leaving just families. Clusters of people were dotted around, eating, drinking, and laughing. Kids played, and the babies and toddlers were huddled on the ground, surrounded by blankets and toys.

It was weird. I'd have been in town a year ago, partying and looking to get laid. Now, I couldn't think of anything worse.

I wandered toward the planks of woods that some of the men had laid to create a makeshift dance floor. The girls were already up there having a good time.

I watched Kitten's hips swing in time to the music and smiled at how happy she seemed.

I felt a presence beside me. Turning, I watched Bowie sidle alongside. "I was just thinkin' how a year ago it was me watchin' Layla dance with you and wantin' to Hulk out."

A lump formed in my throat, and I nodded, "Yeah. I remember."

"Even though you were more ill than I ever realized, you gave me some good advice that night. I'll never forget how you helped me back then, Kit. I dunno if I'd even be with Layla if it wasn't for you."

I turned to my brother, chest warming. "Yeah, you would. You two would've got it together eventually without anyone's help. You were already into her; you just needed a push."

He laughed. "Needed a rocket up my ass, you mean."

I shrugged, "Maybe that, too."

My brother gestured toward the dance floor. "You love her, don't ya?"

I stared at Kennedy's happy expression and jerked a nod. "I've loved her for ten years, Bo. And I'll love her for a hundred more."

"I notice you stayed away from her today. Why?" Bowie asked.

I cleared my throat. "We had a come-to-Jesus moment earlier. I gave Kennedy an information dump, and she needed time to process it. She's angry with me about all the women. I can't blame her. She probably wants to rip my head off."

"Fuck!" Bowie muttered. "I worried about that with Layla, but she never said anythin'."

"You weren't together, Bowie," I reminded him. "You were a single man."

"So were you," he pointed out. "I'm assuming your whorin' ways resulted from the PTSD. You weren't yourself, Kit. I could see it a mile off, but I was caught up in getting my head straight after Sam and let it slide. You need to stop bein' so hard on yourself. Kennedy seems like a smart girl; she'll work it out."

I thought about the anger pounding from her while we sat in the car earlier, yelling at each other. Knowing I'd caused her heartache left me cold. I knew my sins were mounting up, but I'd have done anything to be the one who wiped away her tears and made her smile again.

"This is why I like my sweet girl," Bowie muttered. "Couldn't deal with all this shit. My Layla always heard me out, even when I pissed her off."

I rested my hand on his shoulder. "Bullshit. I remember first the time she came here with Cara. She wouldn't give you the time of day."

My brother smirked. "Remember what you told me?"

"Yeah," I replied. "I told you to take your chance. I said you had an in with her kid and not to waste it."

"Bingo," he muttered. "I rest my case."

My gaze slid back to Kennedy, who was waltzing around the dance floor with Abe. She was laughing up at him with sparkling eyes. My woman looked so happy and alive that I couldn't help smiling.

"Layla came around because I proved she could rely on me," Bowie continued. "Seems to me you've got two amazin' kids who need their dad. Step up and show up. It's the only way a woman like Kennedy will take notice. Grovel. Prove you won't give up on her again, 'cause let's face it, last time the goin' got tough, you disappeared and left her holdin' the babies."

"Groveling won't work with her, Bo. She doesn't care about material things. She cares about her people."

"So start with the two people she loves most and go from there," my brother suggested. "It's not rocket science." Bo patted me on the shoulder before sauntering to the dance floor to pull Layla into him for a dance.

He was right.

All I'd thought about for weeks was getting Kennedy back, but I knew it wouldn't be an easy fix. She knew the boy I used to be and still was in some ways. I had to show her the man I'd grown into, prove he was worth the risk. It would take time and hard work, but as Dad said, nothing worth having ever came easy.

I had to stop telling her I loved her. The words were simple to say, but she needed proof. And even if it took me the rest of my life, I'd show her.

Starting now.

My stare caught on Kai, who sat away from everyone, alone. My heart went out to him because he looked the same way I often felt, like a misfit. It was already clear that Kai wasn't an average boy. He walked around like the weight of the world lay on his shoulders.

It was a lot for such a young guy.

Without a thought, I weaved my way toward him. It was time for me and my boy to have a chat.

He was eight years old, too young to be so world-weary. He should've been running around with Sunny and his sister, having fun instead of moping around.

I reminded myself Rome wasn't built in a day. Still, I needed to lay the foundations now if I wanted to end up something worth having.

I greeted him with a chin lift, and to my surprise, he returned it, probably without thinking. Still, I'd have taken anything by that point.

I sat next to him, staying quiet at first, watching the dancing.

Kitten moved just like she used to, and it was fucking incredible. She could make me pop a hard-on at thirty paces ten years ago and hadn't lost her touch. All I'd found myself doing all day was adjusting my crotch. My woman still did it for me like no other.

"You perving on my mom?" Kai asked, tone bitter.

"Can't help it, Son." I nudged him gently. "You know, she was dancing the first time I saw her. Your mother was the most beautiful thing I'd ever seen. I think I fell in love with her there and then, on some level."

"And then you left her," he accused.

I nodded, trying to find the best way to explain everything to an eight-year-old. I slid my hand across the back of his chair, eyes still fixed on Kennedy. "I know it's not what you want to hear, but if it meant protecting her again, I'd do the same thing."

His head whipped around. "Protecting her?"

I nodded. "I was sick. Have you heard of PTSD?"

"Yeah," he confirmed. "Mom told us you had it. It's not an excuse."

"I agree, Kai. It's definitely not an excuse."

His lips flattened. "My mom's smart and strong. She could've helped you. You didn't hang around to find out."

"You're right," I agreed. "But your mom was a lot like Kady ten years ago. She felt everything. I didn't want her to experience what I was going through. She was only nineteen and hadn't been to college or law school. Your mom wasn't naïve, but she still needed protecting and still does in some ways. I know you're aware of that."

"You're right," he told me. "She does, but I still need to work out if my mom needs protection from you."

His words punched inside my chest, but I hid my reaction.

Kai was right to be wary of me. I'd never shown him anything trustworthy. Getting him onside would be difficult, but I knew where to start. He was mine, after all.

"Thank you for protecting them, Son," I said huskily. "You did my job, and I'll always be grateful, but there's still a lot you need to learn."

He froze. "I've done alright so far."

"You've done amazing," I agreed. "But I can teach you more. I can help build your strength and endurance. Show you techniques that'll put a man twice your size on his ass. If your mom agrees, in a few years, I'll even teach you to load and shoot a gun."

His eyes widened. "I asked Grandpa, and he said no."

I grinned. "Yeah, 'cause Grandpa knows it's my job, not his. That's gonna be a few years away yet, but in the meantime, why don't we start with some boxing moves and buildin' your stamina?"

He nodded suspiciously.

"We start tomorrow mornin'. Want you up at six-thirty doin' stretches, then we'll run a few miles together."

He puffed out his chest. "Easy!"

I laughed. "It won't be, Kai. You'll wish you never started some days, but I guarantee it will help you focus and build self-confidence. I'm not always gonna be around. Part of my treatment program includes traveling to Rock Springs. Sometimes, I may have to stay overnight. Knowing you're home to look after our girls will put my mind at rest. We start tomorrow mornin'. Okay?"

"Yeah." His lips tipped up. "We start tomorrow mornin'."

A spark of happiness warmed my insides.

It was a small victory, but it was still a step forward. I wasn't confident I'd won Kai over—that would take a lot of hard work—but I was determined to keep the faith.

My family was worth the fight.

Chapter Fifteen

Kennedy

The car ride home was surprisingly chilled and friendly. Kai had stayed away from Snow all day. Whenever they gravitated toward each other, my son walked away. So, when Kai answered Snow's questions during the drive back to the rental, I did a double take.

My brain scrambled as I got out of the car. I held back with Kai, walking behind Snow and Kady as we made our way toward the porch. "Who are you, and what have you done with my son?" I whispered. "You said more than two words to your father. Have you been abducted by aliens, and really, you're an imposter taking over the body of my grouchy boy?"

Kai looked up at me as if I was crazy. "Why are you so embarrassing? I thought you wanted us to get along."

"I'm a mom; embarrassing you is my job," I told him. "Anyway, stop changing the subject. What happened to make you acknowledge your dad all of a sudden?"

Kai shrugged. "He's gonna teach me how to box, and when I'm older, he'll give me shooting lessons."

My stomach dropped. "I don't fucking think so." My eyes caught Kit's ass, and I imagined throwing darts at it. "You're too young to be around guns." I raised my voice for Snow to hear.

Kady craned her neck. "Mom's mad," she warned, looking up at her dad. "What did you do now?"

He took her hand, walking her up the steps to the house. "She's always mad at me, Kadence. Your mom never shied away from busting my chops when I met her. You'll be shocked to hear I'm glad she hasn't lost her touch." He glanced at me over his shoulder, smirking. "I love her fire."

My lips pursed.

Asshole.

We approached the door, and Snow held out his hand for the keys.

I huffed, dropping them into his palm. "Still a male chauvinist, huh? You'll be surprised to learn that women learned how to turn a key centuries ago."

Kady looked up at her dad with a furrowed brow. "Are you a chauvinist?" she asked, tone confused.

My stomach panged, and I immediately berated myself for being such a bitch.

"No, baby girl," Snow replied pointedly. "There's nothin' wrong with lookin' after the people you love. Doin' nice things and makin' sure they're okay is good. Not what I'd call chauvinist."

Snow opened the door and held it. "Need to talk to you without the kids hearing," he said quietly.

As if by magic, the twins disappeared down the hallway and into their rooms. "Looks like you got your wish." I sighed. "Let's go into the kitchen."

As soon as we wandered through, he caught my hand and tugged me into him, tipping my chin up with his finger until I had no choice but to look into his hard eyes.

I lowered my gaze, unable to meet his disappointed expression.

"Don't do that again," he rasped. "Whatever happens between us has nothing to do with them. I made headway with Kai today, and you could've just fucked it up 'cause of your jealousy. I can apologize to you until I'm blue in the face, Kennedy, but it won't change anythin'. I fucked other people, baby, and I'm sorry, but you gotta believe I only ever loved you."

A lump formed in my throat as his words sank in.

Snow was right. I'd purposely done something to turn the kids off him because I was jealous and wanted him to suffer, too. I knew it was wrong and mean, but I couldn't stop. I'd been stewing on our argument all day, and although I understood everything he'd said—sympathized even—it still ate away at my soul.

I knew he loved me, but I was so angry at him that I couldn't think straight.

A shiver ran through me as he bent his neck and kissed from my cheek to my ear. "I'm jealous, too, Kitten, he whispered. "I wanna hunt down every man who's ever touched you and break their fingers. But I can't do shit about it. That's my punishment."

I closed my eyes and tried to breathe through the pain.

Why was it so hard to forgive him?

Maybe my heart bled out because I felt cheated by him. Losing Snow and experiencing so much heartache when all along he was living one big party made me want to punch him. But even as those thoughts swam through my head, I knew I wasn't being fair. He'd suffered, too.

"You're so fucking perfect," he continued. "I knew someone else would see it and snap you up when I left. Can you imagine how shocked I was when I realized you were still single? Though, I gotta say, even if you belonged to someone else, I wouldn't have hesitated in chasing you down. You're mine, and even if you've been with a thousand other men, you'll always belong to me."

My body heated, and I shook my head. "It wasn't a thousand men. It was four."

He stilled.

"The first time was three years after I thought you'd died," I admitted. "Some guy at college pursued me, and I wanted to try and move on. I cried all the way through it because it wasn't you."

He moaned softly as if my words caused him physical pain.

"Two were long-term relationships. Well, I say that, but they didn't last more than a year because, again, they weren't you."

His hands squeezed me tightly like he was trying not to lose his shit.

"The other one was a friend. It was a one-off. We didn't mean for it to happen. I think we were both lost and hurting. We were looking for comfort."

His body locked tight for a full minute as anger pounded off him in waves. A muscle ticked in his jaw before he let out a low growl and pushed me away, storming out the door into the backyard, leaving me staring after him, shocked.

I closed my eyes, wanting to kick myself for saying too much.

Honestly, I didn't tell Snow those things to hurt him. If anything, I was trying to reassure him that nobody else had ever measured up. Everything I said was true, and I wanted to lay it all out because he needed to understand there were consequences to all the untruths. Because of a tiny lie, we'd both stumbled through life without ever really being able to move on from each other. But in my case, I thought he was dead, so I had at least to try.

Thoughts of Snow with other women had driven me nuts for weeks. A thread of guilt made me gnaw at my bottom lip, dark thoughts whirling through my head.

What if I'd made him relapse?

I winced as I heard something breaking in the yard.
Shit!

Quickly, I moved toward the back door, determined I wouldn't let Kit drown again, especially as it would be my fault. Kady and Kai needed him. I should've kept my big mouth shut.

Hurrying outside, I saw Snow in the darkness, and my steps faltered.

An old falling-down shed sat to the side of the lawn. Atlas told me he'd get it removed, but it seemed he didn't need to because Snow was in the process of kicking it down.

He drew his fist back and punched through a plank of rotting wood. His face was set into a hard sneer as he followed with a roundhouse kick to the door. Over and over, he pummeled the rickety building, relentless in his fury.

I watched him lose his shit, my heart beating out of my chest. I raked a hand through my hair, ignoring the urge to go over and comfort him. Holding all that anger in would poison him. Snow wasn't hurting anyone by getting his frustrations out. Maybe it could even help.

After five minutes of unleashing his anger, he staggered back, air sawing in and out of his lungs as he tried to catch his breath. Eventually, his shoulders slumped, and he hung his head, all fight leaving his body.

My stomach tugged toward him the same way it always did when he was close.

Tears hit the back of my throat when I thought about all the pain I'd endured through the years. It hurt all the more because I could see the same pain streaking across his face, leaving a forlorn expression in its wake.

My feet moved before I even noticed, and within seconds, I found myself beside him.

I prided myself in being a good person, but I'd let myself down. Years of loss and heartbreak had hardened me, but I wasn't petty. I didn't know why he brought that side out of me. Maybe it was true; there was a fine line between love and hate.

My fingers tremored slightly as I stroked his arm. "I'm sorry, Snow. I don't know what I was thinking when

I said those things. You bring out an evil side of me I didn't even know I had." My voice was small, nervous even.

He must have picked up my sorrowful tone through his residual anger because he swung around to face me. "No. No, baby. I caused it all. I knew you wouldn't stay alone forever when I left, but it didn't make me stay. I was so ashamed of what I'd done. I didn't think I deserved you. My insecurities were so deeply rooted that it was easy to believe I wasn't a good enough man for you."

"You *were* good enough," I croaked. "You were amazing. Nobody else ever came close. You left a mark on me that I can never erase. You gave me Kai and Kady. You made me feel more important than even my own mother ever did."

"'Cause you *are* important," he rasped, taking my hand. "You and the kids are *everything*."

"And so are you, Kit," I banded back. "I know I've been difficult, and I'm sorry if I made you so angry that you wanted to murder Atlas's shed. I'm just so frustrated by you."

He let out a snort. "I know. You've got nothin' to apologize for."

I glanced worriedly at what was left of the wooden structure he'd just destroyed. "Did I make you relapse? The way you just killed that poor shed. Is that you needing violence again?"

His lips twitched, and he chuckled. "No, baby. I didn't relapse. I just needed to vent my frustration, is all." He dipped his head. "Maybe you should lay off telling me about other men in future, yeah?"

"Okay," I agreed.

He nodded toward the house. "You got any food in there?"

Breaker

I gave him an exasperated look. "What do you think? I have an eight-year-old boy, Snow. He'd start a revolution if he couldn't find food in the refrigerator."

"All that exercise made me hungry. Will you fix me something?"

"Only 'cause it's you." I tugged his shirt, relieved we were on good terms again. "Come on. Give the poor shed some time to recover before round two."

Snow slid his arms around me, and we started for the back door. His skin felt warm against mine as he shielded me from the cool night breeze. The knot, which had resided in my stomach for the last six weeks, finally unraveled.

Arguing with Snow and watching him lose his shit should've set me on edge, but weirdly I was much more settled. I felt tired and drained, but a ton of weight had been lifted from my shoulders because we'd somewhat cleared the air.

"Can we talk later when the kids are in bed?" he rumbled as we approached the door. "There's so much shit to sort through. The sooner we start, the better."

I ran a hand through my hair, ignoring the twist in my stomach. "Can we not? I agree we need to talk but not tonight. I just want to shower, get my PJs on, snuggle on the couch, and watch TV. You're welcome to join me if you're good with that?"

"Remember when we used to curl up in bed and watch Game of Thrones?" he asked, pushing the door open and gesturing for me to go before him. "Happiest days of my life."

The beautiful memory brought a smile to my face. "I wonder what happened to the Starks and the Lannisters.

His eyebrows snapped together. "You never watched the rest?"

I went to the fridge and pulled out the ingredients for a sandwich. "I promised I wouldn't."

He nodded thoughtfully, drinking me in with his eyes. "It's a date."

"It's not a date," I insisted. "I'm good with spending time with you. We need to be friends for the kids' sake, but we're different people now. We may not even like each other."

"Keep telling yourself that, baby," he said under his breath. "I'll make you remember."

My lips twisted. "Behave yourself, Snow, or you can go home."

He rolled his eyes good-naturedly. "I'm your bodyguard. Ain't goin' nowhere."

The pitter-patter of feet sounded from the hallway. "Can we have a sandwich too?" Kai asked as he ran into the kitchen with Kady.

"You Stone men have got hollow legs," I teased. "You're the only people I know who can spend all day at a barbeque and still be hungry. Didn't you eat?"

Kai sat at the table, watching me assemble a stack of BLTs. "Atlas kept putting that disgusting hot sauce on everything, so we didn't eat much."

"Sounds like Atlas," Snow muttered, going to the fridge and grabbing juice boxes for the kids. "He puts that crap on everythin'." He placed the drinks on the table and went back for water. "I'm sure he's burned his tastebuds off."

"He was funny on the slide." Kady smiled as she sucked her juice through a straw.

Snow and Kai shared a look, and they began to chuckle.

I looked warily between the two of them.

Twenty-four hours ago, Kai wouldn't have peed on his father if he was on fire. What had happened at the barbeque to suddenly make them BFFs?

"What time are we running tomorrow morning?" Kai asked his dad as I handed him a sandwich.

My eyes rounded.

"'Bout six-thirty," Snow replied, taking a swig of water. "Gotta wait for Shot before we jet. Not leavin' our girls unprotected."

Kai took a bite of his sandwich. "Fair enough," he said with his mouth full. "You better keep up, though."

Snow laughed.

For the next hour, we all sat at the table talking.

Kai didn't often speak, but somehow, his dad managed to pull conversation out of him. Kady and I kept shooting each other surprised looks. God only knew how, but Snow managed to zoom in on what Kai loved most: Martial Arts, soccer, and MCs. My boy sat entranced as Snow relayed stories about growing up among the Speed Demons.

He'd just finished making the kids laugh by telling us about the time his Grandpa Bandit filled a rival biker's ass full of buckshot when I reminded the kids it was past bedtime.

Groans of protest went up, but Snow raised a hand. "At the risk of sounding like a dick, I wanna remind you it's been a long day for your mom. Be the smart and adoring kids I know you are, and do as she says." His stare settled on Kai. "We've got an early start, son. Best you get some shut-eye." He turned to Kady. "And you've done nothin' but yawn for the past half hour, pretty girl."

Kai got down from the table and gave his dad a fist bump. "Night, Mom," he said before disappearing into the hallway.

Kady scrambled down and shuffled toward Snow. Her little eyes went wide as she smiled shyly, watching as her dad turned from the table, resting his elbows on his knees.

"You okay, baby girl?" he asked.

Our girl nodded before throwing her arm around his neck and kissing his cheek. "Goodnight, Daddy," She turned and ran down the hallway.

Slowly, Snow sat straight. "Fuck!" He rubbed his chest, looking dazed.

I smiled because I knew that Kadence had the power to put grown men on their asses, and clearly, her dad wasn't immune.

"I'll go tuck them in, shower, and get my PJs on. You find Game of Thrones and set it up." I stood and walked down the hallway to my room, knowing Snow probably needed a minute.

I had to keep in mind that he'd only returned home yesterday. It had been an emotional day. He'd met the kids, and we'd had a massive argument. Even tonight had been a rollercoaster. He probably needed a minute to regroup.

Twenty minutes later, I settled down on the couch next to Snow while the opening credits of Game of Thrones played. "So. Who do you think will win the Game of Thrones?"

"Robb Stark, all day long," he replied. "Tyrion will go out along with Arya and Sansa Stark.

"Catelyn Stark or Daenerys," I mused. "They both kick ass. In fact, no, I'll go with the Mother of Dragons. Nobody's going to get to her through those scaly-winged bad boys. You mark my words; she'll be the last woman standing."

"I guess we'll see," he said, turning back to watch the opening scene.

I settled back to get comfortable, pulling the throw over my knees. "I guess we will."

A whimper startled me awake.

The first thing I noticed was warmth. I snuggled deeper into the couch, willing the sounds to quieten so I could drift back off to sleep.

The scent of fresh sandalwood and clean skin enveloped me, and I knew I was cuddled into Snow's warm hoodie. It took me back ten years to when he was mine, and we thought we could conquer the world. We'd wake up fused together because we gravitated toward each other, even in sleep. Even subconsciously, we couldn't bear to be apart.

Snow released a low moan, and he mumbled, "No, Benny." His body jerked.

My eyes slowly opened, lifting to see his expression contorted in pain.

My teeth sunk into my bottom lip.

Was I supposed to wake him from his nightmare or let him relive it? I'd read somewhere that you should never wake people from their dreams because it was dangerous.

I pressed my hand gently against his heart and lifted my face from his neck, whispering, "It's okay, Kit. I've got you."

I was startled by a loud buzzing noise coming from his pocket. My jerking must have started a chain reaction because Snow's eyes snapped open, and he jackknifed to a sitting position, taking me with him.

"What the fuck?" I yelped, sliding away to a more comfortable position.

Snow looked around, his eyes dazed and confused. "Fuck!" he croaked. "We fell asleep." He leaned his head back as his cell buzzed again. "Who's that? What's the time?" he muttered, holding a hand to his stomach.

Leaning forward, I checked my cell on the coffee table. "Just gone two A.M."

Snow rested his head back again. "Jesus. That BLT finished me off. My gut's churnin'..." He froze for a few seconds, then tilted his head down again. "The kids. Where are they?"

I frowned at the panicked edge to his voice. "They're in bed. You know they are."

"We need to check." He leaped to his feet and hurried down the hallway.

I stared after him for a few seconds, wondering why Snow was acting so strangely. Was he still half asleep and inside his dream? He seemed awake, but he behaved almost like something terrible was happening.

I stood, heading after him. As I got to the hallway, I saw him close Kai's door. "What's going on?" I asked. "The kids are fine."

He turned toward me and nodded; his expression confused. "Yeah. I've got a gut feelin' about somethin'. It's like a built-in antenna. Whenever my stomach churns, it's usually a sign of danger." His cell phone buzzed again, and he pulled it out, stabbing the answer button. "Atlas. What the fuck's goin' on?" he demanded, clicking it onto loudspeaker.

"Get your asses to the compound," Atlas ordered through the phone. "Shit's hittin' the fan."

Without hesitation, Snow threw Kai's door open again. "Son! Get up. Put somethin' warm on and get your sister." He went to Kady's door and kicked it open. "Kadence. Up, now. Get warm clothes on and stay with Kai." He caught sight of me at the end of the hallway. Shoes on, Kenny," he ordered.

Heart racing, I ran past him into my room, perched on the side of the bed, and dragged my sneakers on. My hands tremored so hard it took me four attempts to lace them up.

Something big had happened. I didn't know what, and if I was honest, I didn't want to hang around to find out. I just needed to get my kids somewhere safe.

Suddenly, a deafening crash sounded from somewhere in the house.

I leaped up and ran for the hallway where Kai and Kady waited, holding hands.

Kady looked up. "Mommy!" she cried. "I'm scared. It's the bad men."

My blood ran cold.

Kai pulled his sister closer to him. "Mom?"

My chest tightened painfully as I ran back into the living room. "Snow?" A scream caught in my throat as a wall of heat hit my face. I lifted my wide eyes to see angry flames licking up the drapes. The fire danced in the muted light, fanned by the night breeze blowing gently through the smashed window.

"It's caught, Atlas," Snow shouted into the cell phone. "I know enough about fire to know the house is about to go up. Gonna have to risk goin' outside. We'll burn to death if we stay here."

"We're minutes away, Breaker," Atlas said, voice thick with anger. "If they come at you, don't give 'em a lick of mercy. Shoot to kill."

"Hurry, brother." Snow clicked the cell before turning and hurrying toward me. "Come on. Kitten. Let's get the fuck outta dodge."

"What's happened? What's going on?" I squeaked as we headed back down the hallway toward the kitchen.

"It's the Sinners, baby. They've hit all the club's rentals, even Layla and Soph's houses. They tried to take Cara's folk's place out, too, but Seth had a fire extinguisher in the kitchen and snuffed it out before it caused too much damage."

"Are they okay?" I demanded. "Snow! What's going on?"

"They're all fine," he said as we rushed into the kitchen, where Kai and Kady waited. He pulled a gun out of the leather jacket he'd worn earlier and crouched down to talk to Kai.

His following words made my heart stop.

"Whatever happens to me. You all get in the car and lock the doors. Do you understand, Kai?"

Snow waited for our son to nod his agreement before he stood, grabbed Kady, and swung her into his arms. "Hold on tight, baby girl."

Kady wrapped her arms around her daddy's neck and held on for dear life.

He handed me the car keys. "Ready?" He waited for my nod, then turned the key in the lock and swung the door open. "You two, hold onto my jacket and stay at my back.

My pulse raced.

"Kennedy, Kai. If anythin' happens to me, get to the car, lock the doors, and drive. Any fucker tries to stop you, run 'em over."

We stepped into the cool, dark night and swiftly made our way down the side of the house toward the SUV parked out front.

My heart thumped so hard I heard it in my ears.

I'd been in some precarious positions once or twice, but never like this. My fingers curled tighter onto Kit's jacket, my other hand sliding across Kai's back.

As we got to the gate, Kit set Kady down, placing her hand firmly in mine. "Take her and get to the cage," he ordered. "They're gonna be out there, waitin'." His face twisted into a blank mask. "Take the kids; whatever happens, don't look back."

We slowly emerged into the street, and I screamed as a dark shadow approached us from the side.

"Run!" Snow's bellow rang through my ears before he turned toward the figure, raised his arm, and fired.

The bang was so deafening it cracked through my eardrums, but I was so intent on getting my babies to the car the pain didn't even register. With my heart banging against my ribs, I grabbed the twins and sprinted for the vehicle, not allowing myself to look back at the sounds of fighting slicing through the air.

The keys to the SUV were in the same hand holding onto Kady's. I let her go for a split second to click the key fob, but when I went to grab her again, she was gone.

My heart nosedived as my girl's high-pitched scream rang out.

Breaker

I whirled around to see some guy hurtling toward a vehicle with Kady in his arms. I turned back and threw the keys at my boy. "Get in the car, Son, and lock the doors." I set off after them, my lungs squeezing so painfully it made me nauseous.

An ache enveloped my chest as I watched him sprint. Even carrying Kady, he was faster and stronger than me.

I was still lagging behind when the car door opened, and he dived into the backseat with Kady.

I cried out as tires squealed on the asphalt, and the vehicle sped away.

My heart cracked inside my chest.

"Snow," I screamed. "They've got, Kady!"

Two more gunshots cracked through the night air, and within seconds, Snow sprinted past me, arms pumping as he hurtled forward. He pointed the gun toward the vehicle, aimed, and fired.

It was too late, though. The big, black SUV's tail lights glowed in the darkness as they turned left and disappeared from sight.

Still staring after the car, I fell to my knees, a pained wail leaving me. It was the sound of my heart breaking.

Strong arms went around me. "No, Kitten. I'll get her back," Snow whispered. "Don't fall apart. Our baby girl needs us. I promise I'll get her back."

I heard his words, but they didn't register. The only thing in my head was my baby's sweet face. "Kady's sensitive, Snow," I cried. "She feels everything. She'll be so scared." My entire body shook as the pain of losing my daughter ravaged me.

Snow tugged me into his chest. "Stop, Kennedy," he croaked into my hair. "I'll find her, but I gotta get you and Kai safe first. I can't help her if my mind's elsewhere. I need to think straight. I can't if I'm worrying about you, too."

As the words left his lips, I caught the distant sound of tailpipes.

"The boys are here. Get up, Kennedy." Snow banded his arms around my waist and hauled me onto my feet. "I need you to be strong. Go to the clubhouse. I'll get Kady." His hand cupped my cheek, and he angled my face to look him in the eyes. "I'll get her back. Trust me." His golden orbs glowed with emotion for what seemed like an age as he took in every inch of my face. After a minute, they dulled as something dark moved behind them. Kit's beautiful face blanked, lip curling as my golden boy's expression morphed into a sneer.

My shattered heart curled in on itself when I saw the emptiness in his eyes.

That was when I knew.

Just like all the bad shit he'd suffered, this had marked his soul. All the work he'd invested in himself was now wasted. The pain of losing our girl had altered his core, his aura.

A shiver ran down my spine, and I brought a hand to my chest as it twisted with a sudden realization.

My Snow was gone.

The beast was back.

Chapter Sixteen

Breaker

Every sliver of humanity slid away as I stood helplessly watching my beautiful baby girl being bundled into a strange car by a sick piece of shit. All warmth left my heart, and a familiar dark void settled in my gut.

It was the Sinners. I'd recognized their Road Captain, Ratty, when he'd just tried to jump me. His beady black eyes stared at me, stricken, as I raised my gun and pulled the trigger, my blackened soul singing with elation at getting a kill after so long.

In that split second, the monster inside me came back to life.

Suddenly, it didn't matter if my kids lost me. I didn't care if I had to lay my life down. The only thing of importance was getting Kadence back.

I needed the beast in control if I had a hope of completing my next mission. Dying didn't scare me. I didn't care if I got wiped off the face of the earth. Kady was the only person I needed to live because the alternative would destroy her mother, her brother, and me.

I closed my eyes, pushing my emotions down to make room for the monster to rise. It roared to life, filling me with the craving for violence, blood, and death. My jaw clenched with the desire to feed it until its belly was sated.

"Kit." Kennedy's pain-filled eyes lifted to mine. "If they hurt her, I'll die." Her hands went to her hair, and she tugged hard, a low moan escaping her throat.

"I'm gonna kill 'em all." I turned toward the burning building, feeling its scalding heat radiate through me. The heat burning my skin took me straight back to the EOD, the task force, and the death missions. Drawing on the soldier was the only way Kady could be saved.

A roar of engines filled the air as my MC brothers rode down the street toward us. The pop-popping of Atlas's engine drew closer until it stopped beside me.

"They've got Kady." My nostrils flared. "Those sick bastards took my little girl."

He dismounted, kicked his stand on, and immediately pulled out his cell phone. Stabbing it, he held it to his ear. "Yo. Prez. Get me Colt. They've got little Kady girl. Need eyes on the cameras we've got runnin'."

Shouts and bellows emanated from the phone as my dad lost his shit, but I didn't care. It meant nothing compared to saving my little girl. I had to concentrate my thoughts on a rescue plan.

"Where have they taken her?" I demanded in a dangerous voice.

"They took the turnin' toward Mapletree," Atlas confirmed. "That's where Beetle's house is, the one his mom left him in her will."

I looked around to see who'd accompanied Atlas and spied Reno leaning into the car window, urgently talking to Kai. "Brother!" I bellowed.

He stood straight and turned to face me.

"Take the SUV and get Kennedy and Kai back to the clubhouse," I ordered. "I need your wheels."

The SUV door flew open, and Kai jumped out, running toward us. My boy's face was streaked with tears as he ran to his mom for comfort.

A familiar red mist descended over my eyes.

Kennedy braced as Kai barreled into her. "It's okay, Son," she murmured. "Your dad will get her back. Won't you?" She looked at me pleadingly.

"I need my sister," my boy cried, burying his face in his mom's stomach. "I need Kady."

Something panged in my chest. Kai's shattered peace of mind affected me, but I didn't wanna feel it. Emotions wouldn't serve me. I needed to push everything down and become soulless if I wanted to get my baby girl back.

I nodded toward Kennedy and Kai as Reno approached. "Get 'em in the SUV and get 'em safe," I ordered. "Gimme your keys and your piece. I need firepower."

Atlas ended his call. "He needs his piece in case they run into trouble, Breaker. Prez, Colt, and Cash are already on their way. They're bringin' weapons and a lil' somethin' special for you." An evil grin spread across his face. "They've razed Layla's house. Reckon they were tryin' to snatch Sunny, too. But luckily, they stayed at the club last night."

A noise escaped Kennedy's throat.

She grabbed my sleeve, dragging me around to face her. All color had drained from her face. My heart turned to steel as I caught a flash of fear in her cornflower blues.

"Do what you have to do," she spat. "Make those sick fucks feel half the pain they've made me feel." She leaned up and quickly kissed my cheek. "Be who you need to be, Snow. Just make them suffer." She looked deep into my eyes before grabbing Kai and turning for the SUV with Reno.

The monster roared with satisfaction, the words weaving a thread of sick happiness around my heart.

Kennedy Carmichael was my one. My other half, my mate. For her, I'd paint the town red with the blood of the cunts who'd taken what was mine.

The sound of car doors slamming filled the cool air.

I turned, watching Reno drive away, my boy's face staring at me through the window.

Another set of lights appeared as the club's SUV passed them, approaching us. Dad didn't get a chance to turn off the engine before Cash, Bowie, and Colt leaped out of the car.

"They definitely took her to Beetle's new place," Colt confirmed, holding up his cell. "I tracked 'em all the way there. They're clueless to the fact we know about Beetle's new place, so at least we'll have the element of surprise on our side."

Cash dropped a colossal burlap sack at my feet. "We've brought some hardware, and Colt included some little toys for you, Kit."

I crouched down and looked inside, smiling as I saw knives, shotguns, and rifles. Also, glass bottles, rags, and fuel.

"We're stepping up the war." Dad's eyes met mine. "You're gonna make up those Molotovs before we extract our girl. Then we'll shoot dead every motherfucker who touched a hair on her head. I'm prayin' Bear's there, so we can take him out, too."

I dug deeper into the sack, heart leaping at the scale of pandemonium we could cause with all the weaponry inside. Over the years, I'd walked a fine line between being a killer and a stand-up citizen. There'd be no confusion tonight, though. The Sinners would be sorry they'd crossed me.

Atlas cracked his neck from side to side. "Get in the car and start settin' those Molotovs up. Me and Cash'll throw those fuckers in the house. They can burn with it."

I stood, and we started toward the car. "Have you noticed, no cops, no fire engines?" Colt said thoughtfully.

Dad nodded. "The rentals are set away from town, but they'd still see the fire and smell the smoke. There's not been a peep from the authorities even though six houses have gone up in flames."

My gut panged. "Was anyone hurt?" I opened the car door, sliding into the back seat with Colt.

"There was only one other house occupied, and he got out okay," Dad assured me.

I opened the bag, took out four bottles, and lined them up as I felt for the rags and the can of fuel. "If no cops showed, it means they're dirty."

Dad nodded. "We came to that conclusion after the shootout, Son. They didn't show then either."

I shrugged. "At least if the authorities turn a blind eye to the club war, we can kill without repercussions."

Colt smirked. "True."

"We don't involve cops in our business anyway," Dad pointed out. "Even if they wanted to help, I wouldn't be callin' 'em."

"So it's just us and the Sinners?"

"Yeah," Colt confirmed. "And the twisted asshole who's been doin' their dirty work since Henderson's demise."

"Brett Stafford?" I asked.

Colt nodded. "Yeah. He's involved but hasn't got any pull with the cops. There's gotta be someone higher up the food chain."

The car doors flew open. Cash jumped in the back seat with Colt and me while Atlas slid in the front.

Dad started the SUV and pulled away. "How's it goin' back there, Kit?" he asked.

I slipped the leather gloves from my pocket, putting them on before dousing the rags in accelerant. "Nearly done," I confirmed.

"So, now all we need is a plan," Cash stated.

"It's simple," I retorted, my stomach burning as I thought about my next move. "You give me time to get in there and extract Kady, then we go back in and kill whoever's left."

"You're not goin' in there alone," Dad argued. "It's crazy. You'll be a sittin' duck."

My thoughts turned to all the missions I'd completed during my years in the military.

Tight spaces and dark holes were the places I felt most comfortable. I'd only given the club a hint of the terrible things I'd done and all the demonic people I'd sent back to Hell. They didn't know this shit was my specialty.

But they would soon enough.

The monster roared in my chest as my thoughts turned to all the soft, buttery throats I was about to slit. "Don't worry, Pop. I know what I'm doin'."

The muttered conversation went on, but I ignored the chatter, instead getting my head in the zone.

Dad and the brothers could make plans, but I already knew my role. Get in, get Kadence, and get out, killing as many people as possible along the way.

My body felt buoyant like before when I'd got a high from my missions. Without a thought, I breathed in through my nose and mouth, eradicating all the love that swirled through my heart. I needed to be a soldier again; a machine. Feelings would be a liability when I made my move on the scumbags who snatched my kid. When I slit their throats, there wouldn't be a trace of regret.

Over the next twenty minutes, I shut down completely. It was crazy how it had taken months of hard work and therapy to vanquish the monster and bring Kit Stone back but only minutes to do the opposite.

Sure enough, Kit Stone had disappeared by the time we sped past the sign welcoming us to Mapletree.

Breaker

Dad drove another few miles while Colt gave him directions to our destination. Luckily, the house was past the woods, a few miles from town. Mapletree, much like Hambleton, was rural. Though, they had a mall and other amenities that Hambleton didn't due to our Mayor's aversion to growth.

Eventually, Dad cut the lights, using the moon's glow to guide us toward a dirt track marked with a postbox, the only indication a house was close by

A rush of adrenaline flooded my bloodstream.

I reached inside the bag, removing two knives and a Glock, sliding them inside my pockets. Then, I opened the door, glancing at the other men who followed me out of the car.

"Wait, Son," Dad hissed. "You don't have to do this alone." His eyes widened a fraction as he stared into my blank eyes. "Kit?"

"If I'm not out in ten minutes, come for me," I said, and without waiting for my Dad's reply, I turned and headed through the thicket of trees surrounding the house where my daughter waited.

It didn't take long to catch sight of the lights from the house, streaming through the windows like a beacon lighting my way.

Approaching the tree line, I crouched down to take stock of the place.

Two men in Sinner's cuts walked around the perimeter, chatting with each other without a care in the world. One was tall and stocky, but it was the other guy who caught my attention.

A muscle leaped in my jaw as recognition washed over me. He was one of the assholes who'd ambushed us on the road outside town when those bastards murdered Sparky.

My mouth hitched. I'd make him watch his fuckface brother die before I slit his throat. Every Sinner would suffer because their Prez and VP were scummy skin traders who'd given the order to take my baby girl. No mercy would be shown. I'd annihilate every man who wore their patch. It didn't matter to me if *they* didn't give the order—I'd get to the fucker who did soon enough—they were still guilty by association. Every one of those sick fucks were about to face their judge, jury, and executioner.

Me.

Heart thudding a staccato beat, I waited until they disappeared around the side of the house before creeping toward the back porch and taking my position in a shadowed corner. Muscle memory took over, and my hands went to my neck, pulling up the black hood of my sweat top and taking a knife in each hand.

I heard them before I saw them. The sick fucks were laughing about something as they came into view, and I was glad for them. It was good they had no idea they were about to meet their maker.

I waited, at one with the shadows, watching them saunter past my position. Then, I stood to my full height, drew my arm back, and lobbed a knife at the back of the tall fucker's head.

A faint squeak sounded. Fascinated, I watched the blade sink into the back of his skull. It took a few seconds for him to drop to the ground.

His bud jumped before he slowly turned and stared down, horrified at seeing his friend's face in the dirt with my blade gleaming in the moonlight as it protruded from his brain stem.

The monster roared.

I lunged from the shadows, wrapping my hand around the Sinner's windpipe, pushing my second blade against his jugular, slicing into his skin. "Tell me where the girl is, and I'll let you run," I snarled from behind him.

He gulped so hard that I felt it against the palm of my hand. "B—basement," he stuttered, voice raspy with fear. "Door in the kitchen to the right. Takes you to a cellar."

I pressed my mouth to his ear so he was in no doubt of my intention. "How many other sick fucks are in that house with my daughter?"

"Four, including Beetle," he squeaked. Shock set in, and he began shaking from head to toe. "One of 'em's guardin' the girl," he added.

"Where's Bear?" I asked, my voice a deadly whisper.

"Not here." He gulped again. "He doesn't know about this. He went off with his baby girl after he killed his bitch. Those girls were personal. They're for the VP. He's pissed we only got one. Says he's movin' her out at dawn and comin' back for the other."

A ton of weight hit my chest.

Without pause, I slid the blade into the sick fuck's jugular, joy swirling inside my chest as he graced me with a death gurgle. I let him drop to the ground before I bent to pull the other knife from his brother's brain.

My head swiveled toward the back door, my mind immediately assessing where the Sinners' whereabouts might be. I crouched low and moved to the window, positioning myself underneath it to listen for voices.

After ascertaining nobody was there, I peered inside to double-check and saw an empty room. Slowly, I crept to the door, opened it, and slipped inside, immediately spotting the area to the right the dead fucker outside had told me about before moving toward it.

The sound of distant voices filtered in from another room. The dead man outside told me there were four men in the house, including the one guarding Kady.

My fingers touched the handle, silently pulling the door to the basement open and peering down the dark steps.

A muted light shone from the bottom, lighting my way.

The setup was much like the house back in the U.K. Benny and me had blown up years before. The concrete steps were enclosed by a solid wall to the left, with drywall to the right shielding the room where my daughter was being held against her will.

Slowly, I descended, feeling the monster rising, ready for the kill. Everything flooded back to me, and I became a shadow again.

Softly, I hit the foot of the steps and peeked around the wall. My eyes rested on a young dude who sat guarding another door. He looked down at his cell, one side of his mouth hitching as he scrolled with his thumb, clueless to his fate.

Silently, I stalked toward him, knife in hand, darkness swirling through my gut in anticipation of killing my prey. I hadn't felt such euphoria since the military. My body was experiencing such a high that I became almost light-headed.

His stare lifted to meet mine the instant he became aware of me. Brown eyes widened in shock as he opened his mouth to shout for help. He didn't get the chance to squeal because I slashed my blade across his face, slicing it open from left to right.

His hands jerked up to his cheek as blood seeped through his fingers, and he let out a low, animalistic moan. The sicko turned away, trying to shield himself, but as he twisted his body, I grabbed his hair, pulled it back, and sunk my blade into his throat.

A panicked gurgle bubbled until he finally gave one last death rattle as his good-for-nothing life slipped away.

Elation swirled in my chest as I watched his body drop to the floor with a lifeless thud.

My stare fell onto the blood dripping from his neck. I lifted my hands and smiled at the life force coating them. The tight, sticky feeling on my face and neck indicated blood covered them, too.

I froze as a thud sounded from behind the door. "Kady?" I called softly.

The shaky, scared voice of my daughter called out one word. "*Daddy?*"

My hand went straight to the door handle, but it was locked.

Crouching down, I rifled through the dead man's pockets, but all I found was a packet of smokes and a zippo. Thinking fast, I pulled out my cell and called Dad.

He answered after one ring. "We're outside the back door. Just saw your trail of big ugly breadcrumbs."

"Kady's locked in the basement," I explained. "I'll have to shoot the lock, but those bastards will hear. They're in the livin' room. Send Cash down to the basement through the door to the right in the kitchen. You and Atlas round those scummy fuckers up. Don't kill anyone until I get there."

"Right," Dad agreed before the line went dead.

After a minute, footsteps echoed as Cash descended into the basement. "Kit?" he whisper yelled.

"Here," I replied quietly.

My brother's mouth was set into an angry line as he came into view. "Dad's gonna call you and hang up. That'll be your sign to shoot.

"*Daddy?*" Kady called out. "*Is it you? The man said—*"

"I'm here," I called, cutting her off. "Step away. Get as far back as you can. As soon as it's safe, I'll shoot the lock off the door and get you out."

"Fuck" Cash muttered. "I dunno if you're aware, bro, but you're covered in blood. Freddy fuckin' Krueger would be more presentable than you are right now. You're gonna frighten Kady to death."

"Don't matter," I said numbly. "At least she'll be safe—"

My cell buzzed in my pocket.

"Did you step back, Kadence?" I yelled.

"*Yes!*"

I aimed my gun at the lock and fired twice. On the second shot, it exploded. I raised a boot and kicked the door hard until it flew open.

A whirlwind came speeding toward me. I crouched and opened my arms for my baby to fly into. The churning in my gut began to ease, and I buried my face in her hair. "Are you hurt?" I breathed. "Did they touch you?"

Kady stayed silent, thrusting her face harder into the crook of my neck.

"Kadence," I snapped. "Did they touch you?" I pulled her body away, checking to see if her clothes were ripped. Everything seemed fine and in its proper place.

"Did they touch you?" I repeated, pausing as I tried to find the right words. "Down below? I need to know, Kadence."

She pulled back to stare at me, and I froze.

Her little lip had been split, a bruise forming on her jaw. "He hit me, Daddy." My baby's little voice croaked as moisture welled in her beautiful cornflower blues.

The monster roared, my mind filling with images of the hell I was about to rain down on the sick fuckers upstairs. My shaking became so violent that Kady threw herself back into my body.

"No, Daddy. Don't," she begged, her little voice thick with tears.

My eyes slid to Cash. "Take her," I ordered through gritted teeth. "Keep her safe."

My brother's eyes widened as he caught the rage pounding from me. "Kit. Let Dad deal with 'em."

I snarled in my brother's face as the monster unleashed. "Take her!" I bellowed. I lifted my face, trying to keep my shit together while I held Kady. I was so close to exploding that my hands tremored, and my nerve endings burned.

Suddenly, the weight of her was gone as Cash took her from me.

I heard her scream for me, but I turned for the stairs and ran up two at a time. Bursting into the kitchen, I stormed through the door leading to the front of the house, my hands clenching into fists as I heard my dad's voice coming from a room further down the hallway.

I stomped inside, and without glancing at Dad or Atlas, headed straight toward a table at the back of the room where three men sat bolt upright. "Who hit her?" My voice was so low and strangled that it almost sounded demonic.

Nobody answered, but I caught one of them flinching from the corner of my eye.

Slowly, my head swiveled, and I took him in.

The bastard was dressed in black jeans and a hoodie. The same thing the fucker who snatched my baby had worn. My feet moved—almost of their own accord—until suddenly, I was on him.

The bastard slipped and fell with the force I used to drag him from his chair. A cry filled the air as I pulled my foot back and kicked him in the head.

I got down, straddling his chest to grab his hair. Lifting his head, I began to punch the sick bastard's face repeatedly.

A vision of my buds sitting on the gym floor, watching with grins spread across their faces, seemed so real that the room's bright light dimmed as if it was one A.M., and I couldn't sleep. I could almost smell their sweat and hear their grunts as I continued to punch.

"Kill him, Snow!" Benny yelled.

A cold shiver ran down my back. I could feel my friend's presence as he roared, "Make him bleed, Snow! Kill him!"

A whooshing flooded my ears, and the gym I'd been in just seconds before disappeared.

The harsh light in the room stung my eyes. Disorientated, I continued punching. "Is this what you did to my girl?" I roared, my fist connecting with his temple. "She's eight years old, and you punched her as hard as I'm punchin' you! How do you fuckin' like it?" Spittle flew from my mouth as I pummeled his face repeatedly.

Dad's voice cut through the air. "He can't feel it anymore, Son. Save your energy for the other two sick bastards."

Glancing up at the table, I caught Beetle's unbothered stare. "You put a mark on my girl," I rasped, watching his face pale slightly.

Slowly, I got to my feet. "Stand up," I ordered, tone almost dead.

He folded his arms across his chest, his thin lips set in a cocky smirk.

Atlas stormed behind him and kicked his chair so hard that the leg snapped in half.

Beetle's ass fell to the floor, and a curse flew out of his ugly mouth.

"You were told to stand up," Atlas grated out. "And from what I can see, you ain't got much choice in the goddamned matter." The SAA stooped down, grabbed Beetle by his long, greasy hair, and hauled him to his feet.

The Sinner prick rolled his eyes. "Just fuckin' kill me already," he said in his whiny-assed voice.

"You put a mark on Speed Demon girls," I gritted out. "You're a dead man."

He went to roll his eyes again, but as his beady orbs lifted, I grabbed my knife from my back pocket, aimed for his perverted dick, and lobbed it.

Beetle emitted a high-pitched scream, bending over before falling to his knees.

"Bullseye!" Atlas yelled. "You got him right in nut sack! Remind me never to challenge you to a game of darts."

Dad let out an evil chuckle.

Atlas pulled Beetle up by the scruff of the neck, reached down, and pulled the knife out of his groin. "May as well go big or go home." He lunged the knife, stabbing Beetle in the dick again.

An ear-piercing wail filled the room before the Sinner's body slumped, and he passed out from the pain.

My eyes slid to the last man standing.

He looked to be in his early sixties with long, grey hair and a scruffy beard. His blue eyes were wide with shock as he stared down at his VP.

"Are you into little girls, too?" I asked through gritted teeth.

He gave one firm shake of his head.

"But you don't care that your pervert brothers are? You sit there in the company of men who abuse little kids like it's just another day at the office." I nodded toward the table. "You were playin' cards with a fucker who punched an eight-year-old little girl in the face and another cunt who wanted her for evil, sick things."

The Sinner hung his head.

"Your choice, Kit," Dad muttered. "Kill him now or put him in the trunk, take him back, and hang him up like the pig he is. We can bleed him dry while he answers our questions."

My lip curled in repulsion as I took in the evil prick.

The thought of letting him live—even if only for a few days—made my insides twist with disgust.

My hand hovered over my gun, fingers itching to shoot his dick off. Sick bastards like him were better off neutered.

"How 'bout this, Break?" Atlas said. "We take him back, torture him. Then you can kill him any way you want."

I sucked in a shaky breath.

I'd lose the chance if I didn't kill him now. I'd saved Kady, but by doing so, I'd let the monster take over again. Being with Kennedy now could only be a dream 'cause I'd have to leave. There was no way I could be around my kids like this. What if I hurt Kitten again? What if I damaged my kids?

Pain seared through my insides. "Take him," I ordered quietly. "But when the time comes, make sure it hurts."

Dad held up the sack and walked toward me. "Let's blow this house of horrors."

I walked over to Beetle and lowered to my knees behind him. Taking my other knife from my back pocket, I tugged him by the hair and sunk my knife into his jugular.

His eyes snapped open, shocked, and he gargled as his life left him.

Silently moving to the fucker who grabbed my baby girl, I repeated the action, watching his eyes turn from fearful to lifeless.

My shoulders slumped as the monster retreated, suddenly sated.

I lifted my stare to Dad, who watched me with narrowed eyes.

"There's a body in the cellar and two more outside. Bring 'em all in here. They can burn in Hell together," I rasped.

"Where's Cash?" Dad asked.

"Keepin' Kady safe." I went to the burlap sack and rummaged through it. "When they've all been brought in, get to the car while I set this place to blow."

Over the next ten minutes, we'd piled the dead men together and doused the place with all the cheap whiskey we could find. There wasn't a stone left unturned. I even went down to the cellar and threw alcohol around there, too.

As I walked back up the stairs, I lit the rag hanging out the end of the glass bottle containing an inch of fuel

Breaker

and threw it into the room containing the bodies, waiting for the glow of the flames to burn bright.

I took a moment to revel in how the fire razed their flesh as they burned before I turned and walked away, making my way through the downstairs rooms to the back door.

As I exited, I turned and lobbed another Molotov cocktail into the kitchen, watching the hot flames lick up the walls before I turned and walked away.

The car waited for me, its engine already running.

I opened the door and slid into the backseat, staring blankly ahead.

Kady scrambled over, throwing her little arms around my neck before burying her face in my throat. "I love you, Daddy," she whispered, "I love you. I love you. I love you."

Tears sprang into my eyes. I'd never hear those words again after tonight.

The monster was back and stronger than ever. I could feel it devouring all the souls I'd taken that night. My gut twisted painfully because I knew I couldn't be around my family anymore.

It was already too late. I could feel the darkness taking over my heart again, but as much as it ached with sorrow, I knew I'd done the right thing. I'd sacrificed my soul for my family. They were the only specks of light in a world full of darkness, and I'd keep them shining brightly if it was the last thing I did.

I'd protect them and keep them safe. I'd always put them above me, every fucking time. No question. No doubt. But by doing so, I couldn't be the man they needed. I would never bring that darkness to their door.

I closed my eyes, the back of my skull falling onto the headrest as I inhaled the sweet scent of my daughter, silently saying goodbye because something was becoming apparent.

Kit Stone was lost again, maybe this time, forever.

Chapter Seventeen

Kennedy

I sat by the clubhouse window with Kai cuddled into me, fast asleep.

My beautiful boy hadn't left my side since Reno had sped us away from the house we'd lived in for the last several weeks.

I'd never seen Kai like this. He was traumatized by the loss of his baby sister.

The tension gripping my body was so sharp it ate at my flesh. I could hardly breathe. My mind kept conjuring images of my girl crying and calling for me.

Kady was so small, so sweet. I knew her spirit would break if anything dark happened to her. She was eight years old and had been snatched by evil men who trafficked little girls.

I felt like I'd been sliced in half.

A tear tracked down my cheek. All I could feel was the sharp ache in my soul and the nausea threatening to rise through my stomach. My skin felt too tight for my body like everything inside was pressurized and about to explode.

I startled slightly as I felt a warm hand gently grip my shoulder.

"She'll be okay, Ned," Sophie whispered. "They'll bring her back to you."

My eyes remained on the inky night sky. "What if they've already hurt her?" I choked out. "She's so tiny."

"She'll be fine."

My mouth twisted. "How do you know? It's been nearly three hours. They could have done anything."

Sophie's arms slid across my shoulders, her face resting on my head. "*If* Kady's hurt—and it's a big if—I'll heal her. I won't sleep until she's okay. We just need her back, Ned. We can deal with anything else."

A painful moan escaped me, the meaning behind her words sinking into my psyche.

If they'd touched her, I'd hunt them down one by one, and I'd cut their dicks off. I'd go to jail for the rest of my life—I didn't care—I'd happily spend every day of my life in prison just to avenge my little girl.

The echo of footsteps made me look up to see Cara, Layla, and Iris entering the bar.

The room was half full of men moving in and out from the parking lot, getting their bikes ready in case they got the call to ride out. It melted the iciness in my heart a little. I only knew most of these men in passing, so I appreciated their determination to fight for my Kady.

Layla sat on the opposite side of me and took my hand. "I understand you're worried, Kennedy, but I know these men. They won't rest until they've got her back. When I was taken, they weren't far behind. I trust they know what they're doing."

Iris sat opposite us with Cara, who gently rubbed her belly.

"Ned. I know you're a lawyer, so I'm gonna speak plainly," the older woman said. "Our men won't leave anyone alive. We may need you if the cops come calling."

I didn't hesitate. "Done. None of the Demons will go to jail. We'll give them all alibis."

Cara smiled sadly. "Do you understand the implications?"

"Yeah, Car," I snapped. "Probably better than you."

She nodded.

"They were here with us," Iris said quietly. "We stayed in the bar all night. Nobody could be bothered to drive home after the barbeque. Cara, around eleven, you had Braxton Hicks. We all thought you were going into labor, but they stopped after five minutes."

Sophie nodded.

"Got it." Cara smiled.

Layla squeezed my hand.

"It's my fault," I whispered. "I should've left town after what happened when we came out of the salon that day. I knew they'd marked my baby. I should've just taken them back to Vegas."

"No," Sophie argued. "Don't do that. The fault lies with the assholes who took her. Not you."

"I should've protected her better, Sophie," I rasped. "I shouldn't have let go of her hand. I made it easy for them."

"Stop!" Cara ordered gently. "It's not your fault. If they've marked her, who's to say they wouldn't have followed you back to Vegas? It would be easy enough to track you down. Think how much worse it would have been with no support. The guys will get her. Have faith."

I closed my eyes, trying to feel Kady's emotions.

Is she scared? Have they hurt her? Then, darker thoughts took over. *Have they done the unthinkable?*

Another tear tracked down my face.

I knew I should be positive, but Kady was my heart. If anything happened to her, it would destroy me. She was so sweet and kind; I knew this would affect her profoundly. I'd done everything I could to protect my children from the evil in the world. How could this have happened?

My ears pricked at the running feet echoing from the corridor leading to John's office.

Bowie and Abe were down there, waiting to hear from John. They'd mobilized the entire club. The men were ready to ride out for my baby.

Kai stirred, looking up at me, his eyes half-mast from sleep. "Kady's okay, Mom. She's with Dad."

My heart leaped into my throat as Bowie burst into the bar. "They've got her," he yelled. "She's okay. They're on their way back now. They'll be twenty minutes at most."

I sent up a prayer of thanks, my chest suddenly light as pure, unadulterated relief chased away the dark thoughts.

Snow had done it. He'd kept his promise.

A loud cheer filled the air, making Kai stir again. "She's fine, Mom," he said quietly through the noise. "Dad's sick, though."

My stomach tightened, heaviness forming inside it. "Bowie!" I called out. "Are the guys okay? Is Kit okay?"

He nodded. "Dad didn't say anyone was injured. Just said to make sure Soph is on standby to check Kady over." He walked toward our table, Abe by his side. "If there were any injuries, Dad would've said."

My gaze slid back to my son's golden eyes, so much like his father's, except Kai's were bright and full of life, a complete contrast to how Snow's had been a couple of hours before.

Cold fingers crept down my spine as realization washed over me.

Snow's PTSD had a hold of him. I saw it earlier and didn't give it a second thought. I was so intent on him bringing Kady to safety that it had flown from my mind. He'd only been out of rehab for days, and now this. It was no wonder he'd relapsed.

Kai sat up, wide awake, and looked up at me. "He'll be okay, Mom. He's got us now."

I nodded, unable to speak because of the tears heating my throat.

Kai was right. Snow *did* have us now.

Last time, I'd let him walk away from me without a backward glance. I knew he was sick, but I'd accepted it regardless. I'd let him take all the blame, but I knew he was stationed at Fort Campbell. I could've gone to him. If I had, maybe I would've learned his name, and the last nine years wouldn't have happened.

I sat straighter, mouth thinning into a determined line as I made a vow to myself.

Snow had sacrificed everything for our girl, and now we'd do the same for him. He had us, and we wouldn't let him fall again. He'd had our backs when it mattered most, and we'd have his. Bringing Kady back to me proved he was willing to put us first.

I motioned for Kai to get down.

His lips hitched. My boy knew me well enough to see I was about to go into mama bear mode.

"Layla," I barked. "Sunny's only a little smaller than Kady. Have you got a spare nightie or PJs she can borrow?

Layla smiled and nodded as she rose from the chair. "I'll go and fetch something now."

I turned to Cara. "Call Cash. Ask him what's going on with Kit. I should know what I'm dealing with."

Sophie's eyebrows drew together questioningly.

"His PTSD, Soph," I reminded her. "This will set him back."

Awareness washed over her face. "Shit." She went to stand. "I'll grab Freya. We'll hit the books. See if we can do anything to help him, at least until we can get him to his doctor."

"Wait, she's on coffee duty," Iris said, also getting to her feet. "I'll go and take over and send her to you."

"Thank you." I turned back to Bowie. "Where's his room?"

He pointed to a corridor across the bar. "Down there. Wait, you'll need a spare key." He turned on his heel and hurried back down the hall he'd just come from.

"It'll be okay this time, Ned," Sophie murmured reassuringly. "John and Cash have the tools to help him. He's got you, Kady, and Kai. He's in a much better position than before."

"Yeah, you're right." I rested a hand on her shoulder. "I saw it earlier, but I was so worried about Kady that I didn't give it a second thought. It was Kai. He reminded me Snow was sick. You know the bond he has with his sister."

"They do have a special way of communicating. I've heard many twins have a bond, like Kai and Kady. They're probably thinking up ways to try and help him already." She scoffed.

I rolled my eyes, letting Sophie think I was in on the joke, but her words—although spoken in jest—hit the mark.

My kids *did* have a close bond. Kai had protected Kady since he was a baby. I didn't dare to think it went so far that they could read each other's minds, but I knew they could pick up on each other's moods and feelings. I'd witnessed it myself.

The three of us had always looked after each other, not just in the physical sense but emotionally, too. Now, it was time to extend the net.

Snow had given up on all the hard work he'd put in over the last few months to do what needed to be done for Kady. Kai saw it, and so did I.

Last time, he couldn't see a way out, and it had almost destroyed him.

This time, he had us, and we wouldn't let it happen again.

"Gates are openin'," one of the guys called out as a buzz went up around the bar.

Bowie hurried back in. "Come on," he barked. "They're back."

"It'll be okay, "Sophie whispered, grabbing my hand and guiding me toward the door.

My stomach jerked at the thought of what I was about to deal with, not just with Kady but with her dad, too.

Headlights sliced through the darkness as the SUV drove slowly into the parking lot. My heart pounded as I waited for the men to pull up outside the clubhouse doors.

The windows were tinted black, so I couldn't see inside the car until the doors flew open and the men emerged. John opened the door behind the passenger seat to reveal Snow, sitting straight backed, blankly looking forward with Kady attached to his neck.

My heart jolted as I stepped up and reached inside for my daughter. "Hey, baby girl. Come to mommy. Let Daddy get out of the car, sweetheart."

She shook her head, burying her face in Snow's throat.

"Kady. Sophie needs to check you over." I reached in and tried to dislodge her from Snow, but she let out a squeal.

"No! I'm staying with my daddy!"

Slowly, Snow's face swiveled his head and locked eyes with mine.

An ache gripped my chest. I had to bite down hard on my lip to stop a moan from escaping.

Snow had aged ten years in the space of mere hours. His skin held a red tinge from all the blood coating him. He was different. It wasn't him. I mean, it was him, but he wasn't *my* Snow.

"I need to get Kady," I whispered.

His eyes blanked. "I won't hurt her,"

"It's cold," I insisted. "I need to get her into a shower to warm up."

He closed his eyes. "She's warm, Kitten. So fuckin' warm, it's amazin'. She should be freezin', but her heat's seeping into me. I can feel it."

I reached for my daughter again, but she screeched at the top of her lungs. "No! I'm staying with Daddy!"

Snow finally swung his legs out of the car. I watched, heart in mouth, as he slid an arm around Kady's back and exited the SUV. Kady hung from her daddy's neck like a little spider monkey. "I'll take her," he said robotically, starting for the clubhouse.

John stepped up beside me as we headed through the doors. "She won't let him go. We didn't want her all over Kit. He's covered in the blood of the men who nabbed her, but whenever we tried to separate 'em, she screamed the fuckin' car down."

I nodded, thoughts whirring through my brain. "Kady feels safe with her dad, John."

"I'd feel safe with him, too." He snorted. "He'd put three out of the six down before the rest of us even got there."

A thread of something akin to satisfaction warmed my stomach. "Good. I hope he made it hurt."

John jerked a nod. "He did, but it's put his recovery back."

"We've got him, John," I whispered, heading for the doors. "Kit's got us now."

Silence blanketed the bar as we entered the clubhouse.

Kai ran toward us as we headed for the corridor to the bedrooms. "Kady?"

"She's okay, Son," I assured him as we followed Snow and my girl. "Your Dad's got her safe."

Mutters and vows of retribution sounded quietly from the men, but they respected Kady, which I was glad for. She seemed so highly strung, holding her body rigid as she clung to her dad like she was clinging to life. I imagined any loud noises would set her off screaming again.

Layla was leaving one of the rooms. "I've left some stuff for Kady," she explained as we walked past her. "Let me know if you need anything else."

I nodded, squeezing her hand gratefully before closing the door softly and turning to take in Snow's room.

A king-size bed sat in the middle, its black leather headboard against the far wall with a nightstand positioned on each side. A wardrobe and dresser were placed behind the door, and a massive TV had been attached to the wall opposite the bed. An open door to the left of the room revealed an attached bathroom. The room was dark, cozy, and perfect for what we needed.

"Can you put Kady on the bed, Snow?" I asked gently. "You need a shower. You're covered in blood." I touched Kady's back, but she screamed so loudly I was taken aback.

"I'm not leaving Daddy," she cried, her little voice thick with tears. "I wanna shower, too."

"Kady," I whispered. "You can't shower with Daddy."

"I can," she sobbed. "I'm not leaving him."

"Snow," I murmured. "Help me out here." I reached up and gently turned his face toward mine, looking for any response, but he just stared blankly back at me.

"Okay, fine," I said as if to myself. "I'll get in, too." I turned to the bed where Kai sat watching us. "Go in your dad's wardrobe and find some clean tees. I'm gonna help them in the shower."

He nodded. "Okay."

Putting my hand on Snow's back, I guided him toward the bathroom. Honestly, I'd be glad to shower. My PJs stunk of smoke from the house fire, and now that Kady was home safe, I just wanted to wash the entire night away until I felt clean again.

I turned the shower on to warm up. "Okay, let's get you two undressed. Kady, let go of Daddy and lift your arms." I gently pulled my girl, tugging her sweater over her head before I took her little pink yoga pants off. "Leave your underwear on, baby."

"Thank you, Mommy." Kady twisted her face around slightly, and I froze.

Our sweet girl had a cut lip and a purple bruise on her jaw.

My heart plummeted.

I reached out and turned her face toward me. "Baby. Tell me. Did they touch you anywhere in your underwear?"

Her big blue eyes fixed on me, and she shook her head.

My shoulders sagged. The wave of relief flooding me was so powerful that it made me dizzy for a second. I pulled myself together and gently ran my fingers over the cut. "Does it hurt?"

"A bit," she replied, snuggling back into Snow's chest. "I cried when he did it."

"Oh, baby girl," I said huskily, trying to reassure Kady and myself. "Tell me what happened?"

"The man in the car," she mumbled, eyes drooping. "I told him my daddy would make him dead, and he got mad at me."

Tears stung my eyes.

Nobody had ever hit my kids before, not even me.

They didn't need that kind of discipline, and I loved them so much I couldn't even spank them when they were naughty.

My blood boiled when I thought about that evil pig taking his hand to my lovely daughter. How could he slap a tiny thing like her so hard that he left marks on her beautiful face?

"I'm so sorry, baby." A sob wrenched from my throat as tears started to fall. Again, I let out a strangled moan.

"He won't hurt anyone again, Kenny."

I jumped slightly, almost shocked that Snow had spoken.

My eyes lifted to see him staring at me, golden orbs so blank that they appeared like voids in his face. Still, I could see the truth in them, and a sense of satisfaction rolled through me when I imagined Snow taking the lives of all those sick men.

Reaching up, I touched his face. "Your turn." My hands slid down to ease his tee up and pull it over his head. He kicked his boots off while my hands went to his belt.

"Keep my jockey shorts on," he rasped. "Kady."

I pulled his jeans down, doing as he asked and leaving his shorts intact. His skin felt clammy and cold to the touch. I drew in a sharp breath at the sticky blood drying darker on his skin. It was much more noticeable now he'd taken off his tee.

"Get in and wash that blood off," I ordered, guiding him gently inside the glass cubicle.

Whipping my tee over my head, I slid my PJs down my thighs, taking my panties with them. Once I'd kicked them off, I unclipped my bra, dropping it on the pile of clothes on the floor.

Stepping into the shower, I turned my face up to catch some of the spray, getting my hair good and wet before reaching for the shower gel and squeezing some into my palm.

"There we go," I murmured, rubbing it into Snow's bloody skin, watching as rivulets of water ran pink down his body and circled the drain.

For the next thirty minutes, I washed Snow and Kady repeatedly. I scrubbed their hair several times, ensuring I cleaned every drop of blood and every piece of dirt away.

Snow stood tall, holding Kady, watching me as I spoke soothingly, whispering everything would be okay.

Finally, I lowered to scrub Snow's legs and feet.

Something made me look up as I ran the washcloth down his legs. I stilled, watching Snow's golden eyes glow as he looked down at me with a slight grin playing around his mouth, probably because of the proximity of my face to his soaked jockey shorts.

I rolled my eyes. "Trust that to get you back in the land of the living again." I giggled as a deep, throaty laugh rumbled through his chest.

Steadying my hand on Snow's thigh, I pulled myself up. I stifled a yawn before sponging Kit and Kady down one last time to ensure every speck of blood had washed away.

"You need to sleep," he murmured.

"We all do." I nodded to Kady, whose eyes were half-mast with drowsiness. "She's glued to you for the night now. Will you be okay with her?"

He glanced down, his eyes softening as he took in Kady's tired face. "Yeah. She's warmin' me up. I was freezin' not an hour ago. But the cold disappeared as soon as she jumped into my arms."

I turned the shower off, opened the door, and ushered them out. "Well, the sooner we get to bed, the sooner we can all warm up."

"Is her face okay?" he mumbled as my hand went to a pile of towels stacked on the bathroom cabinet.

I glanced at Kady to check her bruise out. "She seems fine. I'll watch her overnight and get Soph to look at it in the morning." I gently patted the excess water from my girl's hair. "I'll dry you off and get Kai to bring the clothes to the door."

"She's asleep, Kenny," Snow murmured.

I stepped over to take her from him, but she gave a low whine and clung harder.

Snow shrugged. "Sorry, baby, You'll have to change my shorts for me." He smirked. "Kady won't see anything; she's half asleep."

I ducked my head. "I know that, but what about me seeing it all? You don't seem bothered about that."

Snow gave a little shrug. "You'll just have to try and control yourself, Kennedy."

Ten minutes later, we were all nestled in Snow's bed together. Kady lay snugged into her dad, her face mushed into his throat. Kai was in the middle, next to Kady, while I was at the other end.

Me and Snow lay on our sides facing each other, whispering about the rescue. He'd just given me what I suspected was a censored account of everything that had happened.

"Your PTSD," I murmured. "You've relapsed."

"Yeah," he replied quietly. "I can feel it again. I had to be like that to do what I did, Kenny."

My throat heated. "I know."

He reached over and rested his hand on my hip. "I'm no good for them. Not like this."

"No," I breathed. "You're everything good for them, Kit Stone. Tonight proved it."

"It's gonna keep happening, Kenny. What if I hurt them or you again?"

The first tear tracked down my face. "Please don't leave us. You'll break our hearts. Go back to Grand Junction. Please, Kit, try again."

His eyes drooped. "I don't know if I can."

"Aren't we worth trying for?"

"You are," he admitted, his eyelids closing with exhaustion.

I lowered my gaze, hiding my expression as my racing thoughts made my brain feel like it was about to explode.

If he took off again, I'd be done with him.

I couldn't let it go again, and I certainly couldn't be the same way with him as I had been. I'd forgiven a lot because he'd explained why he left me and apologized for the fake name. Even the reasons behind the other women made sense. I could see how much he'd grown up over the years and how much he regretted what had happened every time he looked at me.

I hadn't realized until tonight, but regardless of all the heartache, he was still my golden boy.

When he brought Kady back to me, I just wanted to hug him and tell him how much I loved that he kept his word, but now he was threatening to leave again, and it hurt.

How could I trust him not to run when things got hard when it was all he kept doing?

I couldn't live my life walking on eggshells, waiting for the catalyst that would eventually cause him to take off. It wouldn't be fair on me or the kids.

Love wasn't enough when it came to Snow and I; our past complicated things.

At least I'd done the right thing by keeping my distance. I didn't want a man who threatened to leave when the going got tough.

I needed someone who'd stay.

My eyelids drooped, exhaustion taking over my body. My adrenaline spike had finally crashed, and I struggled to keep my eyes open.

The weight of Snow's hand still resting on my hip made me wonder something.

Would it still be there when I woke up, or would it, and him, be gone?

Chapter Eighteen

Breaker

Usually, when I woke up and my skin burned, it was because I'd dreamed about Benny being burned alive in the Humvee on the road just outside Kabul.

My heart would race out of my chest so fast it was painful, and Benny would be in my head screaming, *Save her, Snow!*

When I'd dropped off to sleep the night before, I told myself it was dangerous to stay in bed with Kitten and the twins, especially after I'd killed those men just hours before. But God help me, I was so fucking tired, I couldn't move.

Heat enveloped my chest, but strangely, I noticed nowhere else.

I cracked one eye open and nearly jumped out of my skin when confronted with beautiful cornflower blues an inch away from mine.

"Morning, Daddy," Kady whispered.

I brought my arm up to cuddle her close. "Morning, Kady girl. How do you feel, sweetheart?"

She pulled back slightly, gently patting my face. "I'm okay. My face doesn't hurt anymore, but it feels hot." She cocked her head to one side. "The thunder's all gone from your head."

I froze. Jesus, she was right. My head was clearer than it had been for, well, years. I felt lighter like I'd lost fifty pounds. It was weird because, despite last night, everything seemed even brighter than when I left Grand Junction a few days ago. Even after my treatment, the beast was still inside. I was back in control, but he was underneath it all, waiting to burst free. Now, I couldn't feel the demon at all. All I felt was... me.

My eyes caught on Kai, who'd snuggled into his mom before my gaze lifted, resting on the love of my life.

It was weird how I'd been dead set on leaving last night but this morning had no desire to jet at all. The thought of leaving the other half of me and my babies made me feel sick.

I took in my woman's white-blonde mane fanning out over the pillow, resisting the urge to stroke it. Just like before, her soft pink lips pouted slightly as she slept. I grinned because I remembered how the young, dedicated soldier I'd been ten years ago could never resist kissing her awake. My appraising stare dropped to her chest, where I could see her firm high tits move as she breathed deeply.

I closed my eyes, willing my hard-on to deflate.

My woman looked so beautiful when she slept. It was uncanny how much she resembled the girl I'd fallen in love with ten years before. My dark, blackened heart slowly unfurled, and my newly forged soul thudded back to life.

My mind returned to the night before and how Kitten looked after Kady and me.

She'd washed my enemies' blood from my skin with such reverence it made my breath catch. The girl she used to be was still there and still good to me.

Kady giggled quietly, wriggling her body until she almost laid on me. "I'm hungry, Daddy."

My eyes rested on her lip, which seemed to have healed better than the purple bruise spreading down her face. My jaw clenched. I wished I could bring those sick fuckers back to life to kill them all over again. They'd frightened my baby girl. If there was a God, I hoped he'd ensure they burned in Hell.

"Let's go see Sophie," I suggested. "I want her to check out your bruise. Then we'll bring breakfast back for everyone."

"Can I have bacon?" she asked eagerly.

I pulled the comforter back and swung my legs over the side of the bed. "You can have anything you want, Kady girl."

She stood on the bed and held her hands out, waiting for me to carry her. "I like you hugging me," she whispered. "I feel safer."

I held her against my chest, and we padded across the room, opening the door and clicking it quietly shut behind us.

"Kai likes bacon too," Kady informed me, chattering away without a care in the world as we walked down the corridor and into the bar.

I marveled at how unaffected she was. Just hours ago, she'd been taken by strangers and locked in a basement.

I assumed she'd clung to me for hours because she was too scared to let go. She'd been through a traumatic ordeal, but now she was chatting and giggling like nothing had happened. Uneasiness stirred in my gut at the way Kady seemed so unfazed.

I noticed the bar was more or less empty when we walked in, which was good because I didn't want Kady overwhelmed. Just Dad, Atlas, and Sophie sat at a table drinking coffee.

When Sophie looked up and saw my girl's face, a hand flew to her mouth. "Oh, Kady!" she exclaimed, rising to her feet and rushing over. "Does it hurt?"

My brave daughter shook her head and snuggled into me.

Sophie ran her fingers across Kady's face and jaw. "Does your head hurt?" she asked.

Kady shook her head again.

"There are no breaks or fractures," Sophie murmured, fingers still prodding gently. "I don't think there's any lasting damage, but maybe we should take you to the hospital and arrange a CT scan."

"We should buy one'a them scanner things for your medical wing," Dad suggested. "Want me to put it on your list?"

Sophie turned to face him. "It'll cost a fortune."

Pop rose from his seat, eyeing Kady's bruised face. "I don't care. It'll be worth every dime. There's no point you havin' a medical wing if you haven't got the right equipment. Put it on the list." His stare slid to me. "We're on lockdown. Billy's goin' over to the mall later. Get your woman to give him a list of everythin' she needs for her and the kids for the next week."

"She can wear my shit," I muttered, almost wanting to beat my chest like a fucking gorilla at the thought of Kitten ensconced in my stuff while she was here.

Atlas threw his head back and laughed. "You got a collection of panties back there, Break?" He chuckled. "A few bras?" He shook his head. "I can tell you're gettin' all possessive, especially after last night. But Blondie can't walk around the clubhouse in your tees, asshole. The boys will think Christmas has come early."

My gut hardened at the thought of my brothers getting an eyeful. "Okay. I'll sort it, but Kennedy and Kai are still asleep, and I want to leave 'em that way. It was a long night."

Dad regarded me thoughtfully. "We need to talk about that."

Sophie's eyes flicked to all of us before settling on Kady. "Wanna come in the kitchen with me to see what Iris has cooked up?"

Kady's gaze snapped to mine, but I smiled reassuringly. "Go get breakfast and ask Iris to make up a tray for Mom and Kai. I'll be in soon; I need to speak to Grandpa and Atlas."

Gently, I placed her on the floor and watched as Sophie took her hand and led her down the hall toward the kitchen.

"She seems okay," Dad mused.

"Yeah," I agreed. "Kady's unaffected. I'm frightened she's holding it all in, and it'll manifest later. Or maybe she'll have a colossal meltdown."

"If she does, we'll deal, Son," Dad assured me. "All we can do is allow her time to process it her own way. If it comes back to haunt us, we'll handle it then." His hand rested on my shoulder, and he turned me to face him. "You lost your shit last night, Son."

I shrugged. "I'd do it all over again if I had to."

Pop glanced at Atlas, who cocked an eyebrow as they communicated secretly. "You need to go to Rock Springs for a group therapy session. I'll come with."

"Not leavin' the kids," I announced. "I'll happily talk to you and Cash, but I feel okay."

"You lost your head last night, Break," Atlas said quietly. "We were worried you'd relapsed."

I understood what they were saying. Last night, I would've even agreed with them. I remembered telling Kitty I was gonna walk this morning, and I'd meant it. But since I'd woken up, something inside me had shifted. It felt amazing.

"It's hard to explain. I don't want you thinkin' I'm coverin' up or lyin' so I can stay, but I don't think I need it. Last night, when those fuckers took Kady, I reverted to soldier mode and acted exactly like I used to when I first developed PTSD. Today though, I feel better than I have in years. I dunno what happened, but my head straightened itself out overnight, and not just like it did at Grand Junction. It's more than that. I feel happy, like a weight of bullshit's been lifted off me. Don't ask me to explain it 'cause I can't. I just need you to believe me."

Dad looked closely into my eyes. "Yeah. I can see it," he agreed.

"You do seem bright as a button," Atlas announced.

"I feel the way I used to. Before Afghanistan." I explained. "Like I haven't got a care in the world. I'm not even fazed by the Sinners, at least not after last night. Beetle was the VP, but he had no skills apart from being a sick cunt. It proves they're not a threat to us. We've got more war knowledge in our pinkies than those fuckers. I don't wanna leave Kady, so how about you guys keep a close eye on me for a few days while we work out how big the threat is. When it's safe, I'll go to Rock Springs and talk to Steve."

"We can do that. "Dad clapped me on the shoulder. "You seem good, Kit. Me and Cash are here if you need us, and we'll play it by ear."

Atlas studied me for a minute before giving Dad a slight nod.

"Okay," Pop turned to me. "It's a plan. Now, at the fear of comin' across like a fucknut, I gotta remind ya, we've got the remaining Sinner from last night locked down in the Cell."

"What about Piston?" I asked.

"He's gone. We gave him some green and an old vehicle. He's left to find his wife and girls. The fucker's been lookin' for a way out of the Sinners for years. He became disillusioned when Bear started trafficking, and Slash never took him in hand. The problem is, the Sinners aren't a club you can leave and still be allowed to breathe. They'll think we killed him. We'll hint at the fact, too. He's got a second chance now."

"Are you sure we can trust him?" I asked.

Dad regarded me thoughtfully. "What do you think?"

My mind returned to the night I blew up the Sinner's clubhouse and caught Piston. It was an easy job, maybe too easy. I was good at what I did, but Piston never tried to fight back. Maybe he wanted to get caught. I suspected it'd been his way of getting out of the Sinners.

"He definitely wanted to get nabbed," I said. "But there could be two reasons. Either he wanted out, or he wanted to fool us that he wanted out."

Dad brought a hand up to stroke his beard. "Time will tell, I guess."

I walked over to the table and sat next to Atlas. "Where's Bowie?"

"At the auto shop," Dad confirmed, sitting opposite. "We've pulled half the construction crew to start rebuilding the rentals, so profit will be down. Bowie's gonna work all hours tryin' to bring some scratch in. Cash and Colt are checkin' out the stock market as we speak. Your brother reckons he can make a few hundred thou' to tide us over. It's come at the wrong time, especially since we're negotiating a fuck load of medical equipment for Sophie."

My mind went to my bulging savings account. "I still have Bandit's inheritance if you want it, Pop. Cash played around with it while I was in the military. It's four times bigger than it was."

He stiffened. "How the fuck do you have all that still?"

"I don't really spend money," I explained. "I only bought Veronica. Living here gave me free digs. I don't buy myself much. I live on my cut from the club earnings and my military pension. It's plenty."

Dad shot me a grateful smile. "I may take some, but I'll pay it back with the interest you'll lose. Lemme see what Cash can make us over the next few days first."

"How about I buy a plot down by the creek?" I suggested. "That'll give you some more green for Cash to play with."

"You can by all means, but I'm only chargin' thirty K for those plots," he replied. "There's forty down there.

Take your pick. Cash, Bowie, and Atlas have two each picked out. I want one. Freya, too."

"I'll buy three for Ned and the kids and build a house for them now. Then another four. Two each for Kady and Kai to build houses when they're older."

Dad whooped. "Seven plots makes me two hundred and ten thousand, which I can give to Cash."

"How about I transfer the full amount?" I offered. "I can always pay more lieu of the construction team workin' on the build if needed."

"I can do that too, Prez," Atlas said. "And I'm sure Cash and Bowie would if you asked."

Dad's eyes squinted while he thought. "That would work. It'll give me a decent chunk. If Cash can double it, I'd be able to pay everyone's salaries for the next few months while we rebuild. I can put some of the crew on building the houses for you guys, then swap 'em out when we need different skills."

"Maybe we should do a recruitment drive," I suggested. "Another ten or twenty workers. They could work outside jobs while the most trusted men work for the club. There'll be enough in the pot, surely."

Dad nodded in agreement. "I didn't wanna dip into the club's savings but fuck it. It's there for times like this." He pulled his cell from his pocket, stabbed the call button, and held it to his ear. "Colt! You and Cash. Bar. Now!"

The door opened, and Bowie walked in from the parking lot, wiping grease from his hands with a rag.

"Good timing, Bo," Dad crowed, clicking his cell phone off. "Your brother's had a genius idea, and I wanna run it by ya."

Bowie tucked the rag back into his jeans pocket on his approach. "My head's spinnin' with all this talk. You wouldn't even speak to him a few months ago. Cash was the prince. I was the duke, and Kit was the court jester. Now it 'all hail King Kit' and me and Cash are the fuckin' peasants sittin' out in the cold." He pulled a chair out and sat down.

Dad's lips flattened into a thin line. "Instead of sitting here whinin', why don't you spend your efforts knockin' Layla up? You still owe me a set of twins, remember."

Bowie glared at Dad. "If I use my dick much more, I'll be walkin' like John Wayne."

I chuckled.

Atlas threw his head back, roaring with laughter. "Walking like John Wayne? What the fuck's that supposed to mean?"

"I'd be walkin' bow-legged," Bowie muttered. "Like a fuckin' cowboy who's been in the saddle too long."

Atlas slapped his thigh and hooted.

Dad shook his head disgustedly. "The firstborn's a fuckin' stealther, the second's an idiot. The third born's gettin' better, but he's a man in his thirties who still likes playin' with fire. Thank God for Freya."

Me and Bowie chuckled at Dad's mutterings.

"I thought Kit was your new favorite," Bo challenged.

Dad's lips twitched. "He is, and he'll stay that way until one of you other fuckwits gives me twins. His head's straight now, so it's time he took the same shit I give you and Cash."

Bowie rolled his eyes—though I noticed he did it when Dad wasn't looking. "Got plans for tonight?" he asked me.

"We're on lockdown," I reminded him.

"I already spoke to Dad, and he cleared it. Wanna make a date to tail Brett Stafford?"

"I'm in," Atlas interjected.

Bowie grimaced. "No fuckin way. Shit hits the fan every time you do a stakeout. This is a watch-and-learn mission. You're more into car chases and shootin' a fucker."

The SAA grinned, holding his fingers up in a V shape. "Boy Scout's oath. I shall do no harm."

The corner of my mouth hitched. "First, that's the Vulcan sign for 'live long and prosper.' Second, if you were a Boy Scout, I was Miss America. Third, I'm sure 'do no harm' is a line in the doctors' oath."

Atlas made a sad face. "Promise. I'll be a good boy."

Dad pursed his lips. "Just take him, will ya? He'll be a fuckin' nightmare if he misses out."

Bowie shook his head, obviously pissed.

"At least it'll be interesting," I muttered. "Dad. Do you need me here while you tell the others your plan?"

"Nah." He nodded toward the kitchen. "Go see to your girl."

Kady appeared at the doorway with Iris and Sophie as if I'd summoned her. "Daddy," she called. "Iris made breakfast for us all."

I saw Iris holding a tray of orange juice, bacon, eggs, and pancakes. "Thanks, Ris." Walking over, I took the tray and leaned down to kiss her cheek. "This'll do the job."

She cupped my cheek. "Heard about last night," she whispered. "Good job, Kit."

Heart melting, I winked at her before turning for the bedroom corridor. "Did you eat, Kadence?" I asked my daughter.

"No. I want to eat with you, Kai, and Mo—" She let out a little squeak as the door flew open, and Kennedy ran into the hallway. She saw us and immediately rushed over. "Kady!" she exclaimed, taking our girl in her arms. "I woke up, and you weren't there."

"I went with Daddy to get breakfast," she explained as her mother hugged her a little too tightly. "It's okay, Mommy," she assured her.

Kitten looked up at me accusingly. "I was worried sick." Her eyes dropped to the tray, and she did a double take. "Ooh! Bacon."

I laughed. "Move it inside, beautiful. The sooner you sit down, the sooner we can fill up that sexy little belly of yours."

She stood straight and cocked her head. "I thought you were taking off again?"

"Nah," I drawled. "You ain't gettin' rid of me that easily."

She took Kady's hand and led her inside the room. "Did you hear that, honey? You can be my witness when I take Daddy to court for abandonment."

Kady giggled.

I walked into my room, kicking the door shut behind me. "Breakfast, Kai!" I called out.

After a few seconds, I heard the toilet flush. The bathroom door cracked open, and Kai peered through it. "Just washin' my hands."

Kitten and Kady sat on the bed. "Are you okay today, honey?" Kennedy asked, stroking a hand down her face."

Kady nodded and sipped the juice I'd just poured her.

My woman's eyes slid to me. "How are you?"

A slow grin spread across my face. "Good. In fact, I woke up feelin' better than I have in years. I was tellin' Dad and Atlas, it's like I've got a new lease of life."

"Last night, you were in a trance. Like before... you know?" She looked at me pointedly, obviously not wanting to say too much in front of our daughter. "You told me you were going to—" She cut herself off again, not wanting to let the kids know what I'd said.

My heart grew to double its size, full of love for the beautiful woman before me.

That tiny action proved what an incredible mom Kitten was. She could've easily spoke out about the shit I'd said when I was in a stupor, but she was better than that. She was probably in her feelings about what I told her last night, but she'd never voice it in front of the kids because it would make me look bad, and she didn't want that.

I didn't deserve her, but for some reason, God saw fit to make her mine. It was about time I stopped fucking around and showed her.

My stare fell to her nipples—pointing through the soft cotton of my tee—and my cock stirred.

Seeing her wearing my clothes threw up feelings of possession and ownership I'd never experienced before. If the kids weren't here, I'd have dragged her across the bed, cocked her thighs open, and said thank you in a way she'd never forget.

My heart bloomed for the time in years as I watched Kai leave the bathroom and join us on the bed. He glanced at his mom. "You're in a good mood this morning."

Kitten laughed. "Sorry, Son. Did I disappoint you?"

I nudged Kai. "Your mom's a morning person."

He grabbed a pancake and bit into it, looking at me like I'd lost the plot.

My gaze turned to Kitten inquisitively. "Aren't you?"

She winced. "I guess I was back then. All I had to do was work and study. But since I had the twins, I'm less of a 'morning person,'" she raised her fingers to motion speech marks, "and more of a 'don't talk to me until I've had three cups of coffee kinda girl.'"

Kady popped a piece of bacon in her mouth. "I like mornings. A new day means new adventures."

My lips twitched. "That's nice, Kadence." I leaned forward, looking between my kids. "Do you know, the first night I met your mom, we talked for hours. Then we went up Lone Mountain to watch the sun come up. It was the best night of my life."

Kennedy stiffened.

"I'd never met a woman more beautiful," I continued. "Not just her face, but also her soul. Even though we'd only known each other a few hours, it felt like she'd been mine a thousand times over in every life we'd ever lived. I fell in love with her that night. Then, after watching the sunrise, she took me to get coffee and breakfast and introduced me to her friends. She knew a homeless guy called Ed. She took him and his friend Paulie food and medication. I remember thinking how I'd never known anyone kinder and more caring. She was perfect." I raised my eyes to her and murmured, "She still is."

Tears sprung to her eyes, and she smiled sadly. "Paulie died. He got pneumonia. They found his body at the back of the alleyway when they tore the strip mall down. Martha's mom passed too. She wrote me in law school. After the strip mall was bought out, they couldn't afford to reopen the bakery somewhere else. Last I heard, she'd moved to Ohio to be with family and bakes wedding and birthday cakes from her kitchen."

My gut stirred guiltily as I took her hand, entwining our fingers. "I'm so sorry, baby. I should've done more. What happened to Ed?"

Her eyebrows drew together. "I don't know. I went off to law school and lost touch. Maybe, when Paulie died, he didn't feel he had anyone left. He could be dead, too, for all I know. I felt so bad for leaving them, Snow, but Ed told me I had to go. He said he was happy for me and promised to stay in touch, but he didn't. If I knew it was the last time I'd see him, I'd never have let him go. Some nights I lay awake wondering if he's okay. I'd give up anything to know he's okay. I miss him so much."

Kady scooted across the bed and cuddled into her. "Don't be sad, Mommy."

Kennedy looked down at our girl, smiling. "How do you always make me feel better? I wanted to cry a few seconds ago, then you hugged me, and I'm instantly happy."

My chest panged.

I knew losing Ed would have been a blow for Kitten.

He was a good guy, a veteran who, just like me, was affected by war. In a different life, I could've ended up on the streets. When I first popped smoke, I'd roamed the country, unable to stay in one place. My saving grace was that I had money in the bank, whereas Ed probably didn't.

So many men and women lost everything because they were let down by the same country they gave everything to. It got me thinking. Was there something I could do?

An idea began to form in my head.

The Speed Demons owned businesses and were always looking for workers. Most military men came out with skills that, with a bit of training, could be useful to the club. We had empty properties and could easily buy—or even build—more.

At Grand Junction, I came into contact with men who needed help finding work. Maybe I could speak to Nina and set up some kind of program where patients could come here after their rehabilitation. If anyone could understand them, it would be the brothers. Most of them were ex-military.

It was perfect.

My gaze went to Kennedy, who was in the process of telling Kai and Kady about Ed.

She lit up from the inside when she spoke about her old friend. Her eyes shone with tears as she reminisced about him and Paulie and how bad she felt about their situation. She must've spoken to the twins about social issues such as homelessness because they seemed informed on the subject and the nuances that caused families to lose their homes.

I stilled as another idea pinged.

Pulling my cell out, I texted Colt before getting to my feet.

"Where are you going?" Kitten asked.

I bent down and kissed Kady's head before giving Kai a fist bump. "Gotta go talk to Dad about somethin'."

"What about breakfast?" she called out as I approached the door.

I craned my neck. "Sorry, baby." I grinned, taking in how fucking gorgeous she looked with her hair messy and no make-up. If I could pull this off, it would go a long way in getting my woman back. "Make a list up of shit you need. Billy's goin' to the mall for us later. I'll be back in thirty. Just gotta go sort something out."

I swung the door open and swept through like I was walking on air.

Dad was right; I was a genius. If I could pull my ideas off, it would prove to Kenny how much I loved her and wanted her to be happy.

It was time to start my new mission.

Operation get Kennedy back.

Chapter Nineteen

Kennedy

A sense of melancholy swept through me as I sat at my desk, watching Kady draw in her coloring book. I'd been on edge, even though the week since she'd been taken had been uneventful.

Somehow, Kit and the other guys discovered the sickos who took Kady definitely acted alone. It wasn't an order from the Sinners' Prez, so it meant my girl wasn't marked anymore.

Lockdown ended, but we'd stayed in Kit's room at the clubhouse.

We didn't have much choice seeing as the club's rentals were being rebuilt and weren't ready for occupancy. Kit pulled a couple of air mattresses in for the kids so I could get a good night's sleep. Sometimes, I woke up with him beside me, though it wasn't often, and he never touched me once.

Since the night he rescued Kady, I'd looked at Snow from through different eyes.

I was under no illusion he'd killed every man who dared touch our girl, and as much as I should have abhorred the idea, I didn't. If anything, I loved the lengths he was prepared to go to protect us. I knew what he'd done was a touch psycho, and should've made me run for the hills, but it'd had the opposite effect.

Snow made it clear he wanted us to try again, and a part of me wanted that too, but his words that night hurt me.

It seemed that whenever he reverted to the soldier he used to be, he used it as an excuse to leave. It was like I'd already said to him, he'd never fought for me. I couldn't risk being hurt again. I was never the same after he left me last time. How could I jump in feet first when he threatened to do it again?

I loved him, I always had, but in our case, love didn't heal all wounds. Snow still had a lot of work to do, and until he could show me he'd stick around when things got tough, I couldn't risk it. His threats to leave made me skittish.

However, since that night, Snow started doing something I hadn't seen him do for years.

He laughed.

Years ago, when he'd stayed with me on leave, laugh was all we did. Whether it was watching Game of Thrones, cooking, or just talking, we did it joyfully.

Throughout our relationship, the PTSD, and the responsibilities, fun had fallen by the wayside. But lately, he'd reverted back to that person. Any worries about what kind of father he'd be seemed silly now. He'd turned into the Martha Stewart of bikers. He wrangled the kids when I needed to come to the office. He made sure they were fed and kept them amused. I never needed to worry about their care because they had it in abundance at the club.

The more time I spent with him, the more complicated things got. It was even more complex because he reminded me so much of the man I loved.

Snow was quick to smile and looked at me with so much emotion, sometimes my breath caught in my throat.

It was like he'd gone to sleep a broken man and woken up whole again.

I wracked my brain, trying to determine how such a change occurred. Then it came to me. The night he rescued Kady from the Sinners, she wouldn't let him go.

Kit told me how warm she made him.

The way Kady clung to him that night made me wonder if she knew he was sick again, and in her way, tried to help. She had a sixth sense; Kai experienced it, and so had I, so why was it so far-fetched that she'd infected her daddy with all her goodness?

My girl was small and loving and had a way about her I couldn't explain, but to heal Snow so wholly when he'd battled PTSD for years seemed impossible.

Didn't it?

As a lawyer, I liked getting down to the bare bones of the truth. It was in my blood, and I was well known for sniffing out a lie with one look. I couldn't put my finger on it, but a lot about that night seemed... off. I didn't just mean with Snow—though that was weird enough—but also with Kady herself.

I'd been trying to talk to my girl all week about her ordeal. But she kept saying that she wasn't scared because she knew her Daddy would come for her. I'd tried to delve deeper, but she always changed the subject. Kady was so matter-of-fact that I should've been grateful it hadn't left her traumatized, but I couldn't help the niggling feeling in my stomach telling me there was more to it.

"Kady," I said gently.

She put her crayon down and looked at me.

"Why weren't you scared when the bad men took you?"

She shrugged and picked her crayon up again, returning to her drawing. "I was okay," she whispered.

I cupped her hand with mine. "Kady. Put the crayon down."

She obeyed but kept her eyes lowered.

"I'm happy you weren't frightened, honey, but you screamed when the man carried you off. Then he put you in a strange car and hit your face. Why weren't you scared?"

She lowered her eyes again and whispered something that sent a cold shiver down my spine. "I promised I wouldn't tell you."

Stomach sinking, I grabbed her hand and pulled her from her chair onto my lap. Taking her face in my hands, I turned it up and made her look me dead in the eyes. "Baby. Whatever happened, you can tell me. I know you shouldn't break promises, but I'm your mom, and it's my job to know everything about you. The man, did he touch you and make you promise not to tell me or Daddy?"

She shook her head. "No. He was a nice man. He was in the room they took me to and said not to be scared and that Daddy was on his way to get me."

My face scrunched up curiously. "He helped you?"

She wriggled uncomfortably in my lap, nodding.

"Can you describe him?" I asked, trying to tamp down the swirling sensation in my stomach. "What did he look like?"

Kady thought for a minute. "I was shaking, and he told me not to cry. His hair was black, and he wore a tee like Kai's G.I. Joe."

My head jerked with surprise.

"The man said not to worry because Daddy was on his way with Grandpa to get me. He hugged me and made me warm again, but it was the same way you and Daddy hug me. I didn't feel weird about it. He was my friend."

My hands slid across her shoulders. "Kady, he shouldn't have told you to keep secrets from me or Daddy. I'm glad you weren't scared, honey, and I appreciate him staying with you, but you should've told us about him sooner." There was a sharpness to my tone, which I'd never used with Kady before. But she'd never kept anything important from me, either.

Without thinking, I reached for my cell phone, clicked on Snow's name, and held it to my ear.

After one ring, he answered with a low, "Hey, baby."

Ignoring the heat licking between my thighs, totally evoked by his voice, I murmured, "Kady said there was someone in the room with her."

"Huh?"

"The room they kept her in. Kady said a man wearing some kind of security uniform was there. He made her feel safe and hugged her until she warmed up."

Silence reigned for a minute until Snow asked, "Security uniform?"

"Yeah," I replied, heart beating out of my chest. "A guy in some kind of combat tee reassured her that you were on your way."

After several seconds, Kit barked, "Are you still at the office?"

"Yeah. I—"

"Are the doors locked?"

"Of course," I replied. "But Sno—"

"I'll be there in ten," he snapped. "Don't move."

I was in the process of gathering my things together when my cell phone beeped.

SNOW: Out front

"Daddy's here, Kady." Grabbing her hand, we swept out of the office and down the stairs.

She looked up at me, eyes wide. "I'm sorry I didn't tell you. I don't want Daddy to be mad. The man was nice. He didn't hurt me."

I slipped the keys out of my pocket and unlocked the door. "Daddy's not mad, Kadence; I am. You should never keep important things from me." I pushed the door open to see Snow waiting patiently.

Immediately, he opened his arms for Kady to jump into and walked us to the SUV.

"What about my car?" I asked.

"The boys will pick it up." He opened the back door and strapped Kady into her booster seat. After he clicked her in securely, he took my arm, guiding me to the front passenger side, and helped me in.

"Snow, come on. I can do it," I protested, watching him pull my seat belt across my chest and secure it.

Our eyes locked. "Precious cargo," Kit murmured before dragging his eyes away from mine, standing straight and swinging the door closed.

I watched as he sauntered around the hood to the driver's side.

Today was a faded blue Levi's day, and I took a minute to admire how they hugged Snow's fine ass as he made his way around the car. His Under Armour tee clung so tightly to his torso, I could see the outline of his abs and the bulge of his biceps rippling as he walked.

Not for the first time in the past week, he made my pussy tingle.

Since the night of the fire, I'd been drawn to him more than ever. There was just something so fucking hot about a man who protected his own like a boss. I knew it set feminism back by about a hundred years, but the fact he was so goddamned strong and capable made me wetter than a rainforest in March. Add on the fact he had a face like a goddamned Ralph Lauren model, and I was completely fucked.

Or not, because unfortunately, he hadn't even tried to touch me, and I didn't know whether to feel good or pissed about it.

Breaker

Snow and I had a long way to go before we jumped back into bed.

We weren't together, and I'd never been a fuck buddy kinda girl, but it would've been nice if he tried. In fact, I was starting to feel quite affronted that he hadn't.

Why didn't he want to fuck me? I was hot, damnit!

Back in the day, men used to go crazy for me. I still got asked out a lot, so I knew I hadn't lost my juju. You'd never know it, though, seeing as Snow treated me like I imagined he'd treat a sister.

I folded my arms across my chest with a huff just as Snow jumped into the driver's seat.

He glanced at me, frowning. "What's got you so pissed?"

My lips pursed. "Nothing."

His eyebrows drew even closer together. "Right. Okay." He switched the engine on, checked the mirrors, and pulled out of the parking space. "Kady. Why's your mom annoyed?"

"I think she's mad with me for not telling you about the man," she said quietly.

"No, baby." I twisted around in my seat to look at her. "I'm not mad at *you*."

Snow glanced at me curiously. "What did I do?"

I turned my face forward, my mouth setting in an angry line. "It's what you didn't do," I muttered.

His face twisted as he tried to figure out what I was talking about. "Kitten. Stop talking in riddles. What didn't I do?"

"Forget it." I huffed.

He scraped a hand down his face. "Jesus, fuck. I'm on a time-out for something I *didn't* do. Great!" After a frustrated grunt, Snow concentrated on the road, and silence fell over the car.

I knew I wasn't being fair to him, though honestly, I was also confusing myself.

Since he'd walked into the club that night with Kady in his arms, like a hot, sexy, avenging soldier, I'd started to think up dirty little fantasies in my head. Showering with him hadn't helped. Although he wore his shorts, I could tell his cock was hard.

Lately, he'd been reminding me more of the Snow I'd fallen in love with. He smiled, joked, and gave me shit. But the new Snow also brought a quality of strength to the table that appealed to me a lot.

I was a ballsy girl, and I liked getting my own way. So, I needed a strong man to put me in my place. Of course, I wanted kindness and a hot butt I could sink my teeth into, but I also needed someone strong enough to stand up to me. I didn't want a guy I could push around. I'd get bored.

Maybe it wasn't the most politically correct thing for a modern girl to admit, but I liked a bit of monster in my man.

It seemed that Snow was the perfect guy for me, but I couldn't trust him not to disappear when the going got tough. He'd done it once and threatened it again since, so he didn't exactly inspire me with confidence. He'd almost broken me the last time he'd done it, so protecting my heart was paramount.

I was so deep in my thoughts that I didn't even notice we were already at the club. I watched the gates open, and we drove through them.

As Snow turned the engine off, I went to get out, but he pushed me back into my seat. "Kady." He craned his neck to address our girl. "Stay on club grounds. Okay?"

She hung her head and nodded.

"I won't say this in front of anyone else, Kady," he continued. "But you can't keep things like that secret from me or Mom, you know that, right?"

She nodded sadly. "I'm sorry."

"When it comes to you, your brother, and your mom, there are no secrets, sweetheart. I need to know everything if I'm gonna keep you safe. Never lie to me again, okay?"

Head still dipped, she nodded.

"Now, gimme a hug," he demanded gently.

Her head shot up, a smile flashing across her face. Standing, she awkwardly gave him a one-armed hug.

"Thank you," he murmured in her ear. "Now go inside. I need to speak to Mom for a second."

She stepped back and jumped out of the car, slamming the door behind her.

He watched our girl run inside the clubhouse. "What the fuck did I do, Kitten?"

"Nothing." I pouted.

He turned to face me and cocked an eyebrow. "So why are you giving me shit?"

I looked him up and down and huffed again.

"Carry on, and I'll tan that ass?" he said, a thread of warning in his tone.

I rolled my eyes. "I'm surprised you can bring yourself to touch me. It's obvious I don't float your boat these days."

His face twisted. "What the fuck's that supposed to mean?"

I folded my arms across my chest again, staring out the windshield.

He heaved out a breath. "Kitten. I want you more than I've ever wanted anyone. And it's not just because you look like a walking wet dream. Baby, everything about you knocks me on my ass."

My head swiveled to face him. "You talk utter shit, Jon Snow."

"Kennedy," he murmured, a slow grin spreading across his face. "The next time I touch you, it's gonna be because I'm yours, and you're mine. I know you're not there yet." He reached out, cupping my cheek. "Every time I look at you, I wanna cry. I love you, but you don't feel the same way."

My heart fluttered as he stared deep into my eyes.

"Next time I touch you, it'll be because you'll fuckin' die if you don't feel my hands on you. I warn you, Kennedy, the next time I touch you, I'll never stop. I'll touch you because it's forever." His brow puckered. "I did stupid shit in the past to hurt myself, but it'll never be like that with you." He pressed my hand to his heart. "You're in there. I feel you, and if I touched you and you rejected me afterward, I wouldn't survive."

The emotion in his eyes touched my soul, just like he did when we talked the night away in a Las Vegas diner. He was right. It would never be just sex with us. It would always be something profound. And honestly, if we did sleep together and I rejected him afterward, my heart wouldn't survive either.

"Are you there yet, Kenny?" he asked. "Do you wanna wake up with me every morning? Do you want me to slide a ring on your finger and swear before God that you'll always be mine? Do you wanna raise our kids side-by-side? Will we grow old together and die together because we can't bear to live one day on this earth without the other? Will you wait for me to find you in our next life? And all the ones after that?"

My heart gave a strange lurch at Snow's beautiful words.

Everything inside me yearned to say yes, to take a chance and hope to God the dream he sold me was real. But the words got caught in my throat as an equally beautiful promise from nine years before floated through my mind.

You'll get it all. Good, bad, and everything in between. One day, I'm gonna give you a family. A posse of men and women who'll have your back, and they'll be military, blood, and chosen family. One day, I'll plant my babies in there, put a ring on it, and give you a traditional family too.

I swallowed down the rush of tears because Snow was so good at saying the words but not at keeping his promises. The last time he sold me a dream, he left.

My heart belonged to him and always would, but he was weeks out of rehab. I couldn't trust a man who'd yet to prove he deserved it. If it was just me, maybe I could take the chance, but I had two kids who deserved a mom who put *them* first. Snow still had a lot to prove, not just to me but also to Kai and Kady. We were getting there, but I needed more time.

I gazed into my golden boy's eyes and slowly shook my head. My chest panged at the flash of pain he tried to hide. "I know it's not what you want to hear," I said quietly. "And I'm sorry it's hurting you, but I'm not ready. Honestly, so much has happened. I don't know if I'll ever be."

He gave a little shrug. "If you were the type of woman to let me get away with shit, I probably wouldn't love ya so much, Kennedy. Don't ever be sorry for doin' what's best for you."

"I'm scared if I keep hurting you, you'll relapse," I whispered.

He stroked his thumb across my cheek. "If I relapse, it's on me, not you. Don't take that on."

"If it's too hard for you, I'll move back to Vegas," I offered.

"Babe," he growled. "You're goin' nowhere. This is your home now. I'll deal, and it's like I told you before, anything's better than nothin'. I lived without you for too long, Kenny. Just you, Kai, and Kadence bein' in my life is enough."

Nerves fluttered in the pit of my stomach. "What if it hurts us more in the long run?" I whispered. "What if being close but not being together breaks us?"

One corner of his mouth hitched up. "The only thing that'll break me is losin' you for good. Were you happier without me all those years?"

I shook my head.

"Well then." He grinned a little too brightly. "No harm, no foul." He nodded toward the clubhouse. Dad wants to speak to you in Church. Is that okay?"

My forehead creased. "You allow women in Church?"

He laughed, and the beautiful sound weaved around my heart. "Not as a rule, but you're also our lawyer. Dad wants to run a few scenarios past ya."

"Don't tell me," I snipped. "Prez wants to play a game of devil's advocate with me."

Kit shot me another grin. "Somethin' like that."

We got out of the car. "I'm not giving your dad tips on how to break the law without getting caught," I told him, falling into step as we walked toward the clubhouse.

Kit held his hands up defensively. "Don't shoot the messenger, Kitten." He pulled the door open and motioned me through. "I'm just the lowly Road Captain."

A high-pitched squeal filled the air as Kit opened the door and held it for me.

Weirdly, the bar was busy but with women.

Cara and Layla sat with Sophie at a table by the bar, drinking coffee. My friend held a cup to her mouth while she glared daggers at a redhead not wearing much in the way of clothes, who sat within a cluster of women at another table.

Atlas appeared at the mouth of the corridor. "Come on, Breaker. We've been waiti—" His face fell as his dark eyes rested on Sophie. He took in his wife's glare and cocked an eyebrow. "Stitch, baby. Take it down a notch, yeah?"

She transferred her glare to her husband. "You gonna make me, big boy?" she asked, her tone deceptively quiet. "I just want to check. Did you say these *ladies* can sit in the bar and socialize even though there are kids about?"

He paled slightly. "Err, yeah, baby, but let me explain—"

"It's fine!" she interrupted.

"Stitch, baby—" he began.

"Go. To. Church," she ordered, voice low.

Atlas scraped a hand down his face. "Fuck!" he spat under his breath.

I turned to Sophie and jammed my hand to my hip. "Can somebody please explain why the atmosphere in here is suddenly thicker than Atlas's dick?"

Atlas's pale face reddened as he shot daggers at Sophie. "You been openin' your trap, woman?"

Soph smirked. "I have no idea what you're talking about. Maybe you should ask Cherry if she's been talking. After all, *she's* seen it too."

Atlas winced before plastering a fake smile on his face. "Just goin' to Church, dearest," he crooned, tone suddenly lighter. "I'll kick the girls out when we're finished."

Sophie cocked an eyebrow. "Good call, big man."

The SAA grabbed me with one hand and Kit with the other. "Come on, before she kicks my ass. It's true what they say. Happy wife. Happy life."

"What the hell was that?" I demanded. "When Sophie gets quiet like that, you better run."

You're tellin' me, Blondie." He deadpanned. "Lettin' an old piece mix in the same room as the Mrs ain't the brightest."

I stopped and pointed back up the hall toward the bar. "Is that the girl you made sure Sophie saw you everywhere with before you got together? The same girl who jumped all over you when you courted my friend?"

He did a 'meh' shrug. "That's the craw of it. When a biker gets himself an ol' lady, we're fucked-up the ass without a drop'a lube, seein' as we can't get rid of the whores we fucked before 'em." He held his thumb to an electronic pad on the wall and opened the door. "After you."

I entered the room to see the guys sitting around a big wooden table. "I can't believe you," I hissed, turning to the SAA. "Why would you bring your pregnant wife around your ex fuck buddy?"

Dad's eyes turned to flints. "You did what?"

Atlas went around the table and took a seat. "It's Cheska's birthday," he stated. "The girls asked me weeks ago if they could throw her a special lunch in the bar. Thought it'd be cool 'cause Stitch would be at work, right? Then lo and behold, the Sinners start their bullshit. Next thing, little Kady girl gets taken, our women hang around the club for their fuckin' safety, and Atlas is in the dog house yet again." He sat back in his chair, lips thinning. "Why is it every time I do some fucker a favor, I get bit in the ass?"

John rubbed his beard. "I dunno, brother." His voice rose to a yell. "Maybe it's 'cause you're a goddamned idiot!" The prez shook his head at the SAA. "Why did you say yes to the girls, you fucknut? You told me the whores were only allowed in the bar to party with the brothers at night from now on. And that was only if the kids weren't around." He narrowed his eyes. "I swear to fuckin' God. If those bitches have got their tits hangin' outta their tops in front of Mason and Kai, I'll throw 'em out myself."

Atlas rubbed at his temple. "Nah. They're dressed."

John glared. "Thank fuck for small mercies."

I popped a hip. "Helloooo! Remember me? Did you ask me into Church to make me witness a live episode of The Odd Couple?"

Cash barked out a laugh.

Abe's shoulders shook.

Bowie shook his head.

I waited as Snow went around the table and sat next to Abe before continuing. "What do you want me for?"

"Wanna run some hypotheticals past ya," he said. "You told the girls the other night you'd give us all alibis."

I nodded.

"So, if we've got alibis, we can't get locked up?"

My eyes raised to the heavens as I sighed. "Alibis help with defense. They're always good to have, but remember, they're useless if you leave DNA at the crime scene."

"Interesting." John nodded thoughtfully. "What about if they see our bikes?"

"If you think they've been seen, the best course of action is to report them as stolen immediately," I retorted.

"Okay, and what—"

Perplexed, I held my hand up to stop him. "Look, John. At the risk of sounding stupid, why are you discussing breaking the law?"

"Just thought we could get some pointers," he explained. "It'd be good to know what we're dealin' with as far as the law is concerned."

"Well, don't." I sighed.

John's head reared back slightly. "Huh?"

"How am I meant to effectively defend you in a criminal court case if I already know you've done the crime?" I placed a hand against my hip, raising an eyebrow. "And not only that, it's club business. Do I talk to you about periods, vaginas, and bad dick?"

John shook his head, eyes wary.

"So what makes you think I'm interested in criminal activity, boys' toys, and your weird fetish for leather?" My hard stare went from one man to the next.

John blinked.

Abe cackled.

Cash's shoulders shook.

Kit adjusted the crotch of his jeans.

"I'm a defense attorney," I continued. "*Your* defense attorney. If you want me to give effective counsel, don't question me about the crimes you're about to commit." I jerked my thumb in the direction of the bar. "Do you want to talk to Kady about this latest development?"

John shook his head slowly, like he was in shock.

"Good choice. Now, I'm going out there to have my BFF's back while she kicks some fake redhead's ass." I turned for the door. "Toodles."

A secret smile played around my lips as I walked out, almost giggling at the look on John's face. He turned green when I mentioned vaginas and periods.

As the door closed, I heard Bowie murmur. "Jesus. She's one scary bitch."

My smile widened, and my heart suddenly bloomed as Kit chuckled before replying. "Yeah, bro. Ain't she magnificent? I'm gonna marry that girl one day."

Chapter Twenty

Breaker

"Yeah, bro," I agreed, heart thumping with love as I turned to Bowie. "Ain't she magnificent? I'm gonna marry that girl one day."

Cash leaned back and clapped me on the shoulder. "See? Kit gets it." He shot me a wink, chewing his gum at the side of his mouth. "Fiery women rock, right bro?"

"Works for me," I muttered.

"Me too," Abe waggled his eyebrows.

"Couldn't think of anythin' worse," Bowie said under his breath.

Dad nodded his agreement.

"See me?" Atlas jerked a thumb at his chest. "I got the best of both worlds. My Stitch is sweet as candy, but she still gives me lip when I get too big for my breeches."

"Every time you open your mouth, then," Abe fired back.

Atlas flattened his lips as chuckles rose through the air.

Dad waited for the laughter to die before resting his eyes on me. "How are you feelin', Son? Still no after-effects from what happened?"

I shook my head. "Nothin'. I don't understand. I reverted to the soldier that night, but after a good night's sleep, I felt fine."

Atlas leaned forward to address me. "Never seen anythin' like it, Breaker. You were like the fuckin' Terminator. I half expected one of your eyes to glow red." He sat back, muttering. "Been tellin' you for years the boy's got skills, but none of ya listened."

Dad rubbed his beard. "Gotta say, Son. The trail of bodies you left was impressive. Then I saw your knife work, and I nearly wet my jockeys. My eyes water whenever I think about you stabbing Beetle in the dick. I've never heard a noise like that from a human before. That wail was like an animal dying."

Every man at the table winced.

Atlas jerked a nod. "It was an animal, and Breaker sliced its pervert dick off."

More winces.

"So. What's next?" Abe asked. "No sign of Bear. Beetle and his crew are burnin' in Hell. All's quiet for now."

"Yeah," I muttered. "Except for the G.I. Joe who looked after Kady."

Dad was with me when Kitten's call came through. When I left for her office, he told me he'd fill the other officers in.

Murmurs of agreement went up.

"Any thoughts?" Dad asked the table.

"D'ya think it could've been one of Hendrix's men?" Bowie asked. "He's lookin' to recruit commandos for his chapter. Maybe one got word of what was goin' on?"

"How, though?" Cash rubbed his stubble contemplatively. "And wouldn't Drix have let us in on it?"

"I'll call him," Dad decided. "I'm sure it wasn't him, but there's no harm in askin' around."

I sat back, reflecting on Dad's words.

I'd heard Hendrix went after Kitten while I was at Grand Junction. I'd always liked the guy, but knowing he snaked me while I was vulnerable made me double-guess myself.

Word on the street was that the VP had used Anna from the salon as a no-strings fuck for months, all while dating other chicks. Now, he'd fucked off to Virginia without a backward glance.

"What's the setup there?" I asked Dad. "I've heard he's been makin' some shitty moves lately."

Cash nodded. "You mean Anna?"

"Yeah. And my woman."

"What do you know about that?" Atlas enquired thoughtfully.

"Only what your ol' lady told me. He flirted with her while I was in a Vet hospital bein' rehabilitated for PTSD. The asshole made a move, and he asked her out a few times, but Kitty gave him the red light. Tells me a lot about his loyalty."

Dad nodded slowly. "Drix has been actin' up lately. He's been playin' the fool since I agreed he could open the new Chapter. Hendrix is a good guy, but lately, he's not been. I thought it was 'cause his pop was sick, but I reckon it's more than that."

"Maybe he's lettin' it get to his head?" Atlas suggested.

"Then he'll have to deal with the fallout," Dad told our SAA. "If you do the crime, you do the time. End of."

I shook my head frustratedly.

I saw it a lot, and not just in MCs, either. In all walks of life, people let power go to their heads. Good men—and women—turned into assholes because they believed their own hype. Sadly, it never ended well, but with Drix running an MC, it could prove to be a disaster. Pissing off bikers who used to be commandos was asking for trouble.

"I'm hoping he'll see the light before things get too heated," Dad said with a sigh. "Fundamentally, he's a good man. I hope he remembers who he is before shit goes too far."

"I'm pissed he fucked Anna over," Bowie admitted. "She's a good woman and the only person in this town who helped Layla when she was on her ass. She's held a flame for Hendrix for over a year, and he took advantage of it. Don't expect me to roll out the red carpet if he shows his face here."

"Same," I gritted out.

"You did it to Layla," Abe reminded him.

Bowie's lips thinned. "I disagree. I never led Layla on. It happened. I got spooked and sent her on her way until I got my head outta my ass. Hendrix is playin' puppet master. He knows how Anna feels and uses it to play games with her. The prick's takin' advantage of a good woman who's so besotted with him she'll take what he dishes out."

"Yeah." Abe smiled sadly. "I get it, Son."

"We'll keep an eye on it," Dad said, scraping a hand through his beard. "If Hendrix keeps fuckin' up, I'll go to Virginia and sort it."

"We don't need his shit on top of the Sinners and their shit," Cash mused. "Not many people can shock me these days, but this is so out of character for him. He knows what we're dealin' with, so why's he pilin' on more pressure?" My brother glanced at Dad. "Maybe it was too soon to let him open a new chapter."

"It's done," Dad replied. "I like you all having opinions and holding me to account, but I'm still Prez, and it's my decision. If it proves to be a shitty one, I'll deal with it, along with Hendrix." His eyes snapped to me, then Bowie. "Tonight's the night?"

Bowie's mouth twisted into a smirk. "Yup. I'm lookin' forward to a night on the town keepin' tabs on Stafford. Has Colt got the cameras ready?"

Dad barked a laugh. "Bo. It wouldn't surprise me if the fucker's commandeered Government satellites to zoom in on him. He's like a kid in a goddamned candy store." His stare slid to Atlas. "No bullshit from you tonight," he ordered. "Doin' Recon and goin' Rambo mean two different things, right? No car chases. No shootin's. No shenanigans. Let's keep it on the lowdown, yeah?"

Atlas's lips twitched.

Dad looked to the heavens. "Jesus. Save me from SAAs who think their God-given right is to cause as much fuckin' mayhem as they can muster." His eyes lowered. "Any other business?"

Silence.

"Right! Let's get sorted for toni—" He was interrupted by a knock on the door.

Atlas rose, walked across the room, and pulled it open. "This better be good, Prospect!" he barked, standing to one side.

Billy sauntered in, "It depends, boss. At this precise moment, two groups of women are sitting in the bar. Actually, that's a lie 'cause they're not sittin', they're havin' a strip off."

Atlas's face scrunched up. "What the fuck's a strip off?"

The Prospect looked at the officers, his eyes twinkling with mirth. "Let me set the scene for ya. Tupak versus Biggie. Mariah versus Whitney. Hilton versus Rinna. Out in that bar, we've got the smackdown of all smackdowns."

Atlas's body locked. "Stitch?"

"Not quite. Don't get me wrong, it was your woman tellin' Cherry she had a hole the size of the Grand Canyon and a lot more traffic that started the rivalry. Cherry came back with, 'bitch, at least I've got tits.'" He turned to me. "That was when *your* women got involved."

"Yep." I laughed. "That'll do it. Kitten takes no shit, but she takes even less when it comes to her kids and her girls." I braced myself. "What happened next?"

"She called Cherry Little Miss Silicone before discretely flashing her boobs and declaring, '*These* are tits.'"

Fuck.

I blinked owlishly. "Kitten got her tits out? In a room full of bikers?" I asked, stomach slowly knotting.

The prospect must have seen the dark shadow moving over my face because he winced. "Not quite. There was only me and Colt in the bar at the time apart from the whores, and your woman turned her back while she hoisted her top up."

"Fuck me!" Dad muttered.

Cash busted out laughing.

Bowie slowly moved his chair away from me.

Abe held his hand up. "Whoa. Whoa. Whoa. You came in here sayin' they're all partakin' in a strip off. What the fuck's that?"

Billy thought for a few seconds. "Okay. Ever heard of a dance-off?"

Everyone nodded.

"Imagine that, but with stripper moves. And I'm not talking about just your girl, Breaker. It's all of 'em. Even Iris."

Every chair in the room scraped loudly, setting my teeth on edge, as the men jumped up and ran for the door. Dad and Atlas got there first, almost getting stuck before they squeezed through together and rushed into the hallway.

The rest of us followed Atlas as he roared, "I'll fuckin' kill her," before his ass disappeared into the bar. Another roar went up. "*Stiiiitch!*"

Abe cackled as we hurried after them. "Dunno why he's having a conniption. Can't wait to see my Iris showin' the young'uns how it's done."

"Too fuckin' right," Cash agreed. "The thought of Wildcat shakin' her ass like a stripper has given me a hard-on so big I'm surprised I haven't split my zipper."

Bowie balked, muttering, "Too much goddamned information."

"Can't help havin' a big cock," Cash muttered as the thumping bassline hit my ears. Pharrell's voice sang, 'Everybody get up,' as the opening bars of 'Blurred Lines' blasted through the speakers.

Cheers and shouts went up.

"Shake that ass."
"Baby! Where have you been all my life?"
"Come to Daddy!"

"Sounds like word got around about the strip off." Cash laughed.

My chest tightened. The thought of Kitten showing her beautiful body to my brothers made my hands clench into fists. If she had her tits out, I'd whoop her ass.

"Jesus," I muttered as we stomped into the bar, coming to a halt at the sight before us.

"Fuck me!" Cash crowed. "Go on, Wildcat! Show Daddy how ya shake that ass."

Abe hooted, punching the air. "Show those whippersnappers how it's done, Rissy!"

My eyes went around the room, rounding as they rested on the bar.

At one end, Cherry and Brianne stood shaking their asses in bikinis, though they looked more like newborn calves the way they kept falling over in their ridiculously high heels.

My stare slid right, and my cock kicked at the sight before me.

Kennedy pumped her hips in time to the bassline, her arms seductively lifting above her head. Cara and Iris were dancing beside her and doing pretty well, though Wildcat looked ridiculous with her pregnant belly. I smiled as I saw her give the whores the finger while she pumped her ass.

My eyes slid back to watch Kennedy.

My woman looked incredible. Her blonde hair flowed down to her tiny waist. The swell of her hips accentuated her long, shapely legs. Firm, high, perfect tits were encased in a black swimsuit top, matching the black leather pants that clung to her body.

My palms suddenly clammy, I wiped them against my jeans. I thought about glancing at my boys, just to see if they were as transfixed as I was, but for the life of me, I couldn't look away from that goddamned bar. I groaned, rubbed at the goose bumps trailing down my arms, still unable to wrench my stare away from the sex kitten.

"Jesus, fuck!" Cash muttered from beside me. "It's no wonder your woman leads you around by the short hairs."

My gut twisted.

An urge to pull his eyes out of their sockets hit me. I wanted to stop him from looking at her. My fingers twitched with the compulsion to knock him the fuck out.

The chorus hit, and she twisted just before crouching low, ass to the floor.

As if in a trance, I zeroed in on her body.

Her arms swayed in the air in time to the music, hips writhing as she contorted herself into positions and shapes that would be physically impossible for the average person. But then my Kitten had proved many times she wasn't anything like average whatsoever.

Long blonde hair flew over her features, making it impossible for our eyes to connect. I needed to see her beauty and feel the fire that called to my soul.

Cash was right, I was fucked, and I goddamned loved it.

"Come on, baby girl," I whispered, stepping forward. "Show me what you got."

Breaker

She couldn't have heard me over the music or the baying crowd. But just like before, we connected deeper because Kitten supermodel stomped her ass toward the bar's edge, and our gazes locked.

Big cornflower-blue eyes bored into mine.

My breath hitched as I watched a small smile curve her beautiful, full mouth. Her gaze pulled me in like a fucking tractor beam, making me step closer.

My mind went blank for a few seconds before a fire flickered to life inside my gut. I had to force my ass to stay put, to stop myself from leaping up onto the bar and tossing her over my shoulder.

I watched her high, firm, little ass thrust in time to the music in those skin-tight pants. My mind conjured up images of crawling on top of her, digging my fingers into her hips, and doing some thrusting of my own.

She must've seen the blatant desire on my face because she looked me up and down and licked her lips, shooting me a sexy little wink.

I stopped fucking breathing. My cock pulsed, hard as rebar, as a realization hit me.

I'd sailed through life, never connecting with family, friends, or women, except for Kitten. Since I first saw her on that stage ten years ago, she'd made me sit up and take notice. No other woman had come close. My soulmate danced on top of a bar in a biker clubhouse and weaved a spell on me.

She'd flipped a switch inside me and brought me back to life.

Kitten twirled and thrust, all the while shooting me seductive glances.

It was almost inhuman how her body contorted. She dropped to her knees, head circling so vigorously that her silky hair flew out in all directions. Jumping to her feet, still crouched, she slowly rose to a stand, ass first, glutes undulating as she shook her perfect booty.

My mouth watered at her toned muscles rippling under her black leather pants, cock aching against my zipper.

She was an angel and a sinner. Her light blonde hair gave her an air of innocence, and then she'd whip around, flashing me a devilish smirk. It took everything in me to not jump onto the bar and fling her over my shoulder.

The final bars of Blurred Lines' blasted through the speakers, and a thread of panic twisted inside me. I didn't want it to end. I could've happily stood there watching her for the rest of my life.

She spun around to face us again and smirked, crouching slightly and twerking her ass.

I closed my eyes, cock leaking inside my shorts as another roar rose through the bar. Feet stomped, glasses crashed, and yells of 'Kennedy' pounded the air.

I pulled my collar away from my neck. *Jeez, is it hot in here?*

"Close your trap, Kit." Bowie laughed from beside me. "Anyone would think you'd never seen a hot girl dancin' before."

I gulped.

"Gotta say," he muttered, glancing at me mischievously. "Your woman's somethin' else."

Fire swept through me, and my head swiveled toward him.

He held his arms out to the side. "The day's finally come when I can get ya back for your antics at the barbeque a year ago. You were more of a fucker than I just was."

Cash and Abe laughed.

The song began to fade. Kitten looked at Cara, then Iris, and smiled as they pointed to the whores who's obviously given up on the strip off. Nobody could dance better than my woman. It was stupid of them to even try. My Kitten was a class act.

Breaker

"Let's go get our women," Cash muttered, moving toward the stage, Abe by his side as the opening bars to 'Unfinished Sympathy' by Massive Attack blared through the speakers.

Like they had a life of their own, my feet moved toward the bar. I raised my stare to burn into Kitten's cornflower blues, and my heart unfurled with how she looked back at me. Raising my hands, I held her by her tiny waist, lifted her from the bar, and placed her gently on her feet.

The fingers of one hand laced with hers, and I tilted her chin so I could look into her eyes.

They shone with emotion I knew she didn't want to admit she felt, and what burned me was that I'd done that. I'd made her stop believing in me. I'd gone about things so fucking badly. I'd lied and hurt her heart when all she'd ever done was love me.

But whether she believed it or not, I never stopped loving her back, not for one second.

Watching her move put me in a trance.

Kitten called to me like a siren's song, the same way it did the night I met her all those years ago. Everything inside screamed at me to fling her over my shoulder, take her to a room, and fuck her into the mattress, but I was scared. What if I hurt her again like last time?

My lungs ached with need, and my cock ached with want as I stared down into the eyes that I'd dreamed of since I was twenty-one years old. "I love you so fuckin' much." Before I could stop myself, I dipped my head and pressed my lips to hers.

She opened for me immediately, but how could she not? This was us, pure and beautiful. Together, we were so fucking right that my heart sang with joy at just being so close. Every nerve ending fired as one hand slid up my chest, curling around my nape as she molded her beautiful body against mine.

My cock, still hard from watching her dance, ached painfully as my lips pressed harder, adding pressure, getting even closer. She sighed as my tongue touched hers like she was breathing life back into me.

Kitten's lips were as soft as I remembered. I'd spent hours kissing her as a young soldier, feeling the flush of first love for this incredible woman.

I groaned into her mouth, desperate to taste sweet peaches, uniquely her. I forgot everything. Where we were, even who was watching. There was no sense of anything except us. I was just so fucking content to finally have my woman back in my arms where she belonged.

All too soon, the yells and catcalls permeated my brain. I could've cried because even though it was the first time I'd had my mouth on hers in nine years, I knew I had to let Kitten go.

At least for now.

I pulled back slightly, kissing her gently on her lips again and opening my eyes. I expected her to step back and cuss me out. Even to slap my fucking face, but instead, she giggled.

I cupped her face. "I'm not sorry for kissin' you," I whispered among the shouts and hollers.

"Even though you said you wouldn't touch me until I was sure?" Kitten questioned.

I rested my forehead against hers. "If you makin' eyes at me from on top of that bar wasn't an invitation, Kitten, I'll blow Atlas." I closed my eyes, took a deep breath, and talked from the heart. "What do I need to do, baby? How do I fix this?"

"You show up," she replied softly. "For me *and* the kids. You have to make me believe again."

"In me?" I asked.

She shook her head. "No, Snow. In us."

"I'll make you remember," I vowed.

"Time will tell." She stepped back and turned to face Cherry, who stood with the other club girls. "Consider yourself schooled, bitch. Talk shit to my friend again, and I'll school you some more."

"Nah!" John's voice cut through the room, making it go silent. "Pack your bags now, Cherry, and if any of your minions think they can talk back to ol' ladies, they can fuck off with ya."

Cherry's eyes went huge. She jerked a thumb toward Sophie. "She started it."

"And I'm finishin' it!" Dad bellowed. He stomped toward the club girls, anger pounding off him so forcefully that I almost saw steam coming out of his ears. "It stops now! We've let this shit go on for too long. You're here to open your legs and keep your mouths shut, and before you argue, it's what you signed up for. You're not brothers or ol' ladies. You work *for* us, not *with* us. We treat you all well. Better than other clubs would. You get housed, fed, and you get money to buy your shit. But, if you can't live with where you're placed in the hierarchy around here, it's best you leave, too."

Atlas walked up next to Dad and folded his beefy arms across his chest. "You heard Prez. Get the fuck gone. Prospect, go with her, watch what she takes, and escort her off the premises."

"I'm sick of this place anyway," Cherry spat.

"Well, you won't mind fuckin' off then." Atlas watched as Billy took Cherry's arm and escorted her down the corridor to her room.

Dad stood tall, eyes flicking over the rest of the girls. They glanced anywhere but at him, unable to meet his hard stare. "The April shit show brought home how comfortable some of you are gettin'. Puttin' your noses in places they shouldn't be didn't turn out well for her, and it won't for you."

From the corner of my eye, I noticed Kennedy stiffen.

I closed my eyes.

Fuck. Why did he have to mention April?

"It stops here," Dad continued. "Next one of you to step outta line will be made an example of. Do you fuckin' get me?"

Murmurs of assent went up, and the girls shuffled away, probably to lick their wounds.

Kennedy turned slowly to me. "So, Snow. When *were* you going to tell me about the traitorous bitch who proclaimed to be your baby momma?"

Heart sinking, I glanced around, looking for help from anyone. My eyes turned to slits when I saw Abe, Cash, Bowie, and even Atlas, slink away so quickly that my head almost spun. I scraped a hand down my face, wondering who'd been opening their trap to Kennedy about the April thing. It could've been anyone, but I'd lay my money on one of the whores.

Kitten placed a hand on her hip, glowering at me like I was shit on her shoe. "Well? Are you ever going talk to me about your girlfriend?"

My eyes raised to the heavens, and I pleaded for divine help because I didn't want to relay this story to Kennedy. April was a victim of what happened as much as anyone, but she was still a manipulative bitch.

I had to tell Kenny everything. No more lies, even if it meant losing her. My heart dropped into my ass as I heard her foot tap impatiently, and that was the moment I knew.

I was fucked!

Chapter Twenty-One

Kennedy

Kit's fingers laced with mine. "We need to talk." He tugged me down the corridor toward his room.
"Ya think?" I challenged. "It's been weeks since you've been back. It's not like you've had limited time or anything."

He threw the door open and pushed me into the room. Turning to lock it, he slid the key into his pocket.

I took a step toward him. "Why are you locking us in?"

"Makin' sure you don't flounce out the second I say somethin' you don't like. This story ain't pleasant, Kenny. You probably won't wanna know me after I tell ya. But, I swore I wouldn't lie to you anymore, and I'm gonna keep that promise even if it puts us on the outs."

My heart died a little, but instead of bursting into tears, I pulled my shoulders back. "I don't flounce. I've never flounced anywhere, ever, in my entire life." My face scrunched up slightly. "What *is* flouncing anyway?"

He bit back a smile. "It's when you toss your hair, all snooty-like, and storm outta the room with your nose in the air."

"Oh." My stomach sank a little because he was right. I did do that. "Okay. Maybe I do flounce, but I like to call it making an exit."

Maybe I was being a bitch, but whenever anyone mentioned the name April, my stomach turned over, and my teeth set on edge. I knew she was a traitor to the club, and she tried to trap Snow with a baby, but there must've been something between them for it to get that far.

He sank down on the bed and patted the space beside him. "Sit, baby."

"I don't want to sit."

His golden eyes flashed as he looked up at me pleadingly. "Please."

I let out a slight huff, lowering onto the bed.

He took my hand, lacing our fingers together. "First thing I wanna ask, baby, is why the fuck you're walkin' around a biker clubhouse with a bikini top on?" His voice, which started off gentle, quickly turned biting.

"I'm wearing pants," I snipped defensively.

"Thank fuckin' God," he said with a growl. "Are you tryin'a give me a fuckin' aneurism?"

"Well, I can hardly have a strip-off with two club whores dressed like a fucking librarian, Snow. Do you think I'd let those bitches win after the way they spoke to Sophie?" My lips pursed. "I don't fucking think so."

"So now I have to sit here and talk about April when you're basically wearin' a bra, and all I wanna do is feel your tits up."

I stuck my hands out and waved them, putting on a deep voice. "Oooh. Kennedy's got tits. How will I ever control myself?" I stood, went to the dresser, pulled a tee out, and dragged it over my head. "There. All gone. No tits in sight. Now you can talk without coming in your goddamned jeans."

"This isn't how I thought this would go," he said as if to himself.

I plonked my ass down beside him again, blood boiling. "And I didn't think I'd ever be having a conversation with the so-called love of my life about him being the candidate for a club whore's baby daddy, but here we are!" I glared daggers at him.

Kit's stare hit his boots. "I didn't love her. I fuckin' hated her."

The fire in my organs began to burn out, leaving angry tears in its wake. "But she was still good enough to fuck on the regular. Still good enough to risk impregnating. I could understand you loving someone else. I would've hated it, but I could've understood it. But instead, you betray everything we had for someone you say you detested. It doesn't make sense, Snow."

My gaze flicked over him, taking in his slumped shoulders and hurt expression.

For ten years, Snow had been everything to me, even when he died. I'd never moved on from him. I did my best for my kids and lived for the day I'd see him again.

Weirdly, his PTSD and violent tendencies didn't bother me, but thoughts of all the women he screwed ripped me apart. For weeks, I'd been hearing snippets about April, and every time a part of me died inside, and because I was hurting and angry, I wanted him to suffer, too.

One minute I'd bitch at him; the next, I'd remember how he saved Kady and what a fantastic dad he was turning out to be, and all the old familiar love would flood my heart again.

I'd never acted so irrationally before.

"It started last Summer," he croaked. "I didn't know it then, but she'd been watching and learning everything about me over time." He leaned forward, elbows to knees, and continued. "She was the one who Cash cheated with. Me and my brother have always had a rivalry. Dad favored him from when I was a kid, and I guess the resentment grew from there."

I sighed. "You're not making it seem better, Snow."

"I know. I know. Just hear me out, please." He waited for my nod before continuing. "I talked to her, just to see what Cash saw in the bitch that made him fuck Cara over, and she said somethin' that got my attention. April made it clear she knew about my kink, even encouraged it."

"So, she manipulated you," I stated, chest tightening.

He dropped his head in his hands. "I used to hurt her. She became a regular fixture because she was into the same thing and didn't open her mouth. After a while, April became important, not because I loved or liked her, but because I could choke her out, and she'd take it. I needed it to stay straight in the other areas of my life."

My lip curled. "April fed your addiction?"

"Exactly." He paused for a minute, thinking about his following words. "What I didn't know was that she had an agenda. She was Bear's woman and part of the Sinners. He sent her in to infiltrate and find out what she could about the club."

My stomach dropped. "Snow. You're an explosives expert. You can take out a house full of outlaw bikers without breaking a sweat. How did you not see it?" I jerked my thumb in the direction of the bar. "How did *they* not see it?"

"I did see it, and so did they. We saw April for *exactly* who she was, but in my case, she had me by the fuckin' balls. Over the months, she'd collected evidence from all the times I'd marked her, and eventually, it came to a head. I hardly ever fucked her. Just used to choke her while I got myself off. Last Winter, I strangled her so hard I killed her. I had to breathe life back into her."

My insides churned, nausea rising through my stomach.

"She blackmailed me. Told me she was pregnant. Said I was the father, and if I didn't step up, she'd go to the cops and tell my family about me. I'd been takin' drugs and drinkin' a lot. I had no clue if the condom split. Kennedy, I was so high I didn't even know if I'd fucked her the night she professed to get pregnant." He covered his head with his hands, shaking his head. "That was when I gave up, baby. Even if I found you one day, I knew it'd be too late 'cause I'd be saddled with her."

Tears burned the back of my throat. "Then you all found out she was setting you up?"

"Yeah." He turned his head to look up at me. "Bear came for her and confirmed he was the kid's father. She didn't wanna go with him, the bitch shook from head to toe with fright, but I handed her over anyway."

My body froze as everything slotted into place. "Then, Bear killed and dumped her the morning you returned from Vegas."

He nodded. "I'd just seen you again and found out about the twins. I thought you hated me. You looked at me that morning like I'd betrayed you, and it hit me. I had betrayed you, but not in the way you thought. It wasn't even about the lie. I'd let myself down by goin' off the rails and let you down, too. I couldn't take any more guilt or pain. I'd waited so long for you, Kenny, and in that moment, I felt like it was all for nothin'."

A headache began to stab behind my eyes.

The story Kit just relayed reminded me of a bad TV drama. Good guys, evil geniuses, immoral women, and at the center, a man who made terrible decisions brought on by an illness he had no control over.

I knew I should've been kinder; maybe the Kennedy he loved as a young man would've been, but this older, more jaded Kennedy felt sick with all the information and didn't quite know how to handle it.

"So. Now you know everything," Kit stated. "The good, the bad, and the downright ugly. I know it's messy and hard to wrap your mind around, but you gotta remember, my head wasn't right at the time. When I lost you, I gave up on myself. I let things happen to me because I thought I deserved to be punished, especially after what I did to you."

My heart thumped so forcefully that it probably registered on the Richter scale.

Kit straightened his back. "And behind all the bad decisions, the PTSD was slowly killing me. Kitten."

I closed my eyes, listening as he continued.

"It affected every part of my life. Sleeping was a struggle because, as exhausted as I was, I knew I was about to relive the most traumatic moment of my life in my dreams. So, I did things to stop remembering. Drugs, drink, women, anything to tire my brain out until I was almost comatose. I battled tiredness as well as the demons living inside. Everything was a struggle. Every sudden noise tricked my brain into believing I was back in the place that destroyed my peace of mind. I could smell the burn and feel the heat. It's something nobody could understand unless they've lived it." He took my hand, turning me to face him. "I'm sorry, Kennedy. I'm sorry for hurting you, I'm sorry for walking away, and I'm sorry for April, but please understand I walked because I loved you so fucking much. I didn't deserve you, Kitten. I would've hurt you again, and I would've never forgiven myself. She was there, feeding my cravings, but there was no love, no feeling. You've gotta believe me."

I gave him one nod. "I do believe you, Snow. I just need time to process it."

He slid to the edge of the bed and fell to his knees before me. "You've been it for me since I was a fuckin' kid. I was so arrogant I believed being with you was my right, but being without you showed me it's my privilege." He intertwined our fingers, his eyes lifting to lock with mine. "You taught me that everything happens for a reason, but where was the sense in losing you? Where was the sense in breaking each other's hearts?"

My heart filled with emotion as his words sunk in.

He was right. It was hard to see a reason for what we'd lost, except for one huge point. "Kady," I whispered. "If you hadn't been in the military and gone through those missions, how would you have rescued our girl?"

His brow furrowed.

"Maybe you needed to go through it all, Snow," I continued. "I was so intent on conquering the world and you on saving it. Maybe we needed to do those things first, or we would've eventually resented each other."

"The sacrifice wasn't worth the reward," he croaked. "Not if I can't get you back. How do I make it right? Whenever I think we take a step forward, something else from my past gets in the way."

His question made me think.

He'd done so much work on himself already, and I knew the twins and I were a significant reason why. What else could he do? Was it fair to let Kit believe he had a chance when too much had happened? Could I get over it?

I took in his eyes, full of hope and heartbreak. So much of what he'd done resulted from his illness, but he'd never blamed any of his actions on it. He discussed his PTSD and how it affected him but never once used it as an excuse. It was probably why I didn't give him an outright no. However, I couldn't give him the answer he wanted until I was sure.

I squeezed his fingers. "I don't know, Kit."

"Okay," he leaned against my lap. "Then, I'll go with the fact you just kissed me back and keep on keepin' on." He pulled back, getting to his feet and holding his hand out to help me up. "I just need a chance to make you remember."

I looked up at him, my heart wrenching in my chest because love came so easily to us. But so did hurt, anger, and distrust. I knew I had to either shit or get off the pot because all this back-and-forth would eventually turn what we had even more toxic.

Could I get over the lies, the women, and the heartbreak and just be with him?

Maybe. I wanted him more than any man I'd ever met. I knew his heart was good and that he loved me. What held me back was the constant ache in my stomach and the clench of my heart whenever other women came up in conversation. It was the jealousy that stuck in my craw more than anything.

Could he make me remember the good and forget the bad?

Only time would tell.

Chapter Twenty-Two

Breaker

Atlas craned his neck to look at me in the back seat of the SUV. "I'm bored," he whined.
"For fuck's sake," Bowie muttered. "When we talked about recon. I said you'd be bored. I dunno why you came."

Silence reigned for a minute until Atlas sighed. "Just think, Break. Last time we did recon, you blew up the Sinners' clubhouse. Don't suppose you brought any explosives with ya tonight?"

My lips twitched. "Why would I do that when it's strictly recon?"

Atlas lifted one shoulder in a nonchalant shrug. "You never know. We might end up in a gunfight, or zombies might attack." He paused for a minute before continuing. "I should get myself a crossbow like Daryl fuckin' Dixon."

"Bullshit," Bowie argued. "When it comes to zombies, guns are way more efficient. Ya just need to make sure you shoot 'em in what's left of their brains."

Atlas thought about that for a few seconds. "It's all very well, Bo, but think on this. In a post-apocalyptic world, bullets and ammo would be in short supply. You can fashion arrows out of wood and flint. Never-ending supply right there."

"Like you could fashion anythin'," Bowie scoffed.

The SAA's head reared back, affronted. "I could *so* fashion arrows. Could probably make an outstandin' bow if I put my mind to it, too. You should have more faith." He scraped a hand through his beard. "Out of all the wives, mine would survive the longest. My Stitch would kick zombie ass. A few high roundhouses, and she'd kick their heads right off." The SAA stopped for a minute, thinking. "Though Wildcat could probably nag the fuckers to death. Ten minutes in her company and their heads would spontaneously combust."

"I doubt Cash would agree," I mused, inwardly laughing at the bullshit conversation we were having.

"No," Atlas agreed. "The whipped little bitch wouldn't fuckin' dare. Too scared Wildcat would rip him a new one."

My eyes stayed on Brett Stafford's apartment and I smiled to myself.

There was nobody more whipped than Atlas, though getting him to admit it would be like pulling teeth. Admittedly, though, I was living in whipped city with him. Not that it did me any good, seeing as my earlier conversation with Kitten put us back ten steps.

Every time we began to get somewhere, another hurdle would get thrown at us. Our kiss had made me walk on air, then the mention of April's name made me wanna run and hide. In a way, I was glad it was out in the open. It was the last piece of the puzzle Kitten needed to see the bigger picture. Still, after I told her everything, I sensed her pulling away again, physically, and mentally.

I was at my wit's end. I'd done everything emotionally to show Kitten how much I loved her. Though things I'd been putting into place since I was still at Grand Junction were finally coming to fruition, operation Get Kennedy Back was about to begin. "Have you got your timings set for Monday?" I asked Bowie. "You can't be late to the airport."

My brother tapped the side of his nose. "All sorted. Gave the SUV a service and filled her up with gas. Me and Doe will be ready to rock 'n' roll after we drop Sunny at school."

"How you getting Ned out the way?" Atlas asked me.

"Was gonna ask her to go to Rock Springs with me. Got my first outpatient meetin' at eleven. I don't wanna miss it, not after the whole Beetle business. But after our spat earlier, I'm not sure she'll agree to come."

"You can't miss your appointment, Break. Not if you wanna stay on track." The SAA stroked his beard in thought. "How 'bout I have a little chat with Stitch. Ask her if she likes the idea of a double date with you and Blondie? We haven't had a day out on the bike since before Vegas. The Sinner shit's died down now they're missing a few more members, and we know Bear's outta town, so the coast should be clear."

The knot which had twisted my gut since everything had popped off with Kennedy earlier, began to loosen. "That would be great. If Soph goes, Kitten will, too. Don't you mind that your ol' lady's pregnant, though?"

Atlas thought about that. "Nah. I'd never let anythin' happen to her. It's not even an hour on the bikes, and she's been naggin' me to go out. I'd rather do it now than a few months down the line when she can't hold on tight 'cause her bump's in the way." His eyes lit up. "Maybe I can sell it as our last ride until after she has the baby. That way, Blondie will feel obliged to go."

Bowie laughed. "You're a sneaky fuck."

Atlas grinned. "Yip!"

I glanced up at Brett Stafford's apartment, doing a double take when I saw it bathed in darkness. "Lights are out, boys. Let's see if Stafford's goin' to bed or goin' on his travels—" The main doors to the apartment complex opened, and our target walked out, heading toward the parking lot.

"It's showtime," Bowie murmured.

"Don't start the engine until he does, Bo," Atlas ordered. "And keep the lights off."

"Anyone would think I haven't done this before," Bowie said under his breath as we all watched Stafford jump into a white van and reverse out of his spot before heading down the street.

Bowie started the car and slowly pulled away from the curb, staying way back. "Where's the little fuck goin'? Is he headin' toward Main Street?"

We watched as Stafford indicated and took a left toward the western side of town.

"Nothin' down there apart from the rich folks," Atlas announced. "Looks like he's goin' visitin'."

"At gone midnight?" I gritted out. "And why the fuck is he in that van when he's got that bitch car he cruises around town in?"

Atlas shrugged. "Nothin' else down there, Breaker."

He was right. West Hambleton consisted of big houses and a country club with a golf course, tennis courts, a spa, and rich assholes. Stafford heading down there at this time of night was weird.

I pulled my cell out and pressed to call Colt, putting him on loudspeaker.

He answered immediately. "Yo."

"We're followin' Stafford into the West of town. The area's full of cameras. Can you tap into his position, so we can stay back?"

"On it." The clatter of keys sounded through the line as Colt hacked into the law enforcement surveillance computers. "Okay, he's on the main stretch just past Rose Avenue. Gimme a minute, and we'll see where he's headin'."

"Is he goin' to the country club?" Bowie asked.

Breaker

"He would've turned off by now," Colt explained. "And the club closes at twelve, so he's too late to shoot the shit with his good ol' boys. It's hard to get decent conversation out of 'em when they're sober. It's an impossibility when they're fucked-up on whiskey."

"Like you'd know," Atlas muttered.

"You'd be surprised," Colt said as if to himself.

His words resonated. Years back, he told me he completed OCS at Fort Benning. Men needed a college degree and sometimes a word put in for them to attend. If Colt was a candidate, it could've meant several things. He was super intelligent, wealthy, or both.

I knew he was a fuckin' genius. Online security had tightened up considerably over the years, so for Colt to hack into the places he did, meant he was scary smart, 'Criminal Mind's Penelope Garcia and Spencer Reid have a love child' smart.

I didn't really know a lot about our tech guy. He was a fixture in the club, well-loved, and well-respected. He had perfect aim, held his own in fistfights, and fitted in well. He was popular with the ladies though I never saw him go with the whores. I heard he saw Lucy from the florists in town on and off, but it didn't seem serious between them.

I'd worked out years ago that Freya liked him, but I didn't think he'd go there. He was about mid-thirties, so too old for my sister, and regardless, Dad would hit the roof if he touched her.

It worried me sometimes. Frey was my sister, but I could still see what a fuckin' beautiful woman she'd grown into. The way she looked at him when she thought nobody was watching sometimes broke my heart.

There were real feelings there, but it could never happen, and Colt knew it. At least I hoped he did, 'cause that would cause a shitstorm of epic proportions.

"He's passed Rose, Wisteria, and Carnation Avenue," Colt continued. "There's only Bluebell and Sunflower left."

"Most of Sunflower's owned by the mayor," Bowie said. "Surely he'll turn off at Bluebell."

There was a stretch of silence before Colt said, "He's onto Sunflower. The fucker's at the intercom on Henderson's gates. And there he goes drivin' into the mayor's mansion."

A thread of unease wrapped around my gut. What the hell would Stafford be doing there at this time of night?

Atlas glanced at me. "Gotta bad feelin'."

"Yeah," I agreed. "Me too." I thanked Colt and disconnected the call before turning to the SAA. "Shall we wait and follow?"

"Do bears shit in the woods?" He smirked. "Not such a borin' night after all." He patted his pocket, making sure he had his piece.

We drove slowly toward the street where the mayor's mansion stood, tall, white, and imposing in the darkness. It was a vast place and looked much like the White House but smaller, although probably not by that much.

Bowie parked down the side of the street, avoiding the cameras positioned on top of the metal barred gates. "Can't see the van."

"We know he's in there," I said quietly. "It's just a waitin' game. What's the plan for when he comes out?"

A low growl emanated from Atlas's chest. "I say we follow the fucker." He turned his body to face me. "You got your piece?"

I pulled my cut open to show him my gun underneath.

"You?" He nudged Bowie.

My brother jerked a nod, eyes still on Henderson's place. "Message Colt. This area's lit up like a Christmas tree. If we follow the little prick, he'll see us. Want eyes on the little fucker."

I tapped out a message and sent it to Colt, asking him to keep watch through the cameras for when Stafford made his move.

"Maybe we're readin' too much into it," Bowie suggested. "Stafford works for the mayor, has done for a while. If he's a gopher, it's only right he'd be at the mansion."

"I disagree," Atlas argued. "If it was daylight and Stafford was drivin' his pussy car, I'd go with it, Bo. But it's one A.M., and here we are, on a wild fuckin' goose chase followin' fucknut's A-Team wannabe wheels."

"He ain't no B.A. Barracus." Bowie chuckled.

"He's more like Peewee than B.A," Atlas agreed. "But it don't make him less dangerous. Put a gun in any prick's hand, and he can do damage, especially when he's backed into a corner."

Bowie nodded his agreement.

"I better call Pop and fill him in." My gut jumped at the thought of Dad's reaction. "He specifically told us, no shenanigans. No car chases. No trouble."

Atlas's mouth set in an angry line. "Prez'll be okay. After what happened to little Kady girl, he wants to step it up."

After a few rings, Dad answered. "What?"

I clicked the cell phone onto speaker. "Pop. We followed Stafford to the Henderson mansion."

"So, he works for him," Pop said defensively.

"At this time'a night?" Atlas questioned.

Dad released a breath before conceding, "Good point."

"He's drivin' a van instead of his car," I explained. "It feels off. We wanna follow him, but chances are, it'll turn bad."

Silence fell over us as Dad thought for a minute. "If it turns bad, it turns bad. Check your weapons and be on your guard. Is Colt on top of it?"

"Yeah," I confirmed.

"I'll go in his office and help keep tabs," Dad said tightly. "Someone call and keep the line open so we can hear what's happenin' in real-time."

"Got it," I murmured.

"End the call for now. Contact us when Stafford's on the move," Dad ordered. "And boys, this business is dangerous. If Stafford's involved in trafficking, we gotta be on our guard. He'll have friends in low places. Feel me?"

We murmured our assent, and the line went dead.

"Prez is right," Atlas mused. "Stafford, even the Sinners are at the bottom of the food chain. We gotta remember the higher-ups are better connected, and way more dangerous."

Bowie nodded, deep in thought. "It could lead to all-out anarchy. We need to start thinkin' about the women and kids. If things get too hot, we need somewhere to send 'em."

"What about Vegas?" I suggested. "Kitten's kept her house there. It's big, she's got amazing security and a pool. It'd be like a damned vacation."

"Good idea," Atlas muttered. "Vegas works for me. Stitch still has buds there, and Hustle would get the Three Kings on the job for security."

My spine straightened slightly. "What's Hustle gotta do with it? If I need to protect my woman, I'll go straight to Tote."

Atlas turned to face me. "Why? Blondie's Hustle's property."

My mouth went dry. "Kennedy's my fuckin' property!" I snarled.

Atlas raised his hands defensively. "Calm the fuck down, Break. I'm just sayin' until you make her your ol' lady, Hustle's got rights, too."

My gut started to boil and my hands involuntarily clenched into fists.

Kennedy told me she'd been with men, but I didn't suspect for one minute it would've been a biker, especially one with an ol' lady. "She's been with Hustle?" I grated through clenched teeth. "I'll kill him."

Atlas's eyes snapped wide. "Whoa. I never said that."

I sat forward, flaying him with a look. "Then what the fuck are you talkin' about?"

Atlas scraped a hand down his face. "Blondie's his niece!"

I froze. "His niece?"

The SAA's lips curved into a smirk. "Yip. She's a King's princess. Hustle's her Uncle. He's the one who tracked Kyle Simmons down and told her he—umm, you—were dead. His ol' lady, Katie, was in the delivery room when the twins were born."

I sat back, a sudden coldness taking over.

Atlas laughed. "I'm shocked the burly fucker hasn't ridden into town with a posse at his back already. I mean, you did fuck over a club princess."

My chest jerked. "Kennedy told me she had an uncle but never gave a name." My eyes widened as they slashed toward my friend. "We were only there a few months ago."

"Yeah," Atlas turned back to look out the windshield. "Small world, huh?"

I raised my eyes to the heavens, tamping down the frustration coursing through me. "Why didn't you fuckin' tell me?"

Atlas's head whipped around. "Thought Blondie would've opened her trap."

"Well, she didn't." I rested my skull on the headrest. My hammering heart made my chest tighten.

I was screwed. You didn't fuck with women who belonged to biker clubs, even allies like the Kings. They could show up any time looking for retribution. In fact,

Atlas made a good point. I was shocked they hadn't already.

My head spun with this new information as well as the knowledge that I'd have a busy day tomorrow, making calls and apologizing until I was blue in the face.

Bowie leaned forward, pulling me away from my thoughts. "We've got movement," he said, tone low.

Sure enough, within seconds, the mansion gates opened, and Stafford's white van slowly drove out, heading back toward town. My hand reached for my cell phone, and I dialed Colt's number. "He's on the move," I confirmed the second he answered.

"We've got eyes on him," Dad said quietly. "Stay back and let us track him. If you're seen, it's game over."

"Got it," Bowie replied. "Tell me when it's clear to move."

After a minute, Colt's voice came through. "He's past the country club now, boys. Start movin'."

Bowie started the engine, pulling away with the lights cut. "We're probably just gonna follow him home, and all this will have been for nothin'," he grumbled. "Wild fuckin' goose chase."

"Let's hope you're right, Son," Pop said through the cell phone's speaker. "'Cause I'd much rather that than the alternative."

"He's not headin' home," Colt confirmed. "Look, Prez."

A few seconds later, Dad spoke. "He's takin' the road to town, boys. Do a left at the end of that road and stay on the main stretch."

My heart thudded in my chest. "Where's the little fucker goin'?" I said under my breath.

"To Hell, if he's really involved in this trafficking business," Colt replied.

Atlas nodded. "Up until now, I gave him the benefit of the doubt. Thought maybe he'd gotten caught up in something too big and was in way over his head. But the little shit's workin' solo tonight. His actions are his own."

"Speed up, Son," Dad ordered. "Try and catch him up on the road leadin' outta town."

Bowie pressed his foot on the gas, making the engine growl as it sped up. He flicked a switch, and the headlights beamed, lighting the road ahead. Within seconds we were going well over the speed limit, Bowie handling the bends in the road with confidence and expertise.

Nobody could handle a cage like my brother. He knew cars inside out and could build them from the engine up.

Adrenaline flowed through my veins, but not overly so, just enough to make my senses hone in on what was happening around me. Usually, when my blood pounded, my head would swim with the craving for violence. But weirdly, I just wanted to deal with Stafford and get home to Kitten.

It was weird; Espinoza used to tell us adrenaline was our friend, and it served a purpose by making our senses more alert. I'd never understood what he meant until that moment in time. Yeah, my fingers held a tremor, and blood rushed in my ears, but I wasn't out of control.

We flew up the main drag, which took us onto the road leading out of town. Me and Atlas remained silent, letting Bowie focus on his driving.

Dad's voice came through the cell. "Lights off, Bo. You're nearly on him."

My brother cut the headlights again, pressing his foot lightly on the brake, and slowing us down to a crawl.

My breaths quickened, and my heart thumped harder in anticipation of what was about to happen.

"You want us to nab, Stafford?" Atlas asked.

"Not ye—" Dad began before suddenly shouting, "Stop the car!"

My heart leaped into my mouth as Bowie pulled the car over onto a verge and cut the engine. "Jesus, Pop. What's goin' on?" he demanded.

"He stopped the van," Dad explained quietly. "Shut up a minute. Lemme see what the fucker's up to."

Silence fell inside the car while we waited for Dad's instructions.

My heart beat so forcefully I could almost hear it drumming through my ears. Stomach jolting, I looked through the windshield to see if I could pick up on anything.

"Stafford just got outta the van," Dad murmured. "He's on his cell. Looks to me like he's freakin' the fuck out. The prick's pacin', almost tearing his hair out by the roots."

"He's uber nervous about somethin'," Colt agreed. "I can see his hands shakin' through the camera."

Atlas twisted in his seat, his face scrunched up, confused. "What the fuck's he doin'?"

"God kno–" Dad began before calling out, "Wait!"

"What?" Atlas asked, frustration lacing his voice.

"Headlights comin' from the other direction," Colt explained. "Got no eyes that far up the road, though, so I can't make out the license plate."

Atlas went to open the door. "I'm nabbin' the fucker."

"No!" Dad shouted. "Stay put—"

"Stafford's getting in the car," Colt exclaimed.

My gun churned. Something wasn't right. "I think we need to get out there."

"Stay put," Dad ordered. "You don't know how many are in that vehicle. They could have guns cocked ready for ya." After a few seconds, Dad murmured. "They're turning back the way they came from. Stafford's gone with 'em. He abandoned the van."

My first thought was that it could be wired to blow. Stafford leaving a vehicle sitting on the road spoke to the explosives expert in me. But Brett didn't know we were following him, so how would he know to blow us up?

That led me to my following conclusion.

I sat forward to address Atlas. "He's either transporting something and got spooked, or it's a drop-off. Someone may be along to pick it up soon."

"That's it!" Dad exclaimed. "Go. Hotwire it if you need to but get it back to the compound."

"I need to see what's inside first," I protested. "It could be a trap."

"Do it, but hurry," Pop ordered.

Lungs burning, I threw the SUV door open and jumped out of the car, Atlas doing the same. Running ahead, I caught sight of the vehicle almost immediately.

Atlas ran up beside me, his breaths sawing. "What do you need me to do, Break?"

I eyed the van suspiciously. "Stay back while I take a look. Gonna check for signs of tampering."

My feet moved, and I drew closer to the target, listening for suspicious sounds. A coil of apprehension weaved through my gut, but I wasn't nervous. Nothing seemed suspicious, and I doubted pussy-assed bitch Stafford would step foot inside a vehicle rigged to blow.

On approach, I crouched to look under the vehicle, but it was too dark. I checked my pockets for my cell, cursing when I remembered I'd left it in the car.

"Here!"

I almost jumped ten feet in the air as Atlas's voice boomed from behind me. "Jesus, fuck!" I exclaimed, "You frightened the shit outta me. I told you to stay the fuck back."

He leaned down, handing me his cell. "If you blow up, I'll blow up with ya. When will you get it through ya head that you're not ridin' solo anymore? You're my brother, and I've got your back."

I took his cell from him and shone it under the van. "I won't have a fuckin' back if this bitch goes boom."

He got down on his haunches beside me, peering under the vehicle. "See anythin'?"

My experienced eye saw no dust or grease spots had been disturbed. "No. Looks clear to me."

Atlas stood, grinnin'. "Fuckin' marvelous!" He tugged his gun from his cut, aiming it at the van's doors. "Looks like I get to play after all." He let out a hoot before firing two shots at the lock.

The mechanism snapped, and the doors flew open, bouncing on their hinges.

My mouth flattened. "You're a gung-ho motherfucker." I approached the doors and peered inside. My heart leaped into my throat as I caught slight movement through the darkness. I swallowed a gulp as shuffling sounds echoed through the metal interior. "Need some light here, brother."

"Gotcha." Atlas turned his cell phone around. The single beam of light from the torch lit up the dank space and let he out a loud growl.

My eyes rounded as I took in the sight before me, and I cursed under my breath.

Two women sat at the rear of the vehicle, bound, and gagged. They were young, late teens, maybe early twenties, both dressed just in underwear and a tee. My eyes widened as I took in their bare feet and terrified expressions, and nausea gripped my stomach muscles.

It was dark, so I couldn't see their faces properly, but I could tell one had black hair, the other red. I met Atlas's shocked stare. "We better get 'em the fuck outta here, now!"

He jerked a nod before he turned back to the women. "You're safe," assured them. "I'm gonna seal these doors shut and drive you to people who can help. Ya get me?"

Both women nodded, obviously scared out of their wits.

I watched as the SAA undid his belt buckle, pulling it through the loops of his jeans. When it was free, he gestured for me to grab one of the doors and close it, while he pulled the other one shut and threaded his leather belt through the handles.

"Can't we just put 'em in the SUV?" I asked.

"Nah." Atlas looped his belt through the gap in the metal handles again, securing the door. "There's gonna be prints all over this fucker. Theirs, and ours. If the pigs pick the van up, we'll get the blame for nabbing 'em. We need to get 'em safe inside the compound then either burn or break up the vehicle." He pulled on the belt, testing how securely it held before heading toward the driver's seat. "We need to get outta here now, Break. If pick-up's been arranged, they'll be here any second."

I nodded my assent and hurried to the passenger side. Heart thudding against my ribs, I opened the door and climbed in.

Atlas checked the cup holder and dash before pulling down the sun visor, catching the keys as they fell into his lap. "Halle-fuckin-lujah," he crowed. "At least one thing's gone right." He fired up the engine and did a U-turn in the road until we faced Hambleton before throwing his cell on my lap. "Six-nine-nine-six. Call Bowie and tell him to follow us, then call Prez."

I picked up the cell, unlocked it with slightly tremoring fingers, and called Bowie.

"Yo! Whatcha find?" he asked.

"We're in the van heading home," I said, heart thumping out of my chest. "Follow us."

Atlas put his foot on the gas, heading toward the SUV, and saluted Bowie, who flashed the lights twice as we drove past him.

Checking my side mirrors, I watched Bowie turn the vehicle around. Within seconds he'd driven directly behind us. My chest jolted as a flash caught my eye, and my gut leaped into my throat as another set of headlights shone from way back.

Ice scattered down my spine. "Is that them?" I wound down the window and looked down the road behind us.

"Call Prez," Atlas ordered, pressing the gas until the engine almost screamed. "Get Colt on the cameras again. Tell him to ID their cage."

I clicked on the number.

Before it even rang, Colt answered. "I've got eyes on ya," he barked. "Keep goin'. Prez, Cash, and Abe are already on the way. Keep your foot down and try and lose 'em. They're definitely on your tail."

"There are two girls in the back of the van," I relayed urgently, checking behind us through my side mirrors. "We don't wanna hurt 'em."

"A few bruises, even broken bones are preferable to getting captured by those sick fucks," Atlas snapped. He pressed on the brake slightly, took a tight bend, and sped up again. "It's game over for them and us if those cunts catch up."

My body locked as two gunshots cracked through the air.

"Jesus!" I exclaimed. I stuck my head out the window again to see the club's SUV veering left to right.

"Fuckers shot Bowie's tires out," Atlas gritted out, eyes darting to his side mirror.

Sure enough, the headlights behind us pulled to the right as Bowie slowed down and stopped the car at the side of the road, making way for the cage behind him to edge closer to us.

My chest heaved as two more shots filled the air but that time from way back down the road. Heart in mouth, I watched as the car chasing us veered across the street.

"That was Bowie," Atlas shouted. "He shot at those fuckers."

I reached inside my cut to grab my weapon. My eyes clamped shut as a sharp stab of pain ripped through my skull, taking my breath away. Hollister's voice snapped through my head. *"We've got two on our tail. Help me take 'em out."*

The burn from my throat sank into my gut. An all-encompassing fire spread through my chest, destroying everything in its wake. My body began to shake, not with fear, but rage, as the monster inside me roared to life.

Pings sounded as bullets glanced off our vehicle. I squinted, trying to aim for the fuckers who'd fired on us. More bullets sprayed the van but the metal held fast; their weapons not strong enough to penetrate.

I took aim and breathed until the world around me narrowed—my vision tunneling to a pinprick—and I focused on the black car racing behind us. My breath and racing heart were loud in my ears as I fired toward the flickering lights of the enemy fire lighting up the darkness.

The car chasing us swerved to avoid the bullets.

I aimed and fired again, popping three rounds off. Sure enough, it skidded but soon recovered and held fast on our tail.

"He's still at our six," Hollister shouted. *"We're not outta the woods yet, Snow. We need more of that hotshot shooting.*

Again, I aimed and shot off a few more rounds. It turned into a scene from the Wild West. The men in the car behind us were trying to take cover while firing shots.

A loud roar began to fill my ears, and the pain hit inside my skull again. It was so sharp I had to grab at my forehead as the pain streaked through it.

The world around me narrowed again, and a loud whooshing sound filled my ears. My eyes lifted, and I watched Dad's bike roar past me toward the enemy, his hand outstretched, firing on the car behind.

Atlas let out a loud hoot. "Calvary's here. Just in time!" He bounced in his chair excitedly as Abe and Cash roared past us the wrong way down the road, guns cocked, following Dad.

"Fuckin' beautiful!" Atlas hollered, eyes shining with happiness. "They're retreatin'. Look!"

I glanced in my side mirror, and sure enough, the enemy car turned in the road and sped off in the opposite direction." I heaved out a relieved breath, the heavy weight in my chest lightening.

That was too close for comfort.

Atlas slowed the van to a stop and let out another loud hoot. "I fuckin' love my life!" he yelled, punching the air.

I turned to look at him incredulously. "You're a fuckin' lunatic," I barked. "We could've all died.

"Nah." He twisted to face me. "Nice fuckin' shootin', bro. You held 'em off nicely. You did better than Bowie."

"He was drivin'!" I cried. "Hard to shoot and keep your eyes on the road."

Atlas threw his head back and laughed, obviously on a high from the adrenaline rush.

I sat back, skull falling on the rest behind me.

For the first time in months, I wished my emotions weren't so goddamned prevalent. My heart beat out of my chest, and I ran clammy palms down my jeans, swallowing the effects from the adrenaline spike I'd just experienced. I breathed deeply, trying to regulate my heartrate.

I'd just relived the day Benny got killed. Though, at least I'd been spared watching as his Humvee exploded.

My gut stabbed as I realized I wasn't so goddamned cured after all. It was weird because I didn't have a total blackout. Unlike when I beat Cash, I knew where I was and what I was doing; I could just hear Hollister in my ear.

I jumped as someone banged on the side of the van. "You okay in there?" Dad called. "We're takin' ya somewhere safe." He appeared at my window, his stare hardening on Atlas. "I should'a known you'd have a giant hard-on with all this. It's like you've got some built-in radar that attracts trouble."

Atlas grinned. "Made my fuckin' night."

Dad skewered him with a look before his eyes softened on me. "You okay?"

"Yeah," I rasped. "But I've realized I really need to get my ass to Rock Springs."

"Yeah," he agreed. "Stay with me tonight. We'll talk the hours away if we need to. I'll keep your mind occupied."

"Thanks." I smiled.

"We'll escort you back to the clubhouse," Dad continued. "They've probably got buyers for these girls already. We've just cost them thousands of dollars and caused a big headache. It wouldn't shock me if they came back. Abe's pickin' up Bowie now, and we'll all ride back together." He ran a hand down his face, stressed out to all hell.

My heart went out to him. Pop was pale under his tan, a look of worry behind his eyes.

My arm slid out of the window, and I gripped his shoulder. "You okay?"

Dad's mouth set into a thin line. "Yeah, Son." His eyes slid back to me, and smiling sadly, he uttered words that sent a cold chill down my spine.

"But we can safely assume the war just stepped up a notch."

Chapter Twenty-Three

Kennedy

Throwing the clubhouse doors open, I strutted into the parking lot like I was walking the runway at a Victoria's Secret fashion show.

I felt good wearing my skin-tight, black jeans, pointy-heeled boots, and a leather biker jacket with a black lacy camisole top underneath.

When Kit and I dropped the kids off at school a half-hour earlier, I'd looked like a lawyer, but seeing as we were about to ride up to Rock Springs, I thought I might as well look the part. So, I changed into my biker chick gear, glossed my lips up, and put my hair back in a headband à la Brigitte Bardot.

My gaze fell on Snow, who sat astride his bike, chatting to Atlas, and my steps faltered.

Kit Stone was one sexy man.

Like me, he wore black jeans that hugged his muscular thighs and a black leather jacket with the Speed Demons patch on the back. His beautiful, tanned face lit up as he laughed at something Atlas said. Aviator sunglasses covered his golden eyes, but I could imagine them glinting with humor as the SAA continued to make him chuckle. Almost mesmerized, I smiled as he thrust a hand through his curly black hair, the silver rings on his fingers glinting in the sun's rays.

He was every inch the hot biker. Handsome, confident, and in control.

My mind went back to Saturday night when he, Atlas, and Bowie rescued those poor, traumatized girls. Sophie had woken me, explaining what had happened. So, I switched into lawyer mode and called a few safe houses in Vegas—who I'd done pro-bono work for—to see if they could help.

Sophie and I'd waited in the bar, almost biting our nails to the quick.

Suddenly, the doors flew open and Kit swept in, carrying one of the girls safely in his arms, barking orders to the other guys who followed him.

My pussy clenched because Kit Stone did it for me like no other man.

It wasn't because he was handsome and hot, though those qualities didn't go amiss. Rather, his confidence and strength seemed to ooze from every pore as he ensured those girls were safe and comfortable.

Something about him hit me deeply.

When he'd first left Grand Junction, he'd had a quiet assurance about him that I liked. The way he spoke about his feelings with no trace of embarrassment proved he didn't give a fuck what anyone thought. He believed that I was his and he was mine; even though I'd held him at arm's length, secretly, it appealed to me.

Over the weeks, I'd watched Kit's confidence soar, especially when he made decisions involving the club. He seemed to be in his element and the way the brothers showed him such respect made me proud he'd fathered my children.

It also made me hotter than a solar flare.

Kit Stone was a man's man, and I liked it a lot, as did my lady parts, which had started to quiver whenever he was near.

Breaker

My heart bounced as he slowly turned toward me. "Mornin', beautiful," he greeted me huskily. A slow grin spread across his face as his covered eyes raked down me. Despite his sunglasses, the heat of his stare made my skin tingle with awareness of the handsome man who sat before me.

A sense of contentment filled me, and my stomach gave a little tug toward him.

And just like that, I was transported to ten years before when his gaze burned into me as I danced for him in a Vegas strip club.

Memories assaulted me, running toward him and jumping into his arms as he sprinted through the arrivals lounge at Harry Reid. Staring at his beautiful face as the sun raced toward us on a mountaintop. Sheets tangled around us as we lay in bed watching TV, making the most of every minute before he left me again.

Slowly, he was creeping back into my heart.

My feet floated, my body moving as if magnetized toward him, making me feel like I was walking on air as his eyes pulled me in like golden magnets. The scent of sandalwood filled the warm Summer air, and my thighs clenched at the more X-rated memories it evoked.

"Hey," I breathed, squirming slightly at the heated clench of my pussy. "You look good today."

He raised a hand and whipped his aviators off, still grinning, aka Maverick from Top Gun. I almost sighed with pleasure as his golden-brown orbs burned into mine.

"Finally, I get my girl on the back of my bike," he said with a possessive growl. "I've waited years for this."

My brows drew together in question. "It's been years since a woman's been on your bike?"

He nodded. "The only girl ever to grace my back was Freya, and that was only 'cause I needed to learn to carry a passenger. I've saved your throne for you, my queen."

My gaze dropped to take in the black and chrome beauty, and I froze.

The bike was sprayed matt black apart from the muted chrome handlebars and pipes. But what drew my attention was the design across the bulbous fuel tank.

A pin-up girl.

She sat with her long legs stretched into a seductive pose, wearing a red lacy bra and panties. Her hair was long, blonde, and tousled into a sexy mane. What made my throat constrict was her blue eyes. They were the exact color I saw every time I looked in the mirror. Her lips had a natural pout caused by how they downturned on each side, identical to mine.

"It's you," he murmured. "Told Bowie to do it the day I got back and started prospectin'."

My throat filled with emotion as I examined the image. The underwear resembled the set I'd worn the first night he saw me dance.

"Why haven't I seen this before?" I wondered out loud.

"Been runnin' you and the kids around in a cage since I've been back. The only time I rode her was on my journey home from Grand Junction, but you weren't around when I arrived."

Reaching out, I gently traced my fingers over the smooth, colorful paintwork. I knew a biker's motorcycle was sacred to them. The Kings spent tens of thousands personalizing their rides with things that meant something to them. "I can't believe you did that," I murmured.

"It was the only way I could have you with me, baby," he replied simply. His hand caught mine, and he laced our fingers together. Golden eyes bored into mine so intensely it made my breath catch.

"Yo! Stitch baby," Atlas called out from beside us. "Get your ass over here. These two are makin' my back teeth ache." He swung his leg over his bike to dismount before walking toward Sophie.

"Trust that fucknut to ruin the moment," Kit grated, letting go of my hand and putting his shades back on.

Soph shrieked as Atlas swung her into his arms and carried her toward his bike. "My husband says he doesn't do romance, Ned," she called out. "But he's a true romantic at heart."

Atlas gently placed Sophie back on her feet next to his bike. "Don't tell 'em that shit, Stitch baby. I gotta rep to protect." He looked between me and his wife. "You two ready to roll, or we gonna stand here gabbin' all day?" He swung his leg over the saddle and held his hand out to help Sophie on behind him.

"Come on, Kitten. Let's jet." Kit took my fingers, guiding me behind him.

Holding tight, I swung my leg over and settled in. My seat was slightly elevated, but Kit was much taller than me so it put us at the same height.

My arms slid around him, and I splayed my fingers across his hard, muscular stomach.

"Fuck!" he muttered. "This is gonna be torture on my dick." He turned his head, buried his nose into my hair, breathing deeply. "Fuckin' peaches. Every time I catch the scent, my cock sits up and takes notice."

I giggled, blushing like a fucking schoolgirl. "I'm the same way with sandalwood."

"I'll douse your goddamned pillow in it, so you can't resist me," he promised. "That way, you'll ravish me when I come to bed."

"You're getting ahead of yourself," I said accusingly. "We're not even together."

Kit winced slightly. "Yeah. I know."

I put my helmet on. As I pulled the chin strap tight, Atlas called, "Ya ready, Road Captain?"

I felt Kit's body stiffen. He put his helmet on, fastening it up before flicking a switch and making the engine roar to life. A crackle sounded through my helmet as synths played through the speaker carving out the intro to 'Dakota' by the Stereophonics.

My arms tightened around Kit's body. "I love this song," I squealed.

He craned his neck and smiled at me before raising his arm and twirling his index finger. The Harley set off, and we sailed through the open gates with Atlas and Sophie following.

Tipping my head back, I smiled as the sun's warmth hit my face.

I loved riding. When I was a girl, Hustle used to take me out on his bike all the time.

I adored the freedom of the road and the deep-down thrill it gave me. I'd always understood Hustle's favorite saying, 'It takes a whole tank of gas before you can think straight.' I got it. There was nothing like a long ride to clear your mind and open your heart.

Not even the thought of April bothered me.

Since we'd argued about her, I felt like a weight had been lifted from my shoulders. For weeks I'd worried about the nature of their relationship, so when John mentioned her, I jumped at the chance to dig deeper.

Initially, I felt sorry for Kit. However, I still wondered how a guy as smart and streetwise as him had fallen for her manipulations. In a way, I thought he was ridiculous for allowing it to happen until I realized a few things. First, he wasn't the only one; the other men had also missed it, indicating she'd done her job well. Second, I remembered his state of mind at Soph's wedding. His eyes were crazed, and it was clear he suffered mentally. Add drugs and alcohol into the equation, and I could understand how she'd taken advantage and how he'd let her.

The ride to Rock Springs was beautiful; we'd picked the perfect day. The sun beat down but not uncomfortably. The end of Summer brought with it ideal temperatures for riding. The scenery was amazing, too, boasting forests and farmland. All I had to do was hold on and enjoy the view.

The hour ride seemed to pass quickly because we hit the signs for Rock Springs in no time. We took the exit before turning at the sign pointing us toward town. The music playing through my helmet fell silent, and Kit said, "Gonna drop you off before I head off to the Vet Center."

I squeezed his waist, stroking his abs to indicate I'd understood. Maybe it was overkill, but he did have sexy abs, so what was a girl to do? I may not have given him the green light, but it didn't mean I couldn't cop a feel when the opportunity presented itself.

We rode through to the central part of town, finally finding two parking spots and pulling over. Kit turned the bike off while I sat back and removed my helmet.

Kit pulled off his helmet and turned to me. "How's your ass?"

I smirked. "Never had any complaints."

He waggled his eyebrows and laughed. "Is it sore from the ride?"

"Yeah." I placed my hand on his shoulder and dismounted. "I'll be walking like I've shit myself for five minutes, but I'll live."

He chuckled to himself. "You're my kinda girl; looks like a fuckin' film star with a mouth like a biker chick. You give no fucks unless I make you pissed, then you turn into a she-devil. You bitch me out, then feel guilty for it and turn all soft and squidgy again. Gotta admit, Kitten, from the minute I saw you, I've been both confused and compelled."

I couldn't help the smile that split my face. "I aim to please."

Atlas approached, holding Sophie's hand. "Coal Train Café's just up that street. We'll wait there for ya." He rubbed his hands together excitedly. "Their java's phenomenal, and their bagels too."

I popped a hip, looking him up and down. "Do they sell cans of Coke?"

Sophie immediately turned away, raising a hand to her mouth.

Atlas's face scrunched up in confusion. "Yeah. Course they fuckin' do, Blondie. You and your Coke cans. You're fuckin' obsessed."

Biting back my laughter, I turned to Snow. "You heading straight off?"

He checked his watch. "Yeah. The meeting's in thirty minutes, and I still gotta find the place."

Without thinking, I leaned forward and kissed his cheek. "Good luck." I pulled back, and our eyes locked. His swirled with questions I still didn't have all the answers for.

"Be back in an hour and thirty," Kit told me before checking his phone for directions. After finding what he needed, he fired his bike up, gave us a salute with one finger, and pulled away from the curb.

I watched him ride up the street, head suddenly filled with the same what-ifs that had haunted me for the last ten years.

A group of girls walking toward us craned their necks, giggling as he rode past. As much as it burned me to see, I couldn't blame them. With his motorcycle, leather jacket, and a cocky grin, Kit Stone was every girl's wet dream, and I certainly wasn't immune.

Today was the first time since finding each other again that we'd been so physically close. I'd pressed my fingers into Kit's stomach all the way here, familiarizing myself with all the ridges and indents of his muscles. His left hand had been glued to my thigh. Sometimes he'd tapped along with the beat of whatever song played through our helmets, or, he'd stroked up and down gently.

It wasn't easy, I still had April and all the other women in my head, but I was starting to come to terms with what had happened. It was no longer the first thing I thought about every morning and the last thing I cried myself to sleep about at night.

It looked like the healing process had begun, finally. Only time would tell if it would be enough.

Nearly two hours later, I checked my watch.

"He won't be long," Sophie said reassuringly. "It's Kit's first meeting with this group. He'll be finding his feet."

Atlas slid his arm across her shoulder, manspreading across the bench. "I may have one'a them bagels."

"You've already had two," his wife admonished. "And a waffle."

He rubbed his muscled stomach. "I'm a growin' boy."

I sighed with concern for Snow. Meetings usually lasted an hour, and okay, they could go over, but not by this long. I looked around the old-fashioned diner, which had charmed me so much when I'd first walked in. The wooden floors, rustic dark paneling, and iron furniture gave the place so much character that I immediately fell in love with it.

I glanced through the windows and froze when I saw Snow's dark hair and broad shoulders approaching the door. "He's here," I said, tone relieved.

Atlas half-stood and waved him over, calling out, "Yo!"

Looking over my shoulder, I watched as Kit weaved through the tables, nodding polite greetings to people as he went. He looked okay, maybe a little pale under his tan, but that was to be expected after starting a new support group. Snow wasn't the sharing type. The Speed Demons were typical alpha males who beat their chests and threw women over their shoulders.

Were they better than other biker clubs? Sure. John encouraged therapy. Cash and Cara saw a therapist in town together and apart. John had even joined family therapy at Grand Junction—one week making Kit's mom fly down from New York to join them, too—but you could lead a horse to water but couldn't always make it drink.

"Hey," I breathed as Kit pulled out the chair next to me and flopped down. "How did it go?"

His mouth twisted wryly. "Okay. Steve, the group counselor, is great. I met him on Skype back at Grand Junction. It was all part of the transition from inpatient to out. The other men seem cool."

The waitress came over and took Kit's order, plus another one from Atlas. When she'd gone, Kit turned to me. "I'd gotten used to my group in Grand Junction, so I felt like a fish out of water at first, but I settled eventually."

"Did you discuss your relapses with the counselor?" I asked.

"Yeah. Steve said it could happen for the rest of our lives. PTSD doesn't just disappear with therapy and medication. It's somethin' I've gotta live with. We had a long chat about it. Relapses are expected; it's the recovery I need to monitor.

My eyebrows drew together. "How so?"

He reached for my hand, threading our fingers together. "I guess it's like this. I've relapsed twice, but my recovery has been much easier both times. You and Kady brought me around the first time, and I felt better the next day. Then the other night, during the car chase, my mind went back to the day Benny and Simmons died. I could hear my LT yellin' orders, but I still knew where I was and what I was doing. The treatment and the meds have helped, even after just a few months, so maybe after a few years, the relapses won't affect me so badly at all."

"Right," I breathed. "So, they're not great, but also not as debilitating?"

He jerked a nod, staring down at his fingers playing with mine. "The day I beat Cash and grabbed Hendrix's gun, I was in another world. I was back in the military gym Kitten, reliving every second. It wasn't like that the other night."

I smiled. "That's good, right?"

He shrugged. "It's progress."

"And you think it's the medication?" I asked.

"Among other things. I'm less stressed now the club's aware. Dad and Cash are on hand if I need 'em. Soph and Freya are checkin' in, too. Being around you and the kids keeps me goin' 'cause I can see what I'd lose if I gave up. The meds help, but so do all those other factors."

The waitress appeared, carrying a tray filled with coffee and plates of food. She placed them down with a smile before disappearing again.

"I'm starving," Kit mumbled, taking a sip from his mug, then picking up his sandwich and taking a bite. The second he put it down, his fingers entwined with mine again.

I gently pulled my hand away from his. "Eat your food," I ordered, providing a cover for my actions. The last thing I wanted was for Kit to realize he'd gotten under my skin. We were behaving like we were together instead of friends and co-parents.

Kit hadn't put a foot wrong since he'd returned from Grand Junction. Sure, we'd argued, but it was always about the past, not the present.

He was in the process of turning himself around, and the way he was doing it was admirable. His club loved him because he was so capable and intelligent. The men looked up to him for a variety of reasons. Kit was there for everyone, and lately, I'd noticed more brothers approaching him for guidance rather than going to John or Cash purely because they believed in him.

It was understandable that the Prez and Vice Prez needed the line drawn between themselves and the other men. Therefore, Kit had become their voice in meetings instead of Atlas and Bowie.

Kit seemed to be the new Abe: calm, competent, and available, and I loved that for him.

On a more personal level, he was becoming a much-loved father, too.

Kai flourished under the love and care of his dad. I'd never once heard Kit tell his son he was too busy for him. In fact, he always stopped what he was doing to talk to Kai or help him with something. They boxed together, jogged together, and even hit the gym together. Kai loved that his dad and his newfound male brethren spoke to him like an adult, not a kid.

Kady was blooming, too. There was so much love around her to ingest. She was the happiest I'd ever seen despite her recent ordeal. She had Sunny and JB to play with and was looking forward to meeting DJ and Gabby, who were currently on vacation in Idaho. She loved the ol' ladies, especially her auntie Sophie and Iris, and had struck up a strong friendship with Seraphina. The three of them baked with her for hours in the kitchen.

It was true what they said. It took a village to raise a child. I'd never had a family before, so I hadn't missed it, but I knew we'd be lost if I took the kids away now.

I liked living in Wyoming, and once the practice opened, I knew the career woman inside me would be fulfilled, too, but there was one thing I still wasn't sure of.

Kit Stone.

Snow was gone, and Kit had taken over. I admired the man he'd become, but something still held me back. Granted, I'd thrown caution to the wind and jumped into things without weighing up the pros and cons all those years before, but all it'd got me was a broken heart.

If Kit wanted me back, he'd have to go the extra mile. He'd have to do something that blew me away, something that exceeded materialistic things. Kit needed to speak to my heart if he wanted our relationship to progress.

Sitting in that café in Rock Springs, I wasn't sure we'd ever move forward.

Except then, I didn't know then what was in the pipeline.

I should've believed my soul recognized its mate when it entwined with his all those years ago. I should've known that the other half of me would step up and claim me in ways that took my breath away.

I should've believed in Kit Stone.

"We can't stop," I reiterated. "It's the kid's first day of school. I need to get home and see how it went." I looked down Main Street at the coffee shop and huffed loudly.

"Dad's bringin' 'em here to meet us," Kit advised me. "Thought we'd eat out tonight as a family treat."

I watched as Sophie dismounted Atlas's bike, and he kicked on the stand. "We should've got back earlier for them. I've always been there for their first days before."

Kit threw a leg over his bike, took my helmet from me, and hung it on the handlebars alongside his. "They're not four, Kitten. They're old enough to understand shit happens sometimes. And believe me when I tell you for the hundredth time, my mom's probably in her element."

I bit my lip, thinking about his words.

Kit's mom flew in earlier. Bowie and Layla picked her up from Laramie. She and her boyfriend had been away on a cruise. Adele had visited Kit at Grand Junction when he got treatment. Now, she was here for a few days, and from what he'd told me, she was in full-on grandmother mode.

I was looking forward to meeting her, but nervous too. I'd been told how Kit was close to his mom, and she'd favored him and Freya over the other two, who John had favored instead.

"You two ready?" asked Atlas, lacing his fingers with Sophie as they approached us. "Need somethin' to wet my whistle."

Kit pointed out one of the club's SUVs parked across the road as we walked up the street. "Looks like Pop beat us to it."

"Hope the new owner makes coffee as well as Magnolia did," Sophie said as we walked toward the coffee shop."

"Heard she makes out-of-this-world pastries," Kit muttered. "Believe it or not, I went to her old place years ago and can confirm the rumors are true."

I looked up at him, eyes glazing over as I thought back. "I've never tasted pastries like Martha used to make. Do you remember them?"

Kit grabbed the door handle, gesturing for us to go inside. "Yeah, Kitten. They were the best."

"I'm surprised you remember." I smiled. "A lot's happened since then."

"I remember everything now." He waited for Soph and Atlas to enter before he let the door go and took my arm. "I didn't for a long time, though; maybe I didn't want to because remembering hurt too much. But now you're here, and every little thing's coming back."

I went to assure him that he hadn't lost everything but was stopped by the shouts of "Mom" filling the air. My body twisted to see Kai and Kady bouncing excitedly on their chairs, waving us over.

Waving back, I started for them, weaving through the crowded coffee shop as I moved toward the kids. As I got closer, I saw John sitting at the table with a beautiful dark-haired woman.

"Mom!" Kit called.

The woman stood and turned, smiling joyously as she opened her arms for her son to walk into. Her arms went around him, and I saw her squeeze tightly as they embraced. She pulled back, her hands going to cup both sides of his face as she stared deeply into his eyes. "Oh, my boy. You look so much better. The shadows are still there and probably always will be, but I can see *you* again."

I smiled because I agreed.

Adele swept her arm around the table at the kids. "It's no surprise you're healing so well. You've got the best medicine a man could ask for. I've never met more beautiful or smarter children." She glanced over Kit's shoulder and widened her eyes at me. "Oh, my God."

I raised a hand, giving her a little wave. "Hi. I'm Kennedy."

I jumped as the woman lurched forward and threw her arms around me. "Thank you!" she whispered.

My heart warmed. "What for?"

She pulled slightly, her blue eyes swimming with tears. "For Kai and Kadence. For giving Kit a chance to be their dad and sticking by him when he never gave you a reason to. For bringing them here, and lastly for raising them alone, without help from any family, and still helping them become the magnificent little beings they are."

Emotion choked my throat. "That's the nicest thing anyone's ever said to me."

She flashed me a dazzling smile just like Freya's. "I think you and I will be the best of friends, Kennedy. Our spirits are kindred." A devilish smirk took over her face. "Do you believe in past lives?"

I squeezed her hand, glancing at Kit. "Yeah, Adele. I think I do."

"Jesus," John muttered from the table. "Not that mumbo jumbo bullshit again."

Adele's eyes narrowed. She dropped her hands from me, turned toward the table, and popped a hip. "John Stone. You're a heathen. It's about time you got your head out of your fat ass and looked at the world around you. I mean, all this time, Kit and Kennedy lost touch, then ten years later, they met at their mutual friend's wedding. What are the odds of her best friend—who's incidentally a doctor—moving to Hambleton and ending up with *Atlas* of all people? How many times have I said you can't fight fate?"

"I heard that," the SAA rumbled, appearing with two more chairs and motioning for Sophie to sit down.

"You were meant to," Adele retorted. "You're lucky to have her."

I walked around the other side of the table to sit with the kids, Kit following.

"Right," Pop exclaimed, rubbing his hands together. "Who wants what?"

Atlas perused the menu. "Large cuppa java. Two of them BLT bagels, and three of them custard Spandau Ballet pastry things."

I froze, mind working overtime as a memory pinged. Martha used to make them. "Do you mean a Spandauer?"

Atlas shrugged. "If that's how you say it, Blondie, then yip."

"Can I have another pastry, please, Grandpa?" Kai asked.

"You can have whatever you want, Kai," John boomed. "What about you, little Kady girl?"

My girl looked up with big eyes. "May I have another juice and a Spandauer, please, Grandpa?" She turned to me, almost bouncing on her seat with excitement. "The lady said they used to be your favorites, Mama."

My skin prickled.

Breaker

There was only one person in the world who knew that.

"Which lady?" I whispered.

Kady beamed, showing her straight, white teeth. "The new lady in this place. She said she knew you, and you once helped her mom with legal stuff."

My heart stopped, just for a beat, before it began to race out of my chest. Goosebumps scattered down my arms, and something made me look around.

I turned, lifting my eyes, and caught sight of a woman standing behind the counter, openly smiling straight at me.

Her hair was shoulder length, with natural corkscrew curls framing her round, pretty face. My mind stuttered as I tried to place her familiarity. A second passed until my throat seized, my mouth falling open as shock punched me in the chest. "Martha?" I choked out.

Kady giggled from next to me, but the sound hardly registered. I stood so forcefully that the chair clattered to the floor behind me, and my hand flew to my mouth.

Martha headed around the counter, hurrying toward me with her arms outstretched.

Tears welled in my eyes.

I didn't dare believe what I was seeing. Martha was one of my oldest friends, but when her bakery closed, she'd moved away, and we'd lost touch. I'd thought about her over the years, wondering how she was and if she was happy. Somebody told me she went to Ohio with her mom, but nothing more concrete than that.

How could she be here?

What was going on?

I almost lost my shit when her arms surrounded me, and she whispered, "Oh, Kitty. I've missed you so much."

Sniffing, I let out a strangled cry, not quite believing what was happening. "I've missed you, too." I hiccoughed, letting out a shocked laugh. "What are you doing here? Is this a dream?"

"More like a dream come true," my old friend murmured. "But I'm really here." Martha pulled back slightly, smoothing my hair down with the palms of her hands. "You're still beautiful, Kitty, and your kids are exceptional." Her eyes darted around my face, taking me in before her eyes lifted over my shoulder, and she smiled widely.

Heat hit my back. I shivered as Kit's voice said quietly in my ear, "I'll follow Mom and Dad and deal with the kids. You stay here and catch up with your friend."

I turned, eyeing him, bewildered. "You don't seem surprised by all this."

Kit popped a kiss on the tip of my nose. "Dunno what you're talkin' about, baby." He gave Martha a knowing wink. "Everythin' go okay, sweetheart?"

My stomach leaped as Martha beamed at him and replied, "Perfect. Thank you."

I pressed a hand to my stomach to calm the butterflies inside.

Kit had arranged this.

Somehow, he'd found Martha and moved her to Hambleton. I couldn't work out how he'd done it, but he'd managed to bring someone back into my life who I'd missed for years.

Material things had never impressed me. Cars and jewelry were nice, but they didn't speak to my soul like the people close to me did.

My heart grew to double its size, filling up with love.

Without even thinking, I turned to him, rolled up on my toes, and kissed his cheek, trying to pack all my emotions into one tiny gesture.

Kit had thought about the things that made me tick and, by doing so, made my heart swell with joy and contentment.

My golden boy had given me back a connection.

My throat burned so hot that even if I knew what to say, I couldn't have uttered the words, so I just murmured the one thing my overflowing heart told me to.

Reaching up, I cupped his handsome face, smiling as a happy tear tracked down my face. "Thank you, Kit."

Chapter Twenty-Four

Breaker

The weeks passed in a flurry of school, homework, and babies. The latter was because Cara gave birth early to a bouncing baby boy who they named Wilder.

Cash walked around the clubhouse half-dead with exhaustion, but I'd never seen my brother happier or more settled. He and the woman he'd loved for seven years were finally making a go of things again, and I could see his determination to make it work.

I never thought Cash would have a lick of sense when it came to babies, but he took pride in every diaper change and night feed. Like he said, Cara hated being pregnant, so Wilder may be his only chance.

It seemed his boy gave everyone baby fever.

Atlas became so overprotective of Sophie that it got on *my* last nerve, never mind hers. Whenever she went to walk up or downstairs, he hauled her into his arms in case she tripped and fell. Our SAA wrapped his wife in so much cotton wool I was surprised he even allowed her out of their room to go to work sometimes.

Bowie and Layla announced they were pregnant again, and yep, Dad nearly fainted. It wasn't every day you saw a six-foot-four, two-hundred-and-sixty-pound hairy biker skipping for joy.

Jules Ford

I was happy for Bowie. My brother was a husband and father through and through. Though, I reckoned he started too young when he got his first steady girlfriend pregnant. I wasn't fond of Samantha and thought Bowie was taking too much on, but it was still sad when she died.

However, Layla was perfect for him. You could see the love between them whenever they looked at each other, and now he'd knocked her up again, my brother doted on her even more.

Kennedy opened her law practice to a lot of fanfare.

Her list of clients had gone through the roof. Dad kept her busy with conveyancing and taking over the legal side of all the Demon's businesses. On top of that, she still worked for the Kings and sometimes had to fly out to Vegas for meetings.

Earlier that day, Scotty had flown in to check out the new offices and introduce Kitten to some hotshot young lawyer who wanted to work at the Wyoming branch of Clarke and Carmichael Law. I was on my way there now to make sure everything was okay.

I parked my bike across the street from Kitten's office, switched off the engine, and kicked the stand on. Taking off my leather gloves, I smiled up at the old, white building.

My woman had done well for herself, but I always knew she would. Kennedy Carmichael was a force to be reckoned with, and I'd never loved her more. She knew what she wanted and took it without apologizing, despite what anyone thought. There wasn't another woman on this earth who I'd want to raise my kids. Kitten was a fucking lioness who fought for the people she loved with fervor and determination.

I'd loved her before she'd realized her potential, but now, seeing the woman she'd matured into took my breath away. I'd tried life without Kennedy, and it didn't work out well. Now, I was trying life with her and reaping the benefits of having her by my side.

My idea to bring Martha to Hambleton brought us closer—but Kennedy continued to make it clear we weren't together. Weirdly, though, she was fast becoming my best friend, and I loved and loathed it in equal measure.

We talked, laughed, joked, and grew closer every day.

The kids loved it. Kai even asked if we were getting married again. Everyone thought we were a couple, but we weren't. It was confusing because we acted like boyfriend and girlfriend without the sex.

I could feel us drawing closer to it, but Kitten held herself back.

Maybe she was right to. God only knew I wanted her to be sure, but my poor cock was suffering. Three cold showers a day and jacking off until my dick chafed slowly became my normality.

As horny as she got me, I wasn't even tempted to go anywhere else for relief. It was Kitten or nothing and would remain that way until they put me in the ground.

I dismounted and made my way to the offices.

It was September, and temperatures had cooled. The leaves on the trees were turning vibrant oranges and reds in anticipation of the colder weather.

My gut panged with a sense of yearning for everything Fall and Winter would bring.

I'd never done Halloween with the kids and couldn't wait to dress them up and bring them into town for trick-and-treating. Me and Kitten, Bowie, Layla, and even Cash and Cara were making a night of it with the kids. It was crazy. Last year me and the boys hit the bars in town to celebrate, but this year, the thought of doing the same left me feeling sick.

I opened the door to Kennedy's building, cursing under my breath.

My woman hadn't hired a receptionist yet, so anyone could walk in unannounced. I'd told Kitten to lock the door and come down to meet clients when they arrived, but she'd obviously forgotten.

Head shaking, I walked up the plush, carpeted stairs and headed for her office, thinking about how much I'd enjoy putting her over my knee.

I was about to call her name when the sound of voices made my steps falter.

"Does he know about us?" A deep tone asked.

I froze.

"No. He's not going to either, Scotty. It's not his business. Snow and I aren't together, so he doesn't need to know the ins and outs of my sex life."

My heart dropped into my gut, making it churn with nausea.

"He's obviously trying to get you back, Ned," the guy muttered. "Don't you think you should tell him how close we are?"

I heard Kennedy sigh before she replied. "It'll hurt him, Scotty. I don't want to cause any drama. Who I sleep with isn't anyone's business but mine. You told me we could keep it private, so keep it private. The last thing I want is for Snow to relapse because of me and you."

My body jerked like someone had struck me before I slumped against the wall. My fingers tremored slightly as I raised a hand and scraped it down my face.

Kennedy and Scotty?

Fuck.

I never put two and two together before. I'd assumed Kennedy was single; she'd never mentioned she was seeing someone, and I'd never asked. My heart began to ache, pain pounding through me.

Was this why she wouldn't commit to me?

Whereas I thought we were heading toward something special, Kennedy didn't. She probably only moved here under duress for the kids. Heat stained my cheeks because I felt like a fool. Why did I think I could get her back after everything I'd done? Kennedy was a strong woman who didn't take shit, so why would I believe for one minute she'd take mine?

I was such a fucking idiot.

Before I knew what I was doing, my feet moved toward the open door of her office. My jaw clenched as a familiar burn weaved through my chest. I didn't need her pity and didn't need his leftovers. Kennedy should've told me the truth from day one.

Storming into her office, I braced in case I saw them in a lover's embrace, but my steps faltered when I saw Kitten behind her desk and a tall, blond guy sitting by the window.

Kennedy looked up at my entrance, her face falling as she sensed my fury. "What's happened? Is it one of the kids?" She looked up and shook her head, exasperated. "Please don't tell me Kai's started fighting again."

Glowering, I breathed deeply, trying to keep my shit together despite my chest combusting. "You and him?" I demanded, jerking a thumb toward the slimy fucknut at the window.

Slowly, she closed her eyes. "Oh great!"

"Yeah," I gritted out. "I heard everything."

"Wait." Kennedy's eyes widened. "Were you eavesdropping?"

A muscle ticked in my jaw. "I heard you talkin' with your snaky, underhanded prick of a boyfriend over here."

"Hey!" the asshole sitting at the window protested. "I'm not a prick?"

Kennedy shook her head disappointedly. "That's a bitch move, Snow. Men don't eavesdrop. Men find out what's really happening before they get all murdery."

Heat fired my organs, my hands curling into fists. Leaning forward, I glared at Kennedy and bellowed,

"What do you care? You're in a relationship with somebody else!"

The room fell silent for a minute before Kennedy scrunched her nose up. "Huh?"

My breaths sawed in and out as I tried to keep ahold of my temper. Unable to stop myself, I leaned forward, getting in her face, and repeated her words back to her. *"Who I sleep with isn't anyone's business but mine.* What the fuck, Kennedy?"

"Ohhhhh," she said knowingly. "I get it now."

Scotty's stare darted from my head to my feet and back again. Mouth tipping up, he flashed his fake white teeth, and then, the dead fucker chuckled.

Snarling like a wild animal, I stalked toward him. Fucking Scotty was about to learn that taking my girl from me and then laughing about it was a bad move. This wasn't Vegas; the asshole wasn't protected here. He was on Demon's turf, not the Kings, and I'd show him how demons dealt with pricks like him.

Chest exploding, I hauled him up by the collar. "You're a fuckin' dead man." I pulled my fist back and clocked him hard across the jaw.

He went down like the sack of shit I suspected he was, hitting the floor with a pained groan.

"Fucking great!" Kennedy snapped. "Look what you've done. Now I'll have to take him back to the clubhouse and get Sophie to check you haven't broken his jaw." She stomped over, looking down at Scotty sprawled out on the floor with pursed lips. "Last time some ass punched him, I didn't hear the end of it for two weeks." She twisted her body toward me and poked me hard in the chest. "You've got it all wrong."

My blood pressure spiked. "I heard you!" I grated out. "You said you slept with him."

"I did." A pink flush stained her cheeks. "But it was once, years ago, remember? I told you about it."

My body locked.

"That night in the rental. I spoke about the time I needed comfort, and the guy was there, and he needed comfort too? Well..." Her eyes bugged out as she gestured toward Scotty.

My blood suddenly cooled.

I looked down at the slick-looking lawyer still sprawled on the floor and winced.

Fucking oops.

Okay, so maybe I'd got the wrong end of the stick. Still, I wasn't sorry.

My lungs heated again at the idea of Scotty's smarmy hands all over my woman.

The prick had it coming. No self-respecting man would stand by and not punch out the lights of some asshole who'd fucked his girl.

Scotty let out a moan. "I'll sue your biker ass," he muttered, sitting up. "You assaulted me." Gingerly, he got to his feet, rubbing at the spot on his jaw where my fist had connected. "They'll throw away the fucking key by the time I've finished with you. I'll arrange for some big fucker in jail to make you his girlfriend. Your sphincter will never be the same again."

My eyes turned to slits. "May as well make the fuckin' most of it then."

Quick as lightning, I pulled my arm back and punched him again. A satisfied grin spread across my face as I watched him drop to his ass.

"For fuck's sake, Kit," Kennedy snapped, exasperated. "Stop punching Scotty out."

I pointed down at the heap on the floor. "He started it."

"I never did a fucking thing!" the asshole protested from my feet.

I lifted one shoulder, shrugging nonchalantly. "Sorry, not sorry."

Kennedy's lips twisted. She thrust her hands to her hips and looked up. "It's like dealing with children," she complained good-naturedly.

"Preach, sister," Scotty said from the floor.

Kitten's eyes lowered, her mouth twisting into a smirk. "Got to admit, though, babe. It's kinda hot."

My lips tipped up.

This fucking girl did it for me.

Kennedy's soft hand slipped into mine, and she gazed up at me. "It was only one time. I'm sorry I didn't tell you it was Scotty. I was afraid this would happen if you found out." She glanced at the snake, still on his ass. "If it's any consolation, it wasn't very good. Honestly, it was so bad it kinda put me off sex for a while."

"Hey!" he exclaimed. "I heard that."

"You were meant to," she said dismissively. "I hope you've gained more stamina since then."

My blood pressure increased again, and I tugged Kitten to me. "Probably best to keep your mouth shut, baby. If you keep reminding me, I'll probably punch him again."

"Is it wrong that I'm tempted to keep talking?" she mused.

"Thanks, Ned," the fucknut whined.

I nuzzled my nose with hers. "When you're ready, I'll fuck you into the mattress," I vowed. "You already know I fuck good, and with me, at least you know you won't get no short dick man."

Her lips twitched. "I love it when you're romantic."

I cupped her beautiful face in my palm, leaned down, and pressed my lips to hers, groaning as her mouth opened slightly as she allowed my tongue to slip inside.

I was rusty at this. I'd never kissed another woman in all the time we were apart. But somehow, with her, it was like coming home.

My lips moved over hers, tasting her sweetness. The feel of her soft lips against mine made me forget everything except having her in my arms. Feelings surged inside me; love, possession, and outright need for my beautiful woman who belonged to me heart and soul.

All too soon, she stilled and pulled back slightly.

"I love you," I breathed against her cheek, needing the words to sink into her skin so she'd never forget she was mine.

"I know, but now's not really the time or place," she motioned toward the floor, "seeing as Scotty's watching our every move. It's ruining the mood for me."

I'd never wanted to take a man by the scruff of his neck and eject him from a room as much as I did at that moment. It didn't help that the same man once had his hands on what was mine. My eyes slid downward, and I sneered as he straightened his back, staring at us with interest.

"You sure you two aren't back together?" he asked, holding his hands up defensively as Kitten cocked an angry eyebrow. "Just saying because the chemistry you two put into the world tells me it ain't over."

Kennedy turned to me, her mouth set in a thin line. "I've changed my mind. Do you want to punch him again?"

"Can I?" I grinned, bouncing on the balls of my feet.

She laughed. "Do you think if we ignore him, he'll go away?"

My mouth twisted into a grimace. "Doubtful."

Scotty got to his feet, dusting himself off. He clicked his jaw from side-to-side, making sure it wasn't broken. Grinning like a smarmy Cheshire cat, he sauntered toward us, holding his hand out for me to shake. "I think we got off on the wrong foot. Nice to meet you. I'm Scotty, Kennedy's partner."

I folded my arms across my chest, ignoring his outstretched hand.

Sheepishly, he dropped his arm. "Not the friendly type, I see."

My stare flicked over him dismissively.

He was good-looking in a preppy way, but too pretty and too stuck-up. God only knew what she saw in the snaky bastard. The fucker only needed to look at me to see what her type really was. My woman only fucked him because she'd thought I was dead.

"I'm glad you're finally here." He gestured toward Kennedy's desk, all trace of humor leaving his face. "I think we need to sit for this."

The need to clock him again morphed into dread as I took in his serious expression.

It hit me that this guy put on an act to the world, but deep down, he was much more than a smarmy lawyer on the take. Maybe Scotty cared more than he let on, at least about the people in his circle.

I went to the window, picked up the chair the other man had sat on earlier, and carried it to Kennedy's desk, "Sit!" I ordered.

His lips flattened, but he did as he was told, watching me closely as I pulled another chair over, sat my ass down, and skewered him with a glare.

Kennedy sat in her beat-up leather chair on the other side of her desk, biting her cheek as she regarded Scotty closely. "What's going on?" she asked quietly.

Scotty leaned forward to address my woman, resting his elbows on his knees, hands dangling down. "I had an appointment two days ago," he began. "A Mr. B. Rawlins booked in to see me."

Something pinged in the back of my mind. *Rawlins?*

"New client," he continued. "He spoke to Lorraine, told her he'd just moved to the area, and wanted to throw some business my way." He sat straight, his stare hardening. "Turned out he wasn't a new client. Instead, he told me to deliver a message specifically to *you*."

I closed my eyes, uneasiness swirling in my stomach. Warning bells went off as a face suddenly flashed behind my eyes.

"He told me to relay how he had nothing to do with taking the kid but wished he'd thought of it. Then he went on to say he'd picked the wrong girlfriend," Scotty's eyes flicked to Kennedy, "and that he wished he'd waited for this knockout to arrive instead of settling for the other used-up old gash."

Kennedy's face paled.

"Then he said, in his world, it's an eye for an eye. You killed his VP, so the first man he's going after is yours. Told me to warn your brother he'll enjoy killing him the same way you killed his second-in-command. And after he's finished off every Speed Demon, he'll take their old ladies and do the same to them as he did to April."

My heart plummeted into my gut while Bear's sick threats floated around my head.

Visions of Kennedy laid out dead in the parking lot flashed behind my eyes, and I felt the monster awaken inside me, yawning as he lifted his head.

I didn't push him down, though. Bear's threats made it clear I'd need him to keep Kennedy, the twins, and the people I loved safe. The difference was, now, *I* was in control, not the demon. I could keep him dormant until I needed him to murder every Sinner who crossed my path.

I vowed to paint my skin with the blood of any man who dared to touch what was mine. The Sinners were no match for me or my brothers. Because there was one thing they'd forgotten about my club.

Mess with a Demon, and we'd raise hell like they'd never seen.

Chapter Twenty-Five

Kennedy

Shivering, I wrapped my coat tighter around my body, trying to keep a barrier between my skin and the cool Fall air.

The foliage down by the creek had been completely cleared to make way for the building work. The groundwork was in progress, the builders rushing to finish laying the foundations before Winter set in.

Kit had already picked out a vast plot of land, backing onto the stream for the house he was building me. We'd come down earlier that day to discuss the plans the architect had drawn up for us.

It was quiet here. Though I doubted the peace would last much longer due to the construction work commencing in Spring.

Foundations had been laid for eighteen plots: including mine, Layla's, Cara's, and Sophie's. More brothers and their ol' ladies wanted to build down here too but were still deciding where they wanted their houses to be situated.

All of the Stones, and Atlas, had managed to get in early.

Our houses would be side by side, all backing onto the creek, including the plot John had gifted Freya to build on when she finished Med school.

My stomach suddenly tugged.

I turned to see Kit walking down the steps of the makeshift hut where the building manager's office was.

He looked like Mr. GQ, in black jeans, a leather jacket, a scarf, and gloves. My heart fizzed as I watched how he took charge of the conversation, pointing out things on the plans I'd asked to be changed.

These days, his quiet confidence was probably one of the things I loved most about him. It reminded me so much of the young soldier who'd swept me off my feet and made me fall in love with him on a mountaintop. He was older, more mature, a stunning father, and a beautiful friend.

In just four months, he'd proven himself in ways I couldn't comprehend.

Kai and Kady were content, settled, and the happiest I'd ever seen. They'd bloomed under their dad's care and attention.

Kai would always be older than his years; after all, he had an old soul and had been here many times. But now, instead of taking on adult responsibilities that weighed him down, he was a kid again.

My little Kady girl never stopped smiling. She was like a sponge, soaking all the love and beauty into her shiny new soul. She wanted to see and learn everything she could. Life excited her, and I knew one day she'd wander because she yearned to experience all the new things.

Music continued to weave joy around her heart. Billy, the prospect, who'd turned out to be a gifted musician, spent hours with her, playing guitar and singing.

All in all, everything was ticking over nicely. Despite Bear's threat, there'd been no sign of the Sinners, but it didn't stop the club from preparing for war. Even the ol' ladies and I partook in shooting practice and drills in case of an attack. The girls and I worked with Sophie, learning self-defense techniques. It turned out that Layla was a natural with a gun. Her aim was perfect, and her instincts were second to none.

I'd thought about renting a place in town but decided to stay at the clubhouse, which was bursting at the seams with families. I knew it wouldn't be forever, though, and at least I could go to bed without worrying about a nighttime attack.

The only significant change to our lives was that we couldn't leave the clubhouse unaccompanied.

Sophie and I were shadowed at work. The women couldn't even grocery shop without a couple of bodyguards looking on.

I'd discussed it with Kit and decided to hire security for the office. That way, my clients wouldn't be frightened off by a big, burly biker giving them the evil eye when they came in for an appointment. It had taken some time, but with the help of Colt, Kit had managed to track down a guy he knew—ex-special forces—who, luckily, was in between jobs. In fact, we were about to leave the club to go and meet him.

I watched Kit check his phone before his eyes lifted to meet mine. Sensual lips hitched into a grin that almost made my panties spontaneously combust.

My heart fluttered, and my stomach tugged just like it did the first time I'd ever danced, just for him.

After he'd brought Martha to town, I started to see him in a new light.

He wasn't my Snow, the soldier anymore. He was Kit Stone, biker, dad, brother, and son, loved by everyone and everything in between.

When I fell in love with him as a nineteen-year-old girl, I was dazzled by his looks and big dick energy.

What we had now was more mature. It wasn't based on golden eyes, a blinding smile, and young, all-encompassing love. It was based on friendship and mutual respect.

His PTSD still affected him, but the difference now was that he talked to me, his dad, and his brothers. If he felt like he was slipping, we'd jump on his bike and ride up to Rock Springs so he could go to a group counseling session.

A few days before, we'd laid in bed whispering so as not to wake the kids, and he admitted the monster was still inside. He worried it would come out and hurt me or the kids one day, but I had faith it wouldn't.

I'd met his dark side the night he saved our baby girl, and I didn't think it was so bad. It was clear to everyone that Kit Stone loved me and our children with his heart and soul. So, it stood to reason that whatever demon lived inside him loved us too, which I was glad of.

Over time, the Speed Demons had saved eight girls just from patrolling and stopping strange vehicles. The club had disrupted the Sinner's lucrative business, so it would only be a matter of time before Bear brought war to our door.

Kit warned me he'd need his demon at its most destructive if the club was to prevail.

I understood, especially when I thought back to the night he brought my Kady back to me. I reassured him that if the monster could save us, I welcomed it. Plus, it was like I always said, I liked a bit of monster in my man.

The corners of my mouth turned up as I watched Kit saunter toward me, his thighs flexing under the denim of his jeans. My nipples tingled just watching him strut his fine ass towards me, all leather, smirk, and sin.

"Sorry, Kitten. Needed to make sure Kevin understood the changes. I told him you'll sue his ass if your closet's too small."

"You know me well." I laughed as his hand caught mine, and he splayed our fingers together. Warmth radiated from my fingertips and up my arm, finally settling around my heart that had always beat just for him. We still weren't 'together.' I loved him and knew it wouldn't be long before I gave him the green light. I just wanted to wait for the right moment.

He pulled me toward his bike. "Come on. We gotta meet your new security guy in a half hour."

I fell into step beside him. "I can't wait. If Atlas scares any more potential clients away from my office, I'll be broke."

"That's a bit dramatic, Kitty." He grabbed my helmet from the handlebars and handed it to me. "My Dad's and the King's business alone will keep you in designer shoes for the rest of your days."

"Hey! I've got two kids to put through college," I reminded him, pulling my helmet on and fastening the chin strap tight.

He threw a long, muscular leg over the bike. "You mean *we've* got two kids to put through college." He settled his ass and held out a hand, helping me on.

Leaning forward, I slid my arms under his jacket and around his waist, stroking my fingers over the ridges of his hard abs.

The sexy asshole flexed them, showing off.

"Behave yourself," I murmured through the built microphone in my helmet.

He turned and shot me his sexy smirk. "No fun in that, Kitten. Your turn to play DJ. What's it gonna be?"

I slipped my hand inside my coat, pulled my cell out, and looked for a song. I wanted to play something that would convey to him how I felt. How I was scared of jumping in but excited at the same time. How crazy he drove me, but also how much I loved it.

Something that was us.

My eyes fell on 'Sunshine Baby' by The Japanese House, and I smiled.
Perfect.

The ride to town was exhilarating but cold.

I'd become a real biker chick lately. Kit often brought me to work and picked me up again on his bike. It had turned colder, and Kit told me this bike would be put away soon for Winter. It snowed heavily in Southern Wyoming, and it was almost impossible to ride for three months of the year.

Because of that, Kit wanted to make the most of out of riding.

I loved being on the back of his bike, especially as it gave me an excuse to touch his hard stomach. A tiny thrill ran through me every time I looked at my face painted onto the teardrop-shaped fuel tank. It proved that throughout the years apart, the heartbreak, PTSD, and his actions resulting from it, he'd remembered and kept me close the only way he knew how.

It didn't take long to ride into town. The flowers planted by the roadside had died. Orange, brown, and yellow leaves now covered the street instead of the verdant green colors produced by the Summer months.

I held on tight, resting my cheek against Kit's back. Despite the biting wind whipping my cheeks until they were stinging and red, I'd never felt warmer inside.

We turned onto Monument Street, heading slowly toward my office. Kit pulled over and parked, sitting back, idling the engine. We both took our helmets off and hung them on the handlebars.

"You're freezing," He murmured, enveloping my smaller hands in his. "Maybe we should take your Range from now on."

"We meaning you?" I deadpanned.

I'd paid for someone to drive my Range Rover to Wyoming. It was nice having my baby back. I'd missed her luxury and secretly enjoyed turning heads whenever I got behind the wheel. She was tricked out to fuck with color-coded everything. The only good thing about putting Veronica away was that the Range could come out to play instead.

I watched Kit's face light up as he laughed. Something he did more and more lately. "You know I always drive, Kitten," he reminded me. "I like to look after you."

I rolled my eyes good-naturedly. "So, that's your excuse."

Snaking a hand across my shoulder, he pulled me closer. "Yep. And I'm sticking to it."

We kept throwing playful jibes at each other as he took my keys and unlocked the door, ushering me inside. Thanks to the thermostat I'd set the day before, warm air hit me, and I smiled contentedly. "What time is the security guy coming?" I asked as we headed up the stairs.

"'Bout ten minutes," he replied. "There's time for you to set up. He'll buzz me when he's close, and I'll go down and let him in."

My head cocked to one side. "Where do you know him from again?"

Kit's face paled slightly. "A military bud from way back," he mumbled cagily.

A bright red flag started to wave inside my head. Usually, he was open and honest, even when discussing things he knew I wouldn't like, such as the week before when he took Kai for a ride on the back of his bike around the fields and woods surrounding the clubhouse.

I made my way toward my desk, plonking myself in my chair. "You're up to something." Steepling my fingers, I narrowed my eyes. "You're looking decidedly shifty."

He parked his ass on the side of my desk. "I'm nervous introducing you to him. I guess I don't know what your reaction will be when you meet him."

"You don't need to worry about that, Kit," I argued gently. "Is he a good, decent man?"

He stared deep into my eyes. "Yeah."

I picked up my diary and started to flick through it. "Then I'm sure we'll get along fine."

A dull buzz came from Kit's jeans. He reached into his pocket and checked his cell phone. "He's early."

"Not a bad thing," I murmured absentmindedly, reviewing the day's appointments. "I like good timekeepers."

Kit finished tapping into his cell and got to his feet. Leaning down, he kissed the top of my head. "I'll send him up and make myself scarce, so you two can talk."

Taking in Kit's voice, croaky with emotion, I pulled back slightly. The red flags waved inside my head again when I saw a telltale sheen in his eyes. "What's going on?"

Silence fell upon us as he stared at me with golden eyes, making my knees weak and my blood pump faster.

"Always remember I've got your back," he murmured thickly. "Whatever you need, you get. If it makes you happy, it's yours, baby. Don't ever forget that. I don't care if you're not my ol' lady. I wouldn't give a shit if I never got a ring on your finger. I'm always gonna give you beauty. I took from you for a long time, Kitten, but not anymore."

Our eyes remained locked.

His words and actions all pointed to the fact he was up to something, but it didn't worry me. I'd watched Kit evolve into a decent man in the past months.

Quite simply, I trusted him.

"I know you've got my back," I assured him. "Now, let my new employee in, and I'll see you around three."

He shot me a roguish grin, turned on his heel, and left the room.

Getting my notepad handy, I looked over the interview questions I'd set out the night before. My stomach began to fizz, and a slight tremor shook my fingers. Deep murmurs carried up the stairs, and I stilled as a weird feeling washed over me.

What was the matter with me? Why did I feel like something big was happening?

It was weird; over the years, I'd lost a lot of my spirituality. Life as a working single mom got busy, and it was easy to get bogged down with everyday things. Somewhere along the way, I'd become jaded. Maybe it was because I lost the love of my life so young; who knew?

But lately, I'd noticed my soul starting to speak to me again. I found myself feeling people out and taking notice of signs. Maybe it was being around Kit again. Perhaps my soul felt whole now it had reunited with its other half.

With him, I wasn't afraid to be me.

Footsteps muffled by the thick pile of the stair carpet pulled me away from my thoughts. I went back to my notes, doing the last preparation for the interview ahead.

Meeting Kit's military friends brought an automatic smile to my face. I'd met a few back in the day, but we were all in a better place now, and I couldn't wait to hear all their old war stories.

I looked up as a shadowy figure appeared at the door.

He stood about six feet tall with one of those body types that seemed thin, but you still sensed strength and power underneath. At first glance, he looked to be in his mid-fifties, but his face was so weathered he could have easily been ten years younger. He exuded a calmness that I liked immensely. I suspected he wasn't a man who said much, but when he did talk, everyone listened.

Smiling, I exited my chair and walked toward him, hand outstretched. "Hey," I said brightly. "My name's Kennedy. Thanks for coming in today..." My voice trailed off as our gazes met. Every muscle in my body froze, and my mind began to reel because I knew those blue eyes.

My hand flew to my mouth, and I drew in a stuttered gasp as recognition hit me.

The man before me was older and more worn, but his face had been in my mind so often over the past ten years I could never have forgotten it. I could see by the lines of exhaustion etched into his skin that he'd struggled. My heart went out to him because a man with so much goodness deserved more.

Tears welled in my eyes.

I'd missed him so much. For years I'd searched, even paying the firm's PIs to scour the country, but they always came up empty.

Something loosened inside as tears burned the back of my throat. My fingers reached for his, just to ensure he wasn't an illusion. I'd thought of him over the years with an aching chest. I'd prayed he was safe somewhere. I'd prayed one day I'd see him again.

"Ed?" I choked out. "Oh, my God!"

He reached out and wiped away tears I didn't realize were falling. "Don't cry, Kitty."

A loud sob escaped me as emotions I couldn't hold in filled me to the brim. I lowered my head and wept.

Ed's strong arms came around me, and he gently pulled me closer. "Please don't cry. I'm here now, Kitty."

"I can't believe it." I hiccoughed through my tears. "I've looked for years."

His hand rubbed my back reassuringly. "After Paulie passed, I hit rock bottom. Ended up in Arizona, which was too hot, so I tried New Mexico. Eventually, I got some work and shelter, but the old guy I helped out passed away. Went to Colorado, got sick and thought I would die, but someone found me and helped me. She was a nurse at a hospital in Denver; helped me register my name to get treatment. That was when your Snow found me."

My heart bloomed at his words. After a minute, I pulled back slightly. "Snow found you?"

"Yeah." Ed's blue eyes twinkled as they darted between mine. "He had an alert out in every hospital in the country, searching for a homeless guy with variations of my name."

I pressed a hand to my throat, tears tracking down my face. "Kit did this?"

Ed's eyes clouded. "He found me three months ago. Got me enrolled in a Veteran's clinic in Grand Junction. Did nine weeks there, and they helped me, Kitty."

My hands slid up, cupping his weathered cheeks. "I'm sorry I let you down in Vegas. I couldn't find you. Then I got offered a place in Duke and left."

"No, Kitten," he retorted. "I've never once blamed you for what happened. You were the only person in the crowd who ever saw me. You stopped me from starving to death."

My bottom lip quivered before a newfound sense of determination took over. "You're staying." It was more of a demand than a request.

A haunted look took over his face. "If you'll have me, Kitty. You're the only family I've got left."

His words hit me in the stomach, and I lost it. Letting out a soft moan, I threw my arms around him and sobbed.

"It's okay, Kitty," he whispered soothingly against my hair. "We're here now. Somehow fate smiled on us." His hands went to my shoulders, drawing me back slightly. "I'm gonna be here with you, protecting you. Your young man told me everything, and I want to help."

Another lump formed in my throat. "You're really going to work here?"

"Yeah. I'm even gonna work your reception until you get someone else," Ed confirmed. "Nobody will get through those doors without getting past me."

My mind spun with shock, disbelief, and so many questions. "Where are you living, Ed? Are you okay? Do you need anything?"

"The Vet Center helped me claim my military benefits and pension. I've taken an apartment in a complex just outside town, and your young man loaned me a car until I can save up for one."

"I'll buy you a car," I offered.

His fingers, still gripping my shoulders, tightened slightly. "No. You won't."

I sighed frustratedly. This remarkable man had looked out for me when he should've been looking out for himself.

His country had treated him poorly, even after he gave up the essence of himself to protect it.

I'd dreamed about finding Ed. After I became a partner, I searched for him, wanting to look out for him the same way he always did me.

And now I could.

"I want to help, Ed," I insisted.

"No," he repeated. "I've got a job and a roof. I wouldn't take money off your Snow, and I'm not taking it off you."

"Where are you gonna sleep? On the floor?"

Ed laughed. "I've got a bed. Got a stove, fridge. TV, cups, plates, knives, and forks. If I need anything else, I've got money in the bank. Grand Junction got me a government grant to help set me up." He bent toward me slightly, no doubt to drive his point home. "I'm good."

A burst of giggles bubbled from my chest, and I felt myself beam.

"Let's sit, drink coffee, and catch up," I suggested.

Ed jerked a nod, smiling right at me. "Sounds perfect."

Breaker

And that was what we did. I made a pot of coffee, cracked open some cookies, and reconnected with one of the people I loved most.

I was walking on air, head in the clouds, away with the fairies happy, and it was all because of one man who, instead of telling me he loved me, was actually showing me.

My newfound faith wasn't just in myself or even Kit, although he'd repeatedly proven himself. He made me yearn for something I never thought I'd want again, not after all the hurt and pain.

Kit was making me believe again, not just in myself or him.

He was making me believe in us.

Chapter Twenty-Six

Breaker

I couldn't get Kennedy's reaction to being reunited with Ed out of my head, even though it had been a week since I'd taken him to her office and left them to it.

Later that day, when I picked her up, my palms were sweating in anticipation of how she'd react to me finding her old friend.

It wasn't a recent thing. I'd started to put feelers out while I was at Grand Junction. It was Ken who gave me the idea, and once Colt got involved, it was just a case of sitting back and crossing our fingers.

The day after we got the hit, Colt flew to Colorado and spoke to Ed. Once we got the go-ahead, we took him straight to Grand Junction for treatment.

I didn't tell Kennedy because Ed wouldn't commit to relocating here until his treatment was over. Maybe he worried it wouldn't take and didn't want to get her hopes up.

The second Nina confirmed Ed's rehabilitation was going well, I offered him a fresh start, and he jumped at it.

Cash picked him up the day before he reunited with Kitten and brought him back to Hambleton. By then, I'd kept so many secrets from her that when she found out what I'd been up to behind her back, it could've gone either way.

I'd waited outside her office until three fifteen that afternoon, biting my nails until they bled.

When she finally strutted from her building, I held my breath, suddenly double guessing myself. But I should've known better.

Kitty pulled the passenger door to her Range open, jumped in, grabbed my face, and gave me the most tender and beautiful kiss of my life. While our lips tangled, I felt tears on her face. My woman was so touched, so fucking happy and relieved Ed was close again that she was lost for words the entire drive home.

Her kiss blew me away.

It was the first time since we'd found each other again that she'd instigated anything like that, and it made my heart fill with fresh hope that we'd be okay.

It hadn't escaped my notice that Kitty never instigated physical contact; it was always me. The only time she'd ever touched me was in the shower the night I got Kady back, and when she slid her arms around my stomach whenever we went out on my bike.

She was my best friend in the world. The one person I knew I could talk to about anything, and she'd still love me, regardless. She'd proven it time and again.

Even now, sitting up at the bar in the clubhouse, watching her talking and laughing with Iris, I couldn't believe how well she fitted in everywhere she went. You could put her in a courtroom and watch her fight for the underdog, or let her loose in a dingy dive bar, and she'd still be the brightest light in the room.

Sophie wandered over, her gaze sliding from me to Kennedy. She smiled and clambered onto the stool next to me. "How are you doing?" she asked.

"Never been better." I shifted my stare to her. "You okay?"

Her eyebrows drew together thoughtfully. "I've never seen anyone look at another person the way you look at Kennedy. It's like you're scared to take your eyes off her in case she disappears. Every time you're in a room together, I see it. It's beautiful."

"She's my light, Soph," I murmured. "But there's so much more to her than what's on the surface. I can't look away from her because I see everything she is, and it pulls me in."

She cocked her head slightly. "What do you mean?"

I nodded to where Kitten and Kady giggled with their heads together. "Kennedy's got insecurities but would rather die than show them. She hates being vulnerable but loves people all the more for trusting her with their vulnerabilities. She grew up lonely, so she gets emotionally attached to people and loves them with all she's got. She's a dreamer who's nostalgic and has a heart full of hope, even when assholes like me break it. Kennedy Carmichael believes in people and thank God because if she ever gave up on me, I'd wither away," my stare turned back to Sophie, "like I did before."

Her wide eyes had a telltale sheen to them as she thought about my words. "I love the way you see her."

My throat thickened with every sliver of emotion in my soul. "I love that *she* sees *me*."

A huge smile spread over Sophie's face. "Stick with her, Kit."

My gaze went back to my beautiful girls. "Always."

"She'll come around. She's nearly there. I can see it."

I smiled. "I know, but what Kitten gives me now is enough. Anything more's a bonus."

Soph's sniff made me look at her again.

A tear slid down her cheek and she swiped at it. "Don't mind me. This pregnancy's turned me into an emotional wreck. I cried when Jolly Batman got told off the other day. He looked so sad." Her eyes lifted over my shoulder and softened. "Hey, big man."

I jumped as a big, meaty hand smacked down on my shoulder. "I swear to fuckin' God, Break. If you've upset my woman, I'll knock you from one end of this room to the other."

"Oh, stop it, Danny." Sophie sniffed. "He says such beautiful, amazing things; it makes me emotional. Why can't you say romantic things like Kit does?"

Atlas sauntered to his wife's side and jerked a thumb at his chest. "'Cause I haven't got a fuckin' vagina."

Her eyes narrowed. "Maybe if you said nice things to me, you'd get more action."

I smirked.

Atlas's mouth thinned. "Dunno why you're lookin' so smug. It's not like Ned's let you lay a finger on her, right?"

"You'll know what being celibate's like soon if you don't shut your big mouth," Soph hissed, her whiskey-brown eyes hardening.

Atlas ducked his head, suitably ashamed. "Prez wants us in Church." He glanced at me. "Move your ass."

"Why can't you just be nice?" Sophie snapped.

Atlas turned and stepped between her legs. "I *am* nice to you, Stitch baby." He palmed her pregnant stomach. "How's the Demons next SAA doin' today? He makin' you antsy?"

Her eyes softened. "What if it's a girl?"

"Then the Demons better change their policy on women bein' members 'cause I'll make sure my little princess can kick every ass in this club."

I bit back a laugh because I didn't doubt he meant every goddamned word.

Atlas and Soph decided to not find out the sex of the baby. Even so, I reckoned the doc could tell from the scan pictures, though she swore she couldn't.

Taking a last look at Kitten, I slid from my stool, purposely catching Billy's eye.

The chin lift I sent him was a silent request to keep an eye on my girls before I started for the corridor leading to Church.

I caught a flash of black, and I slowed down to look at the myriad of cuts decorating the wall.

They all belonged to brothers no longer with us, including Grandpa Bandit's, which took pride of place in the top spot.

It was mind-blowing how much the club had changed since Dad took over.

We still had originals like Abe, but he'd be the first to say how much better things were now. Bandit was a lunatic by all accounts. Back then, he'd shoot members if they got out of line. Nothing fatal, but many a brother had a bullet hole scar in his shoulder with a crazy story to accompany it.

Club life was more brutal back when the members were true outlaws. Every man at one point served a prison sentence, some quite a few. The law constantly rode the brothers' asses.

Since Pop took over, things had quietened down, except now we had a potential war with the Sinners knocking on our door.

Bandit would've been in his element.

Approaching the meeting room, I pressed my thumb to the pad on the wall. A loud buzz filled the air, and I opened the door to Church.

I gave Dad and Abe a chin lift before my stare went to Cash.

"She left you holding the baby?" I laughed.

My brother had Wilder laid out on the table in a blanket, fast asleep.

"Is he okay on there?" I asked. "I'm sure I've read somewhere you shouldn't leave babies on tables in case they roll off."

"Well, I'm not gonna let that happen, am I?" Cash retorted. "I can't keep holdin' him. He's gettin' heavy."

"Why didn't you bring his stroller thing in?" Dad got to his feet with a *tsk*, pushing Cash out the way to get to his grandson. "Stupid fucker." He picked him, placing Wilder on his shoulder with his hand to his back. "Where's Atlas and Bowie?"

"At's seein' to Sophie, and I guess Bo's on his way." I walked around the table and took my seat.

"Everythin' okay with Ed?" Cash asked. "He's a good guy. Glad you got him here, bro. Knows his shit, too. Told me there's not much he doesn't know about weaponry. He could come in handy if the Sinners start shit."

"He's here to protect Kitty, not us," I argued. "She's out all day at her office."

"Cara's at the gallery," Cash pointed out. "And Sophie's at the hospital."

"And they're guarded, too," I reminded him. "If you want a war Vet who's a specialist in weaponry to guard your ol' lady, hire one like I did."

"I think I preferred you zombied up," my brother muttered. "At least you didn't answer back."

"You can't keep up with him, boy," Abe interjected. "Now he's clearheaded; he runs rings around ya. If you're not careful, Prez may rethink who's sittin' to his right."

Cash cursed at Abe under his breath, folding his arms across his chest just as the door opened and Atlas came striding in, Bowie following.

Dad checked his watch. "Nice of you to join us. Sent you out fifteen minutes ago. How long does it take ya to fetch two officers?"

"Sorry, boss." Atlas took his seat. "Had to find Bo."

"I was in the can," Bowie explained, sprawling out in his chair and rubbing his gut. "Thought I was havin' a fuckin' food baby."

Chuckles rolled through the room.

Breaker

Dad shook his head. "It's bad enough that you fuckers are obsessed with your dicks and reality TV. Do we really have to add your shits into the mix?" His lips thinned as he patted Wilder's back gently. "We've got a future prez here; let's try to be a good influence instead of fuckin' animals."

"How do you know he's a future prez?" Abe challenged, nodding toward me. "Our Kai looks to be a born Speed Demon. By all accounts, we've gotta future prez there, too."

"Agreed!" Cash announced.

Silence fell over the room, every eye snapping to him.

"If Wilder doesn't wanna be Prez or even join the club, I'll support him," he added. "Not puttin' my boy through what I went through. Don't give a fuck what he does; just want him to be happy."

Dad glowered. "The eldest son of the eldest son, Cash. It's the way it's always been."

Bowie scoffed. "It's only been that way for one generation, Pop. Bandit handed it to you, end of story."

"But it's tradition," Dad argued.

"We're not exactly the British Royal family," Cash pointed out. "You took over from Gramps. That's it. The club only started in sixty-eight." His lips twitched. "It's hardly been sworn on the fuckin' Constitution."

Pop looked affronted. "Bandit would roll over in his grave."

"Bandit would want to gavel to go to the craziest motherfucker who liked shooting people," Abe retorted with some side-eye. "You made that so-called tradition up. Not Bandit."

Dad raised a hand to rub his beard. "I better start groomin' Kai for the gavel. Looks like things are gonna change around here."

"You're not grooming him for shit," I argued. "He's eight years old. Let him be a kid. If he wants it when he's older, he'll have to earn it. Until then, leave him be."

Abe chuckled. "Mark my words; Kai will be an asset to this club. It's in his blood. Your woman's kin is a King. Your boy's gonna rule the fuckin' roost. He's smart and strong. Have you seen him in that ring already? He's a fuckin' natural."

Dad looked at me thoughtfully. I could almost see his brain going into overdrive.

"Kennedy will flip her lid if you start pressuring Kai, and I'll back her all the way." I sat, leaning forward, elbows to the table. "If she leaves and takes the kids back to LV, I'll be on the same flight."

Dad held his free hand up. "Alright, alright. I'll back off."

Cash laughed. "Sure you will."

I scraped a hand down my face, suddenly exasperated by Dad, though I understood why he was desperate for the next generation of kids to take an interest in the club.

It was simple; Pop was proud of the legacy.

Although it didn't appear so, I was, too, as were Cash, Bowie, Abe, and even Freya. We all loved the club and what it represented, but we also knew from experience that you couldn't force things.

Cash opened up to me about the pressures he'd always felt weighing on his shoulders.

Our grandpa made him believe it was weak to have feelings, show love, or even mercy. Bandit taught him to hurt others before they hurt him, which explained a lot.

Cash was the heir, and Bowie the spare, which meant I was at the bottom of the food chain. But I hadn't thought about how being the heir and the spare affected my brothers growing up, too. I didn't have the same pressures, so I'd enlisted, but Bowie and Cash hadn't had the same choices.

It helped me gain a new understanding.

Life gave everyone demons that lived inside us, put there for different reasons. I wasn't so goddamned special.

"Bro," Cash said, pulling my thoughts back into the room. "Is Ned's birthday surprise all set? Anythin' you need me to do?"

I grinned.

There was one more ace up my sleeve, and if it didn't bring my woman back to me, I'd give up the ghost and just accept things as they were.

"Nope. All I need is for you to do what I've already asked. We'll go to Giovanni's for a birthday dinner, then all back here for the big reveal."

"She's gonna fuckin' weep," Atlas mused. "Gotta say, Break. Even I'm fuckin' impressed with this one. God only knows how you've pulled it off."

"Yeah," I agreed. "But Kennedy's worth it."

Dad's lips thinned again. "Soppy cunt."

"There you go again," Cash berated. "He's doin' somethin' nice to get his woman back, and you're tellin' him he's an idiot for it. Leave him alone."

Dad's eyes softened, and he shot me a wink. "He knows."

My heart warmed because Dad was right.

I finally had his approval, maybe in some ways I always did. Still, I had to be proud of myself before accepting another's belief in me.

A knock sounded on the door. A buzz filled the air, and Colt walked in.

We all exchanged chin lifts before his stare rested on Dad. "We gotta problem."

Dad stood and placed Wilder gently back in Cash's arms. Taking his seat again, he regarded Colt thoughtfully. "Out with it then."

Colt blew out a breath before placing three grainy images on the table. "These are the pictures of the car chasing Atlas and Kit." He pointed to the license plate. "See that?"

Cash's brow furrowed. "Yeah. What about it?"

"The chase happened weeks ago. Since then, I've been tracking that plate down and getting nowhere fast. After getting nothin' but dead ends, I decided to take a peek inside a few top-secret databases."

Dad's eyes bugged out. "Don't tell me, the Men in Black are on their way here to arrest you for getting' caught hackin' into their fuckin' computers."

"Those ball sacks couldn't catch me on my worst day, Prez." Colt tapped one of the photos and looked at us all in turn. "The way that license plate's laid out reminded me of somethin', so I did a bit of digging and just got a hit." He paused, his gaze settling on Dad. "It's a government plate, Dagger. FBI, to be exact."

A few seconds of shocked silence settled over the room. Suddenly, curses and shouts rang out as the severity of the situation sunk in.

Dad held his hand up for silence. "Quiet! I need to think." His hand went to his beard, and he rubbed it contemplatively for a minute.

My stomach felt like a heavy weight had settled inside it. The ramifications of Colt's words hit me over the head like a sledgehammer.

"What the fuck's goin' on?" Bowie breathed. "Why were the FBI tryin' to traffic women?"

Dad closed his eyes. "God knows."

"I've thought about it," Colt muttered. "Every agency from the local PDs to the President's Office is filled with people with an agenda. Believe me, boys; when it comes to extreme wealth, the rich are so fuckin' terrified of losin' everythin', they'd sell their sons and daughters to stay on top. The social elite is a club that's impossible to infiltrate but also impossible to turn your back on if you're one of 'em."

Dad rested his elbows on the table and held his head in his hands. "This could be bad. If the FBI's involved, we've gotta watch our backs, not only with the Sinners but with the law, too."

Cash thrust a hand through his hair. "They could storm this place and get rid of us with no comeback whatso—fuckin'—ever."

An uneasy feeling washed over me.

Cash was right.

If dirty government agencies were involved with all the bad shit taking over Hambleton, things ran way deeper than we'd realized.

We were a biker club, and yeah, we had support from the locals. But we were no match for the fucking FBI. If there was a darker element at force here, we'd need backup, and I didn't mean allied clubs like the Kings.

The Demons needed to make friends in high places. We had kids, ol' ladies, and people who depended on us. The Demons needed to find a way to take on the big guns because if the FBI were involved, our hands would be tied into knots we couldn't escape from.

A feeling of dread settled in my chest because this latest threat was no joke. If we had to take on the Government, the club would be tied up in so much red tape, it could prove fatal. If we had to take on the FBI, there'd only be one outcome.

They'd annihilate us.

Chapter Twenty-Seven

Kennedy ~ November 1ˢᵗ

Quiet giggles and sounds of whispering roused me from my sleep. As I snuggled deeper into the comforter, I heard throats clear before my three favorite voices began to sing.

"Happy birthday to you. Happy birthday to you. Happy birthday, dear Mommyyy. Happy birthday to you."

I cracked one eye open, and my heart leaped at the sight before me.

My three Ks were standing by the bed, holding colorfully wrapped gifts, flowers, and a tray that I really hoped was loaded with my breakfast.

"What's all this?" I croaked, sitting up, still half-dazed from sleep. "Are they roses?"

"Daddy got them for you," Kady told me excitedly. "And he got you perfume and a load of that skin stuff you like. Tonight, we're all going out for a family dinner."

I smiled as Kai cocked his head the exact same way his father did. "You're not supposed to tell her what her presents are, Kady," he chastised.

Kady's face fell. "I'm sorry."

Kai's eyes clouded at the realization he'd upset her. His face reddened, and he hung his head.

Kit glanced between them and barked out a laugh. "Are you two actually fighting?"

"This is as far as it gets." I smiled. "They tell each other off, then feel guilty for being little assholes to each other."

Still chuckling, Kit stepped forward and dropped a kiss on my cheek. "Happy birthday, Kitten."

I took the steaming mug of coffee he handed me from the tray and took a sip, letting out a moan of appreciation as it slipped down my throat. "Thanks."

Kady crawled on the bed next to me, followed by Kai.

Kit placed the tray on the nightstand and climbed onto the foot of the bed, resting his hand on my leg. "Open your gifts."

Smiling, I placed my mug on the tray and grabbed the first parcel. "Hmmm." I tapped my finger to my lip. "I wonder what this could be."

Kady bounced next to me excitedly. "Open it!" she squealed.

Kai rolled his eyes at his sister. "You already know what it is," he grunted. "What ya so excited for?"

Kady's little body slumped against mine.

"Hey," Kit said gently, staring at our son. "We don't put our girls down for being happy and excited. Seein' 'em smile makes *us* happy."

Kai thought about his dad's words briefly before turning to his sister. "Sorry, Kady."

"It's okay," my sweet girl replied. "Sunny isn't really mad with you. Give her time. She'll like you again soon."

Mine and Kit's eyes met. "What happened?" I asked.

Kady looked up at me. "Sunny wanted to stretch out over the pool to save a drowning bug. Kai wouldn't let her, and she got angry with him."

Kit's gave our boy a fist bump. "You did the right thing. She's not allowed near the pool without an adult to watch her. Well done, Son."

My boy's little chest puffed out. "I know. These women need to listen to us men more. We'll keep 'em safe."

I suppressed a rising bubble of laughter, glancing at Kit. "You've created a monster."

He grinned. "Nothin' wrong with a bit of monster in a man. Eh, Kitty?"

"Nope." I looked down, concentrating on pulling the wrapping paper off the box in my lap. A smile curved my mouth when I saw black leather, pointy, high-heeled boots with red soles. "Whoop!" I yelled, punching the air.

"They're from Daddy," Kady told me, a sage look on her face. "He said they're right up your alley."

I smiled down at my girl. "Daddy's right." My eyes lifted to Kit, who was watching me intently. "Thank you."

He smiled and mouthed, *I love you.*

My heart fluttered, a single thought filling my head, making my inner voice whisper, *I love you, too.*

It took me no time to unwrap a beautiful charm bracelet from the kids, an expensive skincare set, and a pair of designer strappy heels. As I opened them, I smiled because I immediately saw the sentiment behind them. They were exactly like the pair I'd worn the night we'd watched Raven DJ at Underground.

I loved that he remembered. I loved that he reminded me of what we had before all the bad stuff got in the way. My throat kept choking up because there was no pain anymore. Just beauty.

Eventually, I got to the last gift after oohing and aahing over my presents. My fingers lovingly peeled the paper off to reveal a flash of dusky pink. I took hold of the silky material, held it up, and stilled.

It was a replica of the dress I'd worn for him that night.

Kit's eyes roamed over my face tenderly. "Kids. Your mom wore a dress like that ten years ago, the first time I told her I loved her." The pure emotion in his voice wrapped around my heart and squeezed lovingly. "Wear it tonight?" he asked.

Somehow, his meaning filtered through my psyche, and my heart unfurled like petals on the first day of Spring. He wanted to return to that perfect night and change what happened next. He intended to rewrite the bad years, but this time, with our kids along for the ride.

I'd lost my Snow once, and it left me empty. Somehow, since he'd been back by my side, he'd filled me up to the brim again. The beautiful words he'd once whispered came back to me again.

"You're gonna know everything about me. You'll get it all. Good, bad, and everything in between. One day, I'm gonna give you a family. A posse of men and women who'll have your back, and they'll be military, blood, and chosen family. One day, I'll plant my babies in there, put a ring on it, and give you a traditional family too."

For years, I thought he'd lied, but I was wrong. It took longer than we'd anticipated, but my golden boy had finally kept his vow.

"You look beautiful, Kitty," Ed said proudly.

Tristan clapped his hands together. "Like a movie star."

"Gotta say, Tris. That's what I call a blowout," Anna commented, eyeing my hair.

I smiled as I took in Iris's soft curls, Cara's funky corkscrews, and Layla's poker straight do. "I think you're both hair geniuses."

"Abe's gonna be all over me like a rash," Iris murmured, fluffing up her locks.

"Lucky bitch." Tristan pouted as he twirled Kady's hair with the brush while angling the blow-dryer onto it, "Wish a hot biker was all over me like a rash."

"You're a good-looking man," Iris assured him. "Have you met Arrow?"

"Hmm," Tristan replied. "He likes both sides of the coin. Crossing swords and stroking the kitty. Sorry, but I like rods of steel, not soft pussy cats."

"Has Arrow got a pussy cat?" Sunny asked excitedly. "Can I play with it?"

I busted out laughing.

Kit had arranged a late salon appointment for all of us girls. So, we'd showered and driven there to get spruced up for my celebratory birthday dinner at Giovanni's.

"I love that dress," Layla said softly, stroking her baby bump over the flowy maxi dress she wore. Her stomach seemed big for three months. "I wonder if I'll *ever* be able to wear something like that again," she added.

"Doubtful," Cara snipped. "I've gotta feeling that man of yours will keep you barefoot and pregnant for the next few years."

Layla blushed, smiling serenely.

"Don't threaten her with a good time." Tristan turned the blow-dryer off, fiddled with Kady's hair, and grinned. "There you go, sweet little biker princess. You look just like your mama."

She did, too. Tristan had given her a mini-blowout and teased her hair into a toned-down version of mine. Kady was like me, except my girl was prettier.

Kady would turn heads when she grew up.

Kai was furious the boys at school noticed her already, but I'd told him to chill. Love was a beautiful thing, even at the tender age of eight.

"It's nearly seven," Anna announced. "Have you all got everything you need? The prospect's coming tomorrow to pick up everything you leave. Just make sure you've all got your purses."

"Are you sure two can't come?" I asked her. "It'll be a good time."

"We've been invited to a party," she responded, her eyes not quite meeting mine. "Thanks, but tonight's strictly a family thing. We'll arrange a night out soon, though."

I took in her pretty face, a touch thinner than usual. Anna had lost weight, and dark smudges resided under her usually bright eyes. My heart ached for her, probably because it recognized the turmoil raging through the organ in her chest.

"It *will* get better," I murmured so the others couldn't hear.

Tears sprang into her beautiful hazel eyes. "I hope so, Kennedy, because it hurts."

"Some men don't know what they've got until it's gone," I advised her. "You're a catch, Anna. If he doesn't see you, someone else will."

She smiled sadly. "Thanks, Ned. Everything happens for a reason, right?"

I touched her arm. "Right, honey. You can't fight fate."

She went to reply, but Iris interrupted us with a shout of, "They're here!"

Kady sidled up and took my hand. "Does my dress look okay?" she asked.

"You look pretty as a picture." I glanced at the dress Kit had bought her when they'd gone shopping for my birthday presents.

She told me there was no hesitation and no embarrassment when they went into the kid's department of the store. Her dad and brother accompanied Kady and helped her choose her outfits with no complaints.

When I asked Kit about it, he said he felt grateful for the chance to take his daughter clothes shopping. He loved spending time doing things with Kady and making her happy.

Breaker

The bell above the door tinkled.

"Daddy!" Kady called out excitedly.

I turned to see Kit walking through the door with his hand resting on Kai's shoulder. Atlas walked behind him with the other guys, all making a beeline for their women.

My pussy clenched as I watched my golden boy prowl toward me, a sexy smirk plastered across his face. He wore black jeans and a blue Tom Ford button-up, like the one he'd worn on our night out in Underground. His muscles flexed under the thin cotton, large biceps rippling.

Kit's eyes dragged from my head to my toes. Then he grabbed my waist and pulled me against him.

"You're stunnin'," he murmured, voice so husky it was almost a growl. He leaned forward and whispered in the shell of my ear, "You in that dress and those heels gets me so fuckin' hard it hurts."

I bit my bottom lip, heat pooling between my thighs. "You look beautiful, too," I breathed, resisting the urge to rub my thighs together to alleviate the ache.

"Wanna go on a date with me, Kitten?" he rumbled, his molten lava eyes burning into mine. "We'll go for dinner, then back to the clubhouse for a few drinks. The boys wanna celebrate with ya. You only turn thirty once."

My nipples ached for his touch.

He leaned forward to kiss my cheek. "You look just like you did that night. The girl back then belonged to me as easily as breathing, and the woman you've become does, too. I love you, and I'm not waitin' anymore. I know you're ready. I know you're mine." He whispered the words against my skin, his fingers resting on my exposed collarbone, leaving warmth in their wake.

My legs trembled with the need to have my man inside me again.

If I could've dragged him out of the salon and taken him home, I would've. He was right; I was ready.

Honestly, I'd been ready since the day he brought Ed back to me.

He didn't need to keep proving himself. I didn't need that anymore. I'd just needed to believe in us again, and right then, I knew I'd never been more sure of anything.

It was time to move on as a family.

"Right!" John called out. "Now you've all reunited after a goddamned afternoon of being without each other. We've got a reservation. Let's jet!"

Kit crouched to talk to the kids. "Right. Your grandpa's a tightwad, so I want you to order the most expensive food on the menu, yeah?"

Kady giggled.

Kai rubbed his little belly, smirking. "I feel a nice big steak comin' on."

Kit laughed, sending our son an encouraging little wink. "That's my boy."

Our celebratory dinner went by in a flash. I'd never laughed so much in my life.

Everybody had colluded to order the most expensive thing on the menu, seeing as it was John's treat, and he'd nearly had a conniption at the dinner table.

I thought he was about to pass out when Atlas ordered a third bottle of Champagne—even Sophie almost stood up to go and check on him—but he just sighed, shook his head, and took Atlas's banter like a champ.

The only time Kit let go of my hand was when I went to the bathroom halfway through the night. We even ate one-handed because we couldn't bear to let each other go.

As the night went on, something weird happened.

A lady called Elise Henderson came over and introduced herself. She was the mayor's wife and was at

Giovanni's having dinner with a couple of friends from her country club.

I liked her immediately.

Her green eyes sparkled with excitement as she shook my hand. Elise was softly spoken and very sweet. She reminded me of Layla in some ways. My eyebrows shot up when somebody told me Elise was in her early fifties. She didn't look a day older than thirty-five.

She seemed to generate a kind of maternal warmth that I'd never felt before. Her eyes shone brightly, but underneath it all I could sense crippling sadness, especially when she looked at John.

Kit's dad never took his eyes off her. Even when she returned to her table, he kept sneaking looks across the room.

I didn't know why, but I wanted to cry for them. There was history there; I could feel it, but I also felt that something had gone horribly wrong.

Kady noticed, too. I caught my girl staring at her grandpa, then craning her neck to watch Elise. Her forehead scrunched up, her expression turning puzzled.

My girl was too young to understand the nuances of adult relationships. She believed that if two people were in love, they should be together. In an ideal world, she was right, but unfortunately, as I knew from experience, shit happened.

But I also knew something else from experience, something I believed down to my bones.

Fate would *always* find a way.

"I miss them already," I sighed, watching Kai and Kady wave to me through the window of Abe and Iris's car as they drove away from the clubhouse.

"I don't want them in the bar after nine P.M, Kitten," Kit rumbled. "That shit's not for kids. I'm all for sex-ed, but not so up close and personal."

He was right, of course, and it was eleven at night, way past their bedtime, but I hated them sleeping away from me. Iris and Abe loved having the kids, though. They were great with them, too, and I knew the twins would have so much fun that they probably wouldn't want to come home.

"Make the most of it," Cara said from behind me, where she held hands with Cash. "We've got a night off, and I've expressed enough milk to feed Wilder for the next week. I'm going to drink, dance and be merry."

"She's right," Sophie said, carefully picking her way toward us from her car, arm in arm with Atlas. "Me and Layla will live vicariously through you and Wildcat tonight."

"Come on," Cash said, nodding toward the clubhouse doors. "We all whine that we don't get to do whacked-up shit anymore, but as soon as we get rid of the kids so we *can* do whacked-up shit, we whine that we miss 'em."

"Just think, a year and a half ago, we were all doin' whacked-up shit," Kit interjected. "Now, I'm settled and happy, and I wouldn't change it for all the money in the world."

"Yep," Cash agreed. "Who'd have thought that one day we'd all be wifed up with kids," he gestured toward Atlas, "especially fat ass over here."

The SAA cocked a disdainful eyebrow. "Told ya. I ain't fat. I'm big-boned."

"So I've heard." I laughed.

The girls began to giggle.

"Fuckin' women," Atlas said under his breath. "They're all more trouble than they're worth.

"Hey!" Sophie cried, slapping him across the chest.

He rubbed at the sore spot, grinning, "Not you, dearest. You're the light of my life."

Smiling, I lifted my eyes to see a large figure looming by the door. I couldn't make out any features, but I could tell he was a big, black guy with a shaved head. He stood with his arms folded across his chest, looking mean.

My steps faltered as something pinged in my chest.

The man seemed familiar. His stance and build, the way he stood with his massive, muscular arms flexing, reminded me of...

My eyes rounded, and my mouth fell open. "Ty?" I shrieked.

His mean look morphed into a colossal smile, white teeth glinting in the moonlight. "Evening, Kitty. Soraya sends her love. She wanted to come, but our fourth is due any day now, so I told her to keep her beautiful ass where it was."

Emotions flooded my bloodstream.

I took in the wonderful man standing before me. I hadn't seen him for years. Knees almost buckling, I held on to Kit, who helped me stumble to the door.

Ty's strong hands cupped my face, turning it up to meet his gorgeous brown eyes rimmed with thick eyelashes. "You're still as beautiful as you were then, Kitty," he murmured, kissing my forehead.

My brain spun.

I'd lost touch with Ty years ago. When I returned to Vegas from college, everything had changed. Marcus had lost the club in a poker game he'd sworn was fixed, and everyone scattered. I'd tracked a few of the girls down—including Raven, who'd moved to Ibiza as a resident DJ at a club there. Others I'd contacted had either stopped dancing or had moved away to settle down.

Crimson Velvet was such a special place to all of us that I doubted any of the girls would've wanted to dance anywhere else. Our time there was magical.

"I've missed you," I choked out, throat burning with all the memories flooding back to me. How had this happened? What was going on?

"You're all set up. Get your ass straight in the VIP section. Your bill's comp'd tonight." He grinned. "Order the best." His eyes slashed to the person behind me, who heated my back with his warmth. "Snow can afford it."

Dazed, I watched Ty open the door with one arm and gesture us through with the other. "Happy birthday, Kitty," he murmured as Kit pulled me into the clubhouse.

The first thing that hit me was the lighting. The second was the crowd of women who squealed as they crowded around me. My heart soared as I was pulled into a large group hug of women who were crying through their happy laughter.

I looked around the faces of my old friends through the tears welling in my eyes, not quite believing what I was seeing. "Oh. My God!"

"Happy birthday, Kitty," Heaven cried. "I've missed you so much."

A sob rose through my chest, tears falling freely as I lovingly looked around the group of women one by one.

They were all here; Heaven, Ruby, Chloe, Star, Lola, Kiki, Maya, and Venus. They were older, and a few of their bodies had changed with age and, no doubt, pregnancies. It didn't matter, though; they'd never looked more gorgeous to me. These women looked after me and made me feel safe back when I needed it most. They were better mothers to me than my own had ever been, and to see them again was a dream come true.

Turning to Heaven, I raised my trembling fingers and curled them around her nape. "I've missed you, too." I looked around, beaming. "I've missed all of you."

Another sob rose through my throat. "How did this happen?"

Ruby looked over my shoulder knowingly. "Your handsome soldier found Raven. She put the call out to all of us, and we thought it would amazing to have our very own Crimson Velvet reunion." My beautiful friend looked to my side and smiled. "Isn't that right, Marcus?"

I froze for a split second, then slowly turned to my right.

The man standing there was as tall, dark, and handsome as he'd been ten years ago when he'd seen me in the street and instantly decided I was worth something.

Marcus hadn't changed one bit. His gorgeous face still held a look of boredom, a disguise he used to cover up his big, beautiful heart. To look at him, you wouldn't think he gave a shit about anyone but himself. But I knew better; this man saw something in me and had my back when I needed it most.

A thread of warmth weaved through my chest, wrapping around my joyous heart. "Marcus!" I cried, throwing my arms around his neck. "I—I—m—missed you," I stuttered.

"Yeah, yeah, yeah," he drawled in a bored voice. "Still wearing your heart on your sleeve, I see." He curled his fingers on my shoulders and pulled back slightly, looking me up and down. "I got Crimson Velvet back last week. If you ever wanna make some extra bank, you know what to do."

A loud growl sounded from behind me.

Marcus cocked a dismissive eyebrow. "But don't bring soldier boy. You know I can't deal with jealous fucking boyfriends all up in my grill."

I smiled, shaking my head.

My old boss would never change.

Thank God.

"Going to get a drink," Marcus informed me. "Happy fucking birthday." He turned and disappeared through the crowd.

I watched him walk away, lips still hitched in a wondrous smile.

Nothing would ever beat this night. How could it?

Warmth hit my back again, and a shiver ran down my spine.

"Baby." Kit's voice was a growl in the shell of my ear. "I know this DJ. She's great. I'm in awe of the way she controls a crowd. She starts off all slow and sensuous, taking her cues from 'em and working 'em up slowly. She has them in the palm of her hand until they feel whatever she wants them to feel."

I turned to face Kit, heart fluttering as he tucked a lock of my hair behind my ear.

"Raven says there's a perfect speed she works up to." He gently kissed the tip of my nose. "When she hits it, the track starts to resonate. At that point, she and the crowd are on a journey together, and there's no better feeling."

I slid my hands up his chest. "How you describe it sounds sexy as all hell."

My man laughed. "It is sexy. She says it's just like fuckin'. You start slowly, then build up until your blood sings and your nerve endings tingle with sensations."

As if on cue, the music lowered, and a pulsing beat began to thud.

I closed my eyes, feeling the pumping bassline punch through my body.

"Dance for me, Kitten," Kit murmured. "Go with your girls and show me you never forgot."

I stared into the golden eyes I'd loved since I was a nineteen-year-old girl. The same eyes I saw every time I looked at my beautiful son, who was so much like his dad.

The emotions flooding through me felt so forceful that I couldn't stop the tears from filling my eyes again. "I love you," I told my Snow with a watery smile.

"I know," he replied gently. "Now go."

Chapter Twenty-Eight

Breaker

My boys had done me proud.
The clubhouse looked nothing like Crimson Velvet back then, but the atmosphere was just as electric with the proper lighting and music.

It had been relatively straightforward to track Raven down. Once I had her on board, it was just a matter of time before she contacted the other girls and Marcus.

Flying them here was easy. After that, it was just a case of finding them places to lay their hats, which worked well because all the club's rentals were rebuilt and ready to go.

When we got the girls out of the clubhouse, the boys set up the lighting and built a makeshift DJ booth for Raven to do her thing.

I wasn't a man who blew smoke up his own ass, but I was proud of what we'd accomplished, and it worked. Kitten finally admitted she loved me.

The instant she said the words, I'd had a revelation.

Kennedy Carmichael belonged to me.

She'd belonged to me, mind, body, and soul, ever since we'd sat on a mountain, watching the sun's rays race across the city. I'd known it then as plainly as I knew it now.

She should've never forgiven me for the lies and hurt I'd caused, but against all odds, I'd shown her there was nobody else in the world for me. She was my one. The other half of my soul, which had been missing since the day I left her broken-hearted in a small Vegas apartment.

I'd fallen in love with a girl within twelve hours of meeting her, just like a Stone man. There was no rhyme or reason when it came to the way I felt about her, and I fucking loved it.

Somebody clapped me on the shoulder.

I whirled around to see Heaven's husband grinning at me. A few of the girl's men had come along for the ride. It was good to see Leon and the other guys. I remembered how they accepted me into their circle the night we went to Underground and was forever grateful.

He gestured toward the other guys, leaning back against the wall. "Raven's about to come on. She always plays this track before she does her thing. I saved your spot. You can thank me later."

I followed him to the wall, leaning my back against it. A flash of pink caught my eye, and I settled in for the show.

Cash sidled next to me. "What we doin' over here?" he asked, taking a swig from his beer bottle.

"Just watch," I told him, giving Bowie a chin lift as he sauntered and took the space next to Cash.

"You're gonna love this," I promised. "These girls will put on a show you'll never forget—" I was cut off by a steady beat pulsing through the vast room.

Every nerve ended tingled as the *thud, thud, thud* resonated through my chest, and a loud roar went up from the crowd packed onto the dance floor.

Like ten years before, the air was thick with smoke and anticipation. The smell of clean sweat and booze hung in the ether. Calls and shouts came from the crowd as they yelled their appreciation.

My heart jerked as suddenly the music cut, and everything stopped dead.

I glanced up at the DJ booth, suspended eight feet in the air, and my mouth curved into a grin.

Raven stood with her arms outstretched wide, like a God bestowing her grace on the crowd. She wore a gold dress with sequins that caught the lights flashing all over the room. Her hair had been plaited into tiny dreadlocks that looked cool as hell. My throat caught as suddenly, every beam shone, lighting her up like an angel from above.

The single, hard beat began to *thump* louder through the room. The crowd started to move almost as one. Excitement flickered through the air, making my senses tingle. The deep, pulsating thump resonated, and I turned to my brothers, repeating the exact words Kitten had spoken to me ten years before. Words I'd never forgotten.

I pointed toward the DJ booth. "That's Raven, one of Kitten's oldest friends. Like every good DJ, she starts off slow, taking her cues from the crowd and working them up slowly."

Cash's head bobbed in time to the beat. "It's cool as fuck, bro."

Elation snaked through my chest as another loud roar went up.

Beams flashed around the room, tiny pinpricks of light turning everything from light to dark and back again.

The beat pulsed harder until a chorus of synths came in, carving out a sweet melody and the echo of bongo drums that added an extra layer of bass.

Every light in the place shone on Raven.

The crowd yelled as she raised one arm high in the air, made a fist, and pumped it in time to the beat, building higher and higher. Harder and harder. Suddenly, she stilled, almost suspended, as the resonating thump hit a crescendo before she crashed her fist down hard and dropped the bassline.

The crowd went crazy. Every person on the dance floor moved just as a man's soulful voice sang over the music.

My chest swelled. It was so fucking euphoric that my throat filled with heat. For the second time in my life, I watched as Raven captured the crowd in a trance-like state of depthless bliss, the atmosphere of it all making the blood hammer through my veins.

I caught a second flash of pink from the corner of my eye. My stare sliced to where Kitten danced with her girls, and my heart doubled in size.

She was moving just like she'd done on that life-changing night.

Her hips swayed and thrust in time to the banging beat. Her entire body moved like molten liquid as she ground and bumped along with the song.

I knew she could dance; I'd seen her move many times, and she was magnificent. But watching her thrust and grind in the pink satin dress, which clung to her body like a second skin, was even more enthralling because she was still mine despite everything we'd been through.

Kitten swung around to face me head-on.

My eyes lifted from her ass and caught her shining cornflower blues, and my dick kicked hard against my zipper.

"Fuck me," Cash mumbled, elbowing Bowie and staring open-mouthed between me and Kitten.

My woman must've noticed Cash's reaction to the fire between us because she smirked and carried on dancing for me.

Then, with a slight smile playing around her lips, they began to move as she sang along, mouthing the words at me.

My heart stuttered as her lips curved, ass still twisting and pumping along with the bassline, which was turning funkier and heavier the longer the song played on.

More emotion filled my overflowing heart as the resonating beat continued to thud through me.

In five short months, I'd gone from pushing everything down and everyone away, to my heart bursting with love and gratitude for my bountiful blessings. But I couldn't help feeling a hint of sadness at the darkness we'd gone through over the years.

I'd been half a man without my Kitten next to me where she belonged.

Kennedy Carmichael and the two incredible kids she'd given me were at the center of my universe. I was the luckiest man in the world to have them gracing me with their love and care.

My eyes narrowed on a figure moving toward my woman as she danced in her own beautiful world.

Hendrix and a few of his brothers had turned up at the club earlier.

We'd invited them to the party—we were still brothers, and he'd been a massive part of the club. We wanted to be close to our second chapter, so why not include them in our celebrations?

Hendrix hit the bottle as soon as he arrived. Even Ice and his other brothers, Smoke, and Pyro, seemed exasperated with their prez.

Dad tried to talk to Drix, but he became belligerent, so Dad walked away. Kai was there, and I knew Pop wouldn't want to punch a man's lights out in front of my boy.

Hendrix had already snaked me, so watching him making a drunken beeline toward my woman made my hands clench into fists. My girl was a beacon of everything good in the world, so I could hardly blame him for trying his hand, except, I didn't want her touched by anybody but me. Hendrix may have been a hit with the women, but he'd be disappointed this time.

I straightened my back and stalked toward my woman.

Hendrix was very drunk and, therefore, sloppy. I made it to Kitten, tagged her waist, and pulled her into me, baring my teeth at the asshole who used to be my brother.

The new prez's glazed eyes caught mine, and he laughed drunkenly, continuing to stumble through the crowd toward us.

I took Kitten's elbow. "Get behind me, baby," I ordered, tone hard.

She glanced over her shoulder, saw Drix, and flew straight to my back, holding my waist with both hands.

Hendrix barreled toward me. He pointed his beer bottle and slurred, "I juss wanna birthday dance with Kitten."

"Fuck off, Drix," I snarled, my tone a warning for him to stay the fuck away from my woman. "You're wasted. Go to bed."

I watched a shadow flicker over his face. "You should fuckin' know all about bein' wasted ya little pissant." He turned to the crowd, waving his arms to get everyone's attention. "Hey!" he bellowed. "See this little motherfucker. He was wasted off his ass for ten goddamned years, and now he thinks he can tell *me* what to do." Spittle flew from his mouth, his face turning an angry red. "I'm a goddamned *president*. You motherfuckers need to learn some *respect*!"

The music lowered.

Mutters and whispers filled the air, the entire room craning their necks to see what the latest drama was.

My head reared back, and I stared at him in disbelief.

This wasn't Hendrix. The man I knew was the most level-headed guy I'd ever met. That coolness made him a good VP, he could challenge Dad in a way that didn't ruffle his feathers.

But this version was an asshole.

Breaker

My fingers twitched as Hendrix stumbled closer. Glaring at him, I pointed to the door. "Get the fuck out."

"Fuck you," he grated out.

"You heard him," Cash called out from my back. "Get your drunken ass outta that door before you embarrass yourself even more than you already have."

Hendrix threw his head back, laughing manically. "Here comes the fucknut VP who thinks he's all that." He smirked. "You're a bigger cunt than him," he spat, nodding at me.

My body locked, my chest burning. The fucker had gone too far. This was a slight against the mother chapter. President or not, he was gonna get his ass beat.

My breath sawed through my chest, and I waited for a sign to jump into action. Our angry glares clashed for what seemed like hours as we stared each other down, both challenging the other to make a move.

It didn't take long. Suddenly Hendrix let out a roar and barreled toward me.

Shouts cut through the bar as my brothers yelled warnings, but I didn't need help. I was ready. Bouncing on the soles of my feet, I waited until the last minute before spinning to the side just as Drix reached me.

The move—and no doubt all the beer he'd drunk—knocked him off balance.

As he began to fall, I grabbed the back of his collar, pulled his head up, and threw a quick jab at his nose. I heard a satisfying crack as my knuckles connected, and blood flew everywhere.

A loud roar filled the air as Hendrix hit the deck.

I knew it wasn't so much the punch but more the skinful of booze that rendered him useless. He'd been drinking since the moment he'd arrived.

Earlier, I'd watched him go into a room with one of the whores. My mind kept going over it because Hendrix never went with club snatch. He always said he liked beauty in his bed, and the whores weren't that.

Ice appeared at my side. His hands went to his hips, lips flattening into a thin line as he shook his head. "I fuckin' told him not to cause trouble," he muttered, eyes lifting to mine. "Sorry, Breaker. He's got some shit goin' on. He's not himself."

I looked down at a knocked-out Hendrix. "No fucks given, Ice. That fucker came into our clubhouse and talked smack to me and my VP. You know that shit don't stand."

Ice eyed me. "Hear you took my spot."

"Yeah," I confirmed. "You didn't want it. Seems you made your choice, and it went all the way to Virginia."

He nodded thoughtfully, eyes burning with regret as he turned toward the bar. "Pyro!" he yelled.

The big fucker came lumbering toward us, his massive pecs peeking out from under his cut.

"Help me shift the prez," he ordered. "He got himself into more shit."

Pyro gave Ice a chin lift as he sauntered over, grabbing Hendrix by the arms. Ice took his legs, and together, the men hauled their prez through the bar and out into the parking lot.

"Where's the party gone?" Bowie bellowed. "Let's keep it movin'."

Raven went back to her turntables, and with a flip of a switch, the music started. Happy shouts filled the room, and everybody began to dance again.

Cash came up beside me again, clapping me on the back. "You did good. He's been walking around actin' the prick all day. Even Dad had enough of him at one point, and he thinks the world of him. I've told Pop he needs to get on top of it. We can't let Drix go around givin' the Demon's patch a bad rep."

"Where's Atlas?" I asked, looking around for the SAA. "Usually, he'd be the first person to wade into the middle of a fight." I was right, too; wherever trouble was, our SAA wasn't far behind.

Breaker

He looked around, trying to catch a glimpse of our brother.

As if by magic, Atlas walked out of the corridor leading to the bedrooms wearing his jeans, his cut, and a self-satisfied grin.

"Where the fuck have you been?" Cash demanded as the SAA approached our huddle.

At's grin got wider. "My ol' lady needed a little somethin'." He clapped Cash on the shoulder. "She's at the stage in her knocked-updom where she's horny all the fuckin' time. You remember it, right?" He brought a hand up to rub his beard. "Oh, yeah. Wildcat wouldn't let you touch her, then would she? Sorry, bro." He smirked, his expression not sorrowful at all.

"You're a funny fuck, aintcha?" Cash's eyes narrowed. "Well, wipe the smile off your ugly face 'cause you just missed Hendrix gettin' all pissy and Breaker here breakin' his fuckin' nose." He looked at me. "D'ya get it? Breaker breakin' his nose?" My brother chuckled.

The smirk fell from Atlas's face. "What the fuck!" he shouted. "I miss all the goddamned fun. Why didn't you call me?"

"And catch you balls deep in Sophie. Don't fuckin' think so." Cash nodded toward the doors. "You better get out there and make sure he's cooled down."

Atlas punched his hands to his waist, looking to the heavens and shaking his head. "What a fuckin' fucker," he bellowed again. He shot us both a death glare before turning on his heel and stomping through the bar toward the parking lot.

"Jesus. You'd think I'd just told him the tooth fairy don't exist," Cash muttered, his stare remaining on our SAA as he disappeared. "He's such a fuckin' baby."

A warm hand slipped into mine, and my chest warmed.

"You okay, Ned?" Bowie asked.

"Yeah. I'm good," Kennedy said, tugging gently on my hand. "Can I talk to you?"

I leaned down, Cash suddenly forgotten. "What's up, Kitten. You pissed 'cause I fought Hendrix at your party." I shrugged. "Sorry, baby, but he's an asshole."

She bit her lip, looking up at me wide-eyed. Rolling up on her toes, she leaned toward my ear and whispered, "It was hot."

My dick hardened.

She rolled up again. "You've recreated the best night of my life, Snow. But the part I lay awake at night thinking about hasn't happened yet."

My cock turned to iron.

I gripped the back of her neck and pulled her close, letting her feel the effect she had on my dick. "Is *that* want you want, Kitten?"

She nodded, eyes boring into mine, not saying a word.

Jesus. This girl.

"If I fuck you, baby, there's no goin' back. I want it all. Marriage, more babies, and you, forever. Is that want you want, too?" My words were direct and to the point. She needed to understand that if we fucked, she'd be mine forever, no takebacks.

Kennedy tossed her hair and smirked. "Well, duh."

A low hum warmed my blood, which seemed to be concentrated in one particular area of my anatomy. Without a word, I bent my knees, banded my hands around the back of her thighs, and pulled her legs up around my hips.

"My dress is riding up." She squealed as I walked us toward the corridor to my room.

I planted a kiss on her mouth. "Gonna rip the fuckin' thing to pieces in about two-point-four seconds, baby. Who gives a fuck?"

She whooped and punched the air as we approached my door. "Yessss. Chop chop. We're wasting valuable time here."

A bubble of laughter escaped me. Placing Kennedy gently on her feet, I fished the key out of my pocket, unlocked the door to our room, and pulled her inside. My mouth fell on hers the instant I kicked the door shut behind me.

Her lips were as soft as always but more demanding. She gently sucked my tongue into her mouth, her hands going to my jeans and undoing my belt.

I moaned as the urge to come hit me already. There was no goddamned way, though. I stepped back, grabbed her dress, and ripped downward until it came apart.

My eyes drank in my woman who stood before me in silver sandals, a white lace thong, and a smile.

My mouth watered as my eyes roamed over her tits, just as beautiful as they were the last time I saw them. Actually, better because they were bigger, probably due to nourishing my kids.

The thought of that made my cock kick hard.

Grabbing Kennedy by the waist, I picked her up and threw her on the bed. As she bounced, I sat on the edge, whipped my sneakers off, and stood, shucking my jeans down my legs, and kicking them away.

My woman owned *me*, heart, and soul. No monster took me over, no demon came out, and I was determined it wouldn't. I needed to be coherent whenever I was with her like this. Kennedy needed to feel safe, and I wanted to hear every gasp, and revel in every moan.

Nine years without her. It was no wonder I'd died inside.

I stood again and slowly unbuttoned my shirt, eyes taking in Kitten's beautiful body as I threw it behind my head.

"Hurry up and fuck me," she demanded.

My hand slid down, grabbed my burgeoning cock, and fisting it, my eyes on her tits and tiny white thong. "You want this, baby?" I asked, tone husky with need as I pumped my cock.

She replied by knee-walking to the edge of the bed, lowering her head, and taking the tip into her mouth, sucking it hard.

I threw my head back and moaned, electricity coursing through my groin.

She moved my hand, replacing it with hers, and started to jack me off. Her grip tightened, and she twisted her hand as it moved toward the head, making me shout my pleasure.

The base of my spine began to tingle, a telltale sign I was about to come.

Gently, I pulled away, her mouth releasing me with a loud pop.

"On your back, spread those legs and show me my cunt." I growled, satisfied, as her nipples hardened into tight peaks.

Gracefully, she laid down, stretched out, opened her legs, and showed me Nirvana.

My knees hit the mattress, and I moved between her legs, gripped her ankles, and pulled them wider. I raised them high, the silver straps of her sandals glinting in the room's lamplight before settling them over my shoulders.

"You're so fuckin' beautiful," I rasped. My cock was so thick and hard it felt like it would explode if I didn't get inside my woman soon.

"You're beautiful, too," she murmured.

I slid down until my face hovered over her pussy. I nuzzled it, breathing in deeply, my memory going crazy with the familiarity of her scent.

Peaches.

"Open up nice and wide for me," I ordered. "Show me how ready you are."

Breaker

Her hands skated down to her pussy, pulling it open gently, allowing me to see its pink, swollen glistening beauty. I growled again, the monster roaring inside, needing his mate. "We can get you wetter than that, baby," I murmured.

She let out a whimper as my tongue flicked out and touched her hard little bud. I had every intention of teasing her, of making her scream with need, of making her beg for me, but the taste of her drove me so fucking crazy that I dove in and licked her from cunt to clit.

At that minute, I realized something.

I'd never fucked my girl bare before.

The day we argued in this room, and I told her all about April, I'd shown her the clean bill of health I'd got from Grand Junction.

The night I got her pregnant with the twins was a daze. She said she heard me open a condom packet, but my mind was so fucked-up that a bomb could've gone off, and I wouldn't have known.

Tonight I was goin' in without any protection. I assumed Kitten was on the contraceptive pill, though not much longer. I made a vow to myself. The following day, I'd find those fuckers and flush every damned one. The sooner I knocked her up again, the better. I'd missed everything with Kai and Kady.

My cock kicked at the thought of her belly growing big and round with my baby. I wanted to experience the excitement, the ultrasounds, and even the morning sickness. A deep purr rumbled through my chest at the mere thought of impregnating my woman.

My face and hand were soaked from where I fucked her with two fingers while I sucked and licked her pretty little pussy. I couldn't get close or deep enough to satisfy the intense hunger burning in my gut. The taste and scent of her pussy made me heady. I wanted to wring everything out of her.

I continued to suck, lick, and gently nip like a crazy man, doing everything I could to pleasure my woman. It paid off because it didn't take long for her pussy to start clenching around my fingers.

"I'm so close, Kit," she moaned. "Jesus. I'm gonna come so hard."

I lifted my head, and raised my fingers, circling her clit to keep the momentum going. "I wanna feel you come on my cock," I said huskily, my fingers continuing to work her to orgasm as my body slid up hers. "You ready, baby?"

"Thank God." Kennedy sighed, her cornflower blues half-mast with desire.

"You look so pretty gettin' finger fucked," I murmured, easing my hips between her thighs, still working her. I dipped my head and kissed her left nipple. "Love the pink flush you get here when you're close."

She whimpered again. "Please," she begged. "Fuck me, Kit."

Something loosened inside my chest, and I released a grunt of pleasure. I loved how well our bodies fit. Like the Gods had created every plane of muscle, and every curve of flesh, to click together perfectly. Finger still circling, I eased my cock inside her tight slickness, letting out a low moan as her silky heat got a choke hold on my cock. "Fuck, yeah," I murmured, feeding every inch into her tight, clenching pussy.

My hand left her cunt and trailed to her knee, hooking it over the back of my thigh. "Dig those fuckin' heels into my ass, Kitten. Show me you much you love me fuckin' you."

Her pussy clenched tightly again, and I groaned out loud. "Fuck, yeah. Love this pussy." I circled my hips, grinding against her clit every time I made a pass. Her head fell back on the bed, and she lifted her hips, fucking me back just as hard as I fucked her.

Breaker

The sting of her heels scraping my ass made my teeth grit at the bite of pleasure-pain she inflicted on my skin. I loved it. I loved the feel of her and the fact I'd carry her marks for days like a brand of ownership.

I felt her orgasm creeping under her skin. She met every thrust, even though the tightness of her pussy told me she'd be sore tomorrow. I didn't care. I wanted her to feel me for days. My woman needed to remember who owned her pretty cunt.

Kitten's head thrashed from side to side, her orgasm building to a crescendo. I bent my neck and sucked hard on a nipple, kissing across her chest to the other and doing the same before smothering her body with mine.

Moaning, I fucked her hard into the mattress. "Come on my cock, Kitten. Soak me, baby."

She let out a loud cry as her climax hit her hard.

The base of my spine tingled like crazy. My balls drew up so tight they almost hurt. "Fuck, yeah!" I yelled as I planted my cock as deep as it would go, almost blacking out with pleasure as my cum spilled inside her. Still deep, I circled my ass, trying to wring as much as I could out of the brain-numbing orgasm she'd pulled out of me.

Kitten whimpered as her orgasm continued to rip through her. I felt her tight pussy contracting like a vice around my cock. "Jesus, fuck!" I moaned, fucking her through her climax for as long as I could before my thighs gave out, and I flopped down, giving Kennedy all my weight.

Kitten thrust her face into my neck, kissing below my ear. "That was the hottest thing I've ever experienced," she panted. "My legs have stopped working."

I pulled back, still dazed from my earth-shattering orgasm.

It was the first time in ten years I'd fucked for pleasure, and the beauty of it caused a lump to form in my throat. Our souls were finally together again where they belonged.

Dropping a kiss on her beautiful lips, I spoke from the heart. "I fuckin' love you so much."

"I love you, too," she told me softly.

"Wanna sleep with my cock inside you, Kitten. Never wanna leave again."

"I can't give it a suck if it's stuck in my cooch." She giggled playfully.

Chuckling, I nuzzled her neck. "There's always tomorrow, the next day, and the rest of our lives." My eyes locked with hers. "Love you more for giving me another chance, baby. I won't let you down." I touched my mouth to hers, my heart finally knitting back together again with all the love in the world.

Finally, I'd come home.

Chapter Twenty-Nine

Kennedy ~ One Week Later

Kit widened his legs and watched me suck as much of his hard length as I could get inside my mouth.

My eyes slid up and hit Kit's golden orbs, dark with desire. "Jesus, fuck!" He moaned. "Goddamned mouth's the eighth wonder of the world."

I twisted my hand around the base of his cock and hummed as I sucked harder.

His head fell back against the pillow, and he circled his hips upward, trying to force himself deeper into my mouth. "Fuckin' love it when you play, baby. Ain't nothin' sweeter in the world."

I swiped my tongue across the silky head and dipped lower, taking all I could into the back of my throat.

"Jesusssss," he said with a long groan before pulling his cock out of my mouth.

"Hey," I said softly. "Where you going?"

"Won't last much longer." He shifted himself up the bed until his back was flat against the headboard, then spread his legs, allowing me full access. "Hop on, Kitten. Time to take your man for a ride."

I tossed my hair over one shoulder and crawled up my bed.

I'd missed the California King in my Vegas house, and now, I was finally getting to fuck Kit on it.

"Never seen anythin' more beautiful," he whispered, watching my every move. "Can't believe how my life has gone from hollow to overflowing with love, baby. I'm the luckiest man in the world."

I sat over his groin and leaned over him, looking down into his golden orbs. "Baby. I belonged to you before I knew what belonging to somebody meant. That wouldn't have changed even if we'd never got this back. Fate brought us together, then it drove us apart. But deep down, I knew I'd be with you again, even if I had to wait until the next life."

His hands rested on my bare hips. "You're still my fire," he croaked.

I angled my hips until the tip of his cock notched against my opening, then slowly, I sank down until my pussy felt full of everything that was Kit Stone. "And you're still mine," I whispered against his lips.

Resting my palms on his muscular pecs, I began to circle my hips while grinding my wet heat up and down my man's hard length.

Kit's fingers dug into my hips hard enough to make me wince, and my heart contracted. "Baby," I whispered. "Stay with me."

Kit's eyes flew open, stared at me, dazed, his fingers relaxing as awareness flooded his beautiful features.

It wasn't the first time he'd zoned out during sex.

It was to be expected, really. My golden boy would always suffer from PTSD, and the thing he called his monster would always be there, ready to emerge. Sex was an issue because it was easy for him to get carried away and fall into a trance. But it was like his counselor said, as long as he could control it, he could progress.

The first time it happened, we had to stop. Kit didn't want to risk hurting me.

Breaker

After I thought about it, though, I was determined never to let it beat us again. We had to learn to live and cope with everything his condition brought to the surface, and it was like I kept telling him. I liked a bit of monster in my man.

I moved my hands up to his jaw, stroking it reassuringly. "You okay, honey?"

He jerked a nod. "Yeah. You wanna stop?"

I sank down on his cock again, lowering my lips to suck on the soft skin where his neck met his shoulder. "Never."

He thrust his hips upward to meet mine. "The Gods sent you to me, Kennedy," he whispered. "Nobody in this world knows me like you do."

I raised my head and took his mouth. "Love you." I pressed the words against his lips, grinding harder on his hard, silky cock. Pulling up, I sat, leaning back to alter the angle so his dick hit the walls of my pussy as he thrust harder into me.

Kit's fingers teased a path up my leg, hit my clit, and pressed hard. "Come for me, baby." He growled.

I cried out with pleasure.

My skin prickled as fingertips brushed over my hard nipple, and my heart stuttered as it puckered under his touch. I reached for my climax but couldn't quite grasp it.

Soft fingertips continued to skate over my clit. Goosebumps scattered down both arms, and a warm shiver trickled down my spine. Fingertips pressed again before moving down and touching where we were joined. My hips bucked, the elusive orgasm drawing closer,

"Look how well we fit, Kitten," he said, groaning his pleasure. "You're pussy's so fuckin' perfect and so fuckin' mine." Kit's hips bucked harder, causing a bite of pain to claw at me deep inside. Long fingers gathered the moisture from my core and moved up to circle my clit again slowly. "I love how wet you are for me, baby." He let out another low moan.

My muscles gave an involuntary clench, my man's dirty words working me up in tandem with the hard thrust of his cock.

"Fuck, yeah." He grunted. "Need to get deeper."

Suddenly I was airborne.

Kit twisted until my back hit the mattress and was on me in less than a second. One hand slid under my knee and pulling it until my calf hooked over his shoulder.

With one hard thrust, he was inside me again; the angle he had me at allowed his hard cock to almost hit my cervix. I threw my head back and wailed.

His palm covered my mouth. "You'll wake the kids," he grunted, pounding inside me harder. "My Kitten's so fuckin' tight." His neck strained with the effort of holding back. "Baby, you gotta come," he rasped. "I'm so fuckin' close."

My back arched off the bed, and I keened.

I lifted my hips, meeting his every thrust. My pussy ached from how hard and deep he fucked me. A familiar pressure began to build in the pit of my stomach, and I continued to push up to meet him. "Please, don't stop," I begged.

"You're so fuckin' perfect," he bit out, brutally thrusting inside me, grunting every time his hips pounded against mine.

The build wasn't gradual. Within seconds he sent me hurtling off a cliff edge. My orgasm slammed through me. I let out a low moan, my pussy contracting hard over his cock. I pushed my head back against the bed as I arched my body again, electricity shooting through me as the peak of my climax hit.

"Fuck yeah." He planted deep and stayed there, warmth filling my womb as he spilled his cum inside me. He buried his face in my throat, and I felt a sharp sting as his teeth nipped me gently, his lips sucking hard on my skin. Slowly, he began to move again, sliding his cock in and out, desperately trying to make his orgasm last longer.

"I just saw fuckin' stars," he mumbled, still lazily circling his hips.

Every nerve ending came alive. Tingles shot across my skin, my pussy still contracting with aftershocks as I came down from the best climax of my life.

Kit's hand released the back of my knee, his fingers softly rubbing feeling back into it as it rested on the bed.

Our gazes locked, and we stayed there, gazing into each other's eyes.

My heart swelled, fit to burst, as we took each other in. The air around us became charged with pure, unadulterated love, so warm I could almost feel it.

"I was broken without you," he whispered. "I was half a man stumbling through life, missing half of my broken soul. I left it with you for safekeeping, baby. I didn't want it, not without you."

Tears sprang to my eyes at the emotion in his voice.

"The only reason I didn't blow my brains out was because I knew you were somewhere in the world. I didn't think you'd want me after what I'd done, but your light stayed with me. Then, when I saw you again, I was so scared that I pushed you away. I knew I'd fucked-up. That was why I held a gun to my head, baby."

A sob escaped my throat.

"I'm not in the same place now; I'm better," Kit assured me. "But I know if I ever gave up again, you'd leave, and nothin' makes sense if you're not with me, Kennedy."

"Ditto," I whispered.

"Want you to know I'll keep on keepin' on," he told me. "There's no life for me without you and the kids. Want you to know I'm a safe bet. Want you to know, you and my babies give me everything I need to keep myself right."

"I know you won't let us down," I choked out.

He took my hand and held it to his chest. "It's still inside me. You need to know the risks."

"No!" I grated out, spreading my fingers over his breastplate. "Your demons walked into a house and saved our daughter. They made sure the men who took her could never do it again. I'm not afraid, Kit. I don't think your demons will hurt us. I think they'll keep us safe. You went through all that shit so you could gain the skills to save Kady, maybe even others. Everything happens for a reason."

His eyes burned into mine. "There's a war comin', baby."

My heart fluttered. "I'm not scared if I'm with you."

Kit nodded, his eyes searching mine before they softened. He waggled his eyebrows playfully. "It's still early, and the kids are asleep in their rooms. Wanna get the last four episodes done? We'll do that and get some shut-eye. Early start in the mornin'."

A few days ago, Kit told me about his ex-lieutenant living alone and isolated in the woods of California. Since he'd left Grand Junction all those months ago, he'd thought about whether to visit and talk about what they'd gone through together.

I canceled all my appointments, told the kids to pack for a road trip, and set off early the following day, hitting the I-80 heading South West.

It took us nine hours to drive through Utah before we finally reached my house in Vegas. We decided to stay and give the kids a break before heading to San Bernadino, California, to see Hollister the following morning.

Colt found his address with no problem. The tech guy confirmed that Hollister wasn't quite living off grid but wasn't exactly integrated into society either. His old lieutenant had no family to help him deal with his demons. He kept himself to himself, living off his military pension and the money he'd inherited from his folks in his twenties.

Kit hadn't warned him we were on our way. He thought it best to surprise him. I doubted it was a good idea. Personally, I'd have hated someone from my past turning up at my home with a wife and two kids in tow.

In the end, Kit convinced me it was for the best. He was worried Hollister would tell him to stay away if he called. Maybe he was right; I mean, Kit knew the man better than I did.

My golden boy pushed himself up on his firm, muscular arms and rolled over, grabbing the remote control from the nightstand. "Can't believe we've gotten through so many episodes," he muttered, pressing the button, and switching the TV on.

I shuffled to the side of my bed. "I'll clean up while you get it ready."

I let out a yelp as he slapped my ass playfully. "Can't fuckin' resist you, baby."

Smiling, I shook my head, heading into my adjoining bathroom. It was about the same size as Kit's bedroom back at the clubhouse. I held a washcloth under the warm faucet, looking around me wistfully.

"Kit," I called. "Are you sure we can't stay here until the house is built? I miss my bathroom, my bed, and the heat, even the sand."

Kit came sauntering through the door, gesturing for me to hand the washcloth over. "We can, Kitten, but I guarantee Pop, Cash, Bowie, and Atlas will turn up within a week, women and kids in tow."

I handed him the cloth. "Don't threaten me with a good time," I perched my ass on the side of the bath.

Kit gently cleaned between my legs, tossing the washcloth into the laundry basket when he was done. "We wouldn't have a minute's peace. And what about Ed?"

My mouth twisted. "I guess you're right. He won't step foot in Vegas again. Too many bad memories."

Kit's fingers entwined with mine, and he pulled me to my feet before leading me back into the bedroom. He went to his rucksack, pulled out a tee, turned around, and slipped it over my head. "He asked me about Hendrix's chapter."

A burn hitting the back of my throat. "Does Ed want to join?"

"No, baby. I had a chat with him and explained the pros and cons. After he thought about it, he decided he'd never leave you. He wants a fresh start, and with Hendrix building up his membership, it appealed. But he knows the work would put him back in his recovery. Same as it would me."

After the trouble Hendrix caused at my party, John had called him into Church and laid into him.

It came out that Drix had a lot on his plate and had started to buckle under the pressure. His VP—a good buddy he used to serve with—had stabbed him in the back. He'd also had a come-to-Jesus moment concerning Anna, but when he approached her about starting something, she'd told him to eat shit and die.

He'd screwed up with her big time and hurt her terribly. It seemed Anna had a come-to-Jesus moment all of her own, and it didn't bode well for Hendrix.

A tug of my hand pulled me away from my musings.

Kit led me toward our bed, both climbing on and settling back against the headboard.

"Can't believe we've finally got to the end," my man muttered, nodding toward the TV. "When I asked you to wait for me to watch it, did you ever think it would take us ten years to get through this motherfucker?"

My head swiveled right until I met golden eyes. "We got there in the end."

His arm slid across my shoulders, pulling me into his chest.

"Yeah, baby," he murmured into my hair. "You're right. We got there in the end."

Five hours later

"What the fuck?"

I looked at Kit's bewildered expression, probably a mirror image of my own. "I don't know what to say."

His head reared back. "Can you believe we waited ten years for that bullshit?"

I sighed frustratedly. "I'm pissed. I can't believe they built up Daenerys to be a strong female lead, only to ruin her with what seems like a severe bout of PMS.

"And Arya killing the Night King like that." My guys lips flattened into an angry line. "Why put her through all that bullshit training in Bravos, and train her to be an assassin when she does the fuckin' job with a move she learned from Syrio Forel back in season fuckin' one?"

My lips pursed. "Glad you caught that. The lighting was so dark while they battled for Winterfell; I almost missed it."

He grabbed the remote control and switched the TV off. "Come on, baby. We gotta get up in seven hours."

We shuffled down the bed until our heads hit the pillows.

"Love you, Kennedy," Kit said, leaning over me and clicking off the lamp before pulling the comforter over our bodies.

Laying in the darkness, my mind returned to the TV show we just watched. "Kit?" I murmured, snuggling closer to my man.

His fingers stroked the small of my back. "Yeah?"

"Would you fight dragons for me?" I asked.

He chuckled into the darkness. "No, baby. But I'd stand by your side, and we'd fight them together."

I smiled, heart unfurling with love for my man, finally with me after years of heartbreak.

Kit fought for me, slaying his own personal dragons in the process. God only knew what dangers were coming for us. The Sinners could launch an attack any day. Nobody knew what would happen or even if everyone would make it.

But through it all, there was one thing I'd never been more sure of.

My man, and his monster, who I loved so much, would keep us safe.

Six and a Half Hours Later

"Baby," Kit whispered. "Kady's talking to someone in her room."

My sleep-addled brain came awake with a start, and a cold shiver ran down my spine. I sat up and blinked as my eyes adjusted to the dull orange hues that signaled the rising sun.

"Thought I heard a noise on the stairs a few minutes ago," he continued, voice low. "Gonna see what the fuck's goin' on."

My man slid out of bed, grabbed his jeans, and pulled them on. Then, bending down, he went into his rucksack. The sound of a zipper opening whispered through the air, and I saw a glint of metal as he stood, holding his gun.

"If anything happens, get into Kai's bedroom, grab him, and get inside the wardrobe. Is the panic room there secure?"

I nodded, a wave of sickness roiling through my gut. "Yeah. There's a line straight through to the security company."

He came over and kissed my head. "I love you."

Breaker

"I love you too, "I croaked, voice husky from the tightness my lungs. "Be careful, please."

My hand went to my aching temple, and I rubbed it, trying to get my thoughts together. I threw back the comforter, swung my legs over the side of the bed, and followed Kit to the bedroom door.

Slowly, he opened it and peeked into the hallway.

I looked around his body to see whether Kady's bedroom door was open.

I gulped, willing my knees not to buckle when the sound of Kady's melodic voice floated across the landing from her bedroom. "Bye!"

My breath seized.

Is someone in Kady's room?

Heart hammering, I watched as my beautiful, courageous man crept down the hallway, gun up, ready to shoot.

I held my breath, trying to regulate the rush of blood in my ears as my eyes followed Kit inching towards Kady's room. Even through my panic, a part of me still marveled at his capability and strength. My man was fearless. All I could sense from him was a determination to eliminate the threat.

Following his cue, I crept after him, my insides trembling.

Kai's room was just past Kady's, separated by their bathroom.

By then, Kit had reached Kady's door. Back still to the wall and holding his weapon up with both hands, he twisted his body, turning to point the gun into Kady's room, and froze.

Kady's sweet laugh filled the air. "Don't be silly, Daddy. It's too early to play cops and robbers."

Kit craned his neck until his eyes met mine and jerked his head, motioning for me to follow him.

Heart pounding, I started up the hallway, almost dreading what I was about to see. Kady had been through enough in the last few months. My baby was sweet and sensitive. She didn't deserve all the crap being thrown her way.

I released the air from my lungs, trying to calm my insides. Then, I walked into Kady's room, steeling my spine.

The room was empty apart from Kady, who sat up at her desk coloring, still in her nightdress.

My eyebrows snapped together as Snow appeared from her walk-in closet, looked at me, and shrugged. "There's nobody else here," he said, tone puzzled.

My gaze settled on my daughter, questions racing through my mind.

When Kady was four or five, she used to have imaginary friends, but I thought she'd grown out of all that years ago. She certainly hadn't spoken of any lately.

My daughter must've felt my stare because she lifted her eyes to mine.

"Who were you just talking to, baby?" I asked.

She lifted one shoulder in a little shrug. "It was the man."

Quickly, I moved toward Kady, settling on my haunches next to her desk. "What man?"

She cocked her head. "Don't be mad at me." She reached down to her notebook, carefully tore off the top page, and handed it to Kit. "He made me write it down, so I didn't forget."

Straightening to my full height, I watched Kit step forward and take the note, his eyes frantically reading the words. After a few seconds, his face blanked, all color draining from it before a guttural moan tore from his throat.

A knot formed in my stomach. "What is it?"

He raised his arm, handing me the note with tremoring fingers.

I took it and read the words scrawled in Kady's childish handwriting.

Breaker

I looked out for your baby. Now you look out for mine.
You gotta help her, Snow.

I reread the note before turning to Kit. "What does it mean?" I asked, eyes rounding as I noticed Kit's entire body start to shake.

His eyes met mine, the usual golden iris's dull with shock. "Kady," he croaked. "Who was in here?"

She looked up at her dad. "He said to tell you his name was Sol and that you'd know what to do."

Kit's body jerked like something had punched him. He stumbled, almost falling, before burying his head in his hands.

My mind raced. Something inside me screamed to get Kit out of there before he lost his shit.

Throwing Kady a reassuring glance, I grabbed his hand, slid my arms across his back, and slowly walked him back down the hallway and into our room.

The note had affected him deeply. Though I had no clue why.

I kicked the bedroom door closed softly behind us and dragged him to the bed, making him sit. "What was that?" I demanded. "What the hell's going on?"

Kit leaned forward, elbows to knees, grabbing his hair with both hands. "Benny!" he gritted out.

My face scrunched up. "What about Benny? You're scaring me. Tell me what's wrong."

He looked up at me, his skin grey, and sweat beading his forehead. Then, he choked out words that turned my body as cold as ice.

"Benny was his nickname, Kitten. My best friend's real name was Sol."

Chapter Thirty

Breaker

Big Bear Lake was about forty miles north of San Bernadino, California.

The place was beautiful, surrounded by reservations and national parks.

We'd been driving around town, asking for directions for about fifteen minutes before we worked out exactly where Hollister's cabin was situated. The lake had a thriving community, but LT's cabin was so far out of town I didn't doubt he'd purposely isolated himself.

The drive had been quiet.

Kitten and the kids napped most of the way, which gave me some time to think over the events of earlier that morning, and at least *try* to make sense of them.

After the initial shock had worn off, I told Kitten about how I'd seen Benny in my head even though he'd died alongside Simmons and Espinoza. I didn't leave anything out. I even told her the words that ran through my mind whenever his black eyes stared at me, hands held out imploringly.

Help her, Snow. You gotta help her.

The apparition I saw wasn't anything good or pure. Instead of my best friend's open expression and cocky smile, I saw a tortured spirit with voids for eyes and smelled the stench of burning flesh.

Kitten suggested that maybe my PTSD had built Benny into something dark and horrific in my head due to the nature of his death and the trauma of witnessing it.

Perhaps she was right.

Benny's death was one of the worst days of my life. The deep and jagged scar it left sliced away at my soul. The months following my friend's demise were the darkest ones of my life, full of pain and loss.

I couldn't understand how Kady knew Benny's real name. I'd never told anybody he was called Sol, not my brothers or even the guys at Grand Junction. It wasn't a case of me holding the information back. I just never saw him as Sol. He'd been Benny to me and everyone else since we'd met, so that was his name as far as I was concerned.

So, how could Kady have known?

Had she picked up something I'd said and ran with it in the beautiful, innocent thing she called an imagination, or had she really communicated with Benny's ghost? Had he told her to mention Sol on purpose to make me believe?

All this time, I thought he'd been haunting me to torture my soul and punish me for the heinous acts I'd carried out, but what if he'd needed my help instead?

A soft hand rested on my knee, pulling me away from my heart-wrenching deliberations.

"Call Colt," Kitten murmured.

I glanced at her before turning my eyes back to the road. "And tell him what?"

"You say your military brother, who you witnessed die on a mission, may have gotten a girl pregnant, and you need to find her."

My throat thickened. "I can't remember his girl's name. How fucked-up is that, Kitten? I remember my best friend telling me about a girl he'd met. She was too young and innocent for him back in their high school days, but they'd reconnected when he was on his downtime." I shook my head. "I think it began with a C. Carla, Coraline, something like that."

My mind went back to the day Benny picked me up from Nashville airport when I'd returned to base after my week in Vegas with Kitten. We had a whole conversation about her.

"I used to see her in the halls and have to look away. She was too young and, like your Kitten, too sweet. Plus, I had a fucking terrible reputation. We were worlds apart. Always thought she was beautiful, though. You wanna see her, Snow. Long jet-black hair and eyes the color of a stormy Summer's day. Tiny, curvy, and cute as a button."

"What's her name?" I asked.

"Carina."

"Pretty," I murmured. "You gonna make her yours?"

My heart jolted. "Carina! Fuck! It's Carina!" I glanced toward the passenger seat. "Call Colt, baby."

Kitten grabbed my cell phone from the dash and pressed a few buttons.

The low music playing through the car speakers was replaced by ringing. It stopped after a few seconds, and Colt's voice filled the car. "Yo! Breaker."

"I need you to find someone for me," I stated.

"Well, you've come to the right place, bro. Shoot."

"Okay, my military brother, Sol Benedetti, met a girl from his hometown while on leave. She was three years younger than him, and her name was Carina. I need to find her, stat."

The tapping of computer keys clacked through the line as Colt got to work. "What was his hometown?" he asked.

"Woodbury, Connecticut."

A few more taps. "Okay, so that district's school is Nonnewaug High. Let me check their records." He paused. "Aright found ya, boy. Lemme check one more... Okay, gotta hit. Carina Lombardi. The only female with that name who ever attended the school. Born July ninety-six. Gimme a minute; I'll see what else I can get."

Kitten squeezed my thigh comfortingly.

"Okay. Carina's a tenant at Lakewood Apartments, Bristol, Connecticut. She's a waitress in a diner close to where she lives. Single as far as I can tell." He tapped some more. "Wait!"

I froze.

"She has a daughter. Giselle. She'll be eight in January. Sending all the intel to your cell." Within seconds, it buzzed with a notification.

I allowed a minute for Colt's information to sink in, my mind racing with images and conversations from the past. Through it all, one glaring fact remained that blew my fucking mind.

Benny had a daughter.

Through my whirring thoughts, I caught Kennedy thanking Colt before ending the call. Though, it hardly registered through the shit pinging inside my brain.

Benny took some leave a couple of months before he died. I remember him going to see Carina. She lived at her folk's house, so he'd rented a hotel room for the week.

I wonder—

"I think we should extend our trip," Kitten murmured. "Why don't we fly up to Connecticut and talk to her? I bet her daughter is Benny's."

My chest felt like it might explode. All this time, had Carina been desperate?

"We'll help her," Kitten reassured me. "Even if we move her to Hambleton and find her a job. We'll take care of her."

"What if she's suffered?" I rasped.

Kitten let out a quiet sigh. "I know how it feels to lose the man who owns your heart, Kit. She probably suffers every day. But if Benny is her child's dad, I guarantee it's kept her going."

My gut clenched. "I should've done more, Kenny."

"Maybe," she agreed. "But what happened wasn't your fault, Kit, so get that shit out of your head now. If she needs us, we'll be there. We'll move heaven and earth to help her and make Benny proud."

I nodded, memories bombarding me of that fateful day and everything we'd all lost.

I could've pulled over and wept for all the death, heartache, and damage we'd endured. That fucking war ruined so many people, and what made me burn was that it had all been for nothing.

We'd been sent to a place we had no business being for a cause which, over time, became convoluted. So many lives had been destroyed, not just military but civilian lives, too.

And really. Who'd won?

Not Benny, Carina, Simmons, or Espinoza. The little girl I found torn apart by a VBIED hadn't won, and neither had the thousands of innocent civilians who'd gotten caught up in a war they didn't understand.

So many minds and bodies had been broken, and for what? We'd left Afghanistan in a worse state than we'd found it.

And it would happen again.

In years to come, young men would see the next set of towers burn on a TV screen and want to keep their countries safe. The crazy thing was, if the POTUS needed me, I'd fight again, but not for the bureaucrats making decisions in Washington.

I'd fight for my family.

But would the military even have me? By their standards, was my mind too broken?

My thoughts immediately turned to Hollister and what I was about to do. Maybe I should've given my LT a heads-up.

Glancing at the GPS, the corner of my mouth hitched. If I'd fucked-up by coming here unannounced, I'd know about it in about three minutes.

Fuckin' oops.

Nate

It had taken me ten years, but finally, I'd worked out how to chop wood while wearing my blade without losing my balance.

Nobody understood how dependent we were on our limbs. I hadn't until I'd lost one. I was a man who'd always thought if I lost an arm or a leg, I'd just learn to live without it. The day it finally happened, though, I didn't cope well because the consequences of becoming an amputee weren't just about wearing a prosthetic.

They were much worse.

My dad was an Army man, and his dad before him. I had no intention of signing up until I'd lost him and my mom in a car crash. Dad always told me how the military gave him a brotherhood and friends for life, so I enlisted when I lost everyone who ever meant anything to me.

I was twenty-four with a college degree, so I'd fast-tracked straight to officer training school. Four years later, I fought a war in Iraq. Four years after that, a war in Afghanistan.

Maybe I was jinxed because, again, I'd lost anyone who meant anything.

After rehabilitation, they sent me home with a few medals, and a pension which kept me in food, and utilities, but not much else. I had money my folks left me, so I wasn't destitute, but still, a man needed a purpose.

I'd lost that, along with the lower part of my left leg, just over eight years ago on the road outside Kabul.

A bark filled the air as my Border Collie, Roscoe, came bounding out of the woods. Prowling to the front of the cabin, he stood, muscles tensed, barking and yapping at the road.

Sighing, I looked down at my gym shorts, then lower at the blade I'd had fitted to a prosthetic attached to my lower left knee. I didn't care about showin' it off, but, unfortunately, visitors never ceased being shocked.

I raised the axe and smashed it down hard into the tree stump I'd been chopping into firewood. Turning toward the road, I watched as a white Range Rover drove slowly up the dirt track leading to my cabin.

My chest knotted as it stopped, and two people emerged.

It wasn't that I hated visitors; I just couldn't be bothered with assholes, and that white Range Rover screamed asshole from the treetops.

I stood a little straighter as a blonde knockout exited the passenger door, all tight jeans, wild hair, and big tits. Cock twitching like a motherfucker, I gave her a chin lift and my best 'come hither' look. "Hey, darlin'. You lost?"

"No. She fuckin' ain't," a deep voice called out. "And if you keep lookin' at my woman like you wanna bend her over, I'll pick up that goddamned axe and chop your other bastard leg off."

My breath seized, a wave of familiarity washing over me. Eyes squinting, I saw a big, dark-haired fucker walk around from the driver's side of the Range and slide his big, beefy arm around the knockout's shoulders.

The sun dipped, bringing the guy's features into focus. My gaze met golden eyes, and my body jolted as memories assaulted me from all sides.

Jaw on the ground, I watched SPC Kit Stone snap his back straight and salute me, just like he used to ten years ago.

"Sir!" he barked. "Sorry for coming unannounced. Sir."

Almost lost for words, I shook my head disbelievingly. After eight long years, this fucker still surprised me. "What are you doing here, SPC Stone?"

He dropped his hand from his temple. "Wanted to look you up. See how you are." He grinned, eyes darkening with emotion. "It's been a while, huh?"

The corner of my mouth hitched as I took in the man before me.

Snow was older now—and certainly rougher—but still the same good-looking bastard he'd been as a young soldier, full of burning need to make the world a better place.

My eyes dipped to the knockout with him, and another flash of familiarity hit me. She was the stunner from the pictures Snow had shown to anyone who would look. He was so fucking proud to call her his. Now I saw her in the flesh; I understood why.

"I see you got the girl, soldier. Happy for ya. You deserve all the good shit." I nodded toward the cabin, suddenly desperate to connect with the one man alive who'd gone through the same bullshit I had. "It ain't much, but you're both welcome. Wanna come in? Catch up after all these years?"

"Kids are in the car," he replied. "They welcome, too?"

"Roscoe will be all over 'em. Get them out. There's a lot of woodland for them to blow off steam in. The mutt will look after them."

His eyes fell to my blade. "My boy's gonna think you're a God wearing that."

I let out a quiet chuckle, chest prickling with a warmth I hadn't felt in a long time. "Damned straight he will. You've seen me in action. I am a fucking God."

"I love your dog!" a sweet voice called through the open window of the Range. "Does he like kids?"

The knockout turned, opened the car door, and helped a pretty little thing out who stood beaming up at me.

I side-eyed Snow. "How the fuck did you make her?"

"That's my Kadence. She's all her mother." Another door slammed, and Snow's doppelganger sauntered from the other side of the car to stand beside his dad.

Snow rested a hand on the kid's shoulder. "This one's called Kai." He nodded downward. "He's all me."

The kid folded his arms across his chest. "Your leg's cool."

I leaned down, rubbing where the fitting met my skin. "Go to war, boy. If you're brave enough, you may earn yourself one." Standing straight, I grinned at the best blast from the past I could've wished for. "I'm glad you came, Snow."

He nodded slowly, eyes softening a touch. "Yeah, Lieutenant Hollister. Me too."

Twenty minutes later, Snow and I sat at the kitchen table, drinking strong coffee and reminiscing about old times.

I couldn't help marveling at the man he'd become.

I'd seen the PTSD he'd suffered toward the end of our military careers, even gave him orders to see the Army shrinks, but somehow he kept convincing them he was okay.

There were shadows in his eyes. The same shadows I saw every morning when I looked in the mirror. When a man witnessed what Snow and I had, those shadows were our reminders.

We talked about the people we'd served with at both Fort Cambell and Eggers. Then, we moved on to those fateful missions.

Stone told me about his struggles with PTSD and how he'd lost contact with his woman, only recently discovering he had twins.

Eventually, we got onto the subject of that fateful day when we watched our brother's Humvee explode.

"It's what pushed me over the edge," SPC Stone explained. "After that, I was a lost cause. The EOD wouldn't have me, so I popped smoke and bummed around the country. Lost my mind, LT. I couldn't sleep or act normal. I hardly functioned unless I had a skinful of booze, drugs, and some asshole to fight every night. It wasn't pretty. You taught me to shut everythin' down until I stopped feelin' anythin'. That was when my troubles started."

I nodded, rubbing at the pang in my chest. Snow's words took me straight back to that time and my own training. "It's what we were taught to teach *you*, Snow. Our directive was to keep you alive so you could fight the good fight. Emotions were surplus to requirements. It's the way it's always been and probably always will be."

"Yeah," he agreed. "At first, I think I resented you and Espinoza. But Grand Junction opened my eyes to a few things. We were all just cogs in a huge wheel, which was impossible to escape." He regarded me thoughtfully. "Have you received counseling?"

I almost rolled my eyes because I'd probably had more than him, but not because of what I'd done back then. No, my issues started when the opportunity to do what I loved was ripped away.

"I lost a limb, Snow. That shit qualified me for extensive counseling alongside my physical therapy. My issues had to do with my military career being cut short. My Achilles heel was being pensioned off like I was useless and no good to anyone anymore. I yearn for the life and the action. It's weird because I've never been fitter despite my leg. I can run faster, shoot straighter, and punch harder than ever. I've got all this knowledge and experience, and it's useless." My throat tightened. "*That's* what haunts me."

His eyes glazed over as his brain deciphered my words. "Not sure if I could go back, Lieutenant."

My heart sank into the pit of my gut.

Unlike Snow, going back would be a dream come true for me. "It was all I had, Stone. You boys were my kids, my peers were my brothers, and my superiors were my parents. The military's in my blood; it's what fulfilled me. Losing it was just as bad as losing a fucking limb. The day they discharged me, I cried like a baby, and it still hurts as much eight years later as it did then. My life's empty without the military. Got no purpose."

Snow sat back, his eyebrows knitting together in thought. "There's gotta be somethin' you can do. How about private security? We're always hearing about those rich bastards with private armies."

Stomach heavy, I lifted the leg with the blade attached. "Nobody will touch me, Snow. They see this and think it's a liability."

"Assholes." His expression was almost incensed. "You're a talented leader. Put you in a room full of other LTs, and you'd stand out as the best. It's a fucking joke–" He stopped mid-sentence, pausing for a few seconds as a lightbulb went off inside his head. "Wait. I may know someone."

I laughed. "Don't tell me. You've got an army."

A slow smile spread across his face. "Not exactly. But I do know of an MC whose business is security. And I don't mean night watch at the mall. I'm talkin' government jobs, extractions, guarding important people. Sensitive shit." His grin stretched wider. "You ever thought about joinin' an MC?"

"Can you see me prospecting?" I gave him some side-eye. "Don't fuckin' think so."

"What if you don't need to? Hendrix is building a brand new chapter, and there's a small window where, as long as a member vouches, you get a patch. He'd jump at the chance to recruit you; your credentials speak for themselves. You say you miss the brotherhood? You won't find a better family than the Speed Demons."

I stared at the patch on his leather cut. "Your club's looking for security specialists?"

"Yeah, LT," he replied. "My club is, but it's not the Wyoming chapter. It's our new chapter out in Virginia." He leaned forward. "The prez there's recruitin'. I bet he'd love to give you a shot."

Over the next ten minutes, SPC Stone told me about his old VP who'd opened a new chapter but then been betrayed by someone he thought was a friend, a man he'd made his VP. He'd lost half the club. Now, he was in the process of rebuilding.

I scratched my chin, questions pinging around my head.

It was exactly the kind of opportunity I'd been looking for, and in many ways, sounded almost too good to be true. The problem was I'd been out of the game for a while. I'd had a bike in my early twenties and loved riding, so I was set there, but wouldn't an ex-military officer be too set in his ways to become part of an MC? Hell, would I even be able to ride a motorcycle?

Still, something inside niggled at me, a feeling that maybe I should talk to this guy Snow knew. I mean, it couldn't hurt. It'd be good to jump in my truck with Roscoe and set off on a cross-country road trip. I'd be no worse off for meeting the guy and talking.

Snow pulled his cell phone out of his pocket and held it up. "Yes or no, LT?"

There was no second thought, no hesitation. I nodded to the cell phone and met Snow's cocky grin with one of my own.

Breaker

"What are you waiting for, soldier? Make the fucking call."

Breaker

"And Hendrix offered him a place just like that?" Kitten asked as we sat in the rental. We'd arrived in Connecticut an hour ago and driven straight to Carina's apartment. She wasn't home, so we sat in the car to wait for her to show. I'd just hung up on Drix, who called me to say thanks for sending Hollister his way.

I nodded, watching the street through the teeming rain pounding on the window. "Yep. Took him and Roscoe five days to get from Big Bear Lake to Quantico. Hendrix took Nate into Church and offered him the VP slot within a half hour. He said Hollister's a born leader, and he's desperate for a VP he can trust. I vouched, so Drix fast-tracked him past the prospecting stage. Nate's already lookin' for a bike with adaptations for his prosthetic." My lips set into a hard line. "Guess what the lucky bastard's road name is?"

Kitten looked at me questioningly.

My eyes narrowed. "Blade."

She raised a hand to hide her laughter.

It was a massive bone of contention. My road name was bullshit. I'd told Dad I wanted to change it, but he'd told me to fuck off. Nobody in the club's history had ever changed their moniker, so it looked like I was stuck with it.

Kitten rested a hand on my thigh. "Look on the bright side. It could've been worse. You were lucky they never called you chlamydia or herpes the way you went through women."

My eyes narrowed. "Never had an STD in my life."

She dipped her chin, looking up at me through her lashes. "From what I've heard, the fact your dick hasn't fallen off yet is more to do with good luck than good judgment."

My gut panged at the hard note to her voice.

We were about to accost a young, single mom in the street. I needed my Kitten to work her magic, not get pissed about my old manwhore ways.

"Love you, my beautiful baby," I crooned.

"Hmm," she hummed, gazing through the car window. "Love you too, Heartbreaker."

Silence blanketed the car for a few minutes before Kitten sighed. "Hope the kids are okay."

"It's one night, and I think they prefer staying with Abe and Iris than us. He'll have Kai out in his garage building a fuckin bike, and Kady will have cooked up a storm by now with Iris. Fuck a career in music; she'll be storming that Top Chef show at this rate." I stared at the road behind us, watching a lone figure walk hand-in-hand with a little girl. "That could be her."

"Stay here," Kitty ordered. "I'll get out and talk to her first. It'll be less intimidating if I approach her by myself."

"Be careful," I told her. "This area's a fuckin' disgrace. Benny will kick my ass when we meet again for letting his girls live here."

Kitten leaned across the seat and kissed my cheek gently. "It won't be for much longer." She opened the car door and slid out. "Wait here."

Holding my breath, I watched Kennedy run across the street in the pouring rain to intercept the woman I suspected was Carina Lombardi. Peering through the window, I took in the black hair she'd fastened up and her threadbare coat. My stare lowered to take in the little girl holding her hand. *Her* coat looked warm and waterproof against the pouring rain, at least.

A heavy lump formed in my stomach as I saw Carina raise a hand to her mouth. After a few seconds, she swiped at her eyes.

Fuck.

I rubbed the ache in my chest. Why hadn't I checked on her before?

I'd been an asshole to live with for the past week, my bad mood a result of almost hating myself for letting my friend down so badly. Benny had been vocal about Carina in his last weeks, telling me they were serious. Why hadn't he said anything about the baby? I knew I wasn't in any fit state to look after her emotionally—probably would've scared the girl outta her wits—but I would've moved heaven and earth to make sure she had money at least.

The heaviness on my shoulders pressed down a little harder, almost suffocating me. It was weird how I loved my emotions being back in full force, but I would've jumped at the chance to keep guilt out of the equation.

I was so deep inside my own head that I didn't realize Kitten had wrapped up her convo. I almost jumped out of my skin as the door flew open, and she launched into the passenger seat.

"Jesus," she sighed. "I'm soaked."

"Not yet, baby," I crooned.

"Behave." She turned to me, taking down her hood. "Okay. She's meeting us in that diner we drove past down the street. Half an hour."

"What did she say?" I enquired warily.

"She knew you. Benny told her to reach out to you if anything happened. She did look you up but was scared because you were part of a biker club."

The heavyweight lifted off my shoulders. "Jesus."

Kitten nodded. "I know. She's sweet but very skittish. I had to show her my ID and give her my card to prove I wasn't someone trying to take her somewhere and rob her blind."

I scraped a hand down my face. "I can't fuckin' believe this. Why didn't Carina reach out? Even with just a phone call. If I knew she'd had a kid. I could've done something to help, looked out for her."

Kitty squeezed my arm. "It's not so black and white for us girls, Kit. Especially young women on their own. The world isn't geared toward helping the helpless. She's probably got stories coming out of her ears about how she's been let down, used, and left to fend for herself. It affects your spirit and confidence. After a while, you start expecting the worst from people."

I rested my hand on hers, my chest almost caving at the thought of my woman being poorly treated. "Is that what happened to you?"

"No, but I was lucky. People tried to take advantage of me, but I had my tribe behind me. I knew where I was going and had goals and ambition." She swept a hand down her body. "I cashed in on everything I had to get where I needed to be. Not everyone has that, though." She leaned over and kissed my cheek. "We'll help her, Snow."

I turned to meet the gaze of the woman I'd love until my dying day. I'd lucked out the day I met her. "Yeah, baby. We will."

Twenty minutes later, the door opened, and a pretty black-haired, olive-skinned pocket rocket hurried into the diner. Carina Lombardi looked around furtively before her stare landed on Kennedy, then slowly, she approached.

Kitten leaned over and whispered, "Show her you care, Kit. Put her at ease."

I nodded, getting to my feet just as she hit our table. "Carina." Holding out my hand, I smiled. "You're even prettier than Benny told me."

The anguish in her tear-filled eyes hit me in the solar plexus.

This girl had been through the wringer.

Carina was pretty, but it was clear that life had beaten her down. Exhaustion rolled off her in waves. Her blue-grey eyes were filled with worry and had dark smudges underneath them.

She took my hand, squeezed, and swiped at her cheek. "I'm sorry. It's just hearing Benny's name. It's been so long since I heard anyone say it. I miss him." She dropped my hand and sniffed.

Pulling out her chair, I helped her sit, not quite knowing what to say.

It was evident Carina was struggling. She seemed almost at the end of her tether. God only knew what had happened to make her this way. I was scared to ask questions for fear of upsetting her again, but I shouldn't have worried, not when I had my woman by my side.

"Hey!" Kennedy murmured, getting to her feet and moving to the opposite side of the table to take Carina's hand. "There's no need to be upset. I know you've no clue who we are, but we're here to help. You're not alone anymore."

Carina smiled through her tears, her watery eyes resting on me. "I do know you, Snow. He talked about you all the time." She reached inside her purse, pulled out a dog-eared photograph, and handed it to me. "Here," she whispered. "This is all I've got left of him."

I took it from her, closing my eyes against the onslaught of emotions hitting me from all sides. I turned the image over, and the back of my eyes began to burn.

It was a picture of Benny and me in uniform, taken when we were deployed to Camp Eggers. We had our arms across each other's shoulders, laughing at something, like usual. The image captured us exactly how we were when we were young, hopeful men who wanted to change the world.

It hit me then how much I missed my friend. Nobody knew me like Benny. Losing him was a fucking tragedy, not just for me but also for this poor woman sitting before me.

Wildfire burned my throat as my eyes slid over the picture.

"I remember that day like it was yesterday," I croaked. "We'd only been deployed a few weeks. It was taken just after we'd played soccer with some of the local boys. Their smiles were a mile wide. Seeing them like that made *us* smile for the rest of the day, too."

Carina beamed. "It was one of Ben's favorite stories. I tell it to Gigi all the time."

Another pang hit my chest. "Your daughter?"

She nodded wistfully. "I try and tell her a story about her daddy every day. I want to keep him alive for her. I don't want him to just be someone she hears things about and shrugs it off. I want her to feel like she knows him."

Kitten's gaze met mine, and tears filled her eyes.

Heart aching, my stare slipped back to Carina. "Does his mom and dad see her?" I asked. "I bet she's the apple of their eye."

A quiet sob escaped her throat. "They died just after Benny did. There was something wrong with their heating system. They passed in their sleep. Carbon monoxide poisoning." She covered her eyes with her hand. "I always wondered if losing him made them stop caring. He was everything to them... He was everything to all of us."

My throat heated with the effort of holding my tears back.

Carina was right; Benny's folks doted on their only child. Losing him would've crushed them the same way it destroyed me. "What about your parents?" I needed to know if one good thing had happened in her life. "Do they love her?"

She lowered her hand, her pretty face blanking. "My dad's a very strict Catholic Italian. He gave me two choices. Give her up for adoption or get out." She tilted her chin proudly. "I would *never* give her up. She's Benny's legacy."

Kitten made a sound from the back of her throat.

She was the same way. My woman would have burned the world down before she gave our kids up. Kitten and Carina were cut from the same cloth. They were women who fought to survive. Their determination to do the right thing wasn't lost on me, especially when I remembered how easy my childhood had been.

My eyes slid to meet Carina's, my jaw clenching. "What do you need?"

Her forehead furrowed. "Huh?"

I reached out and covered her hand with mine. "You're not alone anymore, sweetheart. We've got ya."

She smiled, her eyes welling again. "*That's* all I need. I'd love it if you could talk to Giselle and tell her about her dad. My girl's like a sponge when it comes to Benny. She soaks everything up."

I ground my molars together.

Why hadn't I sought this girl out? She'd been thrown to the wolves, first by Benny, then me. I looked deep into her eyes to convey the seriousness of what I was about to say. "As far as I'm concerned, you're both family. Move to Wyoming. I'll set you up, we'll get you a job. We'll make sure you never have to worry about anything again."

Carina's smile fell. "I can't leave the East Coast. I have a little sister who goes to boarding school in Virginia. I can't keep an eye on her from Wyoming. She needs me."

Kennedy slid an arm across Carina's back. "How about we put the feelers out and try and get you a better job? Maybe even set you up in business?"

The other woman's eyes widened. "I wouldn't know where to start. I don't have any skills. I went to private school and left at eighteen. I wanted to go to college, but I met Benny and..." Her voice trailed off. "If you know of anyone who needs a cleaner or even a housekeeper who'll give me time during the day to collect Gigi from school, I can do that. I'm a hard worker, and everyone says I'm a great cook."

My eyes met Kennedys, narrowing as an idea formed. "You say your sister's in Virginia?"

Carina jerked a nod.

"Have you ever been to Quantico?" I asked. "I've got a friend there who runs a security company. He's looking for a housekeeper. Someone who'll cook and look after his guys."

Carina's eyes went huge. "That would be perfect." She looked between me and Kitten, eyes glazing over as she dissected the information. "It's closer to Lucia's school. I would've moved nearer to her, but the rents are expensive there." She wrung her hands nervously. "Are you sure? I don't mean to sound ungrateful, but amazing things like this don't happen to me. It seems too good to be true."

I got to my feet and grabbed my jacket. "I'll let you know in about three minutes. You two order, and make sure you get takeout for Gigi," I nodded toward the door. "Just gonna make a few calls."

I dropped a kiss on Kitten's head and started for the door. As I pulled it open, my woman's voice rose above the other patrons.

"You'll love Hendrix and all the guys. You know Nate Hollister, Snow, and Benny's lieutenant? Well, he works there. He'll look after you and Gigi."

I smiled, shaking my head at my girl, who had no clue how correct her prediction would be.

Years later, I'd reflect on that conversation in a small, run-down diner and always grin at the memory.

Breaker

It turned out Kitten was right because Hollister did end up treating Carina and Giselle exactly how Benny would've wanted, with all the care, respect, and love in his massive heart.

And you know what? Nate told Gigi stories about her dad every day, for the rest of his life.

Chapter Thirty-One

Breaker ~ Twelve Hours Later

We didn't end up staying in Connecticut. After we'd left Carina and Gigi, we caught the next flight home.
It had been an emotional day for everyone. It felt like Benny was there, watching everything with the cocky grin plastered across his face that was all him.

Kitten missed the kids, and if I was honest, after finally meeting Benny's little family, I did too. Seeing the beauty my friend had missed out on made me yearn to take Kai and Kady into my arms and never let them go.

Even though we'd lost so much time, I had my babies and the woman I loved. It was a blessing I'd always be grateful for and never take for granted.

We'd left the Range at the airport when we flew out, so getting home was straightforward. I tried to catch some z's on the plane, but mostly stared out the window, thinking. When we landed, I ran an idea past Kitten, and she agreed.

After meeting Carina, my mood turned melancholy.

I wanted to do something that meant something. Nobody knew what tomorrow would bring. Life had taught me to make the most of every moment. So I decided we'd all go to a somewhere we could keep in our hearts and minds for years to come.

We walked through the tiny airport hand-in-hand, not saying much, just being.

What transpired earlier took Kitten back to a place of pain.

My woman never went into detail about the day she'd been informed of my death. But meeting Carina had clearly transported Kitten back there. Earlier, I'd watched as conflicting emotions flickered across my woman's face, not all of them good.

I couldn't imagine what she'd gone through. A world without Kennedy wasn't worth living in. She was my light, my fire, my home.

We drove back to Hambleton in silence.

Emotions burned my chest, and for a split second, I didn't want them ravaging my soul. The day had brought it all back. Benny, deployment, and every heart-wrenching detail that came after.

Kitten turned her body to face me, staring at my face for the entire forty-five-minute journey.

It didn't bother me. I wanted her to drink her fill. If there was one thing I'd learned in life, it was that everything could implode in the blink of an eye. I wanted the woman who owned my heart to etch my face into her memory so completely that it imprinted on her soul.

The vision of Carina sitting in that diner, clutching Benny's picture gutted me.

It was all she had left of a man who was larger than life. His voice, his walk, the way he laughed. One minute we had him; the next, he was gone.

On the road from Rock Springs to Hambleton, I vowed to document everything in pictures, diaries, and journals. I wanted a life we could reflect on with love flowing through our hearts and cherished memories stored in our minds.

Life was for living, and fuck me, my family made every second more beautiful.

Slowly, we drove through the gates of the compound and parked as close to the clubhouse doors as I could get.

I unclipped my seatbelt, leaned across the seat, and kissed Kitten's forehead. "Stay here," I murmured into her hair. "I'll go get what we need."

Sliding out of the Range, I strode through the clubhouse doors and hit the corridor for my room.

Within minutes, I'd filled a small backpack with blankets, and pulled out my army ruck containing my sleeping bag. After grabbing our warm coats, I sauntered through the hallway and into the kitchen for provisions before getting back in the Range and headed it toward Abe and Iris's place.

The pitch-black night air was typical of November in Wyoming. The ground held a layer of frost that would turn into snow within a few weeks. It was the coming of the imminent Winter months that had spurred my plan into action.

"Are you sure Abe will be up this early?" Kitten asked from the passenger seat.

"Probably," I replied. "But if not, I'll break in, carry the kids to the car and leave Abe and Iris a note. I know it's a crazy idea, but I just wanna share somethin' with 'em, somethin' that'll feed our souls and feed 'em together."

My beautiful woman's beautiful lips curved. "It's not crazy, honey. It's us, and it's perfect."

"It's so fuckin' totally us." I agreed, navigating the dirt road leading to our destination. A warm feeling settled over me as we neared the house.

The headlights shone onto the building, lighting up Abe who sat out on the porch, drinking coffee. He sat up, shielding his eyes from the glare of their beam before sitting back again and reaching for his mug the second he identified the vehicle.

"Stay here," I ordered. "I'll be quicker on my own." I threw the car door open, got out, and walked toward Abe.

"Mornin'," he said softly, his deep, scratchy voice floating on the breeze. "You're a bit early for the twins. They're fast asleep."

"We're takin' 'em out," I informed him. "Gonna wake 'em up and carry 'em to the car."

Abe drained his cup and clambered to his feet. "I'll get Kai. You grab Kady," he muttered before disappearing through the screen door.

My hand reached out to stop it slamming in my face. I closed it carefully behind me before moving into the kitchen, through the hall toward the spare bedroom, catching up to Abe as he opened the door.

As I stepped inside, I was greeted by soft snores.

Abe was already at one of the twin-beds, rousing Kai. I went to the other to wake Kady.

Leaning down, I shook her gently and whispered, "Baby. Come on. We're going on an adventure."

"Where to?" she rasped sleepily.

"We're going to the top of the world." I wrapped the blanket around my daughter's body and lifted her into my arms.

Kai stood from his bed; a cover also wrapped around him. "Grab yours and Kady's boots, Son," I ordered gently. "Bring 'em to the car."

He did as he was told, following me as I walked back through the house and outside to the car where Kitten had already opened the doors.

"What's goin' on, Mom?" Kai asked, voice scratchy with sleep.

"Family trip," she whispered. "We're gonna climb a mountain."

And forty minutes later, climb a mountain we did.

Breaker

Kady held my hand, and Kai gripped his mom's as we hiked up the Green River Canyon Rim trail. The kids had fun climbing the canyon, which was well-marked out.

More often than not, I held Kennedy's free hand, desperate not to break our four-way connection. I'd never been a clingy person, except when keeping what was mine safe.

Whenever the terrain got rough, Kai and I would grab our girls, and help them up, especially Kady, who was small and found the going tougher than the rest of us. I loved that my boy wanted to care for them; it boded well for him in the future.

I couldn't help wondering if, one day, my Kai would fall in love like a Stone man: hard, fast, and forever. Maybe he'd find the woman who made him complete and never wanna let go.

My son reminded me of Dad, even Bandit, in some ways. One day he'd be a great asset to the club. I'd wanted to enlist at his age, but it was up to Kai to choose his own path. God broke the mold when he created my son.

My Kady smiled her pleasure with every step she took. Every tree, every flower, every blade of grass was something to be admired.

Kitten told me our girl's soul was brand spanking new, and I could see it in every look of wonder she threw. Kady had an artist's soul. She saw beauty everywhere she looked. I only hoped that she also recognized the beauty in herself.

Kitten pointed to a few large boulders that had lost their frosty layer. "How about we sit over there? It's perfect." She threw he arms out excitedly and twirled. "Look, we've got panoramic views."

I pulled my cell phone out, and clicked on the compass, pointing east. "That's the direction we need to look at."

My sleeping bag was Army issue, warm and waterproof. I laid it on the ground by the rocks and gestured for everyone to sit. The instant they settled, I slid behind them, ensuring they were covered with blankets.

Kitten pointed upward. "The sky's turning purple. Look how clearly we can see the Milky Way."

Every head tilted, following the direction of Kennedy's finger to look at the beauty of the constellations.

My throat caught as I marveled at the stars, more visible because we were miles away from city lights. Millions of tiny bright lights twinkled amongst the hues of blues and purple that made up the dawn sky.

"It's so pretty, Daddy," Kady murmured, nestling closer to me. "It makes me wanna cry."

My arm secured her back to my front, and I laid my cheek against her soft blonde hair. "Me too, Kady."

"We're so small compared to what's out there," Kai whispered. "I wonder if we'll ever get to see other planets like ours one day."

Kitten glanced at me, smiling. "Maybe in the next life."

My heart soared as I held her cornflower-blue gaze. "Or the one after that. We've still got a thousand left to live."

The air between us crackled, swirling with magic, weaving under my skin before settling inside my bones. The same magic that was born on another mountaintop in Vegas ten years before.

Life had tested us, almost to our destruction, but through it all, we'd remained true to ourselves and, in our hearts, true to each other. There was nobody else for me because no other woman was her. Fate chose us for each other, maybe the second we were born. It was only a matter of time before we found each other, against all odds.

Breaker

Twice.

It seemed Kennedy was right. Her soul knew it before mine ever did.

You couldn't fight fate.

The woman who'd taught me how to be me, reached into her pocket and pulled out her cell.

I expected her to play the same song as she had ten years before, when we danced on a mountain top, but like usual, she surprised me.

"Here it comes," she murmured, eyes resting on the spot where the sun's rays pierced the horizon.

Pianos thrashed from her speakers as a soulful women's voice began to sing.

The sun burst into the sky, lighting up the world as it flooded its life force over everything in its wake.

Goose bumps ran down my arms as the song reached a crescendo.

"Wow!" Kady breathed.

"Cool!" Kai muttered.

Kennedy's neck twisted, and she turned back to me, tears welling in her eyes.

A feeling slid deep inside my chest, something elusive I'd chased ever since I'd watched the sun rise over Lone Mountain ten years ago with my Kitten by my side.

Peace.

Epilogue One

Breaker ~ Four Months Later

I puffed my chest out, watching Kai lovingly sponge down Veronica's chrome handlebars, which were gleaming in the March sunshine.

He treated her with so much care, it made my heart unfurl.

Clearly, one day, my son would grow into a steady and well-respected brother.

He loved doing chores around the clubhouse, even helping Billy clean at weekends. He was mature and considerate, not only to the brothers but also to the women. Dad was already actively grooming him for the top spot, which I thought would rock the boat with Kitten. But to my surprise, she just shrugged and told me it was in his blood.

My woman never ceased to amaze me.

We'd had a difficult few months. The Sinners were up to no good, as usual. They were back to their old tricks, trying to get to our women. Unsurprisingly, Kennedy had taken it all in her stride by going out and buying herself a custom-made pink gun and making time to do more target practice.

The other pain in my ass was a certain Uncle called Hustle.

Jules Ford

Three days after we watched the sun rise over the canyon, ten King's brothers roared through the gates, Hustle at their helm. My woman's only blood relative didn't want me going near her or my kids, which caused my Kitten a lot of sleepless nights.

As a result, our alliance with the Kings was on shaky ground, though my club backed me all the way.

Katie told my woman to give him time, and Kennedy agreed, but I could tell it cut her deep.

All I could do was prove I was a good bet and show Kitten she was right to put her trust in me. So, that's what I did, every fucking day, and thankfully, it brought us even closer.

I'd always said I wanted an ol' lady just like Mom and Iris; strong, ballsy, and smart as fuck. Kennedy was precisely that. My woman was an integral part of the club, elevating our standing in the community and making our legal position more robust than it had ever been.

My woman was one of a kind, the other half of my soul, and because I was a wiser man than I looked, it didn't take long for me to lock her down.

On Christmas Day, I'd slipped a rare blue diamond on her finger—the same color as her eyes—and told Kennedy Carmichael she'd be my wife.

She'd rolled her eyes, said, *'Well, duh,'* and started planning.

Our wedding was set for May.

Things hadn't been entirely smooth sailing since we'd been back together.

Kennedy still had dark thoughts about the shit I'd done in the years we'd lost each other. She seemed almost triggered by it.

There was a thread of resentment inside her that would probably never go away. Kitten was nobody's fool; she forgave quickly, but my woman never forgot.

But, if it was what I had to deal with to have her by my side, it was a small price to pay.

The clubhouse doors flew open, and Sunny ran outside carrying a juice box. Kady followed, running so fast that her hair flew out behind her, with JB prancing around her legs.

"Kai. I brought you a drink," Sunshine sang.

My boy straightened and gave her a chin lift. "Obliged," he muttered.

Sunny popped a hip—probably after seeing Kitten do it—and announced, "My mama said the men's gotsta stay vibrated when they work."

Kai's brow furrowed.

Kady giggled. "You mean hydrated."

Sunny shrugged with a laugh. "Oh, yeah."

Kai nodded over at Veronica. "Just gotta polish up Pop's bike, and I'll be in."

"Wanna play in the woods later?" Sunny asked.

My son heaved out a breath. "Don't got no choice with you, Sunshine. Who else'll keep you outta trouble?"

I scrubbed a hand down my face, trying to hide my laughter.

Sunny treated Kai like he was her ol' man, and my son, being the boy he was, just wanted to protect her and make her happy. All the kids—including DJ and Gabby—were great friends, and because their grandpa thought they were the best thing since strawberry-flavored lube, they ruled the fucking roost.

The doors flew open again, and Cash and Atlas stomped outside, laughing as they approached.

"Yo. Break," the SAA barked. "The women not shown their faces yet?"

I shot him a sour look. "Do you see a white Range in the vicinity?"

He got closer, clapping me on the shoulder. "Nah, brother. No pussy car that I can see."

Sunny let out an excited squeal. "Can I ride in the pussy cat car, Assless? Pleeeaaase."

The SAA smirked. "Ask your aunt Kennedy, little Sunshine. I'm sure she'll oblige." His hard stare lowered to Kai and softened. "Yo. Mini biker boy Kit. You've done a stand-up job on my Lana. Worth every dime."

My brow creased. "You're payin' him?"

Kai's lips flattened. "I didn't wanna charge a brother, but Mom told me if I was gonna spend all day cleaning bikes better than a professional detailer, I had to start charging for my valuable time." He shrugged, getting down on his knees to polish Veronica's fuel tank. "She said I don't have to charge *you* though, 'cause you already give me an allowance."

"Damn straight," I muttered.

Cash folded his arms across his chest. "Mine's next in line, right, Kai?"

My boy jerked his uncle a nod. "Yep. Then Bowie's."

We all let out a low groan at the mere mention of my brother.

He'd been insufferable since the Monday after Kitten's birthday party.

Bowie took Layla for her pre-natal check. An hour later, he'd burst back inside the clubhouse with a smile so wide you could almost see his fillings.

"Guess the fuck what?" he'd shouted.

Dad, who sat with Marcus talking business, turned on his stool, staring at Bowie like he needed to attend a straitjacket fitting. "What the fuck are you gabbin' about?" he demanded.

Bowie's body vibrated with pure joy before he let out a loud hoot and bellowed something that made Dad jump off his stool and dance a fucking jig.

"It's twins!"

Since that day, I'd ceased to be the favorite again. Though if Kitty ever got knocked up with twins, I reckoned that would change, the same with Cash and Cara.

Dad was building a legacy, and the more club brats he had to help him do it, the better.

Speaking of the devil, the clubhouse doors opened again, and Bowie came strutting out with Willow fastened to his chest in one of those baby carrier things.

My chest panged.

My biggest regret in life was losing Kitten for all those years, of course, but missing all of my babies' milestones gutted me more. It was weird how one fucking baby carrier contraption could invoke so much sadness. I guess it was what it represented that really cut me.

"Doe back yet?" Bowie inquired, glancing at his watch. "Knew I shouldn't have let her go without me. I'm the father. I need to be there for every one of 'em."

Atlas shot him a smirk. "Shouldn't have played the fool then, should ya?"

Bowie glowered at the SAA. "Didn't want no man up in my woman's fairy garden."

Atlas threw his head back and laughed.

"He's a fuckin' midwife," Cash argued. "Poor guy's there, doin' his job, and you pick him up by the collar, walk through the clinic, and fling him outta the door. It's no wonder you're barred from the place."

"You'd have done the same," Bo told him.

Cash shrugged. "Yeah," he admitted. "Probably."

Atlas cocked an eyebrow. "Told Stitch I didn't want him up in her vag, either."

I stared at them all in disbelief. "You lot are like fuckin' cavemen. He's a fully trained midwife who probably sees more lady bits in a month than you'll all see in a lifetime."

"No fucks given," Bowie retorted. "If he's got a cock then I don't want him up in my woman's hoo-ha. End of."

Atlas nodded his agreement. "My Stitch has got a pretty little." He paused, discretely pointing toward his crotch. "It's hard enough trustin' a woman down there examining what's mine," he shuddered, "so the thought of a male doin' it makes my teeth itch."

I looked up to the sky, rolling my eyes. "Fuckin' idiots. What about their gynos?"

My brothers glanced at each other.

"Same," Atlas confirmed.

"Yep," Bowie shrugged.

Cash held his hands up and pulled a 'meh' face.

My lips twitched. "So. What if their female gynos and midwives and doctors are gay?"

Crickets.

All color drained from Atlas's face.

Cash's eyes rounded.

Bowie pulled his cell out. "I'll get Colt to investigate. He'll sort—" He stopped, closed his eyes, and scraped a hand down his face. "Fuck!"

My lips thinned.

Colt had left the club just after New Year, and I fucking missed him.

Since I'd returned from Grand Junction, we'd gotten much closer. It turned out there was a lot more to Colt than anyone knew. We'd started building a solid friendship until there was an incident over New Year.

To say shit had hit the fan was an understatement.

Dad had rules around certain things, rules he wouldn't bend for anybody. And because of his fucked-up laws, we'd lost a good man who'd had our backs for years. Colt was a major asset, and when he'd walked away, we lost a brother who was integral in fighting the war against the Sinners.

The incident split the club down the middle, too.

Some thought Dad was right in what he'd done to Colt, whereas others, like me and Cash, had been dead against it. MCs were all about living free and not being tied to society's rules, except when it suited Dad.

Now, it had come back and bitten Pop in the ass because Freya was on the warpath, and from what I'd learned about my sister in the last few months, she had bigger balls than all us Stone men put together, including the prez, as he'd learned to his cost.

But that was another story.

A shout came from the gates.

"At fuckin' last," Atlas muttered, watching Kitten's Range glide into the parking lot. "Fuck knows how one little appointment can last all mornin'." The SAA started for the Range, which had stopped a few feet away.

I caught a flash of dark hair emerging from the driver's seat.

Cara slid out, and my gut panged. "Where the fuck's Kennedy?" I called over.

Wildcat jerked a thumb toward the back seat, where my woman emerged from the cage.

I let out a sigh of relief, starting toward her. "You okay, baby? Why aren't ya driving?"

Sophie's lips twitched. "She's had a bit of a shock."

My head reared back, panic clenching inside my gut. "The Sinners?"

"No," Layla replied, grabbing my hand as she heaved herself and her giant baby bump from the back seat. "Nothing bad." She glanced at Kitten. "Or is it? I'm still not sure."

Kitten's eyes locked with mine. "What did you do?"

My throat clenched as I wracked my brain, trying to remember if I'd fucked-up recently. After a few seconds, I came up blank. "Not a thing."

Her cornflower-blues narrowed. "Well, you did something."

My face twisted. "What?"

Sophie walked over and threaded her hand through Kitten's arm. "Okay. So, you know we all went into each other's appointments for support?"

"Yeah?"

"Well," Soph continued. "Kennedy felt faint, so Oliver, the midwife, made her take a pregnancy test."

My pulse kicked. "And?"

Kitten held a plastic stick up for me, eyes bugging out. "You knocked me up!"

Fingers trembling slightly, I took the plastic stick from her and held it to the light.

A pink plus sign showed in the window.

I choked out a growl as emotions flooded my bloodstream, feelings hitting me from all sides. My hand went to the vehicle to support my knees, which had suddenly turned to mush. My voice came out as a croak, "You're pregnant?"

My woman cocked a hip. "Well, *duh*. *And* I take the contraceptive pill."

Moisture hit my eyes. I tagged Kitten's waist and pulled her into me, my hand stroking gently over her still-flat stomach. "I love you so fuckin' much, Kitten. You brought me back to life." With legs like Jell-O, I dropped to my knees, sliding my arms around her back and kissing her stomach. Then, I tipped my face up and let the tears fall.

Kennedy's eyes filled up as she gazed down at my awestruck expression. "I love you, too," she whispered.

Something beautiful sliced through my chest as she laughed, held her hand out, and helped me stand. "I thought you'd say it was too soon."

My hand slid back to my woman's stomach, where my child lay warm, safe, and nurtured. "No, baby—" The clubhouse doors banged shut.

My eyes veered toward the sound to see Dad standing there.

His eyes fell to my hand, still cupping Kitten's stomach. "Baby?" he asked.

I nodded, a slow grin stealing over my face.

His hand flew to his heart, golden eyes like mine widening as his shocked face morphed into a beaming smile. "Really? We're havin' a baby?" he asked, voice husky with emotion.

"Yeah, Pop," I rasped.

Dad beamed, then he opened his mouth and yelled the two words we'd never let him forget for years to come.

"Deary me!"

Epilogue Two

Kennedy ~ Thirteen Years Later

I felt Kit stiffen beside me as the famous TV Network producer slash presenter leaned toward the microphone, and crooned, "And the Grammy for Album of the Year goes to..."

The star-studded audience fell so silent you could almost hear a pin drop, all except for my son, who muttered, "I'll hulk out if that fuckin' prick wins it."

Seated at the other side of me, Kit grunted his agreement.

"Hey," I whispered. "It's Noah's band, too."

Kai crossed his arms over his muscular chest, his lips thinning angrily in an expression identical to his dad's. "It's not him I'll hulk out over, Mom. Don't be dense."

I rolled my eyes and prayed to God for the sixty-third time that night to save me from alpha sons who took after their dads and, as they matured, became even bigger alpha bikers. Thank God for our other son, Kalen, who was a perfect mix of me and Kit. At twelve years old, it was apparent he'd be a biker, too. Except he also had other ambitions, just like his mom.

Our old Prospect, Billy the Kid, aka Noah Thorne, had only been patched into the club for a year before a top music producer from Hollywood discovered his band on YouTube. Within a week, he'd patched out and left Wyoming for the bright lights of the city.

Over time, his band, Dischordium, had grown to be one of the biggest rock bands in the world. Eight platinum albums later, they'd been nominated for their seventh Grammy Award.

And guess what...? He wasn't the only person in our circle nominated for the same Grammy.

A year ago, an incredible young, beautiful woman who wrote a mash-up of pop, rock, and folk music had recently released a critically acclaimed debut album that went platinum in twenty-two countries.

Earlier that night, she'd already won the awards for Best Newcomer and Record of the Year.

A rustling sound came over the mic as the TV network producer slash presenter opened the envelope and slowly pulled out the card.

My heart galloped out of my chest.

Please. Please. Please.

A huge smile washed over his face, and he excitedly held the card he'd just read from up in the air before shrieking two words that filled my throat with emotion... "Kady Stone!!!"

A collective roar built into a crescendo as the thousands-strong audience yelled and screamed, almost lifting the roof off the massive theatre. The air felt charged with electricity as complete strangers shouted their approval for my beautiful, talented daughter.

Kit and Kai jumped to their feet, punching the air and hooting bellows of delight. The din was so deafening I had to cover my ears.

Tears filled my eyes as it began to sink in.

Kady just won Album of the Year.

My eyes snapped closed, mind zeroing in on everything my girl had to endure to get to this place.

You see, Kady had written one of the best albums I'd ever had the pleasure to listen to, an album that spoke to people's hearts. But, she'd had to go through the most gut-wrenching, soul-rendering heartbreak to complete it. My baby girl was a shell of who she used to be. Seeing her so damaged made my soul ache. Kady used to fizz and pop. So full of life and love, but now she was just... broken. *He'd* taken everything from her, and whatever dregs were left had gone into writing and recording the album.

Kady's shiny, innocent, new soul had been marked, and she was only twenty-one years old.

I felt everything she felt because I'd gone through the same thing years before, at almost the same age.

Luckily, my heart had been put back together again, and I'd never regretted giving my golden boy another chance, but I wasn't sure the same happily ever after would happen for Kady.

Kit once told me that Stone men loved hard, fast, and forever.

And in Kady's case, at least, it seemed Stone women did, too.

The stage lights dimmed slightly. A flash of white appeared in the wings, and Kady moved, limbs loose like water, her blonde hair almost shimmering under the beams of white light glued to her as she walked toward the center of the vast stage. She looked almost angelic.

The TV network producer slash presenter seemed awestruck by Kady as she approached. He handed her award over, taking the opportunity to gently touch her hair and go in for a lingering kiss on her cheek.

The deep rumble of three loud growls hit my ears from all directions.

Two of the deep, angry growls came from the men I loved, sitting on either side of me, but interestingly, the third and loudest growl came from a few rows behind.

My heart thudded against my ribs. Slowly, I craned my neck to glance at the five members of Dischordium sitting two rows behind me.

Noah's wide eyes met mine, and he shook his head. A silent plea to keep my mouth shut and not cuss out his asshole bandmate in an auditorium full of people, who no doubt had seen the pictures splashed all over the tabloids showing Luca 'Blue' De Santis coming out of a hotel early one morning about a year ago, with a supermodel on his arm.

And who, by doing so, had shattered Kady's heart.

A soft sigh rustled through the speakers, and I turned back to witness my girl standing alone in front of the mic, Grammy in hand, looking dazed and a little bewildered.

Tears sprang to my eyes at the deep ache resonating through my chest. My girl had lost her sparkle. It physically pained me to see her so lost.

Blank cornflower-blue eyes rested on the sea of faces looking at her expectantly, and her chin lifted as she began.

"I'd like to thank my family..." Kady's voice trailed off.

My throat thickened with tears as Kit's big, strong hand squeezed mine. He knew as well as I did that she was struggling.

I noticed Kai's hands balling into fists. His shoulders stiffened as the same emotions swirling through Kady began to hit him, too.

Kady looked down at her award. "I'd like to thank my manager, Cordelia, and Xavier from my record label, BeatsPM, who allowed me the creativity to write my album my way." Her tear-filled eyes returned to the audience. "I—"

A deep voice cut her off, "Proud of ya, Angel!"

Silence fell over the room for a split second before loud whispers rose from the sea of people who all turned our way.

"What's he doing?"
"Didn't her fuck her over?"
"He's got some balls."

Kady's face paled, her blue eyes flaring as they rested on somebody over my shoulder.

A thousand flashbulbs went off, almost blinding me, and an excited roar filled the ether as the audience went crazy, all eyes still looking in our direction.

"No, no, no. Not now," I whispered to myself as I turned to see Blue De Santis on his feet, gazing toward the stage at Kady. "You did it, baby," he shouted, pointing toward my girl. "To the moon, Kadence Stone."

My girl flinched as though someone had punched her before letting out a low, pain-filled moan.

The air around me turned thick as Kai and Kit's bodies locked.

I groaned. "Oh, shit."

Kit snarled before getting to his feet and bellowing, "You motherfucker!"

"I'm gonna kill him," Kai spat, rising from his seat and turning toward Blue. He raised a hand, pointing at the rock star. "Gonna make you wish you'd never set eyes on my sister."

"Got your back, Son," Kit announced loudly, leaping over me to storm after Kai as my son clambered over the chairs, shouting threats of murder, desperate to get to the man who'd screwed over our girl.

Screams and shouts rang out as people dived to get out of the way of Kai, who'd rounded on Blue, getting in his face, still snarling threats.

Blinding flashes of bulbs hurt my eyes as the paparazzi went into a frenzy.

"Fuck you," Blue yelled, his face inches away from Kai's. "She's mine. I ain't goin' anywhere."

I closed my eyes.

Shit.

I jumped to my feet and whirled around. "Stop!" My heart hammered against my ribs as my shocked stare took in the pandemonium around me. But it was too late; it was every man for himself. I let out a strangled gasp, watching as America's musical elite got caught in the middle of a fucking riot in the middle of the Grammys.

The entire band had jumped in to defend their guitarist, except for Noah, who I saw throw a jab at Blue's jaw from the side.

Kit was trying to choke out the drummer, except one of the band's security guys was in the process of dragging him back by his arm. My husband rounded on him, whipped his fist back, and smashed it into the bodyguard's face before whirling back to the drummer and landing a powerful jab against his temple.

Kai roared, grabbing both sides of Blue's skull and head-butting him straight in the nose.

A loud crack sounded before an explosion of blood flew up, and Blue went down like a sack of potatoes.

Screams and shouts filled the air, the people sitting in the chairs ducking for cover as the sound of fists hitting flesh rang out.

We were at the goddamned Grammys. Photographers were everywhere getting their shots of Kai and his dad beating the shit out of the man who hurt Kady. TV cameras were still rolling, not to mention the auditorium was packed with thousands of witnesses.

It would be front-page news tomorrow.

The footage was probably already making its way online.

Over the years, I'd saved Kit, Kai, and brothers from all the Speed Demon chapters from going to jail numerous times. I was damned good at my job, but not even I could convince a judge not to send my boys to prison when their crimes were being fucking *televised*.

Heart burning with anxiety, I bent down swiftly to grab the silver beaded purse that matched my dress perfectly and pulled out my cell phone.

Scrolling with my thumb, I found the name I wanted and clicked, holding the cell to my ear. After a few rings, a deep voice barked, "What the fuck's going on there? Your man and son are all over the news!"

I let out a deep sigh. "Scotty. That young pit bull lawyer from L.A who's been sniffing around for a job. Tell her she's in as long as she can meet me down at the Hollywood Police Department in roughly thirty minutes." My lips pursed as I watched three security guys pull Kai off Blue, who was sprawled out on the floor, laughing maniacally, his nose pissing blood.

Stomach clenching, my eyes slid to the door where a long line of uniformed police ran down the aisles wielding batons and shouting orders.

My fingers gripped the cell tighter. "Tell her to hurry, Scotty. It's gonna be a long night."

The End

Thank you for reading.
Colt and Freya's book is coming in the Fall/Autumn of 2023.

Breaker's Playlist can be found here ~
https://open.spotify.com/playlist/2YyiAuI7FIhv8UCOUL76vO

Author's Note

This book was a joy to write and a monster. I didn't think I'd get there, Kennedy wasn't giving in, then, Ed came to town. Thanks Ed. X

There's only two (and a half) books to go... We're getting down to the wire.

Nicola, you get the first word this time. I don't think Breaker's book would exist without you. Thank you for working every bit as painstakingly hard as me. I appreciate everything. Thank you for all you do.

Jayne, thanks for your support and all you do in LLMC. You're a queen.

Mylene. I hope you like him. He didn't go the way I thought he would, but they never do, right? LOL.

ARC team... I can't name you all, but I appreciate all the time you take to read and review. You're so encouraging and put my mind at rest every time I release. I love all the laughs we have together. Long may it continue.

Tribe. I had a hard time with this duet, but your encouragement and kindness kept me going. Thank God for such a fab group of people.

A special shout out to Joe for all my lush covers.

Sarah, thanks for sitting on socials, spreading the word, and also Jordi for all the cool stuff you make me.

Beth... Thanks for being you.

And **thank you readers** for giving my Speed Demons a go.

Jules
XOXO

Stalk Jules

Jules loves chatting with readers.

Email her ~
julesfordauthor@gmail.com

Join her Facebook Group
Jules Ford's Tribe | Facebook

Instagram
Jules Ford (@julesfordauthor) • Instagram photos and videos

Printed in Great Britain
by Amazon